The Marriag

Stephen Molyneux

Published by Sites To Suit Limited 2013

www.sites-to-suit.co.uk

Copyright © Stephen Molyneux 2013

Cover design by Samantha Groom

ISBN: 978-0-9576059-0-9

Also available as an ebook
ISBN: 978-0-9576059-1-6

About the Author

Stephen Molyneux, amateur genealogist, lives in Hampshire and the South of France with two metal detectors and his long-suffering wife.

To Sarah

Acknowledgements

I would like to thank friends and family who read my early manuscript and gave me their comments and feedback. I am also grateful to my copy-editor, Sue Shade, for her input and hard work.

Stephen Molyneux
May 2013

Contents

Part One

1.1

Peter spotted the marriage certificate. It was mounted in a clear plastic sleeve just above eye-level and was attached to a blue felt panel. The certificate was one of about fifty printed paper items displayed in similar fashion. These included an impressive gold embossed invitation to a luncheon for some long dissolved Victorian institution, a wartime ration book, a 1920s rates demand, a Post Office Telegram with news of someone having passed away, military service guides to various postings in the British Empire, and several interesting postcards. The display occupied the upper part of a wall within an alcove, the alcove itself being a small open unit in an antiques centre. A sign hung above: 'Unit 14 – Ephemera'.

Unit 14 specialised in interesting paper items from the 1960s and before, although postcards seemed to be the main offering. There were hundreds of them stored in recycled shoeboxes and displayed for sale at table height. Simple handwritten cardboard dividers separated the postcards into categories, which included cities, counties, foreign countries, churches, cathedrals, monuments, and miscellaneous attractions.

Peter cast his eyes back to the marriage certificate … Essex, 1900, he noted, a bachelor and a spinster. It just seemed so sad that something like that should be displayed and offered for sale at five pounds. Placing a monetary value on it seemed inappropriate. Surely, there were family descendants out there, possibly even living children, but more probably grandchildren who ought to have it? How had something so personal come to be offered along with the bric-a-brac of life on a board in an antiques centre?

He was aware that marriage certificates, like birth and death certificates, were documents of public record and that anyone could obtain a photocopy from the General Register Office. However, this was not a photocopy but one completed and given to the couple by the minister who married them. It was the actual certificate produced from the entries in the Marriage Register; the Register signed by the newly-weds and their two witnesses, who were presumably close friends or relatives, signed at St Martin's Church in the parish of Leyton, Essex, on the fifteenth day of January, 1900.

'Marriage Solemnized at ...' the title stated in copperplate script. It didn't seem particularly solemn, Peter thought, not in its present position; just a piece of paper, insignificant now perhaps, but once of huge importance to the two people, whose lives were legally combined into a single entity on that day. A piece of paper, slightly faded, but not worn, so presumably kept safe and secure until, along with other personal possessions, a house was cleared and the saleable items were traded and distributed to whatever niche or market might find them another home.

He detached the plastic sleeve from the board and carefully extracted the certificate from its protective cover. He looked at the names of the couple. It might be interesting to trace their family, he thought. He studied it more closely and for the first time considered purchasing it.

The blanks on the certificate had been completed in black ink and obviously written with a pen or quill. The handwriting had a scratchy, loopy, but quite learned late Victorian style, not at all like the handwriting taught in schools nowadays. It was by the hand of Thomas Walter, who had married the couple according to the 'Rites and Ceremonies' of the Established Church, in other words, the Church of England.

The certificate had a slight odour to it, probably due to age, possibly dampness and he detected something else ... mothballs, he thought ... yes, definitely mothballs, and he recalled the distinctive smell of naphthalene in the school chemistry lab. He remembered too the master, who on leaving for another school told the assembled pupils a farewell joke about an American, so amazed at seeing some mothballs, he remarked, 'Gee, you sure have some mighty big moths in England!'

Back to the present, should he buy it? He deliberated   but why? What would he do with it? Was it some morbid curiosity, nosey

3

interest, or was there a genuinely interesting story here just waiting to be discovered?

He glanced up and noticed the security camera mounted in the corner to his left. If somebody at the payment desk was monitoring him, they might think he was preparing to steal the certificate. Of course, he wasn't, but he'd often experienced an irrational camera-induced guilt when he felt he was being watched remotely in a situation like this. He decided to put the certificate back and tried rather ineptly to reinsert it into the plastic sleeve. After several abortive attempts, the decision was made for him – he would buy it. He took the certificate to the payment desk.

'I'd like to buy this certificate please. Sorry ... I couldn't seem to get it back into its sleeve.'

A very elderly lady assistant smiled at his apology. 'Let's have a look,' she said. 'It was probably folded.' Peter noticed that she had a sort of 'Women's Institute' air to her manner and appearance, typical of a breed of ladies who inhabit the country towns and villages of England. Yet despite having shaky hands, she somehow deftly slid it back into its protective cover. From his wallet, he gave her a crisp five-pound note and in return received a simple brown paper bag, into which the assistant had popped the slightly faded certificate, thoughtfully taping over the opening.

Out he went into the cold late afternoon in January 2011. The light was fading. He felt elated but was not quite sure why. Maybe it was because he had removed the certificate from public view. He was protecting its privacy, perhaps protecting the individuals whose lives were changed forever when they left the church on that Saturday in January 1900. They left with this certificate too, no doubt guarded safely, but surely not in a brown paper bag? What had happened afterwards? If the certificate could tell a story, what might that be?

As he walked to the car, he pondered the circumstances and events of more than 100 years ago. By the time he had turned on the ignition, Peter Sefton had decided to see if he could find out.

1.2

Rose heard the clock, one floor below, strike half past six. It was still dark outside and time to get up. She pushed back the bed covers and stepped onto the creaky floorboards of her small attic bedroom. The other bedrooms were still silent. She was the first of the 'front of house' staff to rise, as was the case every morning, although the housekeeper and servant would already have been up for some time.

She lit two candles before emptying the tepid water from her stoneware hot water bottle into the basin. She topped up with cold water from a jug and washed thoroughly. It was cold in the bedroom, being January in Leyton, Essex, and the east wind blowing from the North Sea over the last few days had reduced temperatures to well below normal. She dressed quickly, a simple neat black dress with a white pinafore and white linen collar, almost a uniform, for it was the dress of an employee in a drapery shop. She lived on the premises along with five other girls who also worked in the shop downstairs.

Rose was a senior member of staff and had a room to herself. She had worked there for eighteen months and was in charge of her own department. She went out into the corridor, pausing and listening at the adjacent doors before knocking gently.

'Daisy, Hilda, Ivy, it's time to get up. Amy, Dorothy, time to get up.' Breakfast was at eight. The shop opened at a quarter past nine.

One floor below, the Crockford family had their rooms, but since purchasing a private house, Mr Crockford and his daughter, Louisa, spent fewer nights at the shop. On the ground floor was the shop itself. Rose went down the narrow staff staircase, passing the kitchen, where she could hear the kettle simmering on the stove. The housekeeper, Ada Jones and the servant, Betty, were preparing breakfast for everyone. Ada had a small room close to the kitchen. Meanwhile, Rose reached the ground floor and slipped out of the back entrance to the yard and the outside privy.

Thomas Crockford, master draper and owner of the building and the business, was her employer. Louisa, now Rose's closest friend, nagged her father continuously about the need to improve the sanitation facilities for the employees, but Mr Crockford's concessions to the new century, for it was 1900, were only those that benefited and impressed the shop's clientele. They amounted to some very modern, if unreliable, electric lighting to the ground floor and the installation of a limited heating system, with radiators warmed by a coal-fired boiler, but again only for the ground floor. He had also recently provided two water closets, one for each sex, accessed via the changing rooms in the shop, but these were strictly out of bounds to staff.

Sidney, the shop's porter, arrived at seven o'clock each workday morning to riddle and stoke the boiler. It was just one of his many duties, which also included fetching stock from the cellar, making deliveries, and collecting goods delivered to the local train station. Aged nineteen, he was 'sweet' on Rose. To Sidney, she was the prettiest girl he knew. Rose may not have been beautiful in the classic sense, but she had a comeliness about her which men found attractive. She was of average height, rounded in just the right places with a trace of southern European colouring to her skin. When she let down her long straight jet-black hair at night and combed it in front of the mirror, she presented a vision, which any man given the opportunity to observe would have agreed was entirely beguiling.

Sidney, generally bright and cheerful in manner, was always ready with a cheeky comment. His father and uncle were both porters at the local railway station, which gave him inside information on the various comings and goings in the town. He liked to chatter and had been reprimanded sternly from time to time by his employer, for 'being held up with the tongue', none more so than when he was caught passing on some titbit of news to Rose. He lived at home but worked for Mr Crockford on a full-time basis, as the turnover of the business had increased steadily and warranted a permanent draper's porter. Rose enjoyed the fuss Sidney made of her, always wanting to help when she needed something from one of the high cupboards or drawers. They dominated the walls behind the counters and were faced in beautiful dark mahogany and all marked with white printed cards indicating their contents.

The shop sold everything imaginable in the drapery line and much more besides. The list of items stocked was almost endless and apart from rolls of cloth and material for clothing and curtaining, the shop stocked hats, coats, mantles, dresses, skirts, blouses, trousers, shirts, ties, undergarments, belts, and gloves. There were several departments: Drapery, Linen, Men's, Women's, and General Haberdashery.

Rose was the head of Drapery. It sounded quite grand, but in reality, Rose and her assistant were the drapery department. Still, it was a big step up in responsibility from her previous employer – a large fashionable London draper situated in the West End of London – where she had spent six years as an apprentice and then four years as one of many assistants.

Her department occupied a corner to the rear of the shop. Apart from Daisy, she had two outworkers she could call on if needed. Rose, although only twenty-five, dealt directly with the customers. In the matter of curtains and drapes, she called in person, if required, to customers' residences, in order to measure up and then afterwards to hang the finished articles. She was ambitious and she saw her present position as a step on the ladder to one day owning her own drapery store.

Rose had been born in Paddington in 1874, out of wedlock. Life had been hard. She had no idea who her father was; only that he was Italian, which was as much as her mother, Edith, knew. In order to keep them both, Edith worked from their small rented room, making and mending clothes. Although Rose was unaware, while she was at school, her mother, out of necessity, occasionally supplemented their income by entertaining men. The occupation of dressmaker was often a euphemism for prostitute in Victorian times and in the case of Rose's mother, the description perfectly covered both her means of keeping a roof over their heads.

Rose worked hard at school. She was bright and by the age of ten was fully proficient in reading, writing, and arithmetic. She was perceptive and early on became aware of her shortcomings regarding background and class. She listened to the way some of the other children spoke, particularly those who came from the more affluent streets in the borough, and at night would talk to herself, copying and practising their accents and intonation. To call it elocution would be an exaggeration, but Rose, through her own perseverance, managed to perfect and use, if required, an accent, which all but hid her lowly origins and the precise location from which her life had begun.

However, education ended prematurely for Rose. She was in her last year at school, just thirteen and unsure what she would do, when her mother fell gravely ill and died a short while later. Fortunately, her schoolmistress had an acquaintance who worked at *Davis & Davis*, a large drapery store in Oxford Street. Rose already had some familiarity with the jargon and the trade of drapery, certainly, as far as rolls of cloth and dressmaking were concerned. On many occasions, she had accompanied her mother to the local draper to buy cheap remnants and roll ends. Her schoolmistress put in a word and secured a position for Rose as a draper's apprentice.

When she started at the prestigious shop in Oxford Street, Rose told any member of staff who asked that she was an orphan. It took time for her to get over the loss of her mother, but Rose found solace in her work. She lived in a dormitory with about forty other young women on the top floor of the shop. The wage was low but they received free board and lodging. They had a Welsh housekeeper who was kindly and sympathetic and tried to make their communal accommodation 'home'. Some were new apprentices like Rose and others were more experienced. They came from all over the country, many were Welsh, and Rose was one of the few local girls. The apprentices staffed the shop, which at the time was growing rapidly into one of London's largest. Rose was something of a chameleon. She had a knack for getting on with people and could adapt her manner and speech should the need arise, to the extent that she soon fitted in and was popular with her workmates and colleagues.

It was discovered that Rose had a natural ability as a seamstress and soon after joining, she was placed in the department that carried out alterations and repairs to customers' garments. Her skills improved and later she progressed to making expensive curtains, ornate drapes, and elaborate mantles. At the end of her apprenticeship, she remained in the bespoke curtaining and drapes department.

London society required that interior decoration should be of the latest mode. Large sums were expended in order to keep up with the trends. Wealthy middle-class ladies, surrounded by servants, had little else to do but concern themselves with renovating their homes in styles determined by decorative fad or technical innovation. Business for the large West End drapers boomed.

Rose started to accompany her senior on visits to customers' houses, where they would measure up and assist in the choice of pattern and material. Rose's confidence grew and she enjoyed working on a face-to-face basis with the clients. These visits showed to Rose a world beyond her crowded dormitory above the shop. She saw first-hand the wealth of London and the sumptuous interiors of some beautiful homes. These revelations started to fuel in her an aspiration to be more than just a draper's assistant, and to have her own emporium. When days were particularly hard or demanding, she consoled herself with this thought.

The reality for an ambitious young woman in a male-dominated world however, was somewhat at odds with Rose's dreams. Most working-class girls were employed in domestic service as maids and cooks or in the mills on weaving and spinning machines. Those who were better educated and intelligent became shop assistants, clerks, or nurses. Girls from more prosperous backgrounds could become governesses, teachers, or authors. In general, women looked to marriage for their financial security. Rose was different. Her eyes were opened when she entered the beautiful homes situated on fine London squares. Despite living in a world run by men, Rose was determined to rise above the status in which she had been born and if necessary, she was prepared to achieve it on her own merits. Marriage and children were not something she yearned for. She decided early on that if possible she would be a commercial success, determined to overcome the restrictions of a man's world.

She worked hard and opened an account at the Post Office Savings Bank. Her wages increased to nearly twelve pounds per year. Each week she deposited a few shillings into her account knowing that if she was ever going to own a business, she would need capital in order to finance it.

It was a condition of employment at the shop that female assistants remain single. Most longed to be married and have children. Marriage provided a means of escape.

'How come you want to save up?' her friend Elsie once asked.

'I want to have my own business, maybe a drapery shop someday.'

'What? You're mad! You've got no chance. If you want to get on you need to find a husband … that's how I intend to get out of this place.'

'I'm not looking to get married,' Rose replied. 'I'm determined to be successful through my own endeavours.'

As the months slipped by, Rose, with more confidence and self-assurance, was allowed by her superior to work with less supervision. Rose realised that where she was, she was a small fish in a very large pond. She decided that if she could find a position with a more provincial draper, she might become the proverbial large fish in a small pond. The idea appealed to Rose. She saw a notice in the *Drapery News*, which the longer-serving members of staff were permitted to read. The paper mainly carried advertisements for new products and lines, but there was section entitled, 'Situations Vacant', where employers requiring staff could advertise.

One such notice, which attracted her attention, read as follows:

Crockford's Drapery Emporium of Leyton, Essex, seeks an experienced and mature drapery assistant to assume responsibility for curtaining and drapes of a bespoke nature, for a growing number of esteemed clients. Opportunity for advancement. References essential.

Rose knew her references were excellent. She did not consider herself mature in age, but believed herself to be mature in experience. Crockford's sounded like it could be a step towards her ultimate goal. Leyton was only about seven miles from central London and although she had travelled little, she understood that the railway service was reliable. If she moved to Leyton, she would be less than an hour away from the world she currently knew, so it would be easy to return if she felt the need.

She decided to apply and posted a letter of application. A week later, she received a response from Thomas Crockford, the proprietor, inviting her to visit his emporium in order that he could interview her and assess her suitability for the new position he was offering.

1.3

The duty officer took the call and wrote down the details: 'Stephenson Street, Leyton, you say ... and what's the house called? ... *Cambria* ... number fifty-nine ... OK, we'll get a patrol car round shortly.'

'George, can you take young Frank with you and go round to Stephenson Street? Just had a report from a worried neighbour about the old man who lives over the road from her. Bit of a recluse apparently and she hasn't seen him recently.'

'Yeah, OK, sarge ... hey, that's a good one ... a recluse and she hasn't seen him!'

Ten minutes later the two police officers drew up behind a milk float parked outside *Cambria*, 59, Stephenson Street. A milkman and presumably the neighbour who had telephoned were waiting patiently on the pavement.

'OK, what's the problem?' asked PC George Palmer as he and his new colleague, PC Frank Meredith, got out of the car.

'It's old Mr Williams,' the milkman answered. 'I can't make him come to the door. There's two pints of sour milk in his porch. He only has one pint a week. I've been on holiday and my stand-in must have carried on leaving his milk. I opened the letter box to shout to him and the smell coming out is awful … knocked me sideways it did … and there's flies too, all over the net curtains at the back.'

'Right, come on,' George Palmer said, indicating to young Frank. 'Let's take a look.' Together with the milkman, they went to the front door. George rang the bell.

'That's not worked for years,' said the milkman. You need to use the door knocker … really hard. Mr Williams is a bit deaf.'

George tried the door knocker … there was no response from within the house.

They stepped out of the porch and the milkman waited while the police officers peered through the front windows.

'Can't see a thing,' said George. 'These windows haven't been cleaned in years … there's more muck on the inside. What's round the back?'

The three of them made their way around the side of the end of terrace house, negotiating with care several rubbish bags and a couple of rusty fridges, all of which looked as if they had been thrown over the sagging garden fence by fly-tippers. At the rear, they could see that all of the windows were closed apart from one small fanlight in the upstairs bedroom. Downstairs, the net curtains and the windowsills inside were covered with blowflies, just as the milkman had described. The policemen tried to peer through the dirty glass and nets into the rear sitting room.

'No good,' said George. 'Still can't see anything. You say there was a bad smell when you shouted through the letterbox?'

'Not arf,' confirmed the milkman. 'Didn't arf hum … the smell I mean, not the flies!'

They returned to the front door. George pushed open the letterbox and peered inside. 'Mr Williams! Mr Williams!' he shouted, before he fell back, bending double and exhaling every ounce of air from his lungs. 'Dear, oh, dear!' he gasped. 'Just got a whiff … it's putrid, absolutely bloody putrid!'

The milkman looked relieved and a little smug. This wasn't going to be a waste of police time after all.

'We'll have to break the door down. Stand away everyone.' Burly PC George Palmer put his shoulder close to the lock and forcibly barged against it a couple of times before the doorframe started to splinter. Then he stepped back and raised his boot to finish off the door. After one good stab, it gave way and flew back on its hinges. A wall of warmer, stale stinking air hit them in the face.

'Stay back. Stay back for a moment. Let some air out and mind the flies!' ordered George. They waited for half a minute. 'OK, Frank, come on, you follow me. Mind how you go. Hold your arm up over your nose, like this.'

George and Frank entered the house, stepping over a scattering of junk mail before negotiating their way through a hallway partially blocked by bulging black bags and bundles of old newspapers bound up with string.

In the shabby nicotine-stained back room, next to the filthy kitchen, they discovered the decomposing body of Harry Williams. He was sitting in a heavy leather armchair, almost worn through in places, his head lolling to one side, reading glasses on his swollen abdomen. His right arm was hanging over the side of the chair, a newspaper strewn across the floor below. PC Palmer noticed that three fingers were missing from the right hand. The nails from the remaining thumb and index finger lay directly below on part of the newspaper. It looked as if Harry Williams had been reading the paper and had suffered a heart attack or a stroke.

For young PC Frank Meredith it was a particularly gruesome sight and his first dead body. Maggots were crawling all over the exposed flesh of the corpse. His boss looked across towards him and lowered his sleeve from his nose to speak. 'Sorry laddie … that your first had to be one like this. Take in what you can and then we'll be out, sharpish.'

Frank looked away from the body and glanced at the newspaper scattered on the floor. It was the *Leyton Chronicle*, dated Friday, 28 June 1996, three weeks before. Had the old man been dead that long? Before Frank could see anything else, George tapped him on the shoulder and inclined his head towards the front door. It wasn't a moment too soon. With rising nausea and an intense desire to get out of the house, Frank stumbled behind his colleague towards the exit and back out into the sunshine, where both were able to inhale cleansing breaths of beautiful, cool, fresh air.

1.4

Rose took a horse-drawn omnibus to Liverpool Street Station, where she caught a Great Eastern train to Leyton. Fifteen minutes later, she stepped down onto the platform, well before her eleven o'clock interview.

As she left the station, with time to spare, she decided to use the opportunity to get a feel for the atmosphere of the town on her way to *Crockford's Drapery Emporium* situated at 41–48 High Street. It was a warm day in early May 1898, with a good number of people out and about, bustling from one shop to another. The town had a fair sprinkling of trades and a pleasing variety of goods on offer. Rose strolled a little along High Street, noting two butchers, a fishmonger, a combined poulterer and fruiterer, a chemist, two hardware shops – their entrances festooned with a brushes and tin baths – a boot maker, a piano and musical instrument seller, a book shop, a tea shop, a grand hotel, and no less than four public houses. Centre place to all of these stood Crockford's Drapery Emporium.

Rose had carried an image in her mind, largely influenced by her previous knowledge of the London department stores, so, it was with some slight element of disappointment that she first surveyed 41–48 High Street from the pavement opposite. She had to admit though that the building had quite an imposing air, when compared to those around. It had three storeys constructed of red brick, Georgian in architectural style, above four large glass display windows on the ground floor, each dressed in a pleasing manner to show the goods on offer to their best advantage. The sign 'Crockford's Drapery Emporium' dominated the upper façade in white wooden letters three

14

feet high on a black background. In fact, the longer she looked at it, the more she felt her early disappointment fade, replaced by a feeling of excitement, that she could make a real start here, that this was an up-and-coming place and if her interview went well, then who knows where she might eventually end up?

Rose took a deep breath and entered the shop.

'Good morning, madam, may I be of assistance?' The question came from an older lady standing behind the haberdashery counter just inside the door. Although polite, her manner was not especially warm.

'Good morning,' replied Rose. 'I have an appointment to see Mr Crockford.'

The assistant's expression darkened marginally. 'Your name?' she asked rather curtly.

'Rosetta Ince … Miss Rosetta Ince.'

The assistant's expression darkened further. 'Please wait here for a moment. I will ascertain if Mr Crockford is available.'

Rose looked around her and towards the recesses of the shop. There were several customers at the different counters. In one corner, she spotted a sign: 'Gentlemen's Department' and it was in that direction that the stern and rather formidable lady assistant had disappeared, presumably to speak to the proprietor. She returned a minute later.

'Mr Crockford will see you shortly. Please take a seat while you are waiting.' She pointed to a simple wooden chair placed at the end of her counter. By then, one or two of the other assistants, all much younger than Rose, had noticed her and she saw one of the girls cover her mouth with her hand to make an aside to her colleague. The other girl stifled a giggle and both quickly returned to their work following a glance full of rebuke from the formidable lady on haberdashery.

Rose noted the orderly nature of Crockford's, and the wide variety of goods displayed and offered. A young porter, shouldering a large parcel, passed one of the counters and stopped to listen to a whispered comment from one of the young girls, before looking Rose's way. As he passed by her, he nodded and gave a cheery 'Good mornin',' before winking and continuing on his way out of the shop. As the porter left, Rose thought she detected a scowl from the lady on haberdashery.

In just a few minutes, she felt she had gained a brief insight into the order of seniority and the politics of working at Crockford's. She was not particularly perturbed however, and felt confident that her previous work experience in a much larger enterprise and the prospect of running her own department ought to mean that she would be equal to the task of coping with the 'dragon' under whose stern gaze she was at that moment seated.

Rose noticed a lady approaching from the interior. She was in her twenties, tall, slim, pretty, fair-haired and, Rose guessed, slightly older than herself. She had an air of confidence and greeted Rose warmly offering her hand.

'Good morning, Miss Ince. I'm Louisa Crockford. My father is ready to see you now. If you would like to follow me ...'

Rose accompanied Louisa to the rear of the shop. Louisa opened a door into a corridor and they proceeded to the end to a room marked, 'Office'. Louisa knocked lightly and showed Rose in, where she was introduced to Thomas Crockford.

1.5

Eric Huntley was the Empty Housing Officer for Leyton Council. It was May 2000 and he was new to his job in Leyton, but had over ten years' experience with a previous council. He had started the week before and had spent the first few days going through the files in his office, familiarising himself with the district and finding out where the empty properties on his books were located. He had decided to spend the second week visiting each property, taking photographs, speaking to neighbours and trying to discover any leads to track down absent owners. It was his job to get as many of the empty properties as possible back into use. One glance on drawing up outside *Cambria*, 59 Stephenson Street, was enough to confirm that this had to be one of the worst cases of property neglect that he had ever encountered.

The end of terrace house was in a dreadful state. The ground floor windows and doors were protected with metal security shutters to deter intruders. The glass in several of the upstairs windows had been smashed – target practise by local youths. One of the bedroom windows was wide open and the wind was pulling at the tattered remains of a faded blue curtain. The windowsill had become a landing pad for a squadron of feral pigeons. A pair were billing and cooing on the sagging gutter above. A downpipe had parted from its fixing, permitting rainwater to soak into the wall, causing a notable damp patch. The garden was strewn with overfilled rubbish bags and various unwanted domestic items. In summary, the house was in a pitiful state. As nature continued its attack, from the weather outside and from the mould, boring insects and vermin inside, it was inevitable that unless something was done to arrest the decay, it would ultimately become a ruin, fit for nothing but demolition.

Eric's secretary had briefed him on the history of the town. She had explained that Stephenson Street was in the 'Falcon Village'. It was one of several streets built by the Falcon Foundry in the 1920s to house its workers. The foundry had closed in 1982 making the workforce redundant. In its heyday, it had built most of the steam engines that operated on the former London North East Railway. Shortly after the foundry closed, the buildings were demolished and the site now remained a large vacant plot.

Eric knocked on the door of the immediate neighbour and a middle-aged lady opened the door.

'Good morning madam, I'm the Council Empty Housing Officer,' he explained showing his identity badge. 'Just wondered if you could tell me a bit about next door, like how long it has been empty and who used to live there?'

'Are the council finally going to do something about it?' she demanded. 'Not before time.'

'Well, I want to get something sorted out. It's obviously been empty for a while and it certainly lets down the other houses in the street, yours included of course.'

The lady softened her attitude. 'That house has been the bane of our lives,' she complained. 'We've had problems with rats, vandals, squatters, drugs – you name it, we've had it. Goodness knows what effect it's had on the price of our house. We can't move, you know. Who'd buy a house with that next door?'

'How long has it been in that state?' asked Eric.

'Years! Harry Williams was the last occupant and he died in 1996, aged ninety-five, I think. The milkman found him, you know. He'd been dead three weeks. We were away on holiday at the time. July it was, so we missed all the drama, but the house was in a shocking state. He was a recluse and he just let the house go, you know … no interest whatsoever in maintaining it properly.'

'So, if I could trace an owner, or failing that, get the council to purchase it with a view to making it habitable again, you'd be in favour then?'

'In favour? That's an understatement if ever I heard one. We'd be delighted! As far as we're concerned, the sooner that house is repaired and reoccupied by a respectable person or family, the better.'

1.6

Peter and Felicity Sefton lived in a stone cottage in Wiltshire, not far from the market town of Marlborough. They'd been there ten years and had chosen it because they liked its pretty appearance and quiet location. Felicity was a schoolteacher at the local primary school, while Peter was a private investor, trading shares from home.

Peter was comfortable researching companies and markets, analysing charts and weighing up when to buy and when to sell. He enjoyed investing, always hoping to make a decent return, but unfortunately not always succeeding. Still, that was investing, impossible to be right every time, but right enough of the time to make it worthwhile.

Apart from shares, he sometimes bought gold sovereigns if he spotted them at a tempting price. He regularly checked jewellers' windows, auctions, and antique markets. In fact, it was a call from a dealer contact in the trade that had sent him to Marlborough that afternoon. The dealer had a couple of coins for him and after they had chatted for a while and concluded their business, Peter had wandered over to the nearby antiques centre eventually leaving with the marriage certificate.

He was no novice when it came to genealogical research. Using the Internet and other records, he had already researched his family tree and often at family gatherings, he was asked about it.

'When are you going to find the blue blood?' Uncle John had once teased. 'I'm sure we're related to that aristocratic family with the same name.'

'I'm doing my best,' Peter had countered in reply. 'Felicity would love to be Lady Sefton but so far I can only find coal in our blood. Most of our ancestors, certainly the ones living a hundred and fifty years ago, were either mining coal below ground or sorting it on the surface.'

'Uncovered any secrets or skeletons in your research?'

'Not really, but I have discovered something quite sad.'

'Oh? What was that?'

'My great-great-grandfather, Francis Sefton, he would be your great-grandfather, was a victim of a coalmining disaster back in 1878. The coroner's report described him as Victim Number 185, identified only "by his trousers and his wedding ring". The deaths were caused by an explosion deep in the mine.'

'How awful. I'm sure I've never heard of it.'

'I'm not surprised. My father hadn't either and yet your grandfather was one of the five children who were orphaned as a result of the accident.'

'Amazing … what happened to their mother?'

'She'd unfortunately died two years before. It must have been pretty grim for the family at the time … no welfare state to provide a safety net. I must admit, it sent a chill down my spine when I first found Francis' name on the list of victims.'

'What about the children afterwards?'

'The eldest son was about twenty-one and he took over as head of the household, but he and his brothers continued to work at the colliery.'

'I suppose there was no alternative. I wonder why my grandparents never spoke of it.'

'I've no idea. Perhaps they wanted to block it out and start afresh.'

'Makes you feel a bit guilty though,' Uncle John had continued. 'We're always moaning about our lives, but hard physical work in a coal mine for low pay can't have been much fun.'

'Exactly what I thought … with genealogy, you just never know what might come to light.'

After dinner that evening, Peter remembered the marriage certificate. 'Just popping out to the car to get that certificate,' he said to Felicity as he got up from his chair.

'Don't be long. It's below freezing, you know.'

He went out to the garage crossing the shingle driveway. It was frosty and the small stones crunched and stuck to his shoes. He retrieved the certificate from the car's glovebox, taking it back into the cottage. He looked at his watch … *probably just enough time to fire up the computer*, he thought, *and run a search on a couple of family history websites*. He called out to Felicity: 'I'm going to have a quick look on the computer … see if I can turn anything up about the couple who got married.'

'OK … that programme you like is on at ten.'

'Yeah, OK … just a quick look.'

1.7

Eric Huntley returned to his office at Leyton Council and took out the folder for *Cambria*, 59 Stephenson Street. Fetching a coffee from the machine, he returned to his desk and began to scan the contents.

Harry Williams, the previous owner, had died in July 1996 with no known relatives. The council's Bereavement Officer had searched the deceased's house for a will or family papers but had found nothing of significance. Police enquiries had revealed little, other than the neighbours thought the deceased's family came from Kidwelly in Carmarthenshire.

Initially the house had been cleared of perishables and locked up. A year later, looking even more dilapidated and unoccupied, the house had attracted a number of uninvited guests. The immediate neighbours wondered if the house had squatters and had contacted the police.

The police found that the lock on the back door had been forced. They discovered signs of damage and vandalism. Someone had tried to bypass the electricity meter and at the base of the stairs, an attempt had been made to start a fire. More alarmingly, they found a number of used syringes in one of the bedrooms. The police had recommended that the council make the property more secure. Eric's predecessor had organised the fitting of steel shutters to the doors and ground floor windows, and the clearing of the house. The folder contained some quotations from second-hand furniture dealers and house clearers. Several pieces of antique furniture had been sent to auction. The net proceeds after deduction of funeral expenses had been deposited in an account pending the tracing of any heirs.

There were copies of two letters in the file from the Council Solicitor outlining the action taken so far. The first letter explained that they had established that Harry Williams had a bank account and a savings account. They had advertised in the local press for relatives to come forward, but without success, this despite the local media interest the death had attracted at the time.

21

Eric briefly switched to some cuttings from the local paper. A reporter had tried to find out what was known of the reclusive Harry Williams, who had died alone in his home and shockingly lain there for three weeks before his body was discovered. Various comments from neighbours were quoted: 'He hardly ever went out, certainly not in the daytime.'; 'He used to get all of his shopping at the small corner shop close by. He usually went in the evening, because it didn't close until ten o'clock.'

One neighbour claimed that she had tried to offer assistance at times, but had always been rebuffed. Another mentioned that: 'Mr Williams never appeared to have any visitors. He didn't take holidays. He'd allowed his house to go to wrack and ruin.'

A photograph taken around the time of his death, showed the house in a slightly better state than when Eric had just seen it, but even then, it was obviously in a bad way.

The second letter from the Council Solicitor gave the address of a firm of probate researchers, Highborn Research, based in London, whom the council had contacted to see if they could trace any descendants with a legitimate claim to the estate. The letter was twelve months old. Eric decided to ask the Council Solicitor whether any further progress had been made. If not, he would recommend disposal of the house via public auction on behalf of the deceased's estate, with a condition of sale being a requirement to renovate the house within a limited time period.

Eric dialled the Council Solicitor's number and was put through after a short delay.

'Hello, Mr Huntley. My secretary's just handed me the details of the Williams' case. What did you want to know?'

'Can you tell me whether Highborn Research managed to find any relatives?'

'Let me have a look ... ah, yes, here's a letter from them. No, they regret to say that they failed to trace any close kin.'

'Right, well I think we should go for a compulsory purchase order. The house is in a terrible state. I've been down there this morning. It really lets down the whole street.'

'Fine. I'll get onto to it right away and get the ball rolling on the legal side. Might take a few months, but at least we can send it to auction, get it off our hands and put the proceeds into the deceased's estate.'

'Excellent. Let me know when the Compulsory Purchase Order is due to be served. I can fix the notice on the property when you're ready.'

'Will do.'

'Many thanks. Goodbye!'

Eric replaced the receiver and felt satisfied that progress was finally being made with at least one of his empty properties. *Ah, one other thing*, he thought. Before putting the file away, he picked up the phone again, spoke to Waste Collection, and instructed them to send a team to *Cambria*, 59 Stephenson Street, to clear all of the rubbish from the garden.

1.8

'Good morning, Miss Ince, thank you for coming. Do sit down,' Thomas Crockford said in a polite and kindly manner. His daughter had left the room after the introduction and closed the door behind her. 'Now let's have a look at your application.' He quickly scanned her carefully written letter.

'This is to be a new position, running the bespoke curtains and drapes department here at Crockford's. We are an expanding business you know ...' He paused to read further and then looked at her references. 'These are very good. I see you've been working at *Davis & Davis* in Oxford Street since you left school and that after your apprenticeship you have been specialising in drapes and hangings – excellent. Now, how old are you, Miss Ince?'

'Twenty-three, Mr Crockford, sir.'

'And where were you born?'

'Paddington, sir.'

'Just Mr Crockford will suffice, Miss Ince. Now, twenty-three is rather young for a position of this nature, but I do see that your department head says that you have had a good deal of experience and that you stood in for your senior while she was incapacitated for a month, recovering from illness. Tell me a little of your customers. What sort of work have you been doing?'

'We have a good number of wealthy customers, Mr Crockford. You can imagine that the area we serve has many households of prosperous means.'

Mr Crockford nodded in agreement. He was listening intently appreciating the description of the type of customers he was also hoping to attract.

Rose continued: 'The lady of the household generally makes the decisions on colours and patterns, but we are often asked to advise and assist. Usually they come to our establishment initially or, in the case of old and valued clients, they prefer that we visit them at their residence and provide a selection of swatches and pattern books for their inspection and perusal. Once the choices are made – these could be for curtains, swags, mantles, counterpanes or door coverings, for example – we take measurements and then obtain the material and make up the order according to the customers' requirements. We are usually retained to hang and install the finished articles.'

'What happens if, for example, you find that the rails for the drapes are inadequate or poorly positioned?'

'We either send a specialist artisan or the customer employs someone to install the requisite fixings, but this is discussed when the measurements are taken and before we accept the order.'

'I see,' considered Thomas, 'and what about the actual making of the items? What is the extent of your experience in this regard?'

'Early in my drapery apprenticeship, it became apparent that I had a talent for dressmaking and seamstressing. For two years, I was engaged on duties associated with alterations and repairs, but later advanced to "made to measure" dressmaking for our wealthy individual clients. My senior, who was also involved with curtains and drapes, started to take me with her on outside visits associated with the bespoke service offered by *Davis & Davis*. She sought permission for me to transfer to drapes and hangings permanently and so for the last four years that is what I have been doing.'

'Excellent! Well, let me tell you a little of what is happening here and how your experience might fit into my plans. Leyton is expanding rapidly with dozens of new villas being built to accommodate a growing population. The wealth and influence of London is spreading here, you know. Affluent citizens looking to move to the district, to escape the noise and smell associated with the city, have discovered that by moving just a few miles out, they can enjoy far greater space and amenity than in the centre of London. I want to provide a drapery service to them, to rival that of the great emporia of the West End.' Mr Crockford spoke with enthusiasm. 'I have increased the size of the business three-fold in the last ten years. We now have five apprentices and a porter. Mrs Robins looks after haberdashery; she's been here for fifteen years. My daughter, Louisa, is in charge of women's attire. For my part, I concentrate on our male clientele, in addition of course to the general running of the establishment. The bespoke curtaining and drapes department will be a new addition to the services we offer, but I believe there is sufficient untapped potential and demand in Leyton to ensure an adequate supply of work and commissions. It may be slow at first, but I am confident that if the quality and suitability of our work is high, then the customers will come to us rather than look further afield. You would have one junior assistant assigned to you and I already have two outworkers in mind who could make up orders off the premises.'

Rose began to get the feeling that he intended to offer the new position to her, but her expression betrayed none of her excitement. She listened attentively.

'I can provide accommodation for you here at the shop with your own room and seniority over the five apprentices who also reside here. They share rooms on the top floor. I am a widower, but employ a housekeeper, Mrs Jones and her servant. My daughter and I also have rooms here. You will be required to exercise a level of supervision over the younger girls, but Mrs Jones acts as housekeeper and housemother to them. Naturally, your experience will put you on a par with Mrs Robins, as far as the seniority within the shop is concerned.'

So he's a widower, thought Rose, *and not an unattractive one at that, but perhaps a little too old for me.* Rose had never had a romantic attachment or relations with a man. Marriage and family were still not something she wished for, but marriage to a successful draper … that could give her a shortcut to achieving her ambitions. She smiled inwardly.

For his part, Thomas Crockford was quite taken with Rose, although any romantic idea was quickly dispelled when he considered the age difference. Mrs Crockford had been dead twenty years. She had died in childbirth along with the second son she bore, both of them dying coincidently on the third day after his birth. At the time, his son David was only three and Louisa was eight. Louisa had provided the tonic and distraction he had needed to pull him from depression and she had given him the incentive to carry on with his life and business.

Thomas Crockford was impressed with Rose's knowledge and experience. The fact that she had worked at *Davis & Davis* in Oxford Street would go down well with his customers. He noticed, to her credit, that she had little trace of a 'London' accent. The more he considered the lovely young lady seated on the other side of his desk, the more certain he became that she could be the right person to take control of his new department.

'I would like to offer the position to you, Miss Ince. Would you like to take a tour of my establishment? If you have any questions then do not be afraid to ask. If afterwards you feel disposed to take up my offer of employment, then I am sure we will be able to agree terms and can set in motion the necessary arrangements to effect your move from your present employer to Crockford's.'

They passed an hour looking around the shop; Mr Crockford describing the way he ran the business and the standards he expected from his staff. His attitude seemed firm but fair and nothing he said in any way caused disappointment or doubt to dampen Rose's growing enthusiasm for what she was seeing and how it suited her ambitions. Louisa joined them. She seemed relaxed and friendly, not stuffy or distant. Rose felt that even though she was her employer's daughter, she and Louisa could perhaps become friends.

At the end of the tour, Rose was entirely content with what she had seen. She confirmed her acceptance of the terms offered and shook hands with Thomas and Louisa Crockford. She was engaged to set up and run the new department on a trial period of three months, with a starting salary of fifteen pounds per year. This was a significant increase on her existing rate of pay. She agreed to give *Davis & Davis* one month's notice and would start at Crockford's on the first Monday in June 1898, moving into her room the day before.

Peter settled himself at his computer and studied the marriage certificate carefully for the first time. He loved to play the detective and he felt the familiar buzz he always got when starting research on a new family. He noticed that the bride and groom both lived in Apsley Street: the groom at number 46 and the bride at number 15. Was that a coincidence or a temporary situation prior to the wedding? Perhaps, they were neighbours and he wondered if that was how they had met.

Certificate of Marriage

Marriage Solemnized at St Martin's Church in the Parish of Leyton in the County of Essex

When Married	Name and Surname	Age	Condition	Rank or Profession	Residence at Time of Marriage	Father's Name	Rank or Profession
15th January 1900	John Williams	30	Bachelor	Leaman	46 Apsley St. Leyton	Arthur Williams	Hotel Keeper
	Louisa Matilda Crockford	29	Spinster	Draper	15 Apsley St. Leyton	Thomas Crockford	Master Draper

Married in St Martin's Church according to the Rites and Ceremonies of the Established Church. By Licence ....By me, Thomas Walter

This Marriage was solemnized between us, John Williams Louisa Matilda Crockford   In the presence of us, Rosetta Price Frank Williams

He looked at the occupations. He initially read the groom's occupation as 'Leaman', but could find no such trade listed. Then he realised that the vicar's loopy handwriting was to blame and that the groom was a 'Seaman', and that made sense, as Leyton was not far from the docks in the East End of London. Louisa's occupation was shown as 'Draper', so perhaps she worked with her father who described himself as 'Master Draper'. The groom's father was 'Hotel Keeper'.

Peter looked up Apsley Street on the 1891 Census Return, nine years before the marriage. It wasn't there, which was odd. He tried the 1901 Census and found it, so it must have been built during the intervening ten years. A quick search of the current property market in Leyton soon brought up a picture of 32 Apsley Street, just a few doors away from the groom's address. The estate agent's photograph showed a typical late Victorian, bay fronted, terraced house with two bedrooms. He wondered whether number 46 looked similar.

Peter next tried a 'persons' search on the 1891 Census and this time had immediate success. John Williams, the groom, was living with his younger brother Frank, along with parents Arthur and Florence in Ventnor, Isle of Wight. Arthur was head of the household and the census recorded that he was 'Keeper of a Boarding House'. John, aged twenty-one, was listed as 'Seaman', and brother, Frank, aged fourteen, as 'Scholar'. Every member of the Williams family had been born on the Isle of Wight.

He also found the bride's family on the 1891 Census. They were living at 41–44 High Street, Leyton. Thomas Crockford, widower, headed the household as 'Draper'. In 1891, he was forty-three. Louisa, his daughter, was twenty, and there was a son, David, aged fifteen. The Census showed two other girls in the household, aged sixteen and eighteen, who were listed as 'Draper's Apprentices'. Mr Crockford obviously had a drapery shop and in 1891, the family and staff lived on the premises.

Peter then tried a trade directory for 1900 and found *Crockford's Drapery Emporium*. It had expanded to occupy numbers 41–48 High Street, Leyton. Presumably, Mr Crockford had prospered and changed his residential address from his shop to a private house, because at the time of the marriage he had the shop and his house at 15 Apsley Street.

He looked more closely at the witnesses: Frank Williams, the groom's brother, was no doubt the best man. Rosetta Price was the other witness. Peter was fairly certain that she would have been Louisa's bridesmaid. He found Rosetta Price too in 1891, living in Islington, London, aged nineteen, a draper's assistant, born in Llanelly, South Wales. *That fits very nicely*, Peter thought. She and Louisa must surely have met through a connection with the drapery trade. Perhaps, by the time of the wedding, Rosetta Price was even working at Crockford's, but he couldn't be sure.

One detail from the certificate stood out: 'Married by Licence'. That was unusual. Church of England weddings normally took place after Banns. That gave anyone who knew of a legal impediment to the marriage the opportunity to make it known. 'Married by Licence' on the other hand, could imply an element of haste, as no Banns would have been read.

Peter wondered about this for a while. Given the groom's occupation, he thought it possible that he could have been on leave and the couple might have wanted to marry before he returned to sea. He checked the date of the wedding ... 15 January 1900 ... a Monday; not quite the traditional Saturday wedding he'd originally imagined. The London docks were conveniently near for a mariner like John Williams. Peter thought he must have being doing reasonably well to live in Apsley Street and wondered whether he was a ship's officer rather than just a 'Seaman'.

Unfortunately, the census returns did not show if the head of a household owned or rented the address at which they resided, but on the question of rank, Peter came up with the answer. Searching crew lists, leaving from London in 1900, he found the following entry.

Date: 19 January 1900
Port of Departure: London
Ship's Name: RMS Kidwelly Castle, Castle Mail Packet Co. Ltd
Name of officer: John Williams, Chief Engineer
Destination: Cape Town

With some satisfaction, Peter sat back from the computer. Just four days after the wedding, John had left London on the RMS Kidwelly Castle, his destination Cape Town, South Africa. That had to be the reason or part of the reason why John and Louisa had married by Licence and on a Monday too. Hang on though, he thought. In 1900, Great Britain was at war in South Africa, fighting the Boers in The Boer War. It occurred to Peter that any vessel sailing from London to Cape Town at that time would probably have been used, to some extent, by the British War Office. He looked up the history of the ship's owners, the Castle Mail Packet Co. Ltd, and his suspicion was confirmed.

In the autumn of 1899, the *RMS Kidwelly Castle* was one of several vessels commissioned by the War Office to transport troops and equipment to South Africa.

1.10

The staff gathered for breakfast, as usual. It was just after eight o' clock. Mr Crockford carried out his daily inspection at nine and everyone had to be at their stations by then. Each evening, most of the fancy window goods were folded up and put away, hence each morning the stock had to be put back on display with labels and price tickets. Amy and Dorothy had already been down to remove the shutters and dress the windows.

Mr Crockford was a stickler for detail. He carried out a thorough inspection each morning before the shop opened for business. Every article had to be clearly marked and displayed in a tidy and orderly manner. The female staff were expected to look clean and presentable, with pinafores freshly laundered and ironed.

That particular morning, there was a growing air of excitement around the breakfast table. It was Saturday, and at close of business that evening, the shop would remain closed until Tuesday morning. The reason, that Louisa Crockford was getting married on Monday and Mr Crockford, after careful consideration, had decided that it would be a kind gesture to give all of the staff a day's holiday so that they could attend the wedding. He could have insisted that they work as normal, but he knew they would be distracted and that it would be easier for all if he closed the shop.

He hadn't been able to give his customers as much notice as he would have liked, due to the short time which had elapsed between his consenting to the marriage and the date fixed for it to take place.

However, Mondays were generally quiet, especially in January.

He liked his prospective son-in-law, John Williams. He understood that John's leave in England was limited. He was a ship's engineer – Chief Engineer, no less – and his ship was under the jurisdiction of the War Office to transport troops and stores to Cape Town, where the war was not going well for Britain. John and Louisa had been engaged for over a year, so a certain amount of haste was understandable and acceptable. He appreciated too that at twenty-nine, Louisa was not getting any younger and marriage opportunities were likely to diminish, as she got older. He felt that it was time she settled down with a husband and started her own life. Of course, he would miss her in the shop, but he had already thought about how he would manage without her.

He was optimistic about finding a replacement. He would advertise again in the *Drapery News*. If that source of potential employees proved to be as fortuitous as it had been in providing Rosetta Ince, eighteen months earlier, then he would indeed be a happy man.

John Williams had spent little time in Leyton during the engagement. His last leave, six weeks before, had been for just five days. He had been at sea during Christmas and New Year and Louisa had missed him greatly. His ship had returned from Cape Town and had berthed at the East India Docks early on the morning of 7 January. The vessel required extra maintenance, allowing him a generous twelve days' leave. The day after his return, he had told Thomas Crockford – with Louisa at his side – that they wished to marry before he returned to sea. John explained to Louisa's father that he had enquired at St Martin's Church and it was possible for the marriage to take place by Special Licence on Monday, 15 January, just seven days away.

Mr Crockford gave his blessing to the wedding and Louisa had set about organising the event. She didn't want a grand affair and the couple decided on a quiet wedding, with guests limited to immediate family, close friends and the staff from the shop. She had asked Rose to be her bridesmaid and John had asked his brother Frank to be his best man.

The time for the ceremony was set at eleven o'clock, followed by a luncheon reception at The George Hotel in Leyton High Street, just a few doors away from Crockford's Drapery Emporium. Afterwards, they would leave by train for John's parents' hotel at Ventnor on the Isle of Wight. His ship was due to leave London the following Friday, which meant that they would have only three nights in Ventnor, before returning to John's house in Leyton on the eve of his departure once again for Cape Town.

Louisa and Rose had been making new best dresses for some time, which were both pale in colour, and Louisa's was perfectly suitable as a wedding dress. Little work was needed to finish them. Louisa had collected John's smartest uniform from the laundry. She had checked to see what her father intended to wear and had made sure that everything he needed was ready and prepared for the big day. She had called at Mr Douglas, the portrait photographer, who had agreed to a special sitting during which he would photograph her and John immediately following the ceremony. It would take about thirty minutes, giving them enough time afterwards to walk the few doors down to The George Hotel for the wedding luncheon.

As Rose sat at breakfast that Saturday morning, listening to the young girls chattering about the wedding, she was not only excited by the honour of being the bridesmaid. She had another reason ... she was thrilled at the prospect of seeing Frank again. Her mind drifted back to their first meeting on the previous Wednesday evening ...

She and Louisa had been invited to dinner at 46 Apsley Street to discuss the arrangements. Mrs Jones, the housekeeper from Crockford's, had been sent over earlier to cook a meal for them, which smelled delicious when they arrived. John showed them into the parlour.

'Rosetta, I would like to introduce you to my brother, Frank. Frank, this is Miss Ince, Louisa's friend and her bridesmaid.'

Rose had always thought John a handsome man, but on seeing Frank, she was even more impressed. She felt sure that Frank must have noticed her cheeks flush when she offered her hand to him.

'I'm delighted to make your acquaintance, Miss Ince. I have heard much about you, all favourable of course.'

'Thank you, Mr Williams.'

'Oh, please call me Frank ... we need to be less formal, especially with our joint responsibilities towards my brother and your dear friend Louisa, my future sister-in-law.'

'Yes of course ... and please call me Rose.' She barely dared to look him in the eye. Louisa had told her that Frank was twenty-four, six years younger than his brother. He stood nearly six feet tall, of average build. He had a full head of fair hair and a very distinctive waxed moustache. He had a presence, which she couldn't at first determine, but as they all chatted and laughed Rose realised he had a confidence and an attitude, which she decided, was most attractive. Frank had been lodging with his brother for nearly six months. He worked as a clerk in a shipping agent's office near the Albert Docks. By all accounts, he was doing well and had good prospects.

It was during dinner that Frank dropped his bombshell. It was news to everyone seated at the table, including John.

'I've been given nine months' sabbatical. I spent this morning at the Guildhall because I've decided to answer the government's call for volunteers to join the City Imperial Volunteers and serve my country in South Africa. I was sworn in and I have to report to barracks next Thursday for the issue of uniform and kit.'

There was silence for a few moments. John looked surprised and dismayed. 'Are you sure you've done the right thing? What about your position at the shipping agents?'

'It's fine. It's all agreed. I'm not the only one; there are several of us who've volunteered. By all accounts it should improve our prospects when we get back.'

'What if you *don't* come back?' asked John.

There was another awkward silence until Frank continued once more. 'Look, I can ride and I can shoot. I've already had military training.'

'But look what happened down there in December,' John said.

'How many was it? Something like 2,800 casualties on our side compared to about 280 Boers, in one week alone!'

Frank, full of confidence, waved aside his brother's concerns. 'Look, I'll be fine. The government has promised to change tactics and update our weapons. They're replacing lances with rapid-fire rifles. The war will be over in no time and I should be back by autumn at the latest. That's what everyone believes. Besides, some of my colleagues might be in the same company and if not, then I'll soon make some new friends and we'll be able to look out for each other. Don't be worried, I'm not!'

'What sort of military training have you had?' asked Rose, interrupting the conversation between the brothers and surprising herself at her boldness. In fact, she was still a little unsettled at her reaction to meeting Frank. Normally so confident and single-minded in wanting to achieve her ambitions, for the first time ever, she was suddenly aware that perhaps there were other aspects to life, apart from seeking goals allied to commercial success.

Frank turned to her. 'I was a horseman in the Hampshire and Isle of Wight Yeomanry. They said that I would be ideally suited to being trained as a mounted trooper in the CIV. We'll probably spend most of our time on scouting duties. It should be fun.'

'When did do you say you have to report to barracks?' asked John.

'The eighteenth, next Thursday; why do you ask?'

'Because we sail from London on the nineteenth and we're due to embark troops for the Cape on the twentieth from Southampton. I'll bet anything that if your enlistment programme goes according to the usual timings, you'll be among the men we take on at Southampton.'

'That's great then. You can make sure that I get special passenger status!'

John said no more on the subject at that point and the conversation moved on to the wedding arrangements. Little did the others know that he had mixed emotions about taking his younger brother to war, to the horrors that would surely await him. He understood that Frank wanted to seek adventure and to see the world, but he wished that he had thought of some other way, rather than joining up. On his recent return from Cape Town they had repatriated over 200 casualties with a variety of injuries, some very serious indeed. He had heard first-hand just how hard the fighting had been and how the Boers, with better equipment and using unfamiliar tactics, had given the British troops an unexpected and thorough bloody nose. The war was no picnic and he truly feared for his brother's safety ...

After the shop opened that Saturday morning, Rose busied herself with her work and it wasn't until later in the day during a quiet spell that she recollected once again the conversation between the two brothers during dinner. What if Frank really was killed or badly injured? That would be awful and such a waste too! Frank was exciting. He had good prospects and John reckoned that if he stuck at his job then he had a good career ahead of him.

Imagine that, she thought, *my husband a shipping agent. Did I just say husband to myself? I think you may be getting ahead of yourself there, Rose Ince.* She scolded herself. *Marriage is not for you! Now, pull yourself together and concentrate. Let's just get these measurements correct for Miss Dalby's curtains.*

1.11

It was Thursday morning in early January 2011 at the London office of Highborn Research, a professional heir-tracing firm. During the night, the Treasury Solicitor's Office had published the weekly additions to the list of unclaimed estates via its Bona Vacantia Division website. After an early start, Highborn's main office was buzzing with researchers trawling the newly published list. They were trying to decide on which cases to tackle, hoping to find missing heirs to unclaimed assets and thereby earn Highborn's commission.

Nick Bastion, a senior partner in the firm, was coordinating efforts, receiving progress reports and making decisions on where to deploy his staff. Carol, his young trainee, stood beside her mentor, watching and learning.

Nick turned to Carol. 'The Treasury list is updated each week sometime between Wednesday night and Thursday morning. At one time the list showed the value of each estate but not anymore.'

'Why is that?' Carol asked.

'Fraud,' answered Nick. 'Crooks cottoned on to the opportunity to impersonate heirs. They went for the higher value estates, so four years ago the Treasury Solicitor stopped disclosing values. Now, we just get the name of the deceased, date of death and where they passed away.'

'So how do you choose which names to research?'

'Two factors mainly: was the deceased a homeowner and how common is the surname? We avoid Smith, Jones, Brown, Evans, etc, if we can.'

Tom, one of the senior researchers, shouted excitedly across the room. 'Nick! It looks like we've got our first heir on that Maidstone case.'

'Brilliant, Tom! Get Fred Howard over there ASAP. Hopefully, he can sign them up. Do we need certificates?'

'Yes, just to be certain.'

'OK, send him to the local register office first and then see if you can make an appointment for him with the potential heir.'

'Will do.'

Nick looked pleased. It was only eight o'clock. He decided he'd go back up to his office. 'Keep up the good work everybody. If anyone wants me, I'm upstairs.'

Nick returned to the relative tranquillity of his desk with a contented feeling. Things were going well, so he decided to spend a little time reviewing the firm's unsolved cases. He scanned a printout of names. The list was long. Normally, he worked methodically in alphabetical order, but for some reason he decided to dispense with convention and he picked one name at random towards the end of the list. The name 'Williams' caught his eye ... 'died July 1996'. *An awful name for an heir hunter,* Nick thought, but nevertheless he brought up the file on his computer and started to read the notes.

Early in 1999, Leyton Council's solicitors had written to Highborn Research asking for assistance. The council had failed to locate any close kin for Harry Williams, who had died in Leyton, aged ninety-five. Reading on, it seemed that Nick's firm had got nowhere either. The surname 'Williams' was the problem. The death certificate showed no place of birth. They hadn't been able to find a marriage for the deceased and therefore had not been able to confirm the names of his parents.

From enquiries at the time of death, the Council believed that the family had a Welsh connection, possibly the area around Kidwelly in South Wales. The house in which the deceased had lived was called *Cambria,* the Roman name for Wales. Due to the large number of 'Williams' in South Wales, Highborn's researchers had been unable to identify either the deceased's birth or any member of his family. There were copies of correspondence to Leyton Council confirming this.

The case had come to Highborn's attention again in 2002 when it was first published on the Bona Vacantia Division list. The value of the estate was shown at £67,000, but they had decided not to pursue it due to the setback three years earlier. Nick supposed that there must have been other potentially easier and more lucrative cases to chase at that time.

Research resources had moved on since 2002 and the Internet was now by far their most useful tool. It gave them instant access to property ownership details, census records, indexes of births, deaths and marriages, and to specialist genealogical websites, with an immense and diverse wealth of information, from electoral rolls to passenger shipping lists. *Yes,* Nick thought, *the choices and options have improved; perhaps we ought to have another look at this one.*

Nick first double-checked to see if the name was still on the latest Bona Vacantia Division list and was pleased to see that it was still there. No indication was given of value, but he already had that information from 2002.

He opened the file on his computer screen and noted that Leyton Council's solicitors had stated that Harry Williams had owned his house. Nick studied a scanned copy of his death certificate for a few moments.

Certificate of Death	
Registration District Essex South Western in the County of Essex	
Date and place of death On or about First July 1996 Cambria, 59 Stephenson Street, Leyton	
Name and surname Harry Williams	**Sex** Male
Date and place of birth 8th October 1900	
Occupation and usual address Patternmaker (retired) Cambria, 59 Stephenson Street, Leyton	
Name and surname of informant John Summerton	**Qualification** Causing body to be cremated
Usual Address Leyton Council Offices, High Street, Leyton, Essex	
Cause of death A) Intracerebral Haemorrhage B) Hypertension **Certified by P Wilkinson, Coroner for Essex** after post-mortem without inquest	
Date of registration Twenty-fourth July 1996	

The place of death was the same as his usual address, so he had obviously died at home. He noted that the death had occurred 'on or about' 1 July 1996. That implied uncertainty and meant that he had died alone. He saw that the informant was an employee of Leyton Council, the Council having assumed responsibility for the funeral arrangements. *How sad*, Nick thought. *Dying alone and having no friend or family member to organise the funeral. What a damning indictment of the world we live in today, an all too frequent occurrence, unfortunately.*

He pondered how they might proceed. Not knowing the place of birth was a problem and of course, the surname 'Williams' didn't help. Those were the main stumbling blocks, but the case had to be worth another look. He buzzed down to Carol and asked her to come up to his office.

1.12

Joan struggled with the wheelchair. It barely fitted into the back of their small car and she always had to take it apart before stowing it away, which in turn meant putting it back together when readying it for her twin sister Margaret. She wheeled it round to the passenger side and opened the door. Margaret was waiting to swing her legs out, as best she could, and with assistance from Joan managed to stand using her crutches before dropping down heavily on to the seat of the wheelchair.

'There we are. How's that? Do you want your blanket?'

'It's fine, don't fuss. I don't want to get too hot. Have you got the list?'

'Yes, of course I have, and I brought the memory stick for your computer, so that we can show them which type it is at the shop. You forgot it, last time.'

'All right, all right, I only asked!'

They set off from the disabled parking bay, with much huffing and puffing from Joan, who was pushing the wheelchair and then proceeded over a rather bumpy set of flagstones, before reaching the entrance to the shopping centre. It was Saturday in Lymington, market day. Traditionally, they always went into town on Saturday, when they stocked up with fresh vegetables, picked up any odds and ends, bought a local newspaper and then had a coffee and pastry at the Marie Rose café. Their lives were very much ruled by routine and each of them liked it that way.

They were spinsters and shared a small bungalow, with Joan acting as Margaret's carer. They were in their early seventies. Margaret's disablement was a result of contracting polio in her teens.

The sisters used to swim during their school summer holidays in the 1950s at their local park, which had a large lake. There was a bathing section, marked by a line of brightly painted cork floats, roped together, and strung across from one side of the lake to the other. Joan was the better of the two at swimming and she constantly nagged Margaret to go with her, because their mother would not allow either of them to go to the lake alone. During a particularly warm spell, the water became discoloured and swimming was suspended. The girls passed the following few days wondering how they could amuse themselves, but all that was put aside when Margaret became ill.

She was admitted to hospital and tests confirmed that she had contracted polio. She had to remain in hospital until she was able to start eating again. She lost a lot of weight and muscle tone. Her right leg was paralysed and she was fitted with a leg-brace to help her stand and walk. When she finally left hospital, Margaret walked with a stiff-legged gait, and never recovered her former mobility.

Joan did not succumb to polio and because she'd been the most enthusiastic to go swimming, she had, ever since, felt an element of guilt that it was her poor twin sister who had been struck down by the cruel illness. Joan was devoted to Margaret and after their father died, she retired early, giving up her librarian's job in order to care for her mother and sister at her home in Lymington. Generally, they got on well and although they bickered and moaned at each other continually, there was actually a good deal of sisterly love between them.

When both of their parents were alive, Margaret lived with them in Wiltshire and managed to do some part-time clerical work locally, but her employer's business failed and she lost her job. Although she tried hard, she never managed to find any further paid employment.

Her condition had worsened noticeably during the last ten years. The medical experts called it 'post-polio syndrome'. She had had to over-use her functioning muscles and joints, in order to compensate for those that were paralysed. The result, as she got older, was a faster than normal deterioration in her muscles, characterised by fatigue and weakness. She had become more reliant upon her sister for care and support.

Margaret had contracted polio during a time when litigation was seldom the option for those for whom possible negligence may have caused them illness or injury. There had been no large payment from the lake's owners in compensation. 'Negligence was too difficult to prove,' they were told by someone their father knew at work. The family just accepted it as bad luck – just one of those things.

Money was tight. It was the luxuries and treats they missed out on, like being able to afford a holiday and perhaps a spell in respite care for Margaret, while Joan took a few days break. A new wheelchair would have been nice, one that was lighter and easier to manage, with electrical assistance to power it along. They had requested one and for the moment, Margaret was on a waiting list, but the government was talking about cutbacks and they had decided not to be too hopeful. The ultimate would have been a new car, specially adapted so that Margaret could remain in her wheelchair, whilst sitting in the rear, but vehicles with a loading ramp and the necessary height clearance were extremely expensive and well beyond their means.

Part Two

2.1

The church stood on a gentle rise and there was a reasonable view of Leyton Parish from the beautiful wooden lych-gate at the entrance to the churchyard. An ancient yew tree stood just inside, thirty feet high, with an incredibly thick, gnarled trunk, full of holes and cavities. Its circumference was almost equal to its height. It was protected by a neat black iron railing bearing a small cast iron plaque, indicating the tree's age at between one and three thousand years old.

A church had stood on the site since the eleventh century and its records of baptism, marriage and death told the story of the parish in that little corner of England. If the ancient yew had been able to speak, what tales could it have told? What countless folk had passed before it?

A gravelled pathway led from the lych-gate, through the churchyard to the entrance of the church. On either side were graves, most neat and well tended, although looking towards the extremities, the grass was longer and a number of headstones were leaning at awkward angles. Several grand oaks towered above the graves, each of them at least three hundred years old. They were leafless in their winter state, but poised to be released from hibernation, as soon as some warmth from the sun and the lengthening of the days heralded the return of spring and life's cycle could begin once more.

The church was quaint and charming to look at; grey stone under a clay tiled roof with a bell tower and short spire. A painted wooden porch on the side, its exterior decorated in relief with bars and arches, sheltered the beautifully carved heavy wooden doors, which opened into the church itself.

On that Monday morning in January 1900, the congregation had begun arriving shortly after half past ten. Louisa Crockford was marrying John Williams. Louisa's mother and baby brother were already there, but not in the church, for they were interred in the family grave, located beneath one of the fine old oaks.

'Not too many guests', had been the couple's wish, but of course all may attend a marriage. The congregation though was small that day, mainly close family and the staff from the shop. There were a few parishioners and one or two customers of Crockford's too: customers who had known Louisa for many years and who wanted to wish her well and be there to see her start her new life.

The choice of which family members to invite had not been difficult. Neither the Williams' nor the Crockford's family were large. Apart from his parents and brother, John's family consisted of his Aunt Beatrice who was his mother's widowed sister-in-law, her son George and his wife Charlotte. George was John's first cousin and six years older. George and Charlotte although married for eleven years, were childless.

There were no relatives on the Crockford side, apart of course from Louisa's father. His only brother, Uncle Frederick, had emigrated to America in 1885. Louisa's surviving brother, David, had joined his uncle in 1894. Neither Frederick nor David had been invited due to the length of time it would take them to make the journey to Leyton. Louisa had promised her father that she would write to them both, sending them a memento of the wedding. As neither had been in touch for more than two years, she would have to hope that they were still at their same addresses.

The front pews easily accommodated both families. As the organist played quietly in the background, the congregation took their seats and awaited the arrival of the bride. John shifted nervously in his freshly laundered uniform. As a chief engineer, he was entitled to wear the uniform of an officer of the Castle Mail Packet Company. He consulted his watch frequently, anxiously hoping that all would go well, wanting to get the ordeal of this day out of the way. He loved Louisa dearly, but weddings were not to his liking. However, society demanded them and for the sake of Louisa's family, he was compelled to comply.

'I hate this waiting,' he confided to Frank. 'I hope she's not too late. I just want to get this over with.'

'Calm yourself. Don't worry. With me in control, everything will be fine.'

'That's what I'm worried about,' John whispered in response.

John had to admit to himself that Frank did seem totally relaxed, somewhat surprisingly, in fact, bearing in mind the amount of alcohol he had consumed the previous evening. That was typical of Frank though: confident, self-assured, able to take his drink, and never one to worry too much about anything.

The organist, who had started to play Wagner's *Bridal Chorus*, interrupted John's thoughts. It meant that the bride had entered the church. The music increased in volume. The Reverend Walter beckoned the congregation to stand. John took a deep breath and sighed quietly to his brother. 'Right, let's get this over with.'

Louisa and her father, followed by Rose as bridesmaid, made their way to the front of the church and the wedding ceremony commenced. Rose cast a glance towards Frank and thought how handsome he looked. Her growing excitement at seeing him again was in no way diminished. Frank for his part, in looking back to Louisa as she had proceeded up the aisle, could not curb the thrill he felt in seeing Rose once more. Frank had decided that he was going to try and make the most of today and with luck Rose Ince would feature prominently in his enjoyment of it.

After the couple had exchanged their vows, John took Louisa on his arm and Frank took Rose on his arm. They followed the Reverend Walter into the vestry in order to complete the marriage register. He handed the four of them in turn a quill dipped in black ink and asked them to sign in the appropriate place. They chatted for a few minutes, Louisa looking happy and relaxed, Frank saying all of the right things. Then John and Louisa led the way back into the body of the church, followed in turn by Frank and Rose, and with bells ringing and the organ playing, they emerged into some unexpected but welcome winter sunshine.

The bride and groom remained outside the church for a while to accept congratulations. Introductions were made; for it was the first time that the two families had met. Then under a shower of confetti,

John and Louisa walked together down the gravel path, past the ancient yew, through the lych-gate to their carriage, for the short ride to The George Hotel via Mr Douglas' Portrait Studio.

There, Mr Douglas was waiting to take the wedding portrait cabinet, which would be mounted on small, embossed cards to be sent to David and Uncle Frederick. Afterwards, they walked the few doors down to the hotel in order to join their guests for the reception luncheon.

2.2

Nick Bastion was in his office with Carol. The 'Williams' file was the first case she'd been given to handle on her own. She wanted to impress her boss and was hoping for success.

'Any luck with the Williams case I asked you to look at yesterday?' Nick asked.

'Well, I've made a little progress,' she replied cautiously. 'I've assumed, as you suggested, that the deceased came from the Leyton area, not South Wales. I've ordered birth certificates for all of the Harry – and Harold – Williams, born in Essex in the fourth quarter of 1900. I think there are about ten possible births. The certificates will be with us later this week. There's a reasonable chance that one of them might be correct, but obviously it could all be a waste of time and money.'

Nick nodded. 'Good thinking about the name Harold,' he said. 'I realise that we could be wasting our time but I'm happy to throw a little money at this one. We might be lucky … actually, there is something else you can do …'

'Yes?' Carol said, wondering what she had missed.

'Try the electoral roll. Find out if the Essex County Records Office has voting records for Leyton. See if you can find out how long Mr Williams lived at his address and whether he was there fifty years ago or so, when his parents might still have been alive. You never know, the record might show other registered voters at the same address and if they were family members, then we may be on to something.'

'I'll get on to that straight away.'

'Let me know how you get on.'

Carol returned to her desk downstairs and looked up the number of the Essex County Records Office. She gave them a call and afterwards spoke to Nick on the internal phone system. 'I've tracked down the voting records for the time period we want. One set is at the Vestry House Museum, just down the road in E17. They're on microfilm. Shall I go down there or ask someone else?'

'Pop down there yourself. It's not far. Go this afternoon. That should give you plenty of time to look thoroughly.'

Nick put down the phone and leaned back in his comfortable leather office chair. He pondered his conversation with Carol. This case was fourteen years old, so competition, at the moment, was unlikely. It had obviously gone cold. He had a feeling though about this one, and the thrill of solving an old case always got his investigative juices flowing ... that and of course the possibility of a nice fat commission.

The hunt was on.

2.3

Louisa and Rose were upstairs at The George Hotel. The reception had gone extremely well. The men had retired to smoke cigars and enjoy a brandy. Louisa, John, his parents and Aunt Beatrice were to leave together, as they were all travelling to the Isle of Wight. It would be Louisa's first trip to the island and she was looking forward to staying at Arthur and Florence's hotel in Ventnor for three nights' honeymoon.

'Oh Louisa, Frank is so amusing and such good company. I can't believe my luck to be paired with him today. We seemed to have so much to talk about. I know you told me he was nice, but I never imagined he could be such fun and so good-looking too. Is the Isle of Wight full of men like John and Frank?'

'I doubt it. I think they're the pick of the bunch. I told you Frank was nice and that you didn't need to worry! Mind you, watch him Rose; I've seen how he looks at you. I think he might be well and truly smitten.'

'Do you think so Louisa, really?'

'Yes I do, and like I say, watch out!'

Louisa beckoned to Rose to come close. 'Rose, I know I can trust you. I want to let you into a secret. You must promise me that you won't tell anyone,' she whispered.

'Of course, of course ... goodness, Louisa, what on earth is it? Have you got some terrible thing to tell me about John? ... or even Frank?'

'Shush, listen ... I'm pregnant,' she whispered.

'What do you mean, you're pregnant?'

'I mean, I'm pregnant. I'm going to have a baby. It happened on John's last leave, back in early December at John's house.'

Rose put her hand to her mouth.

'Look don't look so shocked,' declared Louisa. 'I know it's ... but, well it's happened!' she continued. 'I was so worried at Christmas when I was late, and when I missed completely I was in such a panic. I told John as soon as he came back and he said that we would get married straight away. That's why it's all been a bit of a rush.'

'Does your father know?'

'No, of course not ... and I don't want him to know, at least not yet.'

'So what's going to happen?'

'Well, everything's fine now. We're married and if the baby comes on time, well we can just say that it came early. I'm due at the beginning of September. Mind you, I am worried. I can't stop thinking about my mother and what happened to her.'

'Don't be silly, you'll be fine. You're fit and healthy. I thought you were a bit quiet at Christmas. I assumed it was because you said that you were missing John. I didn't realise you were worried about something. Sorry, I should have noticed that there was more to it.'

'It's fine … don't worry. If you didn't notice, then I'm certain father didn't either.'

'Louisa?'

'Yes?'

'What's it like … you know … doing it … losing your virginity?'

Louisa stifled a giggle and whispered. 'Trust you to ask, Rose … actually it's quite nice … I can't wait until we get to Ventnor tonight!'

The carriage pulled away from the pavement outside The George Hotel and headed towards the railway station. The newly-weds were departing, along with John's parents and Aunt Beatrice. The guests shouted their last farewells and as the carriage rounded the corner at the end of High Street, they all turned to agree with each other on how happy the couple looked and how everything had gone so well.

It was mid-afternoon and due to get dark shortly. The staff at Crockford's had been given the whole day off, but when Mr Crockford said his goodbyes and headed towards his shop, most of the staff soon followed after him.

Back inside the foyer of the hotel, Frank asked Rose if she had a coat.

'It's upstairs,' she said. 'Room number two, where Louisa changed before the journey. There's a bag on the bed too, which needs to go back to the house.'

'Right,' he said. 'You wait here and I'll go up to fetch them. If we need to take her bag back to the house, why don't you come with me? You can hang up her things and tidy up if you like.'

Rose considered the invitation. At least he hadn't asked her to go up to the room with him to collect Louisa's bag. For a single lady to accompany a man into a hotel room would be considered as very unseemly and most improper. What about going back to the house? Surely that would be all right, after all she *did* need to put Louisa's dress away in the wardrobe and she wanted to make sure that the house was in order, ready for her return on Thursday … and obviously she couldn't let Frank touch any of Louisa's clothes or unpack her bag.

'Very well, thank you,' she replied, a little hesitantly.

'Is that a *very well, I can fetch the things*, or a *very well, you'll accompany me to Apsley Street*?'

'It means fetch the bag and that I'll accompany you to Apsley Street, but I won't stay long.'

Five minutes later, they were sitting opposite each other in a Hackney cab. Rose's innermost thoughts were a little confused. Here she was, a single woman, in a cab with a single man, a very handsome man, on her way with him to an empty house, where all manner of things could occur. She shouldn't be doing this. What might he think of her? On the other hand, she thought, *don't be ridiculous Rose! You were the bridesmaid today and he was best man. Your best friend married his brother. So what's wrong if you accompany him? It's all quite innocent. Isn't it? You are merely assisting him in carrying out his duties as best man, to ensure that all the loose ends are tied up and everything is returned to its place.*

Frank looked across at Rose and smiled; a smile she reciprocated before she turned her head to look out of the window.

God, you're lovely, he thought. *John told me you were pretty, but his description clearly did not do you justice. I wonder if you like me, if you find me attractive. I'd love to kiss you. What if the opportunity arises? Should I try, or will you push me away and reject me?*

He considered the situation. She had acquiesced to come back to the house with him. That must say something about what she thought of him; that had to be some sort of positive concession in his favour. She seemed to enjoy his jokes and they had conversed on numerous subjects, both on Wednesday evening and now again today.

As far as age, she was just about right for him, he twenty-four and her twenty-five, not that she'd told him; he'd asked John. He'd also enquired whether she had a male companion or suitor and John had made his day when he replied that as far as he knew Rose had never had a suitor, nor been engaged. She was probably a virgin too, thought Frank, which surely put his chances of seducing her at nought. Never mind, he had one trump card, which if he played it right, might just persuade her, and with luck the evening might yet end in the manner he so greatly desired.

They drew up at 46 Apsley Street. Frank paid the cab driver and opened the gate to escort Rose up the short path to the front door. The house was almost new, the centre one in a terrace of five. It was nearly dark and the drapes were already closed at the neighbouring properties. He patted his pockets several times to locate the key, which his brother had entrusted to him, along with the marriage certificate. He feigned an exaggerated expression of loss on his face.

Rose looked troubled. 'What's wrong? Have you lost the key?'

'Don't worry,' he laughed. 'I didn't lose the ring this morning and no, I haven't lost the key either.' He produced the key.

'Oh Frank!' Rose exclaimed. 'You really worried me then!' She paused a moment, before she giggled and he started to laugh too. He unlocked the door and they went inside.

In the back room, Frank turned on the gas lighting and stoked the fire; a few embers still glowed from the morning. It was nice and warm in the house, especially in contrast to the falling temperature outside, the clear sky heralding a cold frosty evening. He filled the kettle with water and placed it on the single gas ring. The house was well equipped with all the latest conveniences.

Rose, meanwhile, slipped upstairs. The house had two bedrooms: the main one at the front, and a smaller one at the rear, which belonged to Frank, overlooking the garden. Rose went into the main bedroom. Louisa had shown her on Wednesday where to put her things. She unpacked Louisa's bag, hung up her dress and shawl. The bed was unmade. She supposed that John had not had time to make it before he left for the church. She debated whether to touch it and decided that she *would* make it, so that the bedroom would look nice for when they returned from the Isle of Wight.

As she smoothed the sheets, Rose's mind wandered to what she assumed had taken place in this very bed, just a few weeks before. She remembered Louisa's reply to her question of, *what was it like?* She tried to put such thoughts out of her mind, but the problem, she realised, was that she was a little jealous of Louisa. She knew she shouldn't be, but jealousy was a failing with Rose, be it money, position, social standing, or whatever. It was probably deep-rooted and connected with her impoverished childhood and lack of a proper family.

Why should Louisa have all of the fun? Why couldn't she, Rose, just for once experience what Louisa had? Surely, now, this evening, was her chance, a rare opportunity. Here she was, alone in a house, with a lovely man, of whom she was growing increasingly fond. What would be the harm? Should she give him some indication of what she might be prepared to offer him? Maybe she should seduce him, but how? Rose had no experience whatsoever in these matters.

As it happened, Frank took the initiative. When Rose went back downstairs, he greeted her with a large glass of sherry. They sat down and started to chat.

'I think everything went off very well today Rose. Don't you agree?'

'Yes it did. Louisa looked so happy when they left. I know she was really looking forward to seeing the island.'

'Gosh, I nearly forgot.'

'Forgot what?' asked Rose.

'The Marriage Certificate.' He stood and went over to where his jacket hung and withdrew the certificate from the large inside pocket. 'Do you think it'll be all right here on the dresser?'

'Yes, I'm sure it will. They're bound to see it there and of course I can remind Louisa when they return.'

Frank walked over to the fire and turned to face Rose. 'My brother married at last,' he remarked, shaking his head slightly in apparent disbelief. 'Let's raise a glass to John and Louisa, to wish them success and happiness.' He came over to Rose and sat down in the chair next to her. They gently clinked their glasses in a toast.

'I thought your cousin George and wife Charlotte were very nice. I enjoyed chatting with them. They certainly laughed at those stories you recounted, when you and George were children. Before you joined us, they were describing to me where they lived on the island

53

and even invited me to call on them if ever I got the opportunity to go to Ventnor. You know they're staying on in the capital for a few days. They've never been to London before, so I was able to tell them something of what to see and where to go.'

'Oh, well done. George would appreciate that and you're right, they are very nice.'

Rose began to relax, enjoying Frank's company, as well as the warm ambiance of the room and the effect of the sherry. They got on to the subject of Frank's enlistment.

'It's not just John who's worried about you enlisting and going to South Africa,' Rose began. 'I am too, you know. The Boers have inflicted some very embarrassing defeats on our troops.'

'Don't think about it. I'll be all right … but obviously there's no guarantee that I will survive unscathed …' He left the thought hanging just long enough for it to take effect. He decided that this was the moment. 'Rose,' he said gently. 'You and I have become well acquainted with each other these past few days. I think we've become good friends.'

Rose looked at him steadily, not wishing to interrupt.

'I am going to a very dangerous place and there is a risk that I may not return. There is something I would like to do before I go, if you would permit me.'

'And what is that?' Rose asked, barely able to keep her excitement under control, sensing that something was going to happen.

'I would very much like to kiss you.' With that, he stood. He offered his hand to hers.

Rose took Frank's hand and stood up in front of him. For a few seconds they looked at each other cautiously, not sure whether to proceed. Then, Frank bent his head down to her and they kissed a soft gentle kiss. He drew back a little to check her reaction. He was worried that he had been too forward, but his concern was unfounded. Rose put her hand around his neck and pulled his head down to hers. She stood on tiptoes to meet his lips and this time they kissed firmly and with passion.

Later that evening, Frank escorted her in the cab on the return journey to Crockford's. He asked the cab driver to pull up a few doors down from the shop. 'This will do fine. Can you wait a minute? I'll need to go back to Apsley Street.'

'Certainly, sir.' The cab driver descended and opened the door.

Frank stepped down first and when he offered his hand to Rose to help her descend, they both felt again a measure of the warmth and intimacy that they had so recently shared. Rose had given herself completely to this man.

He whispered, 'I'll see you here on Wednesday evening at seven o'clock then.'

'Yes,' she said quietly. 'I usually go to a painting class with Louisa on Wednesday evenings, so nobody here will think any different. They'll assume I'm going on my own, but I will need to be back here by ten o'clock.'

'That's a shame, but at least I can see you. Till Wednesday then?'

'Yes, till Wednesday,' and they kissed gently before Rose turned and walked the few yards along the pavement to the door of the shop's staff entrance.

At breakfast, on the day after the wedding, the atmosphere in Crockford's was still full of excitement and discussion. Nobody seemed to have noticed that Rose had returned quite late in the evening and she inwardly sighed with relief that she'd not had to answer any awkward questions.

Throughout the day, it was difficult to concentrate on her work. She kept reliving the events of the evening before and of course, she still had Wednesday to look forward to. She was convinced that Mrs Robins was scowling at her on one occasion, but decided later that perhaps she had imagined it; after all, it was most unusual to see Mrs Robins with a smile, even when the staff were working hard.

Rose thought about what Louisa had told her in confidence. Frank hadn't mentioned it. Surely, John must have told him, although she couldn't be certain. Still, if he was told in confidence too, then he was unlikely to mention it either, and the fact that he hadn't, meant he could be discreet, another point in his favour and a quality to admire.

Then the big question reared its head: *What if I'm pregnant?* Rose thought. *Hardly likely*, she decided. *Yes, but what if I'm unlucky? Well, in that case I am sure Frank will do the decent thing and marry me, especially if he is like his brother.* This scenario, and the possible outcome, occupied her mind periodically throughout the day. When she weighed things up, Frank was a good catch. She had her own ambitions, but if he served well in the CIV and was then favoured for advancement at the shipping agents on his return, then that could give her the future of prosperity and respectability she craved. It would indeed be an alternative outcome to her life.

It was with this thought in mind that she met Frank at seven o'clock on Wednesday evening and sat close beside him in the cab, on the way to Apsley Street.

2.4

The RMS *Kidwelly Castle* was making good headway. She was off the Kent coast heading east, soon to change course to the south to go around North Foreland and into the Strait of Dover. She would then follow a more westerly track, passing Beachy Head, making for Southampton, where she was due to dock at eight o' clock the next morning.

She'd undergone an overhaul during her twelve days in dock and taken on extra stores, including a large quantity of the latest issue army rifles, ammunition, harness, saddles, and medical bandages. She was carrying a few important civilian passengers too, but the bulk of her accommodation was reserved for the troops who were due to embark at Southampton.

It was a cold clear night and the sea was calm. From his elevated position in the engine room, Chief Engineer, John Williams, monitored the gauges, with a subconscious ear on the rhythmic pulse of the steam pistons in the background. They were at full ahead, making seventeen knots, the Chadburn telegraph connection from the bridge not having moved for the last hour. He watched a couple of men lubricating the bearings and moving parts, winding in the greasers and adding a stroke or two of oil. He observed too, the stokers stripped to the waist. Periodically, they opened the fireboxes to feed in coal to satisfy the voracious appetite of each boiler. The boilers had been inspected for the first time during the twelve-day stopover. All was well, but the gaskets and seals needed to be closely monitored until everything had settled down and bedded in. His crew knew the routine. Daily, until they passed Madeira, they had to tighten the bolts on the inspection plates, or risk a serious and potentially dangerous escape of steam, if one of the gaskets failed.

John considered the events that had occurred since he last stood at his station. He was now a married man, with a lovely wife and a child on the way. He knew they'd had to rush the wedding, but he'd intended to propose before the year was out anyway. He'd worried when he was away at Christmas, about whether Louisa was all right and whether she was pregnant. He could tell as soon as he saw her face on his return, that she had something urgent to tell him. It was the news he thought he might dread, but after she blurted it out and started to cry, he realised how worried she'd been, and his sympathy for her predicament swept away any apprehension he felt.

He loved Louisa dearly and it mattered nothing to him that they had married with so little notice. He recalled the concern he felt about informing her father, unsure as to his reaction, but fortunately he had taken it well, not the pregnancy of which he was ignorant, but the suddenness of their decision to marry. With luck, the birth could be disguised as an early arrival. No harm would be done.

As newly-weds they had passed a very pleasant time at The Cascade View Hotel in Ventnor, owned and run by his parents. Although it had rained each day, they'd still managed to get out and walk along the esplanade after breakfast and again after lunch. Louisa found the sea air bracing and restorative. It was a shame that they could not have stayed longer and at a warmer time of year, but choice was not an option and they'd made the best of it. He had his job to get on with and although it meant time away at sea, his ship normally maintained a strict timetable and they could plan with reasonable certainty when his next leave would be.

His parents were also in the dark regarding Louisa's pregnancy, although his mother had declared that she thought Louisa was blooming. As she had made this remark, she had scrutinised them for some hint of reaction, but they felt they'd got away with it as nothing more was said. They had agreed that there would be plenty of time to tell their respective parents and certainly not before a reasonable time had elapsed after the honeymoon.

Frank, of course, had been his usual self, confident and assured. He'd carried out his duty as best man faultlessly, once he'd managed to get going on the morning of the wedding. John thought that it was something of a miracle, in view of the copious amount of whisky his brother had consumed the evening before.

He hadn't seen Frank when they returned from Ventnor late on Thursday evening. *Goodness*, he thought, *that was only yesterday evening*. Frank had already departed in order to report for duty. He had left a brief note next to the wedding certificate on the dresser and dropped his key through the letterbox. John recalled how he and Louisa had both studied the details on the certificate and appreciated further that they were not only bound in love, but in the eyes of the law as well. He'd put the certificate away for safe keeping in a former biscuit tin, where he kept all of his important documents.

John was distracted from his thoughts by a call from the bridge. It was the First Officer checking that everything was running smoothly. John confirmed that he was happy so far and not anticipating any problems. He'd been with the company for five years and was well respected as a man with sound mechanical knowledge and experience. He'd seen some changes, no less so than that of the status of the ship, because now she not only delivered the Royal Mail, but also was under contract to the War Office. He could appreciate why the War Office had been enthusiastic to retain her. The RMS *Kidwelly*

Castle was just over eighteen months old, the first ship in the Company to have twin screws and at over 9,000 tons she was also one of the Company's largest. His position as a chief engineer, on a ship with the latest developments in propulsion, was something of which he was justifiably proud. He called down to the senior crewman and informed him that he was going to retire to his cabin, but to wake him if need be. With that, he left the engine room to get some sleep.

At five thirty in the morning, he was back up on deck, looking toward land on the starboard side. It was still cold with a black sky, but the lights of Chichester were discernible to the north and he estimated that they would be docking on schedule. Each time he entered Southampton Water, it reminded him of his youth and the number of times he had made the crossing from Cowes to the mainland at Southampton's Royal Pier. He'd started as an apprentice working for Red Funnel Ferries. Southampton Water was always busy. Paddle steamers ferried passengers from several small harbours on the Isle of Wight, crossing the waterway to Portsmouth, Southampton, and Southsea. The presence of these little ships combined with large ocean-going vessels entering and leaving the port, meant that captains had to exercise extreme caution, in order to avoid collision or running aground.

John fondly recalled his early apprenticeship. The little paddle steamer, on which he worked, sometimes made the return crossing five times daily during The Royal Yacht Squadron's Annual Regatta at Cowes. The event attracted a great many visitors and was the highlight of the international yacht-racing year. Its success and popularity was immense, especially as it was conveniently timed on the social calendar, being towards the end of the London season, just before the wealthy went to Europe for the autumn. Vessels came from all over the globe to take on the best. The Regatta attracted British and European royalty, as well as American millionaires, and it was a matter of national pride to win the Queen's Cup.

The Isle of Wight had become a very fashionable place to take a holiday. Queen Victoria had a royal residence at Osborne House. With good rail connections between the Solent and the capital, and a

59

regular ferry service by paddle steamer, the journey to the island was part of the holiday and only served to enhance its reputation. As an island with royal patronage, it had become a destination for those with money and time to spare.

John's mind drifted on to thoughts of Cowes itself. Outside of the hectic Regatta week, it was a quiet, pretty little town, with narrow streets, quaint cottages and shops. John pictured the substantial Georgian building occupied by the shipbrokers where Frank had started his career as a clerk. John could not help but worry about his brother. First, he had given up a good job in Cowes and moved to London. Now, he'd given up his London job too, in order to follow a whim to find excitement and glory in South Africa. John felt that his brother was making a mistake.

Shortly before six o'clock, after a brief breakfast, John returned to the noise and warmth of the engine room. The night watch reported no problems and this was confirmed as he scanned the array of gauges in front of his station. The telegraph bell rang as the instructions from the bridge were relayed to the engine room: 'HALF AHEAD', then some twenty minutes later, 'SLOW AHEAD', followed by, 'STANDBY'.

John could picture the scene outside. By now, the tugs would have the ship under control, gently guiding her to the dockside. The stevedores and crane handlers would be preparing to load further stores and of course, somewhere out there, he expected Frank to be one of the volunteers nervously waiting to embark upon what for some, would be a one-way trip.

2.5

Peter managed to spare some time to further research the marriage certificate. He quickly reviewed his progress to date. So far, he'd found where each of the marriage partners was in 1891, but he needed to move forward ten years, to the 1901 Census Return, taken on the 31 March, fourteen months after the wedding.

He first searched for John Williams' address at the time of the marriage. Two names were listed.

1901 Census Return					
ADDRESS	NAME	RELATION	AGE	OCCUPATION	WHERE BORN
46 Apsley St. Leyton	Louisa Williams	Wife	30	Dressmaker	Leyton
	Henry Williams	Son	6 mths		Leyton

Louisa was there so they'd obviously moved in after the wedding, but where was John? Most likely at sea and away from home on the night of the census, he thought. There was now a son, Henry, who was six months old. Peter did a quick mental calculation. For Henry to be six months old, he would have to have been born before 30 September 1900. Unless he was born early, it was highly likely that Louisa was already pregnant when she married. That might be another reason, Peter reasoned, why the marriage was arranged by special licence at short notice.

He chuckled to himself. For all the morals of Victorian society, women still became pregnant out of wedlock. He leaned back in his chair and thought for a moment on how much attitudes had changed. Nowadays, there was nothing unusual about having children outside of marriage, but in 1900 and even as recently as forty years ago, it was looked upon as shameful. Couples in that position were put under great pressure to do the 'decent thing' and get married.

Returning to his task, Peter looked back six months earlier on the birth indexes. He soon found the entry for the birth of young Henry Williams, during the third quarter of 1900 in West Ham. He ordered a copy of his birth certificate. Once he had that, he would be able to calculate from his date of birth, whether Louisa definitely was 'in the family way' when she married.

Peter also wanted to know what the two witnesses to the marriage were doing in 1901. The census revealed that Rosetta Price was still living at the same address in Islington, as a draper's assistant. That rather disproved his theory that Rosetta Price may have been working for Thomas Crockford at the time of the wedding.

Of Frank Williams, he could find no trace. There was no matching individual of the right age, born on the Isle of Wight. Generally, each census tended to miss out about four per cent of the population, particularly if a person was away from their normal residence when the census took place. Peter knew that it was likely that Frank would turn up on the subsequent census return.

2.6

At six in the evening, *RMS Kidwelly Castle* left her berth and headed down Southampton Water towards the Solent and the English Channel. It was another cold clear night. Darkness had fallen by half past four, just as she had finished loading her compliment of passengers and equipment. In place of her normal first class, second class, and steerage passengers, she had taken on board about 1,500 officers and men, part of the newly formed City Imperial Volunteers. Many of them, like Frank Williams, were clerks or men from the middle classes. Most had some military training. The CIV consisted of a battalion of infantry, two mounted infantry companies, and a Vickers-Maxim machine gun battery.

The men had travelled by train from London and then marched the short distance from the rail terminus to the dockside, where they had formed up in orderly lines, to await embarkation in company order. Loaded with packs and weapons, they had to stand in the cold for some time before ascending the gangplank and being shown to their billets in the warm interior of the ship. John Williams had managed to gain a few moments on deck from time to time during the day. He was certain he had spotted his brother at one point, waiting his turn to board. Unfortunately, Frank had not been looking up in John's direction, but he would of course have known by now that he was on John's ship and would no doubt make himself known at the first opportunity.

An hour after departure, John left the engine room for a few minutes to go back up on deck. Men were to be seen in small groups, discussing where they were and how far out from land. The lights of Ventnor were just visible. For most, this was their first trip on an ocean-going vessel. Looking one deck below, he could see lit cigarettes and outlines of solitary individuals, arms on the railing, lost in their own thoughts. *How many of these poor devils will come back in similar condition to the wounded we repatriated on our last trip?* John wondered. It made him shudder, even more so, when he thought of Frank and where he was going.

He looked across to Ventnor, recalling that only three days before, he had been there with his new wife, looking out to sea from the esplanade. His parents' hotel was somewhere in the distance, just one of the many buildings with a gas light outside, just one among the collection of lights which revealed the location of the town.

John returned to his cabin and found a note from Frank stuck under the door. It confirmed that he was on board and gave his cabin number. John knew he would be sharing with at least three other men. It was late, so he decided to turn in and leave contacting his brother until the following day.

Twenty-four hours later, crossing the notorious Bay of Biscay, the ship was in the grip of poor weather and rough seas. Many of the soldiers were seasick. When his duty was over, John went to Frank's cabin and found him absent, but was told that he was in the temporary mess room. Sure enough, there he was, unperturbed by the motion of the ship, playing cards with a number of comrades. He stood and introduced his brother, adding with pride that he was Chief Engineer. His mates seemed genuinely impressed, for the recently commissioned ship was modern and well appointed, albeit a little crowded, carrying twice the number of passengers for which she was originally designed.

Frank wanted to talk privately, so he passed his hand to one of the others and suggested to John that they go back to John's cabin.

The cabin was small but perfectly adequate. Frank noticed the portrait photograph of Louisa on the bedside locker. He sat down on the bed and John pulled up the single chair, opening the conversation with: 'Well, how are you getting on? You seem to have installed yourself pretty well.'

'Fine, thanks. Beautiful ship, I must say. Do you think you could give me a tour of the engine room sometime? It must be pretty impressive, if the rest of her is anything to go by.'

'Of course, of course, plenty of time for that, but first of all, have you been told where you're going, once we put you ashore in Cape Town?'

'Nothing official yet, but you can imagine the rumour mill is running at full speed. What about you? Haven't you heard something? I thought you might know. I've seen your First Officer talking to some of our officers.'

'Nobody's said anything to me,' replied John. 'They're keeping pretty tight-lipped about it. In fact, I'm not sure they know too much either. I suppose you'll be getting your orders from Lord Roberts or Lord Kitchener when you get down there.'

'I assume so,' confirmed Frank.

'How are they treating you? What happened on Thursday?'

'Well, it was all rather amazing. After reporting for duty, we received our uniforms and rifles. Then we attended a formal ceremony with the Lord Mayor of the City of London. You know that the Financial Institutions and Guilds are sponsoring us?'

64

John nodded and Frank continued. 'We were given Freedom of the City, before a farewell service at St. Paul's, followed by, would you believe, dinner at the Inner Temple.'

John looked impressed.

'We stayed in barracks Thursday and Friday night. Yesterday morning, we had parade at four, which was a bit of a struggle. Then we marched to Nine Elms to get the trains for Southampton. So far, it's all been good. They made a real fuss of us before we left, almost like heroes and that's before we've done any fighting. God knows what it will be like, if they give us a victory parade when we get back … but enough of this military talk, why don't you find that little bottle of whisky I know you always keep for emergencies?'

John grinned and opened a cupboard to retrieve a bottle and two glasses. He poured a couple of generous measures.

'Come on,' continued Frank. 'I want to know how the honeymoon went! Did you manage to escape the cold outside and spend plenty time in bed? Mind you, you'd already had some of that sort of fun hadn't you, but did it continue?'

'We had a great time and it was so nice to be together. Mother and father left us very much to do as we pleased, which was good of them. What about you? Did the lovely Rose succumb to your charm? You seemed to be getting along fine at the reception.'

'Did she ever? I can't believe it John; I think I'm in love!'

'What? You? Surely not!'

'Yes, I mean it. We spent the evening at Apsley Street after the wedding and then again, on the Wednesday evening before I left. John, she's gorgeous and she's interesting and funny. I really mean it! She's the one thing about home that I'm missing. When we get back in the autumn, if she's still keen, I'm going to ask her to marry me!'

John recoiled in shock. 'Good God! You have got it bad! Rose is a lovely girl. Louisa would be thrilled. When you say you went back to Apsley Street, does that mean what I think it might mean?'

'Certainly does! John, she's fantastic, just what I've always wanted. You never told me how nice she was!'

'Well, you know what they say, about beauty and the eye of the beholder. I suppose I'm so besotted with Louisa, I didn't think to mention it, but I agree with you, Rose is lovely and you could do a good deal worse. You'll need to watch her though. She's quite ambitious and there's something else you ought to consider.'

'What's that?'

'Well, what if Rose ends up in the same predicament as Louisa?'

'Ah, yes, I've already considered that.'

'It's possible then?'

'Well, yes I suppose there is that chance, but if so, I will definitely stand by her and marry her, no question. Actually though, there's something I need to ask you?'

'Yes ... what's that?'

'Look, I know I'm going to be all right, but I made a will a few months ago. Well, I don't have much, just some cash savings ... about forty-five pounds and a few shares, but I've left everything to you.'

'Well that's decent of you, but I wouldn't like to think that I would ever actually inherit it.'

'I'm sure it won't come to that, but if the worst did happen and I end up getting shot or something, and Rose turns out to be pregnant, do you think you could give her some of the cash to help her out? I know it's a lot to ask, but when I made the will, I hadn't met Rose and now it just seems that things in my life have changed. I'm sure that if mum and dad knew Rose was carrying my child, they'd help as well. I wouldn't want all the responsibility to fall to you. You've got your own life to get on with.'

'That's good of you to say, but of course, in such circumstances we'd see her right. Don't worry. Louisa certainly wouldn't leave Rose to cope on her own, as an unmarried mother. We'd sort something out ... but anyway it's all hypothetical, let's not dwell on it any longer.'

John refilled their glasses. 'I'd like to propose a toast ... to your safe return and if you don't change your mind and if she is willing to have you, to your marriage to Rose!'

'Cheers!' They clinked their glasses in unison.

Three days after leaving Southampton, the *Kidwelly Castle* docked briefly in Funchal, Madeira. Her stopover gave the men the opportunity to stretch their legs and take a brief tour ashore. Some of them used the short stay to wander around the market, marvelling at the quality and abundance of fresh fish and homegrown produce on display. Many bought fruit and were amazed at how much cheaper it was than back in London.

Out at sea once more, the weather was glorious; blue skies and a moderate swell. The men were measured up for olive drab khaki uniform; gone were the days of crimson tunics and conspicuous accoutrements. It was now about camouflage, making the soldiers a more difficult target, for the sharp shooting skills of the Boers.

A feature of the mounted troopers' uniform was the slouch hat turned up on the left. Apart from greater sun protection, the troopers enjoyed wearing it because it distinguished them from the infantrymen.

The following day, they passed the island of Tenerife, the volcanic peaks capped with winter snow and two days later, they spotted flying fish and porpoises as they passed Cape Verde. The day they crossed the equator and entered the southern hemisphere, they celebrated with an evening band concert.

The ship had a small pool deck, where the men could take a weekly bath. Drill sessions occurred twice daily and late afternoons were given over to sports activities. Church parade took place on both Sundays that they were at sea.

The men were offered inoculation against enteric fever. Frank and his messmates discussed whether or not to opt for it.

'I've heard you get a dose of enteric just from the serum. It can be right nasty,' Charlie Mills warned. 'If it stopped bullets I might be interested, but I reckon I'll take my chances.'

'Must admit, I feel the same,' said Frank. 'I know the disease is pretty rife down there, but I don't trust these injections.'

They both decided to forgo inoculation and felt vindicated when several of their inoculated comrades were feverish for a few days afterwards.

The men were able to buy postcards on board, postcards with a picture on the front of the *RMS Kidwelly Castle*. Frank bought some, as well as asking his brother for some writing paper and envelopes. He had decided to write to Rose, to tell her how he felt.

Finally, seventeen days after leaving Southampton, and exactly on schedule, as required under her duties as a Royal Mail Ship, the *Kidwelly Castle* entered Table Bay and arrived in Cape Town on the 7 February 1900.

The troops and their kit were unloaded and marched directly to Green Point Common where they pitched camp. There in the following few days, the mounted troopers were issued with saddles and horses. Rifle practice and training took place around the clock. Practice parades were held. Two days after landing, they took part in their first fully mounted parade. Dressed in khaki uniform with slouch hats, they trooped their colours before Lord Roberts.

On the eve of their departure into the interior, Frank took out one of the postcards he had purchased on his brother's ship. He wrote carefully across the lower right-hand corner of the front of the card, in the space created by the white foam, displaced by the bow of the steaming ship:

10th February, 1900. Dear John and Louisa. Setting off for Orange River tomorrow. All in good cheer. Love to you both. Frank.

He handed it over for posting, got down under his blankets and tried to get some sleep. The next day, they broke camp, mounted up and set off for the railhead, where along with their horses and equipment, they boarded a troop train and departed for the front.

2.7

Rose got up, as usual, at six-thirty. It was the last day of February. She washed before dressing and going along the landing to wake the other girls. Rose was worried. She was more than three weeks late. She had never missed before and this morning as she went downstairs to the privy, she felt a little nauseous. She was tired too, and the thought of working all day in the shop did nothing to improve her mood.

She ate a small piece of bread for breakfast, anxiously hoping that none of the other staff noticed her lack of appetite. The smell of the hot kippers that Mrs Jones had placed in the centre of the table very nearly made her sick, but she managed to control herself. Fortunately, the steam from the fish rose in a plume, which drifted away from her, towards the other side of the table. The girls chatted and gossiped.

'Here, Mrs Jones, what do you think about this Ada Chard Williams case on at the Bailey? Do you reckon she's guilty?' Hilda asked.

'No doubt in my mind she is,' came Mrs Jones' reply, as she bustled about with more toast and tea. 'Hanging's too good for her … taking five pounds off some poor unmarried mother to find the child another home and then murdering it instead. Baby farming … that's what it is, buying and selling babies for profit. Shouldn't be allowed.'

Rose remained silent during the conversation although inside she felt tormented. Why was it that everyone was talking about babies and unmarried mothers?

'You all right, Miss Rose?' Daisy asked. 'You're quiet. You're not going down with a cold, are you?'

'I'm fine, thank you,' replied Rose. 'Just feeling a little under the weather, but I'm sure it'll pass. If you don't mind, I'm going to excuse myself. I have some things to attend to.'

With that, she left the breakfast table and returned to her room. She still felt queasy, but was certain that she wasn't going to be sick. She sat on her bed and opened the drawer of the washstand. She took out an envelope and unfolded the letter it contained.

69

30th January 1900. RMS Kidwelly Castle

Dearest Rose

I hope you are well. I am writing this to you from the deck of the RMS Kidwelly Castle, John's ship, just as we thought. We are ten days out from Southampton and crossed the equator yesterday. I am fine and in good spirits. The weather is very sunny and the sea is calm.

Dearest Rose, I am missing you such an awful lot. I keep thinking back to the time we spent together. I am so very fond of you Rose and I hope you feel the same way about me. They say absence makes the heart grow fonder and I can truly say that I agree whole-heartedly. I have never felt about anyone, the way that I feel about you.

Will you still want to see me when I return? I hope so, Rose, I hope so very much. Everyone here says we'll be back in no time, certainly by the autumn. It's not long to wait.

I had a chat to John the other evening. He said they had a good time in Ventnor and marriage is suiting him well. Send my regards to Louisa, when you see her.

I will post this on board, so you should receive it around the 26th February, when the ship returns to Southampton.

You are constantly in my thoughts and I am looking forward to returning and to seeing you again.

Yours, most truly,

Frank.

PS. If you care to write, my address is: Trooper F. Williams, 94 Company, Mounted Metropolitan Rifles, CIV, Natal. South Africa.

The letter had arrived the previous day. Rose had cried when she first read it. The tears were of joy mixed with relief. Frank obviously felt the same way about her as she felt about him. The three preceding weeks had been awful. She knew she might be pregnant as soon as she realised she had definitely missed her menses. During those three weeks, a range of feelings from hope to despair had played on her mind, as she had considered her situation. Surely, Frank would stand by her and marry her? That solution was the best and most acceptable, as far as she was concerned, but what if he didn't want to do the honourable thing? What if he didn't want to marry her, or even know her? What if he never returned to England? Worst of all, what if he was killed?

The previous week, the British press had carried reports of the CIV coming under fire for the first time and how gallantly they had behaved. War was dangerous and Rose was fearful for Frank's safety. Being pregnant and unmarried would mean that she would lose her job and her accommodation. With no livelihood and no roof over her head, where would she go? The workhouse, she kept imagining. She would never achieve her ambitions.

She had even considered some drastic solutions. She could try to seduce Mr Crockford. She knew he had a liking for her as she had noticed his admiring glances. One had only to hear the way he jealously reprimanded Sidney if he caught him flirting with her. However, Mr Crockford was far too decent and old-fashioned to fall for any ruse to entrap him and she had discounted the idea as preposterous and totally out of the question. Furthermore, of late, he seemed to have a growing eye for the beautiful Constance, Louisa's replacement, so her chances in that direction were probably fading anyway.

Rose had also thought about ridding herself of the pregnancy. She had heard that Mr Harvey, the chemist, stocked a patent remedy to restore 'irregularity and suppression' but she didn't feel brave enough to make a purchase and certainly tongues would wag. Her best option, if she had to decide on such a course, would be to find a mail order supplier of such remedies.

71

Of course, there was another way: it would necessitate a trip back to central London, to ask if any of the girls she used to work with could put her in touch with a doctor willing to operate on her, but she hoped that it wouldn't come to that. Besides, abortion was illegal.

Rose's most fervent hope, until she received Frank's letter, had been that she might miscarry naturally, but for now much of her despair had dissipated. The feeling of panic and utter helplessness had gone. She was still very worried, but not nearly as much. She needed to write in reply and tell him what was happening.

Rose spent the next evening writing her first letter to Frank. It was difficult for her to know what to say, or how to say it, but she took her cue from the tone of his letter and decided to tell him why she was so anxious.

28th February 1900, Leyton, Essex

Dearest Frank

Thank you so much for your letter. I am also missing you terribly and can barely wait until you return. Life in the shop is different now. Louisa is no longer here, so I don't have her to talk to. Mr Crockford has employed a new girl, Constance, to look after the Ladies' Department. She seems quite nice, but it's not the same.

I don't want to alarm you, but I think you ought to know. I believe that I am going to have a child. I haven't told anyone, not even Louisa. I haven't been to a doctor either, but I am fairly sure. I missed at the beginning of this month and just recently have been feeling sick, which is usually an indication and confirmation.

I have been so worried, but after receiving your letter I feel somewhat relieved. I feel exactly the same way about you, but I hope this news does not reduce your affection and regard for me. What should I do? Will you still want to see me when you come back or will this change things between us?

Please reply by return if you can. I need to know how you feel. It may not be too late to consider the alternative, but time is limited.

I hope you are looking after yourself and keeping your head down. What are the conditions like? Have you seen any Boers? I've been keeping my eye on the news board outside the newsagents for any mention of the CIV.

Please be careful.

Your dearest love,

Rose.

A little more than a week later, Sidney arrived one morning with news, which almost made Rose lose her composure. It was part of his job to bring Mr Crockford's daily paper when he arrived for duty each morning. As he breezed into the shop, he mentioned the morning headlines, unaware of the significance of them to Rose.

'Blimey, those CIV boys soon got stuck in down there. Headline says, "13 CIV Wounded and Taken Prisoner at Britstown". Reckon they might have bitten off more 'an they can chew. They're no pushover, them Boers. My dad told me some of the tricks they've been gettin' up to … shockin', quite shockin', if I don't mind sayin' so.'

Rose almost panicked but tried to remain calm. 'Here let me have a quick look, will you? Miss Louisa's brother-in-law is a trooper in the CIV and he's down there at the moment.'

She quickly scanned the details. At least it seemed that no one had been killed and there was no mention of any mounted troopers being involved. The fighting had taken place two days before and the headlines were testimony to the marvels of the telegraph communication between London and Cape Town. The story unsettled her and she knew her unease, along with that of Frank's family, would continue until it was known definitely that Frank was safe.

2.8

Frank's company left Cape Town for Orange River on 11 February 1900. They arrived three days later and unloaded their horses and equipment. Initially, they took part in scouting activities, reporting any enemy sightings to headquarters.

On 15 February, they joined other British Forces in the attack to regain the town of Jacobsdal. Four members of the CIV were wounded, but the town was taken. Frank's company was unscathed and their contribution mentioned in a despatch sent by Lord Roberts to the Lord Mayor of London. *'The City of London Volunteers under Colonel Cholmondeley came under fire for the first time yesterday at Jacobsdal and behaved most gallantly.'* The despatch was widely reported in the British press.

A few days later, Frank's company found themselves to be part of the main British force surrounding an army of 13,000 Boers under General Cronje at Paardeberg. They were held back in reserve, but still able to witness the British artillery bombardment directed from observation balloons. The barrage continued periodically for seven days.

One night during the bombardment, a Boer relief convoy tried to break through, but it was destroyed by fire. Ordered to remain where they were, the CIV troopers could only watch the flashes of shells in the distance against the darkness. The following morning, a substantial group of miserable, bedraggled Boer prisoners was escorted under guard, past their camp.

'Did you see the age of some those prisoners?' Frank remarked to Charlie Mills. 'One of them was not much more than a boy, and at the other end of the scale there were a couple of them who looked well over seventy.'

'Yes, and all volunteers too, they reckon,' replied Charlie.

'I hope I don't feel the need to take up arms when I'm an old man. Would you want to? Surely, they must have been forced into arms, not as volunteers?'

'Who cares,' said Charlie. 'Doesn't matter what age they are. If they can hold a rifle, then they can kill us, simple as that. All I know is, we've got a job to do down here. Those Boers are going to toe the line. They've got too big for their boots and we're here to teach them a lesson.'

A series of heavy thunderstorms followed over the next few days, soaking both armies, but more importantly, further sapping the morale of the entrapped Boer forces. Their situation was desperate.

Finally, on 27 February, Cronje surrendered, giving the British their victory at Paardeberg. Frank's company was ordered to escort Boer prisoners to the town of Modder River. From there, the captives were forwarded to a specially constructed camp, where they were processed and contained, before transportation to St Helena, Bermuda, or Ceylon.

Frank and his victorious comrades then enjoyed more than a week of relative calm, with scouting duties during the day and sentry duty at night. The men were issued with extra blankets, kit and most welcome of all, mail from home. Frank was delighted to receive a letter from his mother. She described the particularly rough crossing on the journey home after the wedding, and the time John and Louisa had passed at the hotel. He wished he could have had word from Rose, but he calculated that at best, she would only have just received his letter, the one he had written during the voyage south. He wondered about her reaction to the sentiments he had expressed, and whether she would reciprocate.

He decided, that he would continue to write to her in a similar vein, unless she indicated to him that she did not feel the same way. Thus, it was, that during the respite after Paardeberg, he wrote once again to Rose. With luck, he hoped that she would receive his letter sometime in early April.

6th March 1900

Dearest Rose

I want you to know how much I have been thinking of you. I hope you are well.

Things are going well here. I can't tell you too much because of the censors, but we are camped by the Modder, a river, and we have been bathing in it. The fighting for the moment has diminished and we have been scouting and doing sentry duty. We escorted a lot of Boer prisoners last week, when Cronje surrendered. If things continue like this, I am sure that we will be coming home in the autumn, maybe even before that. I hope you wish to see me when I return.

We received mail today, the first since we departed England. I had a letter from my mother. I didn't expect a letter from you, as even if you had replied post-haste, I shouldn't imagine it will arrive in Cape Town before mid-March, and then of course it has to find its way out here. We are a full three days by train from the coast.

Please write to me Rose. It would mean a great deal.

Yours, most truly,

Frank.

2.9

It all happened quite suddenly one April afternoon in the shop. Rose had been dealing with a difficult customer. She was a good customer, but she could be extremely demanding. Rose had shown her the curtains they had made, as per instruction, but the customer had declared rudely, and rather aggressively, that the material was darker than she had chosen and that they were unacceptable. Rose was sure that there had not been an error on her part and reached down behind the counter to look for her samples and order book. Meanwhile, the customer became quite insistent and demanded to see Mr Crockford.

For Rose it was the last straw. She had been feeling unwell for six weeks. She had also received another letter from Frank, but it was written before he had received hers. He said he was fine, camped at Modder River and enjoying a lull in the fighting. He made light, but to Rose he was in the thick of it, and not just there to stand reserve for the regulars. The possibility that he might be killed in action only served to heighten her anxiety over his safety, and her predicament, if he did not return. She was anxious as to how he would react to her letter. She knew she might have to wait another four weeks before she got his reply. The worry was preying on her mind.

When she straightened up, with the large heavy order book to hand, trying at the same time to placate the most unreasonable customer she had ever encountered, Rose started to feel hot and faint.

As Mr Crockford approached the counter to help with the awkward customer, Rose passed out.

She regained consciousness when Mrs Robins slapped her cheeks. Lying on her back on the floor, looking up into the questioning yet unsympathetic face of Mrs Robins, was not the most pleasant way to return to the world. Mrs Robins started to scold Rose almost immediately, but Mr Crockford intervened. He summoned Sidney to help him and the two of them raised Rose carefully to her feet and helped her to a nearby chair.

'Daisy, go and get a glass of water. Miss Ince, are you all right? You fainted. What's the matter?'

'I'm sorry, Mr Crockford, I don't know what happened. I've never felt like that before.'

The irate customer meanwhile had been observing all of this. Her anger had certainly abated and she was feeling a measure of guilt for the way she had spoken to Rose. 'I'm sorry if I upset you. I had no idea you were of such a fragile disposition. Are you ill?'

Mrs Robins was watching the proceedings like a hawk. She took a renewed interest and peered down at Rose. She also enquired if Rose knew of any reason why she had fainted.

'I've no idea,' murmured Rose, 'no idea at all.' She sipped some water. 'I feel better now; I would like to carry on.'

Mr Crockford however, would have none of it. 'I think you should take the rest of the afternoon off, Miss Ince. Go and have a lie down. I'll ask Mrs Jones to send you up a cup of tea. Daisy, please see Miss Ince up to her room.'

Mr Crockford ordered everyone to return to their posts. He listened to the customer's complaint and then consulted Rose's order book. He found the customer's order and saw the swatch of material pinned to the page. He removed the swatch and compared it against the finished curtain. There was no doubt that they were identical. When he invited the customer to accompany him outside to check the colour in daylight, she reluctantly admitted that the mistake had been hers.

For Rose however, any temporary relief that she had avoided the discovery of her pregnancy was short-lived, as Mrs Robins' suspicions had been aroused. She had noticed Rose's slight hesitation when the customer had remarked on her fragile condition. She decided that she would watch Miss Ince very closely over the next weeks.

A few days later, Mrs Robins spotted Rose urgently whisper something in Daisy's ear before hastily leaving her counter and disappearing towards the back entrance of the shop. She suspected that something was amiss and made an excuse to her own assistant, deciding that, on the pretence of needing to use the staff lavatory facilities, she would investigate. Mrs Robins followed Rose and opened the door into the back yard. There was no one about, but she could see that the privy was occupied. She quietly closed the door and tiptoed over to the privy door. She stood and listened. A few moments later, she was smugly satisfied to hear poor Rose being sick.

Mrs Robins crept back across the yard and re-entered the shop. She considered what might be the matter with Rose, but she already had her suspicions, and pregnancy was at the top of her imaginary list. What she had just heard fitted in well with her theory and she speculated on who the father might be. *Mr Crockford? Sidney? No, certainly not. What about the best man at Louisa's wedding? He and Rose seemed to get along very well. Yes, it could be him. He was far too cocky and confident for his own good, a bit of 'ladies' man' if ever there was one. He's the most likely suspect.*

Mrs Robins made up her mind to maintain her watch on Rose. If she found herself free of customers, and if Rose continued to leave her counter in similar circumstances, then she would follow her again.

Several times over the next week, Mrs Robins noticed Rose leave her counter quite urgently. She wanted to follow her, but unfortunately, each time this happened she was dealing with a customer, until early on Friday morning, not long after opening, she saw Rose heading towards the door to the yard. Muttering something to Amy, Mrs Robins left her in charge and followed Rose. Sure enough, the privy was occupied and once again, she was able to hear Rose being ill. She was sure now and a thin smile crossed her normally harsh, scowling face. This was her opportunity to bring Miss Rosetta Ince down a peg or two.

Mrs Robins considered her options for the rest of the day. She had never liked Rose from the start. She had not liked the way Rose had been given her own department and put on an equal standing with her in the hierarchy of the shop. *Imagine that*, she thought. *Me, with all of my experience in the drapery trade and her, nothing more than a young slip of a girl.*

She resented the manner in which Mr Crockford had immediately taken a shine to Rose. It displeased her to witness the way he scolded

Sidney, if he lingered too long at Rose's counter. In Mrs Robins' opinion, Mr Crockford was guilty of jealousy – whether consciously or not – regarding any competing male attention that Rose received. She also detested the fact that Rose and Louisa were such close friends. She regarded the friendship as an element of strategy on the part of Rose, to inveigle herself even more into Crockford's, and ultimately she imagined, her own position as the head of haberdashery might be threatened. She regarded their close friendship as inappropriate. It could mean that Rose became involved in the running of the shop. Mr Crockford had already consulted Rose on several matters concerning the window display, matters upon which she used to be consulted, matters which she considered as being well beyond the knowledge and experience of the likes of Miss Ince.

In addition, with the arrival of Constance, Mrs Robins had felt even more threatened. Constance was another pretty, young woman, whom she believed lacked the experience to take on the position for which she had been engaged. There was no doubt that Mr Crockford was ambitious and she had seen his business treble in size during the last fifteen years. The problem was that he seemed to be employing younger and younger girls and she could not help but wonder how much longer she would have a place at Crockford's. If she had the ammunition, she would have no greater pleasure than to use it to knock one of the young upstarts from their pedestal.

Since Rose had joined the business eighteen months before, Mrs Robins had bided her time, waiting for her chance. She had not done anything to upset Rose, or given her any indication of how she really felt about her, but now she had the chance she needed. There was no doubt in her mind, that once Mr Crockford was made aware of Rose's predicament, he would have no choice but to dismiss her. To be expecting a child out of wedlock was shocking and most unbecoming for a senior employee in a respected drapery enterprise, such as Crockford's. There was no way she could imagine that Rose would be allowed to remain. She smiled inwardly to herself. She was enjoying this and she eagerly anticipated confronting Rose and ensuring that Mr Crockford was informed.

First of all, she needed to corner Rose and ask her outright if she was pregnant. She felt confident that she could extract an admission and would not be fooled by any denial. Secondly, she would enjoy telling Mr Crockford and seeing his face when he heard the news. She needed the right moment to tackle Rose and it presented itself beautifully just after closing time the following day, Saturday.

Mr Crockford had shown the last of his customers to the door before locking up and drawing the blind. Daisy and Ivy had put the shutters in place and had removed the bulk of the items from the window displays. All of the staff had either gone home or retired upstairs. Rose had remained in the shop catching up on her ordering and reviewing the work that she needed Sidney to take out on Monday, to her two outworkers. As she studied her notes, she became aware of Mrs Robins standing before her, dressed in her hat and coat and obviously about to leave. Rose realised that for some reason Mrs Robins wished to speak with her upon some matter before she departed. It was most unusual and Rose instantly felt a little nervous and uncomfortable.

'Spending an awful lot of time in the back yard these days, aren't we, Miss Ince?' Mrs Robins stated sarcastically.

'What do you mean?' asked Rose, a little taken aback.

'Oh, I've seen you and heard you too, retching and vomiting ... a regular occurrence I'd say. You're pregnant, aren't you?'

'No – no of course not,' replied Rose. She hoped her denial was convincing, but she doubted it was so. 'I've had an upset stomach.'

'Upset stomach? Upset stomach, for four weeks? ... I'm not stupid you know! I've had three of my own. You can tell me,' her voice softened. 'I might be able to help.'

Rose hesitated for a moment, before breaking down. It had all been too much, the worry and the anxious waiting for a reply from Frank. She wept into her handkerchief, nodding her head, confirming that she was pregnant and asking what she should do.

81

'Do? ... Do?' Mrs Robins exclaimed, her tone hardening once more to its usual pitch. 'First thing you can do is hand in your resignation to Mr Crockford!'

Rose looked up in alarm from her handkerchief. 'But you said you might help me? If I tell Mr Crockford, he'll dismiss me and I'll be out on the street.'

'Well, that's where you should be, shameless hussy like you, bringing this shop into disrepute. Good riddance, I say. You'd better tell Mr Crockford first thing Monday, because if you don't, then I certainly will.' With that, Mrs Robins pulled her coat around her with a flourish, gathered her bag, turned, and marched off swiftly in the direction of the staff entrance.

Rose watched Mrs Robins' back as she strode away from her. She tried to breathe deeply to pull herself together, but she started weeping once more into her handkerchief.

Mrs Robins could hear Rose's sobs, as she opened the staff door to leave. When she stepped outside, she too took a deep breath, but hers was to exhale a sigh of satisfaction. With a broad smile on her face and a spring in her step, she joined the shoppers and workers on their way home. She was really looking forward to Monday.

2.10

Acting as scouts for the advance, 94 Company, CIV, set out at first light on 8 March. The British target was Bloemfontein, the capital of the Orange Free State. The town had raised a number of enemy commando units and to capture it would be a major step in the defeat of the Boers. Two days later, Frank was part of the British contingent in full pursuit of a large enemy force. The two forces engaged one another and suffered heavy losses on each side, with the Boers coming off worse. Skirmishes continued and the British brought up their heavy artillery pieces once more to shell the enemy. Frank's company formed part of the escort for the important strategic weapons.

The British closed in, and during the evening of 12 March, the Boers evacuated Bloemfontein and withdrew. Lord Roberts made a ceremonial entry the following day. The town was in British hands and became the focus for British reinforcements and military organisation.

The frantic military activity preceding the taking of the town was over and Frank's company was given almost two weeks' break from the fighting. The days were filled with drill, parades, and the continual need to ensure grazing for the horses.

Frank finally received his first letter from Rose. He replied later that evening.

25th March 1900

Dearest Rose

I have just received your letter today and I am so delighted to hear from you and hear your news. You have no need to worry my darling; we will get married as soon as I return.

I am sorry that you have had so much worry and I wish I could be there to share it with you. Have you told Louisa by now? If not, I think you should. Ask Louisa and John to help you. I spoke to John on the voyage out and he gave me his word that he would help you if the need should arise.

I miss you so much my darling. I wonder what you are doing at this moment. I am looking forward to returning to England. The country here is very different and I am tired of being on horseback, but it is far better than walking!

I am sure you will know that we took Bloemfontein last week. We are resting for a spell, before we make our next move. The weather has been mixed, with some torrential storms, the like of which I have never seen in England.

I must end this now as I am on sentry duty shortly. I am in good spirits and cannot wait to see you. Make sure you tell Louisa and John everything. They will see you are all right. I will write to my parents and tell them of our intentions, so they will know too.

When you write can you enclose a photograph of yourself for me? I do so envy the other men who possess a picture of their wife or sweetheart.

Good night dearest.

Love,

Frank.

2.11

Rose pulled herself together, finished the orders, tidied her work away, and went upstairs to her room. Mr Crockford had already gone. He was spending the weekend at his large residence in Apsley Street. She didn't know what to do. Should she tell Mr Crockford? Was Mrs Robins bluffing? Should she go and see Mr Crockford before the shop opened on Monday? If Mrs Robins told him, should she just deny it? Should she take drastic action and find a 'doctor' who could perform an abortion? Rose began to panic. She needed to talk to someone. She needed some help. She decided to go and see Louisa and tell her what had happened.

She took a cab and arrived outside Louisa's house. She didn't know if John was back or not – she couldn't think. She knocked at the front door and waited.

From the other side of the door, Louisa asked hesitantly, 'Who is it?'

'It's me, Louisa … Rose.'

Louisa opened the door. She could see that Rose was upset. 'Good Lord, Rose, whatever's the matter?' She ushered her in and closed the front door behind her.

'Oh Louisa, I'm in such a mess. Have you heard anything from Frank? Is he safe? I've been so worried since that newspaper report about the fighting at Britstown.'

'I think he's fine. Father told me that his unit was not involved in that. They're supposed to be in the Jacobsdal region, which is a hundred and fifty miles away and anyway we would've received a telegram by now if he'd been killed or wounded. Why are you in such a mess?'

'I'm pregnant! It's Frank's! Mrs Robins has found out and I don't know what to do. She says she's going to tell your father, unless I resign on Monday. Oh Louisa, what am I going to do? Should I go and tell your father now?'

Louisa looked worried. 'Sit down. Here, let's have your coat. Let's not be too hasty, Rose. We need to think about this carefully.'

Louisa hung up Rose's coat and returned. 'Now tell me what has been going on. When did you find out? How long have you known? You didn't say anything about this a couple of weeks ago.'

'I know, but I thought I was coping and that nobody need know, at least not until I had heard back from Frank. He's written a couple of letters, but his second letter was sent before he would have received my reply to his first. I'm sure he'll stand by me if he truly feels as he says in his letters. I wrote back straight away and I told him of my condition and asked him what I should do, but I'm still waiting for his response. I might have to wait another three weeks!'

'How did Mrs Robins find out?'

'I fainted in the shop a few weeks ago. I've been feeling queasy and have been sick several times. You know, like you were at the start. I think she must have been suspicious; she said she heard me in the privy one morning. She cornered me after closing this evening and accused me of being pregnant. I was taken aback and caught off guard. She said that I could tell her and that she'd help me, but when I admitted it, she turned on me and said she would tell your father if I didn't resign. Whether I tell him or she tells him, I'll have to leave.'

'I don't know why father keeps her on, you know,' Louisa said sympathetically. 'She doesn't fit in there anymore. I once suggested he get someone younger, but he wouldn't hear of it. Mrs Robins is a nasty piece of work. He said that she brought in a lot of the older long-standing customers and we mustn't forget that they are the bread and butter of the business.'

'I had wondered about getting rid of it.'

Louisa looked aghast. 'No, Rose! How could you? Don't even think of it!' She rested her hand on her own swelling. 'I could never do such a thing and I'm sure you couldn't really. Besides, there are some terrible so-called remedies, which could make you really ill, and they don't work. Surely, you weren't thinking of some backstreet physician?'

'Well, it had crossed my mind,' Rose admitted. 'I don't know what to do. I need to hear from Frank.'

Louisa was quiet for a moment. 'Listen Rose, I'm going to tell you a secret. I've been sworn to secrecy, but I feel I have no alternative.'

'What do you mean, sworn to secrecy?'

'You know John took Frank down to Cape Town.'

Rose nodded.

'Well, one evening during the trip, he and Frank discussed certain matters. Frank told John that he had made a will before he left London and that he has left everything to John. I shouldn't be telling you this really, but you'll understand why in a moment. Frank also told him about how you two became involved and that he is in love with you and intends to marry you when he gets back.'

Rose was looking intently at her now, hardly believing what she was being told. It confirmed the sentiment he had expressed in his letters.

'He told John that if you found yourself in the same predicament as I was, then he would marry you. He also asked ...' at this point

Louisa's voice began to tremble slightly, 'that if he was killed and failed to return, could we use his estate to help you? John assured him that of course we would help you and I think you need our help now.'

'Oh Louisa,' Rose started to sob. 'It's such a relief to hear that from Frank, and to have your offer of help too. Do you really mean it? Will John be agreeable too?'

'Yes, I know he will be. He gave Frank his word; but anyway, it need only be for a few months, until you have your baby. Frank's far too fond of his good looks to go risking any disfigurement or wounding, at the hands of the Boers. When are you due?'

'Well I'm reasonably certain it'll be the third week in October.'

'Right then, in the meantime you can live here. I'm due at the beginning of September. You can help me. We can help each other. Once Frank is back, you can get married. John reckons he'll be back by the autumn … maybe even before you give birth.'

'When does John's ship next return? It should be carrying a letter for me from Frank. Are you sure he won't mind if I stay here?'

'He's scheduled to arrive in London on 16th May. He'll be agreeable. I know he will. You can keep me company. It hasn't been easy adjusting to life here on my own. I know father is up at the end of the street, but he still stays at the shop quite a lot and I miss the hustle and bustle of Crockford's. It'll be fun.'

'But what do you think your father will say?'

'He won't be happy about it, that's for sure. He'll have no choice but to accept your resignation. You know what the customers are like and in the end, Crockford's is everything to him. He'll be shocked and disappointed, but these things happen. Look at my situation. If John hadn't stuck by me and agreed to hurry our wedding, then I dread to think what might have been. No, don't worry, we'll make the best of it, and with luck everything will turn out fine.'

Rose stayed the night at Louisa's house. The following day, Sunday, Louisa helped Rose compose her letter of resignation. It was formal in tone and gave the reason for leaving as a 'matter of personal circumstance'. She resolved to see Mr Crockford in his office during a quiet spell on Monday morning.

2.12

Mrs Robins seemed to be in unusually fine spirits when she appeared for work on Monday morning. She had thought about her strategy over the weekend and had decided to inform Mr Crockford of Rose's plight at the first opportunity. Her intention was to speak to him before Rose.

Rose had risen earlier than normal and spent time packing and organising her things on the assumption that she would be moving out later that day. She appeared in the shop with only moments to spare before inspection, carrying in her apron pocket the envelope containing her letter of resignation.

Mr Crockford made his usual morning assessment of staff and shop, satisfying himself that all was well before telling Sidney to unlock the front door. Rose's counter was extremely busy immediately after opening. She didn't notice Mrs Robins walking off in the direction of the office. Reappearing a few minutes later, looking flushed and with an expression of hurt upon her countenance, Mrs Robins made her way back to the haberdashery department.

Shortly after ten o'clock, during a lull in customers, Rose went to Mr Crockford's office. She tapped gently on the door.

'Come,' he called.

With great trepidation, Rose opened the door and entered.

'I wish to hand in my resignation, Mr Crockford, sir.' She placed the envelope on his desk, before retreating a pace to await his reaction.

He picked it up and using a knife to slit the envelope, removed the one page letter. He read it slowly, showing no reaction, before placing it down on his desk.

Rose was shaking. This seemed like the worst moment of her life.

'Why are you leaving Rose? What are you referring to as, "personal circumstance"?'

'I'd rather not say Mr Crockford, sir. It's personal.'

He hesitated, choosing his words. 'Are you in an unfortunate predicament, Rose?'

Rose hesitated, not sure how he would react. 'Yes I am, Mr Crockford, sir. How did you know? Has Mrs Robins told you?'

'Yes, Rose. She told me earlier this morning and I took no pleasure from it, no pleasure whatsoever. I appreciate that you have had the decency to tender your resignation. You know I can't keep you on here. The customers would not approve.'

'I know, Mr Crockford. I understand your position and how you must uphold the reputation of Crockford's.'

'The problem is, Rose, I don't want to lose you, but I can see no alternative. You are very good at your job and it won't be easy to replace you. What are you going to do, Rose? Where will you go?'

'I'm going to move in with Louisa, until Frank Williams comes back from the Cape. Frank is the father.'

'Is he now? Do you think he'll stand by you?'

'I hope so, Mr Crockford. He has intimated as much.'

'Well, I hope for your sake, he does the decent thing. When are you expecting the birth?'

'October.'

'And when do you ... erm ... when do you think that others might start to notice?'

'Louisa says, end of May.'

'Listen, Rose, I'm going to accept your resignation, I have no choice. However, if you wish, we can defer your leaving for a few weeks until the end of May, but no longer. I can't let you work here, once your predicament becomes obvious. In the meantime, I will try to find someone to replace you. It may be that if you are at Louisa's, you can assist her with some of the dressmaking outwork she's doing, but I make no promises. We will need to keep your presence there confidential,' he stated firmly. 'You are not to say anything to anyone here at the shop of this arrangement. It is a little unusual. Normally, dismissal would be immediate. I have warned Mrs Robins that she is not to repeat the allegation she made of you. I will not have gossip of that nature spread amongst staff or customers. We can say that you are leaving to take up an offer of employment in the West End, a promotion, so to speak.'

'Thank you, Mr Crockford. That is very decent of you. I won't do anything to embarrass you, or tarnish the good name of Crockford's.'

'Very well, Rose, you may go. I will speak to Louisa of this and ensure that she understands my decision.'

'Thank you, Mr Crockford.'

With that, Rose returned to her post, quietly relieved that she could continue to work a while longer and that the shame of her condition was not about to be broadcast all over the shop.

2.13

The troopers were given the order to saddle up and prepare to move out. It was only four in the morning and their blankets had been covered in frost when they awoke. They had received new mounts the previous evening: Argentine horses with a good reputation, but time would tell whether they were suited to the rigours of the terrain and warfare.

It was now early May, and Frank had been in South Africa for nearly three months. Frank, like the men around him, had changed. They were becoming battle-hardened. They had seen comrades killed and wounded. Their early enthusiastic optimism had faded somewhat, appreciating through experience, that the Boer was a formidable foe and not one to be underestimated. Some days, when ordered to march in pursuit of the enemy, they remained in the saddle all day, often under almost continuous fire. They foraged when they had the opportunity, supplementing their rations with local game. During conditions of imminent engagement, the nightly routine also included the chore of digging entrenchments, as protection against shelling.

For Frank's company, that morning in May was a sad one. They had buried two popular members the day before: a sergeant and a private. They had been killed by shellfire during a skirmish with the enemy at Brandfort. Although they had taken the town, any elation amongst Frank's comrades ebbed when the bodies were brought in for burial. The mood of the company was still sombre.

They covered more than twenty-five miles before nightfall, scouting ahead of the main infantry column, looking for enemy patrols. It was hard-going for men and horses. This pattern of activity continued for several days and the general assessment of the men was that the Argentine horses were not up to the job.

They went into action at Zand River on 10 May and drove the enemy from their positions. Frank's conduct, under fire, was praised by one of his officers and he was promoted to Corporal. There then followed two days of calm, during which the horses were watered and grazed in the hope of improving their condition. On Saturday, 12 May, they took part in the successful capture of Kroonstad.

The following day, they rested. During the afternoon, seated in the shade with his back against a rock, Frank wrote another letter to Rose.

13th May 1900

Dearest Rose

I am sending this letter c/o John and Louisa as I am not sure whether you have been able to remain at the shop. Perhaps you have left by now? If any of the staff has found out, I do sincerely hope they treated you respectfully. I do so wish I could be with you, to lend my support. We would be married without delay.

I hope you are well, my love, and coping without me. I feel rather useless here and long to be there with you. Still, I am told that if the campaign continues to go as favourably as it has to date we shall be returning in September. We are making progress.

I have some good news. I have been promoted to Corporal, which will enhance my career prospects when I get back. I have been giving considerable thought to our future. I think it would be best if you have the child on the Isle of Wight. No one there knows of you. I don't think it is fair on John and Louisa to overstay your welcome. Their house is small and they will need the second bedroom for a nursery. John will help you with travel arrangements. I think it best if you stay with my parents.

I have written to mother and father and told them of your condition and my love for you, and of our intention to marry as soon as I return. I think we should consider the island our home. My family has contacts in Cowes and I am confident I will be able to find a job. Cousin George has a senior position in one of the banks and I believe he would help me find employment if necessary.

Before leaving for the Cape, I made a will, leaving everything to John. I spoke with John on the voyage down here. Should I not return, John knows that my fervent wish is that you should receive the benefit of my estate. It's not much, but at least you will have some money to tide you over for a while. I have about forty pounds in my savings and a few shares. I know my parents will help you too. Such talk is melancholy, my love, and I refuse to dwell on that subject any longer, but I needed to tell you.

On a lighter note, I have some good friends here now and we intend to keep in touch when we return. We are going to a concert this evening given by the band. Have I mentioned Charlie Mills? He's from the island too and we have several mutual acquaintances. He shot a Secretary Bird the other day. It looks a bit like a cross between an eagle and a stork and has feathers on its head, which resemble quill pens stuck behind the ear. We cooked it over the fire and it was delicious, if a little tough. There was enough for about eight of us to enjoy.

I am writing to you with my back against a rock. We are encamped on a kopje giving us a view for some distance over the veld. The veld, as the landscape here is called, is a brownish grassy colour, broken by the most amazingly tall anthills and clumps of prickly pear trees.

I will have to stop writing now. I need to check the horses. The new ones we have are not standing up to the conditions at all well. I am looking forward to your next letter. I hope it is waiting for me when we return to the main camp.

Take care my love.

Your most affectionate,

Frank.

2.14

John Williams returned to his home for two days' leave in the middle of May. It was early in the morning as he turned the key in the lock. He was delighted to find Louisa still in bed, just as he had hoped. He was tired and hungry, but not too tired to enjoy the delights of his homecoming with his new wife. Afterwards, Louisa went downstairs and started to prepare breakfast. John shaved and dressed before joining her at the table. He was so pleased to be home.

As they ate, Louisa brought him up to date with events and gossip and of course, the topic most on her mind was Rose. She told John what had happened a couple of Sundays before and that Rose was pregnant and expecting the birth in October. As Louisa anticipated, John wasn't entirely surprised and agreed that they would let Rose stay with them until Frank's return.

Louisa explained that her father could not let Rose continue working for him beyond the end of May when her condition would start to become obvious to staff and customers. He had to protect the good name of Crockford's. He had agreed though, that if possible and if enough work was available, he would employ Rose as a casual outworker so that she could at least try to make a living, but he made no promises.

'Has Rose heard from Frank?'

'Yes, she's had two letters from him. She showed me the first. He wrote it during the voyage to Cape Town. He said he was missing her terribly and had never before had such feelings for anyone. He's hoping that she will want to see him when he returns, but of course, he wrote his letter before knowing her news. She replied immediately, explaining everything and is worried that his feelings for her will change.'

'I doubt that very much. When he spoke to me about what happened while we were away on honeymoon, he seemed absolutely besotted with Rose. I'm sure he'll stand by her. It should all be fine, providing of course that he doesn't get himself wounded or killed. Things are tough down there you know. It certainly isn't a picnic.'

'What if Frank's return is delayed and it drags on past the autumn? Do you think we should consider that possibility?' asked Louisa.

'I think we should. We need to be careful. I know you are very fond of Rose, but this is a small house and we don't want to start getting in each other's way. If she spends her confinement here and has the baby here, then of course the locals may get to hear about it. That could have some unwelcome repercussions for your father. It might be best to see how things go. Don't make any promises.'

'What do you mean, don't make any promises? You're not here most of the time anyway. I've already said she can stay,' said Louisa starting to get angry.

'No, don't misunderstand me. Of course, we'll see her right. I'm thinking aloud ... I may have a solution: what if Rose were to have her baby in Ventnor? Nobody there knows her and she could help my parents with the hotel. They're still refurbishing it and mother was telling Rose at the wedding about her problem in finding a skilled seamstress for all of the curtaining and drapes. That could be the

94

answer. I know that Frank would be agreeable. He even half suggested it himself, certainly that our parents would help out.'

Louisa considered this idea. It had its merits. 'So how long could she stay here, then?'

John thought for a few seconds. 'Rose is due to leave the shop by end of this month and she'll come here, yes?'

'That's right, if all goes as expected,' confirmed Louisa.

'Right, so let's give it until end of July and then review how things are going. We might know by then when they intend bringing back the CIV. Maybe she could stay until after your birth, but leave after that?'

'That might be too late if she's going to go to your parents' hotel,' explained Louisa. 'I'd like her to be here when I have the baby, but from what I've been told, you generally don't like too much gadding about during the last few weeks of pregnancy, so a crossing to the Isle of Wight in September might be too much. If she did leave before I'm due, father said Mrs Jones from the shop could stay for a few days to help me, especially if you can't get leave.'

'Well, let's see how it goes and how we all get along under one roof. If we know Frank's coming back before September, then it won't be a problem. She can stay until he returns. If not, then we can consider sending her over to the hotel.'

2.15

Frank's life as a CIV trooper continued to take him into potentially dangerous situations. He always fought bravely when required and gave a good account of himself. However, since learning that Rose was pregnant, his attitude to life had changed. He no longer volunteered for extra duties without thought or care, especially if it meant possible contact with an enemy patrol, or the likelihood of conflict. It wasn't that he was reluctant to fight or wished to avoid the enemy; it was more a case of realising that he now had responsibilities and a reason to return to England.

He calculated that his odds of coming through the campaign unscathed were improved if he reduced the frequency of confrontation with the enemy. This was not in any way cowardly, for when his company went into action, Frank was there, leading his small group of men, with no less determination than before. It was just that now, he avoided what he considered to be the more frivolous of volunteer activities, such as laying in ambush at night, on the off-chance that a couple of Boer scouts might fall victim to an improvised trap. Such endeavours were not without occasional success and plenty of men volunteered, as much to relieve boredom as anything else. The fact that Frank no longer did so bore no reflection on his character or capability as a soldier. His new attitude merely reflected his changed status. No longer the impatient confident young buck, he was now a wiser more discerning man, with a beautiful prospective wife and soon to be born child, waiting for him at the end of his spell of duty in the Cape.

At night, beneath his blankets, he thought about Rose. He longed to receive her next letter with perhaps a photograph. He wanted to know how she was coping. The shame of pregnancy outside of marriage could not be exaggerated. He was mindful of the taunts and jibes she might receive, after all, unmarried mothers were under great pressure to give up their children for adoption. There was no legal system of adoption and giving a child away was usually the only option for an unmarried mother. Sometimes babies were given up at birth and taken by the midwife to a childless couple. There were adoption societies too, which brought together couples wishing to acquire a child and unmarried mothers pressured to give one up, but money often changed hands and there was no official paperwork.

Frank knew of instances where families made their own private arrangements, with childless relatives taking on the infant of an unmarried cousin or friend. Such arrangements made good sense because the child stayed within the family. The grandparents were often able to remain in contact and of course, a couple desperate for a child had their prayers answered.

Frank even recalled advertisements he had seen in the newspapers at home: '*Offered for Adoption. Three months old, baby girl, all rights forfeited.*' He shuddered at the thought. *No child of mine will be given away or fostered*, he promised himself. He would write to his parents and implore them that if anything happened to him, they would see that Rose and her child – his child – were spared the indignity and cruelty of forced separation.

2.16

John arrived back from Cape Town on schedule in late June. He hugged and kissed Louisa when he came into the house, commenting humorously on her increasing girth. It was mid-morning and Louisa and Rose had been sewing dresses in the front parlour. Cuttings and remnants were scattered all over the rug. After polite exchanges, Rose made herself scarce and went up to her room, so that John and Louisa could talk in private. John appreciated her diplomatic exit, but was disappointed not to be able to enjoy the same welcome home he'd received on previous occasions. Obviously, decorum decreed that he and Louisa maintain a respectable air in front of Rose.

While they were alone, John brought Louisa up to date with events at the shipping company and other news. 'Have you heard of the lying-in hospital in Finsbury?' he asked.

'Yes, of course, the one near St Luke's on City Road.'

'That's the one. Did you know that it was established to assist, amongst others, wives of soldiers and sailors?'

'I know that it's some sort of training hospital for midwives and doctors, but I didn't know who its patients were. Why do you mention it?'

'Because, I'm a sailor and you're my wife!' John exclaimed excitedly before quietening his tone. 'I appreciate how anxious you are about the birth ...' he took Louisa's hand, 'with what happened to your mother and baby brother. George Corbett told me that I should get on to the office, because they have contacts at the hospital and they can arrange for us to have a midwife, to be present when you have the baby.'

'But that means I will have to go into hospital ... and I'm sure I heard that they had some problems a few years ago, with infection and a large number of cases of childbed fever. That's what my mother caught.'

'No, apparently that's all been sorted out and you wouldn't have to go in, because they have some very experienced midwives who go out to patients. You could still have the baby here at home.'

'Really? Do you think so?'

'Yes, that's why I'm so pleased about it.'

'It certainly would be reassuring to have a woman here, who knew what she was doing, but would they come this far? It must be about five miles away.'

'George reckons they would. He says the company has special influence at the hospital and a word or two in the right ear should be enough to swing it. I'm going into the office tomorrow to get the ball rolling, if you're agreeable.'

'Yes, of course, it sounds perfect and I know my father will be greatly relieved too. He's never got over losing mother and when I told him I was expecting, I saw a moment of fear in his eyes, before he controlled himself and offered his congratulations.'

'Good, so that's settled then.'

Later, as Louisa prepared luncheon, John enquired of Rose how she was and how things were going. He could see that she also was now noticeably pregnant, nearly as big as Louisa, in fact. He asked her how she was coping.

'I feel much better now,' Rose said. 'Louisa and I compare notes on our conditions. I left the shop on the last Saturday in May. I didn't have many things to bring with me, because I'd already brought most of my few possessions over the week before. Mr Crockford called me into his office just before I went. He gave me three months' wages, which I think was most generous of him. He said that I had been an excellent employee and was sorry to lose me. He handed me a reference to that effect. The others were kind too, apart from Mrs Robins on haberdashery. She was desperate to tell the rest of the staff the real reason why I was going, but Mr Crockford had been adamant she was not to do so and threatened her with instant dismissal if she breathed a word. At least I didn't leave under a cloud, as far as my other work colleagues were concerned. Sidney even gave me a little present to remember him by.'

John chuckled. 'Louisa said he was very taken with you.'

Rose smiled and continued. 'The staff were told that I was going back to the West End to take up a position in one of the prestigious drapers there. They assume it's a promotion, but fortunately no one asked me too much about it.'

'What if one of them finds out that you are staying here?'

'If anyone discovers I'm here, I can say that the job wasn't as I'd been promised and that I'm helping Louisa for a while, but I really don't think that'll happen. I shan't be going into the town, so it's unlikely they'll know at Crockford's. Anyway, I've had another letter from Frank and he says it would be best if I went to stay with your parents in Ventnor, until he returns and we get married.'

'When was the letter written?'

'May 13, just after they took Kroonstad, I think. He said the campaign was going well and according to camp gossip and speculation, they will be coming home in September. He's been promoted to Corporal. He's decided he doesn't want to go back to his old job in London. He said that your family has plenty of contacts on the island and he should be able to get a job in Cowes.'

'Really? He's made up his mind not to go back, whatever. That's a shame, because I thought he had good prospects as a shipping agent. Did he say anything about the conditions out there? I've heard that a lot of men have gone down sick with enteric. The hospital at Bloemfontein is apparently full of soldiers suffering with the fever.'

'He hasn't mentioned it. Is it really that serious?'

'It can be. It depends how quickly they get onto it. If left too long, you can get abominable complications. It can take months to get over it.'

'Let's not talk of it. I'd rather not know too much about subjects like that.' Rose turned the conversation to other matters. 'Don't you think Louisa's looking well? I'd say confinement suits her.'

'Yes she is. She's looking more beautiful each time I come back.'

'When would you like me to leave?' Rose asked bravely, raising the matter with John. 'Shall I stay until after Louisa has had the baby or go to Ventnor before? Only, originally I thought I would prefer to stay here, if you were agreeable, but I am getting rather big now and perhaps if I'm going to travel, I ought to go before.'

'Let's think … Louisa's expecting around 2nd September. I'll write to my parents about suggested arrangements for you. They're probably quite busy at the moment, with it being the start of the season, but they usually see trade drop off towards the end of August, especially after the regatta ends. In fact, that might be a good time to go. Louisa's baby will nearly be here by then. I've just been telling her that I'm going to arrange for her to have a midwife from the lying-in hospital in Finsbury attend her. Mrs Jones from the shop is on standby as well to help after the birth, so you wouldn't want to be here then anyway, would you?'

'Oh no, not if she's coming. I'll need to be well away before then. Mid to late August should be fine, if your parents are agreeable.'

'I don't think it will be a problem. You might need to keep your head down at the hotel. I mean the circumstances are a little unfortunate, but Frank is the apple of mother's eye you know. She'll probably put any embarrassment aside, as you two intend to marry when he gets back. If you're discreet, there shouldn't be any real harm done.'

'What's Ventnor like? I was reading the other day that it's now very fashionable, with a south-facing climate that's ideal for those wanting to improve their health … you know, clean air and salt-water bathing, and the like.'

'Quite right. It started out as a fishing village, but since they built the railway connection from Cowes, it's grown substantially. It's got lots of things for visitors … an esplanade, a pier with a bandstand, a landing stage, and a lovely beach with those bathing machines, which they push into the water so that the bathers can have some privacy.'

'So, your parents' hotel is quite busy then?'

'Yes, they're doing well. They're quite near the small waterfall known as The Cascade. It's famous for the abundance of plants that grow around it, plants more suited to warmer climes.'

'It sounds lovely. Have you managed to book some leave?' enquired Rose. 'I know how important it is to Louisa to know that you will be here for the birth.'

'I'm supposed to have six weeks, starting from my next return to London. That should be on 2 August. Do you realise that we've hardly had a break since January? Just a couple of days at each end and then back to sea again. There is always the chance that leave will be cancelled. Let's hope nothing untoward happens in the Cape … in fact, thinking about it, I might even be able to go over to Ventnor with you. I haven't seen mother and father since the wedding and I can help you with the luggage.'

'That's very kind. I would appreciate some assistance, but only if you think you can leave Louisa.'

'Oh, I think she'll be able to manage for one night. I can return the following day. I'll write to my parents tomorrow to make sure that they can accommodate you.'

2.17

On 11 June 1900, the British advance reached Diamond Hill, just twenty miles from Pretoria. Frank was part of a large force of mounted troopers and infantry, supported by artillery, which was ordered to attack the elevated defensive positions of the Boer army, under the command of General Botha.

To begin with, the fighting was inconclusive; the British relying on their artillery to pound and break the resolve of the defending force. When the infantry and mounted troops were sent in to the attack, progress was slow. The Boers fired down on the advancing soldiers with sweeping fire, inflicting numerous losses.

It was a Boer tactic to avoid close combat, or hand-to-hand fighting, if possible, preferring to use their superior longer range Mauser rifles from afar. They used smokeless powder shot, which made them difficult to spot. Whenever the British did look likely to overwhelm them, they tended to retire and melt away, saving their forces to fight another day.

In one particular frontal attack, Frank's company suffered a number of casualties. They were ordered to charge on a Boer position situated at the top of a shallow rise. The ground was open and slightly uphill. They were about 1,200 yards away when a hopeful ranging shot took Frank's horse from beneath him. The poor animal buckled and died instantly, throwing Frank heavily to the ground.

Luckily, for Frank, he found he had fallen just behind his horse and realised that he was concealed from Boer snipers by the bulk of the animal lying on its side. He glanced to his left and could see that his friend, Charlie, was also down. He was wounded and lay on his back about twenty yards away. He was groaning and clutching his shoulder. There was no sign of Charlie's horse.

Frank realised that Charlie lay exposed and in a vulnerable position. He stuck his head above the side of the horse to gauge his options. Bullets whistled above and around him. One thudded into the horse's body. Charlie groaned again. Frank knew he needed to act swiftly to save his stricken friend. Keeping low, he dashed out into the open and ran over to him. Charlie was barely conscious. Trying to avoid further injury to Charlie's shoulder, Frank grabbed his feet and dragged him backwards as quickly as he could to the relative shelter created by the dead horse. He pushed Charlie up against it and tucked himself tight up against him so as to conceal himself as well. More bullets ripped through the grass around them.

After a few minutes, Frank realised the sound of enemy fire had ceased. He risked a quick glance in the direction of the enemy and was relieved to see several of his comrades galloping back towards them. He waved to attract their attention.

An officer swiftly assessed the situation and sent one of the troopers to fetch a medical orderly and stretcher-bearers. Happily, for Charlie, the bullet had passed cleanly through his shoulder, without damaging any vital arteries. He was given brandy to sip while his wound was bandaged. He was then evacuated to a field hospital. Later, he was sent home to England and eventually made a full recovery.

Frank's replacement horse was a Basuto pony, bred in the colony and much better suited to the terrain and climate. He was extremely pleased to have been given such a fine mount and found himself on the receiving end of much semi-jealous ribaldry from his comrades. During the following weeks, he and the pony bonded strongly with each other. It was good to be alive. The war was going well and Frank was increasingly confident that he would be leaving for home in the autumn.

Early July found the CIV on garrison duty for several weeks at Heilbron, followed by action in the Fredrikstad area. Yet again, they performed well and although suffering more casualties, the majority survived the fighting to gather near Pretoria at the end of August. All talk was that they would soon be going home.

Part Three

3.1

John's ship docked in London according to schedule on 2 August. The weather that afternoon was very warm. The streets were noisy, smelly, and hot; crowded with all manner of horse-drawn contraptions. During the cab journey from the dockside to Apsley Street, John reflected on what was due to occur during his leave of six weeks. By the time he went back to sea, he would be a father. His life would have begun a new chapter. He hoped Louisa was still as healthy and blooming, as she had been when he'd last seen her and of course, Rose would be there too. He wondered how she would be coping and whether she'd heard from Frank.

As the horse clip-clopped over the cobbles, these thoughts and others occupied John's mind. His ship had brought back more wounded from the Cape. Charlie Mills, one of Frank's CIV friends, had sought him out on the return voyage. Charlie had received a serious but now greatly healed shoulder wound. However, his arm was weak and he had been allowed to return to England. He was glowing in his praise of Frank's bravery, for dragging him out of danger whilst under fire. Charlie believed that he might not have survived if Frank had not intervened.

John meditated on this mention of Frank's courage. He was in two minds whether to tell Rose or not. On the one hand, he was immensely proud of his brother's conduct, but on the other, it served to emphasise the dangers of the war and he didn't want to alarm Rose. *Probably best to let Frank choose whether to tell her*, he thought.

He found Louisa and Rose sitting in the shade in the small garden at the rear of the terraced house. They were drinking tea and chatting happily. Louisa was thrilled to see John. He bent and kissed her tenderly on the cheek. He was relieved to see her looking fit and well, if not a little warm. Rose too looked fine and equally pregnant. She got up slowly and went into the kitchen to make him some tea.

'Did you have a good trip, darling?' Louisa enquired.

'Yes, everything went fine, no major problems to report ... and

I've been given leave for six weeks as we hoped. I've also had confirmation that we are to have an experienced midwife here for you, when the baby comes.'

'Oh, that's wonderful news. Father will be delighted too.'

They chatted together for a few minutes before Rose returned with a tray of tea and some biscuits. She set it down on the table and joined them.

'Any news from Frank?' John asked her.

'I had a letter last week. He says he's fine ... got a new horse by all accounts and pretty certain he'll be leaving for home this autumn.'

'Did he mention any of the fighting?'

'No, he didn't. He never does. Perhaps it's the censor, or he's protecting me and doesn't want me to worry. It's bad enough reading the stories in the newspapers. They say the fighting at Diamond Hill was quite intense, but thankfully, we were victorious in the end.'

3.2

Two weeks later, John, Louisa, and Rose, breakfasted together as usual. Louisa prepared it, while John browsed the morning paper and Rose finished packing. The news from the Cape was good. Pretoria was once more under British control and a large contingent of Empire troops was encamped around the city. It was rumoured that the volunteer regiments, including the CIV, would be repatriated at the end of September.

'I expect we'll be bringing troops back with us on my next trip,' according to the papers anyway,' John announced to Louisa as she busied herself at the stove.

'Perhaps Frank will be one of your passengers again,' she replied. 'You never know, it's happened once, so why not again?'

'You may be right, but there are other ships. There's quite a number of vessels making the run now.'

Just at that moment, Rose appeared. John noticed how beautiful she looked. Her long jet-black hair was clean, shiny, and fashionably styled. Her skin showed a hint of the colour he associated with women he'd seen in the Mediterranean ports of Genoa and Marseilles. Rose had never spoken of her parentage, other than to say that she was orphaned at the age of thirteen. Perhaps she had some Latin blood within her, John mused. She was as big as Louisa. Maternity suited her well.

'Morning, John,' she said brightly. 'Do you need any help, Louisa?'

'No, you sit down; I'm almost ready to serve.'

'Will it be a rough crossing today?' Rose asked anxiously.

'Judging by the sky, I don't think you need worry too much on that score,' John assured her. 'This fine weather is set for the week.'

'I've never been on a boat before,' she admitted. 'Do you think I'll be seasick? Louisa told me she was, when you went over together after the wedding.' She looked towards Louisa for confirmation.

'Yes, but it was January,' said John. 'The weather was awful and the crossing from Southampton to Cowes was especially rough. It was calm on the way back though. You were fine on the return trip darling, weren't you?'

'Yes, I was, that's true. I'm sorry Rose; I might have made more of it than I should have.'

'No, don't apologise. So John, what time is our train from Waterloo to Southampton?'

'Our train leaves at eleven and gets into the Southampton terminal at a quarter to one. We can have lunch there and then catch the ferry and be over to Cowes by around four. I reckon with the train to Ventnor, we ought to be at George and Charlotte's by early evening.'

Louisa brought over three plates of cooked breakfast, with freshly grilled toast and tea. She sat down and they began to eat.

'I suppose the worst part will be getting to Waterloo Station,' fretted Rose. 'I just hope nobody from the shop sees me at Leyton station. They think I went back to a good job in the West End.'

'No, don't worry. We'll only be there for a few minutes. Now, the cabbie is due here at eight-thirty. Our train for Liverpool Street leaves Leyton at nine-fifteen. We need to get another cab to City underground station and then take the underground railway to Waterloo. The journey on the underground only takes four minutes so we should have plenty of time.'

'I've never liked going under the river,' Rose said a little nervously. 'All that water above you and how reliable are those electric trains? You know they call that line "the drain"?'

'Yes,' said John laughing, 'but I'm not sure why?'

'I heard it's because they have to keep pumping water out and it smells damp and musty in the tunnel. It's only been open a year or so.'

'You're right, it does smell a bit damp, but then again it's bound to. There's nothing to be afraid of though. Don't forget, I spend most of my life working below the waterline.'

They finished breakfast and Rose got up to leave the table. John pulled out his pocket watch. 'Right, it's eight o'clock now. Are your bags ready? If so, I'll bring them down for you.'

'Just give me ten minutes to finish,' said Rose. 'I'll call you when I'm ready.'

Considering the number of parts and changes, the journey to Ventnor went without mishap. The weather was beautiful. The section on the underground was a little unpleasant, due to the heat and humidity in the tunnel, but all of that was forgotten when they finally boarded the paddle steamer at Southampton's Royal Pier for the trip across the Solent.

During the journey, Rose had time to reflect on her life. She and Louisa had exchanged a tearful farewell that morning; they had become even closer during the recent weeks and each wished the other well. They assumed that the next time they met would be as new mothers. Motherhood wasn't something that Rose was looking forward to. She had kept her reservations for the most part from Louisa, who by contrast, although worried about the rigours of childbirth itself, was on the whole, very excited at the prospect of having a baby.

At the root of her misgivings, Rose regretted falling pregnant. She loved Frank and thought he was a wonderful man, but she felt a degree of bitterness at having to sacrifice her own ambitions, and wasn't entirely sure she wanted to spend her married life on the Isle of Wight. Once Frank returned, she wanted to discuss their future together in more detail. Making plans by letter, and having to wait up to two months for a reply was not ideal.

She was also worried about her relationship with her prospective in-laws. She'd been surprised when John informed her one morning that his mother had written in reply, advising that the hotel was full and not entirely suitable to accommodate Rose in her condition. This may have been true, but it rankled somewhat with Rose and made her wonder whether she was likely to have a difficult relationship with Frank's parents.

However, this concern was tempered by the alternative arrangement, which Frank's mother had organised: Rose was to stay with cousin George and Charlotte. They had a substantial house, with plenty of rooms, and Mrs Edwards, the housekeeper, had skills in midwifery. Rose had only met the couple once, at Louisa's wedding, but she had taken to Charlotte straightaway, and thought George polite and charming. It was no secret that they had tried for many years to have children but none had been forthcoming. Charlotte was said to be very excited at the prospect of having a baby in the household, should Frank's return be delayed.

John, at times, interrupted her thoughts, to enquire how she was or to point out something of interest. On the ferry crossing to Cowes, he went up on deck. He was in his element, being a seaman and having spent his apprenticeship going back and forth over that very stretch of water. She looked out of the window on the ferry, across the gentle swell, and considered how this same water continued all the way to Cape Town, to Frank. She hoped he would soon be on his way home, to help her and share in her predicament. *Pray that his journey will be a safe one*, she thought.

The child within her kicked and jolted her from her reverie. *Yes, I know you're there, I haven't forgotten you. How can I?* She just hoped that Charlotte and George would be as pleasant to her, as they had been in January. With luck, Frank might be home before she had the baby and her stay with them would only be for a short period. The problem was that Rose didn't know when exactly he'd be returning and her future, for the moment, was out of her hands.

Approaching Cowes, Rose was amazed at the show of wealth before her. Several large private yachts, remaining behind from those participating in the annual regatta the previous week, were riding at anchor. For Rose, the wealth on display was yet another reminder of her ambition to one day achieve something with her life; to be her own boss. She wanted to enjoy the trappings of money and success, yet heavily pregnant, unmarried, and with a far from certain future, her dreams at that moment seemed depressingly unattainable.

When the cab driver finally pulled up outside Brindle Lodge, Beaufort Street, Ventnor, Rose was very tired. It had been a long day and although she had managed to doze here and there, she was physically exhausted.

John helped her down from the cab and paid the driver. He opened the gate and carried her luggage up the short path to the doorstep. Rose followed a few steps behind. They paused within the porch, while he pushed the beautifully polished brass button. They heard a bell ring within the large house. Moments later, the door was opened by an older lady in a black dress.

'Hello, Mrs Edwards.' John had been there before on several occasions.

'Good evening, Mr Williams.'

'This is Miss Ince. Mr and Mrs Morris are expecting us?'

'Yes, they are. Do come in. I'll inform Mrs Morris of your arrival.'

'That won't be necessary Mrs Edwards,' shouted a voice approaching from within. 'I heard the bell and assumed it would be our guests. Come in please. Welcome,' Charlotte said warmly 'You must be exhausted.'

111

Mrs Edwards moved aside, but not before she had managed to have a good look at Rose. The older woman's expression however, gave nothing away.

'Yes, it's been a long day, hasn't it Rose?' John replied.

'A very long day,' agreed Rose, 'but, on the whole, the journey was most interesting, especially the crossing from Southampton.'

'Yes it can be lovely on a good day. Leave your luggage here Rose. Mrs Edwards and Emma will take it up to your room. I'll show you up first. We can have dinner a little later, when you've found your bearings, if you're agreeable?'

'Of course,' said Rose. 'That's most kind of you.'

With that, George arrived in the hall too and greeted them warmly.

'George, can you look after John?' asked Charlotte.

'Certainly, my dear. Come on John, while the ladies are upstairs getting reacquainted, we can sample a nice sherry I keep for special occasions.'

'Sounds good to me,' said John.

After dinner, they all retired. Rose was delighted to have a small bathroom adjacent to her room. It was solely for her use and so luxurious compared to the facilities at Crockford's Drapery Emporium. Her room was light and airy, with a glimpse of the sea from her window, if she peered to the right. It was a lovely room.

The house had three floors and a basement, similar to some of those she had admired so much in London, but on a less grand and smaller scale. She noted that some of the furnishings were somewhat provincial in style, which was not surprising, but there was no doubting the quality of what she saw.

She slept well and the following morning, shortly after breakfast, John left. He bade Rose a fond farewell. 'Don't worry. Frank will soon be back and then you can get everything sorted out and all the loose ends tied up, so to speak. Keep in touch. If you don't have time to write letters, just send us a postcard to make us feel jealous of you here by the seaside.'

'Yes I will, and thank you so much for accompanying me and helping yesterday.'

'Think nothing of it. I'd love to stay longer, but Louisa needs me.'

'Of course she does, and very lucky she is to have you. Now take good care of her and give her my love. Perhaps the next time I see you, will be at our wedding!'

After he'd gone, Rose and Charlotte chatted for a while.

'So how are you feeling Rose? Can you feel the baby kicking?'

'Yes, I can at times.'

Rose didn't speak with too much enthusiasm, because she felt a little guilty. Louisa had told her how desperate Charlotte had been to have a child and how upset she was when a doctor explained to her and George that they were unlikely to become parents. Rose didn't want to upset Charlotte by talking too much about her pregnancy. Charlotte however was unperturbed. She gave no hint of any envy, or her own disappointment, and seemed genuinely interested.

'I'm sorry to have to raise the matter,' said Rose, 'but I must pay for my accommodation whilst I am here. I have a savings account at the Post Office. I assume there is a Post Office in Ventnor?'

'Yes, of course there is, but you really have no need to worry. Florence has given me something in advance to cover your keep, all of course on the instructions of Frank. He apparently was most explicit that you should be taken care of. He is going to assume all responsibility when he returns. In the meantime, you can consider yourself our guest.'

'That's very kind of you, truly it is. I don't really know what to say, but … thank you, and if anything happens to Frank, I will pay my way.'

'We'll cross that bridge if necessary.' Charlotte took Rose's hand to reassure her. 'Besides, the war is going well. The papers are full of our retaking of Pretoria and the imminent return of the volunteer troops.'

'Is Mrs Edwards happy with the arrangement, with her being called upon to assist at the birth?'

'I can assure you that Mrs Edwards is entirely happy. She's had four children of her own and has delivered all of her sister's children. You'll be fine. In the event of any complications, we can always call upon Doctor Kendall. His house is not far away.'

Later, Rose retired to her room. Emma, the maid, had already tidied it. She was unused to such pampering and attention. She lay on the bed to rest and read a book for a while. The weather outside was warm and Charlotte had enthused that they should take afternoon tea together in the rear garden, which she promised, afforded great privacy.

Rose went over her conversation with Charlotte. Perhaps she had misjudged Frank's parents, Florence and Arthur. It seemed as though she had been placed under the care of Charlotte for very sound reasons. She realised that she was extremely fortunate to be here and that the family genuinely seemed to have her welfare at heart. It must be difficult, she thought, taking in an unmarried woman in her condition, someone they barely knew. There was a stigma to her plight and Charlotte was to be all the more worthy of praise and appreciation, for the kind treatment she had bestowed so far.

It was comforting to know that a doctor lived nearby. Rose hadn't consulted a medical practitioner at all, not once. She hadn't wanted any more people than necessary to know and besides, a consultation with a doctor was expensive. She and Louisa had compared notes and helped each other. Louisa had a book, which had answered all of their questions concerning pregnancy. They were aware of recent health advice on diet and ensured that they were eating good food in sufficient quantity. They had also decided to follow the latest medical recommendations regarding corseting. It was that of the Rational Dress Society, which advocated wearing looser garments, more comfortable during pregnancy and birth.

So began a relatively calm and restful period for Rose. Breakfast and lunch were taken in Charlotte's company, because George left early for his office in Cowes. In the evening, he returned for dinner, during which there was much discussion of the war in South Africa. Rose thought she detected an element of frustration that he hadn't

114

been able to volunteer, but age and seniority had ensured that such a course of action was not a practical option for him.

George too, seemed unperturbed by her presence in the household. She imagined that he and Charlotte must have had many friends and acquaintances on the island and she wondered how they would react to her staying with them. Charlotte later revealed that if anybody asked, they had agreed with Florence that they would say Frank's fiancé was staying and the couple intended to marry upon his imminent return.

3.3

Rose's stay at Brindle Lodge during September was marked by three notable events.

Florence and Arthur visited Rose for the first time on the Sunday afternoon, after her arrival. The initial meeting was a little awkward, bearing in mind that they had only met her once before, at John and Louisa's wedding, but Charlotte fussed about with tea and sandwiches and tried to lighten the atmosphere. There was no doubt that Florence worshipped Frank, and Rose thought she detected a slight resentment towards her. Arthur though, was entirely different. He took to Rose immediately. He seemed genuinely interested in her and listened intently as Rose described her experiences as a draper at the stores in London and Leyton.

'I'm sure we could find some way to make use of Rose's talents at the hotel, don't you think, dear?' Arthur asked his wife.

'Yes, I've no doubt we could, dear, if Rose feels up to it.'

'Certainly, Mrs Williams. I would be only too pleased to help in any way I can. I do so need to repay your kindness to me, although I think I may need to wait until after the birth.'

'Oh, don't thank us,' she said. 'It's Frank you need to be grateful to. He's asked us to assist you until he returns, which of course we are happy to do.'

'Have you heard from him in the last month?' asked Rose.

'Not directly,' Florence replied, 'but we have had news …' She let the statement hang in mid-air.

'Really?' asked Rose, a little puzzled. 'What sort of news?'

'We had a visit from Charlie Mills. You know, his friend from the island, who ended up in the same CIV company?'

'Yes, Frank's mentioned his name. What's he doing back here?'

'Our Frank's been a bit of hero,' she said proudly, puffing out her chest and returning her teacup and saucer to the table.

'Gosh, what do you mean?' asked Charlotte excitedly.

Florence had everyone's attention as she explained: 'Charlie Mills was visiting his parents in Cowes last week. He was discharged from the CIV, as a casualty. He was wounded at Diamond Hill; shot in the shoulder by a Boer sharpshooter. Charlie came over to the hotel to thank us, the parents of Frank, his *saviour*.'

'Saviour!' exclaimed Charlotte.

'That's how he referred to Frank. He said that Frank had saved his life. Apparently, when Charlie was shot, he fell from his horse and lay incapacitated in the open, vulnerable to sniper fire. Frank had been unseated in the same attack, but lay shielded behind the corpse of his mount. Spotting Charlie, Frank dashed out across the exposed ground, at considerable risk to his own life, and dragged poor wounded Charlie back to the cover of his dead horse. Then Frank maintained watch over him, until their comrades returned and were able to summon medical assistance.'

'Gosh, how very brave!' said Charlotte.

Rose's immediate feelings were mixed: admiration, yes, for his bravery, but worry too that he had been in a dangerous situation and at great risk. Florence, for her part, seemed unconcerned of any dangers to Frank. She was so proud of him; her pride seemed to outweigh any misgivings she may have had for his safety.

'I wonder if he'll be recognised for a medal, or mentioned in despatches?' asked Charlotte.

'I doubt it,' replied Arthur, trying to bring the atmosphere back to reality. 'It was a brave thing he did, but that's all part of fighting. No, you need to do something really outstanding, to get any form of gallantry medal. I doubt we'll hear any more of it, but it was decent of Charlie to come over and thank us personally.'

The second event of import during this period was far more serious in nature. Charlotte received a note from Florence during the afternoon of 9 September. A Post Office messenger boy had delivered a telegram to the hotel that morning. The telegram was from John. Louisa had given birth to a baby boy the day before, but the birth had been prolonged and extremely difficult. The aftermath had left her exhausted and in great discomfort.

This news was worrying. Louisa's mother had developed childbed fever two days after giving birth and she had passed away before the end of the third day.

Florence had left immediately for Leyton, promising to write to Charlotte by return with more details. Both Charlotte and Rose were greatly perturbed. Rose considered going back to Leyton herself to support her friend, but Charlotte sensibly talked her out of it.

'You are in no state to travel now,' Charlotte said. 'Better we wait for more news from Florence.'

Rose knew Charlotte was right. She felt increasingly tired at times and often needed to lie down and rest. Undertaking the journey back to Leyton would be folly and there was little help she could give, that Florence was not capable of providing.

They worried and speculated for several days, until the post brought a letter from Florence. The news was good. The midwife had been invaluable; it was thanks to her that Louisa and the baby had survived. Louisa was feeling better and coping with the baby, whom they had named Henry. Mrs Jones, the housekeeper at Crockford's, had returned to the shop, while Florence remained at Apsley Street. John was there too.

Charlotte and Rose wondered whether Louisa had suffered complications similar in nature to those that had brought about the death of her mother, when Louisa was only eight years old. They knew that there was nothing practical they could do to help. Leyton was too far away. They discussed the routine and nature of Rose's confinement and agreed that Rose should change nothing. She was clearly following correct advice. Rose wrote a brief note to Louisa, wishing her well and promising to write more fully in a few days.

In the meantime, Charlotte persuaded Rose that they should spend some time on turning one of the rooms into a nursery. The maid was given the task of cleaning and dusting one of the small bedrooms. It was another lovely room, close to Rose's, with its own fireplace to keep it warm in winter. There was an old wooden cot in the attic. Charlotte had it revarnished, while Rose made some new curtains. Luckily, the large house had lots of blankets and sheets stored away in cupboards and drawers. Some of these, Rose cut and sewed to fit the cot. When they had finished, the nursery looked splendid.

Charlotte loved to organise and plan. She convinced Rose that they ought to have in readiness an adequate supply of napkins and other infant requisites, including gripe water. Rose was grateful for her kindness and support.

Ten days later, Rose and Charlotte were relieved to hear that Louisa was fine. John had gone off to sea again and she was looking after Henry herself. Florence brought the news in person, enjoying her captive audience, as they hung on to her every word. The only sad part was that Louisa's doctor had warned her that she might have problems in conceiving again. He couldn't be sure and hoped that it would not be the case.

The third event, which marked the passing of September for Rose, was a letter from Frank. It had been forwarded from Leyton. He'd written it at the beginning of the month. The CIV were encamped just outside Pretoria, waiting with growing anticipation for the order from high command to send them on their way to Cape Town and a ship to bring them home. He made no mention of the incident with Charlie Mills. He hoped that she was on the island by now, but hadn't received confirmation, so he had sent the letter care of John and Louisa to ensure she received it.

Rose reread the letter several times. His affection was still there, perhaps more so. It was obvious he was looking forward to returning

118

home and getting married. He was extremely optimistic about getting a job in Cowes. It was apparent that he hadn't considered the possibility that Rose would be anything other than delighted to live on the island, but for Rose, misgivings persisted despite her attempts to suppress them. She constantly told herself that she wouldn't have long to wait, either for the baby or for Frank, and that shortly after he returned, they would marry, and all would be well. She was lucky. Things could be much worse. In the scale of things, sacrificing her career would be a small price to pay. Why, only six months before, she was contemplating life in the workhouse, as an impoverished and disgraced unmarried mother. *Put any doubts out of your mind,* she reprimanded herself. *Be positive. Frank will soon be home and we will be able to get on with our lives as a family.*

3.4

The CIV remained encamped throughout September and were inspected by Lord Roberts on 2 October. He made a speech and spoke in flattering tones of the strengths and successes of the volunteer forces. During the build-up to the parade, Frank felt increasingly unwell. He had been under-the-weather for a day or two, with a headache at times and he had started to develop a cough. As his company formed up to troop past the senior generals, Frank clenched his stomach muscles to combat the increasing pain in his abdomen. He hoped he was suffering from nothing more than a reaction to disagreeable camp food, but in his heart, he was also increasingly worried that he was developing fever – enteric fever.

He'd witnessed the symptoms several times during the previous months, as comrades had succumbed to the condition. Despite feeling cold and shivery, he maintained his place in line. At one point midway through the address, he thought he might pass out, but he managed to remain in the saddle. However, after the ceremony ended, he slumped forward against the neck of his pony and collapsed. He was put on a stretcher and sent for medical examination.

A camp doctor confirmed Frank's illness as likely to be enteric and he was despatched, along with some other very sick soldiers, to the military hospital at Bloemfontein. The journey took the best part of two days, part of it by slow-moving bullock wagon. At the same time that Frank was enduring his journey to hospital, his healthy comrades in the CIV were embarking on trains to take them to Cape Town.

Frank arrived at the hospital on 4 October. He was delirious, badly dehydrated, and very weak. His abdomen was painful and distended, caused by putrefaction in his intestines. He was too sick to start the regime of four pints of milk per day, the standard treatment of the time. They tried to give him a drink containing arrowroot, but he was unable to keep it down. In the early hours of the following morning, Frank died. Later that same day his comrades boarded the *SS Assegai* and began their journey home.

Frank was buried before sunset, in the graveyard adjoining the hospital. When his headstone was erected later, it gave the following details.

Name: Williams, F
Rank: Corporal
Unit: City of London Imperial Volunteers
Enteric, 5th October 1900 at Bloemfontein.

3.5

The young Post Office Telegram boy dismounted his bicycle and leaned it against the railing outside The Cascade View Hotel, on Marine Parade, Ventnor. He couldn't have been much older than fourteen. He looked very smart in his uniform, as he entered the main door and proceeded to the desk in the hall. He rang a small bell and thirty seconds later, a gentleman appeared from the dark interior of the hotel.

'Telegram for Mr Arthur Williams,' he declared, retrieving a small brown envelope from his leather satchel.

'That's me,' replied Arthur.

'Would you be so good as to sign here, please sir?' The boy opened a page in his receipt book.

'Yes, of course,' mumbled Arthur, distracted as he considered what news the telegram might contain.

'Thank you, sir,' replied the messenger, handing the brown envelope to Arthur. 'Good day to you, sir.'

'Yes, good day,' Arthur muttered to the departing boy.

Arthur sat down at the desk and turned over the envelope. He hoped it wasn't more bad news from John, concerning either Louisa or little Henry. He slit the envelope at the top and then hesitantly started to slide out the single sheet of paper it contained. He'd only revealed the top inch when he paused. His heart missed a beat. It was stamped 'On Her Majesty's Service' and 'WO', which Arthur knew meant it was from the War Office.

With shaking hands, he pulled out the telegram and read the message upon it. He groaned in despair and put his head in his hands. The message was brief and to the point.

To: Arthur Williams, The Cascade View Hotel, Ventnor, IOW.
Date: 8 October 1900.
Regret to inform you, your son 7159896 Cpl Frank Williams CIV died of Enteric at Bloemfontein OFS, fifth October.

Arthur stumbled his way to the private rooms at the rear of the hotel and broke the tragic news to Florence.

She let out an awful wail and collapsed in a chair, holding the telegram before her, barely able to confirm the message through her tears. She was inconsolable – Frank, her beloved Frank, gone. She'd lost him and he would never return from that wretched war in South Africa.

Arthur it was, who later broke the news to Charlotte and Rose. They were together in the parlour, cutting and arranging flowers. He was guided through by Mrs Edwards and was barely able to maintain his composure, when he faced them to deliver the dreadful news. He told them, before showing them the telegram message to read for themselves. It was cold, brief and contained only the bare facts, addressed to him being Frank's next of kin.

Charlotte gasped in horror and then started to cry.

Rose remained quiet, stunned for a few moments. Then she felt again that sensation she'd had in the shop all those months before. She felt sick. Her pulse rate increased and a crackling noise started to build in her ears. Her vision became unclear and finally, relief; she fainted.

When Rose regained consciousness shortly after, she found herself lying on the floor. She had fallen heavily on her side. The others gently lifted her to her feet. Mrs Edwards declared that Rose should have a glass of water and be put to bed without delay. They helped her climb the stairs to her room. Arthur waited in the sitting room downstairs, while Rose was settled into bed.

Charlotte returned to see if Arthur would like a drink. She started to weep once again and it was Arthur's role to console and sympathise. He found the maid and asked her to make some tea. As he returned to the sitting room, he saw Mrs Edwards coming down the broad staircase. She took his arm and ushered him into the room, so that she could address both he and Charlotte at the same time.

'How is Miss Ince?' asked Charlotte.

'I think she's started,' announced the housekeeper. 'I think the fall and the awful news have given her a terrible shock and I do believe the baby may be on the way.'

'Oh my goodness! Should we call Dr Kendall immediately?' cried Charlotte.

'No, I don't think that will be necessary, not just yet. She can't be more than a week or so from her time anyway. I'll go and sit with her for a while and keep an eye on her, if that's agreeable to you, madam?'

'Yes, of course, and if in the meantime there are any complications you will call me straightaway, won't you? I'll join you shortly.'

'Of course, madam.'

Arthur decided that perhaps he ought to take his leave. He needed to get back to the hotel to look after Florence and he would have to let John and Louisa know too. Charlotte showed him tearfully to the door. He went out into the street, pondering the bad fortune that had befallen his family and wondering whether he should tell Florence that Rose's baby might be on the way.

When he arrived home from the office, Charlotte gave George the painful news of Frank's death. He was terribly upset and retired to his study with a glass and a brandy bottle.

Meanwhile upstairs, Rose was in the early stage of labour. Her hip was bruised from her fall, but she appeared to have no other external injuries. Mrs Edwards was reasonably confident that she had no internal injuries either, but only the next few hours would tell. As the evening drew on and the candles were lit in the bedroom, Mrs Edwards gave orders to the maid to fetch clean linen and towels and to keep a supply of hot water in readiness. She was prepared for a long night; this was, after all, Rose's first child.

Rose groaned and grimaced with the pain, which came in waves. Charlotte sat in a chair beside the bed and mopped her brow. As she comforted her, Charlotte realised that Rose hadn't spoken of Frank's death, since collapsing in the kitchen. She could only surmise that she wanted to block it out for the moment, while her mind and body were focused on the imminent birth of her baby.

Rose, however, although not voicing her thoughts, was deeply tormented. She was inwardly terrified. She had lost Frank and now she was going to have his baby, with no hope of marriage or of a father for her child. It would be a bastard child. The shame; the disgrace; whatever would she do? Why had she been robbed of the father to her child? Why was life so cruel?

A very strong contraction brought her back to the present. Mrs Edwards examined her and confirmed that the baby's head was visible. Rose gripped Charlotte's hand tightly. Mrs Edwards kept her surprise to herself that Rose's labour was progressing more quickly than anticipated. A short while later, after Rose had summoned all her strength for a final push, a baby arrived into the world. Happily, it started to cry and Mrs Edwards placed the child in Rose's arms. It was a healthy little girl.

Rose looked beyond the child to Mrs Edwards, who met her eyes and nodded knowingly. 'You've another one in there, my dear. Come on, you can do it,' she pronounced encouragingly. 'I don't think we'll have to wait too long.'

Charlotte wrapped a sheet around the newborn child, put her in the cot, and gave Rose a sip of water. Twenty-five minutes later, a second child was presented to Rose, this time a healthy little boy. Both babies were small, but that was to be expected. Rose was exhausted. She tried to feed them, but fell asleep, so Charlotte and Mrs Edwards each cradled a newborn and fed them with watered down cows' milk, from a small spoon.

The twins were placed 'top and tail' in the cot in the new nursery, where they drifted into a contented doze. Charlotte went downstairs to find George and gave him the news. He looked sad, slumped in his armchair, but managed a smile and gave Charlotte a hug, when he heard that not one, but two healthy newborns were now in the room upstairs. It was good to hear and somehow tempered the bad news of just a few hours before.

Rose did not take easily to motherhood. Although relieved to have two strong babies, she struggled to feed them adequately and Dr Kendall was called upon.

'Assistance from a wet nurse is the only option,' he declared. 'I know of a suitable woman. Sadly, she has recently lost a baby. I am sure she can provide enough milk to make up any shortfall in that provided by mother. I'll arrange for her to call three times a day, until the children are weaned.'

The wet nurse duly called and Rose was relieved to find that she only needed to feed the children herself, if they woke during the night. Charlotte helped with napkin changing and later as the twins began to consume solids, she helped with feeding too. Charlotte took to the role of 'motherhood' with a natural ease, unlike Rose, and displayed great affection towards the two infants. It made it easier for Rose and she was very grateful.

Charlotte also accompanied Rose to the local register office in order to register the births. Rose named the babies Edith and Harold. Edith was her mother's name. Harold was simply a name that she liked. The registrar raised his eyebrows when no name was provided for the father.

Rose had wanted to register Frank as the father, but the registrar took delight in explaining that it was not allowed. She and Frank were not married; nor was he present to give his consent and in such circumstances the law precluded entering a father's name on the certificates. In the eyes of the law, the twins were illegitimate.

Rose and her babies continued to reside at Brindle Lodge. Money was a source of worry to her. She did not feel comfortable living off the generosity of Frank's parents. They continued their arrangement with Charlotte and George, but Rose wanted a long-term solution. She still had the greater part of her savings and John had assured her that when Frank's estate was settled he would pass on everything left to him in Frank's will.

Rose could not get the feeling of resentment out of her mind: resentment that Frank was dead and that she was now responsible for two hungry mouths. Since Frank had declared his love for her, it was a responsibility she had not truly envisaged she would have to face alone. Although she had worried for Frank's safety in South Africa, she mostly assumed that he would return in one piece. She was weighed down with her difficulty in taking to motherhood and the dashing of her ambitions.

When the children were nearly four months old, Queen Victoria died at Osborne House. For a few days, the island was the centre of world interest, before the Queen's body was taken ceremoniously across the Solent and on to London. Her state funeral took place in February 1901. To the nation, it seemed like the end of an era and mourning lasted three months. Rose wore black in public. Black and purple banners were hung from shop windows and business premises, as a mark of respect.

The Queen's death provided an unexpected opportunity for Rose. The Cascade View Hotel wanted to mark the Queen's passing, by festooning mourning banners from the windows on the front façade. Still grieving for Frank, Florence found the whole experience too much and asked Rose for assistance. Rose was glad to help.

Florence gave her some money to go to Marshall's, the best draper in Ventnor. There, she purchased material, before making the banners at Brindle Lodge. Charlotte kindly created a sewing room for her in the attic. She worked late into the evening, with Charlotte happy to attend to the twins. The following day, Rose oversaw the hanging of the banners on the front of The Cascade View Hotel, much to the admiration of Arthur and Florence and their guests.

Several other hotel proprietors, impressed by Rose's handiwork and anxious to show appropriate respect, contacted Florence with similar requests. She passed on their names to Rose, requesting she contact them. Before she knew it, Rose had taken half a dozen orders. This time she charged for her labour, and with Charlotte's blessing, she made all of the banners at Brindle Lodge, before fitting them as required at her clients' establishments.

The opportunity was important for Rose for a number of reasons. Primarily, it proved to her, that work of a bespoke nature might provide a means for her to earn an independent living and to pay her way in the world. If the work expanded, then perhaps it would open the door to her long held ambition of becoming the owner of a draper's shop or related business.

Her frequent trips to Marshall's, owned by the Marshall family, also brought her into contact with Charles Marshall, a most eligible man, she guessed no more than two years older than herself. Whenever she entered the shop, he dropped whatever he was doing to make himself available to assist her at the counter. He was extremely charming, and Rose knew that she had made a good impression, so good in fact, that he agreed to reduce the prices she paid for her material, the reason being of course that she was, 'in the trade'.

He proved to be a very good contact. Wealthy customers looking at materials for refurbishing their houses were sometimes at a loss to find someone with the skills and experience to make and fit new drapes and curtains. Charles started to pass on the name of Miss Ince. It was a useful arrangement for both of them. Rose obtained valuable work and Charles supplied the fabrics.

Rose made sure that she never met with clients at Brindle Lodge. She always went out to see them and this ensured that none had any idea that she was an unmarried mother.

Ten months after their birth, Edith and Harold were baptised quietly in a very private and discreet ceremony, restricted to immediate family. Rose chose to wait ten months, mainly out of respect to Florence and Arthur, who wished to observe a lengthy period of mourning after the loss of Frank. It also allowed sufficient time to elapse after the death of Queen Victoria.

John and Louisa came to the church at Ventnor, bringing little Henry with them for the first time. Fortunately, the baptism coincided with John's shore leave. Henry had been christened a fortnight earlier at Leyton, with John's shipmate and friend, George Corbett, and his wife, acting as godparents. As for godparents of the twins, John and

Louisa agreed to be godparents to Harold. George and Charlotte were thrilled and honoured to be godparents to Edith.

Henry was exactly one month older than the twins were, but when compared to them, it was obvious that he wasn't thriving. He was a sickly child. He cried often and for no apparent reason. Louisa, although proud and protective of him, looked tired and exhausted.

The baptism of Edith and Harold was overshadowed by the loss of Frank. The vicar who presided at the ceremony knew the Williams family well. When he entered the details in the church register, instead of leaving the name of the father as 'unknown', he entered 'Frank Williams, deceased'. He did this at the request of Arthur and Florence. He knew it had no legal standing, because the surname of the children was 'Ince', but he understood the significance of the request and was happy to oblige. Although it remained unspoken, everyone felt that Frank should have been there.

Further information from the War Office had not been forthcoming. A letter had been received from Frank's commanding officer. He spoke in glowing terms of Frank's bravery and conduct, throughout the time he had known him. Naturally, he expressed his deepest sympathy. He explained that Frank had been buried with full military honours in the graveyard at Bloemfontein Hospital. He said that in due course, his grave would be marked with a regimental headstone and a military memorial would include his name, along with those of his comrades, who had also made the ultimate sacrifice, in service of Queen and country.

As far as the family was concerned, there wasn't much else they could do. Charlie Mills had been in touch with them and had said he would try to organise a suitable memorial on the island, but that it may take some time to come to fruition. Some of Frank's personal effects had been returned to the family. In accordance with his will, he left everything to his brother, John. However, John, anxious to fulfil the promise he had made to Frank on the voyage to Cape Town, immediately passed the proceeds of Frank's estate to Rose by depositing the sum in her Post Office savings account.

Rose found that she had enough money to maintain herself and the children for some time. A steady supply of work was coming through via Marshall's. She finally persuaded George and Charlotte to accept a weekly payment to partially cover her keep and that of the infants. It was a gesture really, as they refused to accept more. Rose asked Florence and Arthur to cease their contributions, but they were reluctant to do so. A compromise was reached, in that they agreed to reduce the amount they passed on to Charlotte by the same amount that Rose paid towards her keep. At least Rose felt that she was moving, if rather slowly, in the right direction, towards financial independence.

John's parents continued to visit on Sundays, delighting in watching the development of their grandchildren, of Frank's children. There was no doubting whose father Edith was, whilst Harold took after Rose.

The household at Brindle Lodge settled into a routine. Charlotte began to do more and more of the 'mothering', helping Rose whenever she had the chance. Mrs Edwards too, was very fond of the children and enjoyed feeding them when time was available. Rose managed to find opportunities to write to Louisa. They kept in touch with each other as much as they could.

Louisa's letters were full of the medical problems of poor little Henry. The family doctor in Leyton was baffled and wanted to admit Henry to hospital for tests, but Louisa was reluctant to let him go. She was convinced that given time, he would eventually gain weight and strength more quickly. By contrast, Edith and Harold, although a little underweight at birth, had soon made up any noticeable deficiencies.

The end of the year came and went. Christmas passed peacefully at Brindle Lodge, but events in South Africa had taken a turn for the worse, as fighting had flared up again. For those still grieving over Frank, it was almost as though his contribution had been for nothing.

3.6

The spring of 1902 brought promise of a new summer season on the Isle of Wight and the pace of life picked up, as hoteliers and business owners prepared for the influx of seasonal visitors and day trippers.

Rose and Louisa kept up their correspondence. Sometimes Rose wrote a long letter, but if time was limited, she sent Louisa a postcard. The news on Henry was generally not good. Edith and Harold were walking by early summer of 1902, but Henry had not yet achieved that particular developmental milestone. Louisa had talked about coming over in June, but unfortunately John's schedule did not allow it. As things turned out, it was for the best. Henry became very ill with acute diarrhoea, and in June was admitted to the Hospital for Sick Children in Great Ormond Street in central London. Louisa was extremely worried and had to cope alone as John was at sea. He did not return until early July. The hospital performed a series of tests and observations. They were concerned that Henry was underweight and underdeveloped. However, they could find no particular overriding cause of his illness, and when his bowel movements regained a degree of normality, they allowed him to go home after seven days.

For a couple of months, Henry did seem to be noticeably better. He was less particular about eating and kept down more of his food than previously but Louisa fretted about him constantly. She hoped that Henry was at last starting to grow out of a difficult stage in his life. He gained a little weight and colour, but in her heart, Louisa was convinced that he had some underlying problem.

At times, Henry appeared to be in great pain. He was eating more solids, but often cried after taking food, his little face contorted. The pain only seemed to last for a few minutes and it didn't happen every time he ate. She was puzzled and watched him closely whenever she fed him. She asked a neighbour who had three children, if she had encountered similar problems with her offspring, but was told not to worry, as 'wind' was the likely cause.

Throughout July and August, if the weather was agreeable, Charlotte took the children down to the beach during the afternoons. Sometimes Rose accompanied her, but if she had work to do for a client, she remained at Brindle Lodge. Rose was guiltily aware that she was giving less and less attention to the children and more to her work. By contrast, Charlotte was becoming increasingly involved with them. She seemed especially to adore Edith, her god-daughter, but would never admit so.

This evolving arrangement however, suited Rose well. She was at last able to earn her keep, using the skills for which she had been trained. This inevitably aroused her ambitions even more. Perhaps she *could* build up her clientele to the point where she would need premises and could start to take on staff. She looked around her small attic sewing room. *Empires have been built from more humble beginnings,* she thought. Sometimes, her imagination ran wild, but often it was brought back to stark, guilty reality, when she heard Charlotte laughing with the children in the room below.

3.7

Rose's business world fell apart in early October 1902. It was the day before the twins' second birthday. She entered Marshall's in order to purchase more fabric for a commission she was engaged on. Instead of the normal enthusiastic greeting from Charles, he barely looked up, as she made her way to the counter.

She knew something was wrong, but wasn't sure what it was. She nodded politely, but he snubbed her and retired to the back of the shop. It was a most public rebuke and she couldn't imagine what had warranted such rudeness. She noted also, that the assistants seemed to regard her with a rather frosty attitude. Although they provided her with what she wanted, there was none of the usual warmth or conversation to which Rose was accustomed. She left the shop with a distinct feeling of unease.

Later in the day, a messenger arrived at Brindle Lodge with a note from one of Rose's wealthy clients. The contents were curt and to the point. The client wished to inform her, that she no longer intended to do business with her and would be obliged if she would submit her account to date, in order that it be settled and closed. The following morning, the postman brought two more letters from Rose's clients, requesting closure of their accounts. Neither correspondent gave any hint of why. It was most irregular.

Rose went to find Charlotte. She was with the children in the nursery, who were playing with their birthday presents. 'I've now had three of my best clients request that their accounts be closed. Two letters came this morning. Oh Charlotte, what's going on? What am I to do? Have you any idea why these people are withdrawing their custom?'

'I have my suspicions,' Charlotte replied. 'It might be something to do with Harvest Supper, held last Saturday.'

'Harvest Supper? What on earth is that?'

'Listen Rose, the island, for all its seaside attractions is still quite agricultural, and every year after the harvest, the local parish church here marks the occasion with a service of thanksgiving, followed in the evening by a social gathering called Harvest Supper. Although mainly attended by the farming community, it also attracts the great and the good from the rural fringes of this parish. They see it as an opportunity to mingle socially with the local landed gentry and no person of influence or standing misses the event.'

'But you didn't go, Charlotte. Surely you and George—'

Charlotte cut her off. 'George and I hate occasions like that. There is so much snobbery. Besides, George's business interests are in Cowes, so happily we don't have to subject ourselves to it,' she confessed. 'Many who attend even regard hoteliers with disdain. They are still considered as relative newcomers, you see, and are classed as "trade". It's a good job that Arthur and Florence always take their own annual holiday in Scotland at this time of year, otherwise in ignorance, they may have been tempted to go. Florence has mentioned it wistfully several times and each time I have avoided telling her the truth about the snobbery one encounters there.'

Charlotte continued. 'I mustn't shy from telling you Rose, something I learned on Monday. I met my friend Jane Morton in the town. We wanted to hear each other's news, so we decided to take tea at Mr Topping's tea shop. She told me something concerning you Rose, something that worried me, and I now fear that is behind the loss of custom you are experiencing. I didn't want to tell you, just in case it amounted to nothing, but it seems it may have been significant.'

'What do you mean, Charlotte? What was significant?'

'Apparently, Jane overheard a conversation at Harvest Supper. Mrs Hopson, Mrs Dinwoodie and the colonel's wife, Mrs Cole, all wealthy customers of Marshall's, were discussing you and how pleased they were with the work you have done for them.'

'Oh, that's good, that can't have done me any harm.'

'Well, no, but the problem is that Mrs Roberts, the wife of the parish clerk was listening to their conversation. She's always yearned to be accepted in their circle. Frankly, she hasn't the means nor the house to make use of your talents Rose, but not to be outdone she decided to drop a bombshell.'

'A bombshell?'

'Yes. Jane said she overhead Mrs Roberts ask the other ladies if they knew that you were the unmarried mother of twins, a boy and a girl, and that they were baptised quietly last year at the parish church.'

Rose gasped and brought her hand to her mouth. 'What did they say?'

'Well, nothing for several seconds. Mrs Hopkins apparently went white. Mrs Cole and Mrs Dinwoodie had expressions somewhere between incredulity and horror. Then Mrs Cole asked her to confirm that she really meant Miss Ince, the young lady recommended to them by Mr Marshall. Jane said it was quite amusing to watch, but when she told me, I was worried for you Rose, truly.'

'And did they say anything else?' asked Rose, trembling.

'Yes. I'm afraid the general consensus was that they wished to have no further dealings with you. Oh, I am so sorry Rose. If it weren't so serious, it would almost be comical. According to Jane, one of them was particularly shocked, because when you went to her home in order to measure up, she introduced you to her unmarried son!'

Rose groaned. 'That would be Mrs Cole. What am I going to do, Charlotte? I've always feared the reaction of some of these people, if word of my true situation became known, but I didn't appreciate just how bigoted they are; all because of the silly wife of the parish clerk.'

'Quite so,' said Charlotte. 'By all accounts, Mrs Roberts looked a little guilty after her revelation. She may have overstepped the mark, but the parish register is a document of public record, so it's unlikely she's broken any confidence.'

'They're such snobs,' said Rose, 'but I've lost my three best clients. What am I going to do now? The others are hardly worth working for. I need to pay my way, but how can I with no clients?'

'Don't worry, Rose, something will turn up. It always does. I'll speak to George. He might have some ideas.'

Rose got into bed that night feeling sick and rejected. Why had her life gone so wrong? Why had she been so foolish and reckless with Frank? The business she was now losing had been her salvation. It had satisfied her ambition, enabled her to earn some money, and importantly provided an excuse for her to concentrate on something other than the children. It had been perfect and whilst she was working hard for herself and the twins, allowing Charlotte to take on much of the care and devotion required for the children was acceptable. With the clients gone, she had a double dilemma: no income and no justifiable excuse to do anything other than concentrate on the children. She knew now that she wasn't suited to being a mother. All she could do, as she tried to get to sleep, was console herself with the fervent hope that Charlotte would be right and that something would turn up.

The following morning, a telegram boy parked his bicycle outside Brindle Lodge, before pressing the polished brass button in the porch.

The bell rang and Mrs Edwards went to the door. She returned a minute later with a brown envelope in her hand. She took it upstairs and went to find Rose, for it was addressed to her.

Without tearing the contents, Rose opened the telegram envelope as quickly as she could. Telegrams often contained bad news. *Please, please, please,* she thought, *let it be good news for a change.* Although at that particular moment, she couldn't imagine anything in her life, which might be the subject of good news.

The news was bad – very bad indeed.

Post Mark: Leyton 9 Oct 02
TO: Miss Rosetta Ince. 'Brindle Lodge', Beaufort Street, Ventnor, Isle of Wight.
Henry passed away yesterday. Please return Leyton urgently if possible. Louisa.

Rose managed to catch the four o'clock express from Southampton's ocean terminal, bound for Waterloo. The ferry was running late and it was a rush, but she just made it. Two years had passed since she had last crossed the Solent and on that occasion, in the company of John. She recalled that she was heavily pregnant, with one child as she thought, on her way over to Brindle Lodge for the first time. She remembered how worried and apprehensive she was. On this crossing, her mind was no less preoccupied by what lay ahead of her.

The telegram from Louisa had been delivered earlier that morning, short in words, but long in meaning and consequence. Rose sensed the sad and desperate plea for help contained within its cold, stark message. She opened her handbag and took out the telegram. It was the first one she had ever received and she read it once more. What could have happened to little Henry? In Louisa's last letter he seemed to be improving, eating a little more, and continuing to put on weight. Had he met with an accident or was his death connected with his earlier stay in hospital? She decided speculation was pointless. She was dreading her reunion with Louisa. She knew the first moments would be difficult for both of them, but Rose was resolved to do her best in supporting and helping her friend in her time of need.

Rose was travelling with little luggage. She had hurriedly packed a carpetbag with some essential clothes and something suitable for a funeral. She knew she might need to be away some time. In her handbag, she carried her Post Office Savings Book. She had about eighty pounds, a sizeable sum, so should she need it she would have access to money while she was away.

Charlotte had been so helpful and understanding and of course told her not to worry about the children. She would look after them until Rose returned.

'You go to Louisa. She needs you. Tell her that she and John are in our thoughts. Let us know what has happened and what the arrangements are to be, as soon as you can', were Charlotte's parting words.

Where is John? thought Rose. *He must be still at sea. When is he due back?* She recalled the contents of Louisa's most recent letter and reckoned that he ought to be returning in about three days' time. What a shock for him, poor John. What a shock too for Arthur and Florence when they find out. Louisa must have their holiday address in Scotland. *She'll have sent them a telegram as well*, Rose reasoned.

Although full of concern for Louisa and John, Rose was at times distracted. She kept thinking of the last few minutes before leaving Brindle Lodge. She'd gone into the nursery and kissed the children goodbye. She'd told them to be good for Charlotte, but noted that they didn't seem especially bothered that she was leaving. In fact, they'd hardly glanced up from their play when she went in to see them. They obviously felt secure and happy at Brindle Lodge, with Charlotte and George.

She was reluctant to admit it to herself, because it didn't seem appropriate, but Rose felt some relief to be away from Ventnor and on her way back to London. She realised that she was on her own for the first time in two years. She wasn't sure whether it was the break from the children, or nostalgia for her old haunts, that was responsible for the slight feeling of release.

The express sped past Winchester and on towards Basingstoke. Rose wanted to doze a little. She tried to avoid thinking about how

Louisa would cope and found herself drifting back again to the relative ease with which she had said goodbye to the twins. Was she callous and hard? Shouldn't she be finding the separation more difficult to bear? Guilt and unease caused her to fidget and take in a few sharp breaths. She needed to calm herself.

For distraction, she turned to look out of the window and studied the scenery, as it sped past in the late afternoon sunshine. The Hampshire countryside was beautiful. It was autumn and she noticed the striking and contrasting colours of the leaves on the trees, waiting for the first gales of winter to send them whirling and twirling over the landscape. The train had settled into a rhythm and the fields, the hedges, the woods, the chalk downs, and the sides of the cuttings, pockmarked with freshly excavated rabbit holes, formed the backdrop to her thoughts.

Then into Surrey and after Weybridge, the countryside started to change, with the first indications that they were on the outskirts of the capital. Buildings, a few at first, then more and more concentrated, until they formed a continuous corridor on each side of the track, channelling and drawing the express towards its destination. By then, it was getting dark and the gas lamps illuminated the interior of the carriage. The train had reduced speed, passing through stations at Kingston and Wimbledon, crossing points, changing tracks, all the while getting nearer and nearer, until exactly on time, and with a exhalation of steam, it finally came to rest at platform one, Waterloo Station.

The reunion with Louisa that evening was as upsetting as Rose had imagined. Poor Louisa was distraught. John was still away. Her father was there, but his manner betrayed his unease and the problems he had been having in trying to support his daughter, through such a difficult time. He was clearly relieved at Rose's arrival and hoped that she would be able to comfort Louisa, in a manner in which he had so far failed.

He made his excuses and left shortly after, promising to handle the more practical matters of registering Henry's death and making enquiries about funeral arrangements. He said he would inform the shipping office of Henry's passing and ask them to forewarn John, as soon as his ship berthed. As Rose had calculated, John was due back on Sunday morning in three days' time, but until his return, Rose was being very much relied upon to look after Louisa.

Tearfully, Louisa tried to explain the chain of events leading to Henry's death, caused by 'intussusception'.

'What exactly is intussusception?' asked Rose. 'I've never heard of it.'

'Neither had I,' explained Louisa, still sobbing. 'Apparently it's a condition whereby the walls of the bowel fold in on themselves and cause a blockage. It's very painful. I knew he was suffering. I think he'd had touches of it before, because at times he used to draw up his legs and grimace with pain, poor little dear. He must have been so uncomfortable. I should have made more of a fuss. I feel it's my fault. Oh, I've let him down, and what will John say?'

Louisa was racked with emotion and sobbed out loud. Rose put her arm around her friend to comfort her. 'Come now, Louisa, you can't blame yourself. He was in the Children's Hospital in July and thoroughly examined then. The doctors only allowed him to go home when they were satisfied that he was fine.'

'I know, but perhaps I should have noticed the symptoms earlier.'

'What *did* you notice?'

'Well, Doctor Hawley gave me some medicine for him and the diarrhoea did seem to stop, but when I changed him yesterday morning, I noticed blood in his napkin. I thought I could feel a lump in his abdomen too. I took him back to Dr Hawley immediately and he said that he might have intussusception. He wrote a note for the admissions doctor and told me to take Henry to the Children's Hospital again without delay. I keep thinking that I should have noticed something before. Oh Rose, he was so weak and he was starting a fever. As soon as the doctor at the hospital examined him, I knew from his worried expression that it was serious. They tried everything they could to save him. He only lasted a few hours before

138

he slipped away. I was there with him. I felt helpless. Oh, it was so dreadful Rose.'

'Listen Louisa, from what you've said, it doesn't sound as though you could have done any more. It seems to me, that you acted correctly and in no way can any blame be attached to you. What causes it? Did you ask?'

'Yes, of course, but it's not fully understood. It's more common with boys and most cases affect children up to about eighteen months, but they can suffer from it later, like Henry. They said it could follow a case of severe diarrhoea. What's John going to say? Oh, I wish he was here ...' Louisa choked on her words as she broke down once more.

'What about Arthur and Florence? Do they know?'

'Yes, I asked father to send them a telegram. They always stay with their friends in Dundee at this time of year, the Robinsons, who are hoteliers as well. John's been several times and luckily, the hotel's address was in his drawer. I expect they'll be here tomorrow or maybe on Saturday.'

Rose thought to herself that if John's parents were here when he comes back, it might help.

She lay awake that first night at Apsley Street. All of her problems stemmed from a few of hours of illicit romantic madness, and in this very bed. *Oh, I was such a fool. Was it just the sherry? No, of course not.* Rose recognised that she was infatuated at the time and would have settled down with Frank, but that was not what fate had determined. Now, she had the cold reality of unsupported motherhood and the thwarting of her ambitions to deal with. She churned with guilt again. She should feel like Louisa about children, but the stark fact was that she didn't. *Oh God*, she thought. *Am I selfish? What is it about me? Why am I such an ungrateful mother? What am I going to do?* She cried herself to sleep.

Rose spent the following day looking after Louisa and ensuring that the house was tidy and ready to receive guests. Louisa's father had offered to accommodate Arthur and Florence when they arrived, so Rose was able to remain in Frank's old room. She unpacked her

139

belongings, few as they were, and put them into the wardrobe. With the date of the funeral yet to be arranged, she could see herself being there for some time. She placed the telegram from Louisa in its envelope on the mantelpiece above the bedroom fireplace. She didn't really know what to do with it. It wouldn't be right to throw it away, she thought, and frankly, she didn't want to keep it, as a harbinger of bad news. She decided to leave it where it was and John or Louisa could do with it as they pleased when she returned to Ventnor.

Thomas Crockford arrived at the house after lunch. He explained that he had registered Henry's death that morning and if Louisa wished, he would keep the certificate until John returned. He said that the hospital had consented to retain Henry's body, pending the funeral arrangements. They both agreed that they should not make any funeral plans in John's absence.

As predicted, Arthur and Florence arrived that evening. Although visibly shaken and upset by the event, they were of some comfort to Louisa. It seemed as if the experience of Frank's loss had made grief easier for them to bear. Rose, meanwhile, remained indispensable, making tea and generally helping in the background.

Early on Sunday morning, the RMS *Kidwelly Castle* entered the Thames estuary. John Williams was looking forward to being home with Louisa and Henry for Sunday lunch. When the ship docked at its berth, one of the company's senior officers went aboard and sought out John to impart the tragic news. He was released from duty immediately, so that he could return home with all haste to comfort his grieving wife. His homecoming on this occasion was particularly sad. It was not at all as he had anticipated when his ship had entered the Thames reaches just a few hours before.

3.8

The small funeral procession came slowly up the hill to the church, where it drew up at the lych-gate. The hearse, and subsequent carriages, were each drawn by an immaculate pair of black horses; their bridles decorated with matching black plumes.

Reverend Walter was waiting within the shelter of the lych-gate to greet the mourners and pass on his condolences. Then he led the small procession, consisting of the head undertaker, the bearers with the coffin, Henry's parents, grandparents, godparents, and the remaining mourners, solemnly towards the church. John and Louisa passed the ancient yew tree once more, this time grieving for their son. How stark the contrast in their spirits, when as a newly married couple, they had last passed before its ancient trunk.

The procession entered the church and everyone took their places. Charlotte and George were absent. Louisa had excused them, because of George's business commitments and Charlotte was needed in Ventnor to look after Rose's children. The church was barely half-full, even with the added number of elderly parishioners, who always made it their business to attend whenever a funeral took place.

Rose made sure that she sat well away from Mrs Robins, who was representing the staff of Crockford's. She couldn't bear the thought of a conversation with her. Fortunately, she had not had to endure her company in the carriage, for Mrs Robins had ridden with Thomas Crockford and Henry's godparents.

Rose found it hard to concentrate. As she tried to listen to the vicar's words, her attention wandered. Although full of sympathy and compassion for John and Louisa at their loss, she couldn't help remembering the last time, when she'd sat within the church. Frank had been there then and momentarily she recalled the excitement she'd felt at the end of the service, when, with the organ playing, he had led her by the arm behind John and Louisa.

Things had gone wrong for her; the unwanted pregnancy, the worry, then the reassurance that he would stand by her and then the

141

shock and abandonment, when she learned of his death. Now her fledgling business on the Isle of Wight had fallen apart too, victim to prejudice and moral judgement. How could she ever achieve her ambitions? She was in an impossible situation. She needed to work to support her children, but society wouldn't let her work, because she had the children.

She returned to the present, as the bearers picked up the little coffin and everyone filed behind Henry's parents to the family plot in the graveyard, beneath the tall oaks. Rose stood back and watched. The grave was marked by floral tributes. Henry was lowered to join his grandmother and infant uncle, the brother of Louisa, who had died shortly after birth. Reverend Walter invited the mourners to scatter some soil on the lid of the coffin. After exchanging graveside commiserations, they all left the scene and departed for the home of Thomas Crockford, for the wake.

In the elegant dining room of Mr Crockford's private residence, Rose maintained her distance from Mrs Robins, sipping tea and making polite conversation with George Corbett. She kept an eye on Mrs Robins though, and watched as she cornered Arthur and Florence on the other side of the room. Rose could see that they were in deep conversation. She saw Mrs Robins' jaw drop and immediately glance in Rose's direction. *There we are, my secret's out*, thought Rose. Not only had Mrs Robins confirmed that Rose had a child, but now she'd know that she was the unmarried mother of not one child, but of twins. Now she'd have gleaned that Rose lived on the Isle of Wight and the news hadn't been imparted in confidence. Mrs Robins would be free to inform all and that little piece of gossip would be all over the shop as soon as she returned. Rose's situation was a secret no longer.

3.9

Engine driver, Albert Wallis, reported for duty at the Nine Elms depot at seven o'clock in the morning. He'd worked for the London and South West Railway for twenty years, starting at the age of eighteen. He was appointed fireman, aged twenty-four, and became a driver eight years later. More recently, he had been promoted to express driver status, which made him one of the elite who drove the express trains on the company's network.

Albert was assigned to the principal route between London Waterloo and Southampton. For many of his passengers, this was the fastest and most direct way to the ocean liner terminal at Southampton. He knew the route well and understood the importance the company placed on keeping strictly to journey times, which were measured by the half-minute. Habitual lateness was penalised, unless with good reason, and arriving before the scheduled time was equally frowned upon.

He reported to the traffic office to receive his instructions for the day. As expected, he was to drive the second express, the eleven o'clock from Waterloo to Southampton, before turning round to drive the return service at four o'clock in the afternoon. The company ran two express trains each morning, the first at nine-thirty. Each train comprised three coaches for second-class passengers, one coach for first-class passengers and a combined kitchen and brake van at the rear.

Albert joined his fireman, Edwin Groombridge, in the engine shed. Today was notable, in that they had been assigned a recently built locomotive. Designed and constructed at Nine Elms, she was only six months old and it would be the first time he had driven her. She was the same in layout and controls, but had slightly more power and stood nine inches taller than the older locomotive he usually drove. He was looking forward to the trip. Being trusted with the new locomotive would enhance his prestige in the engine shed.

They set about preparing her for the day's work. Edwin cleared ash and cinders from the firebox, before lighting and stoking the fire. As the fire gained in heat and intensity, the water in the boiler turned to steam, building to an operating pressure of 175 pounds per square inch. Albert attended to the essential oiling and greasing of the massive locomotive and coal tender. She could pull the train weighing over 120 tons, at a speed of up to sixty-five miles per hour.

Once she had sufficient pressure, they moved her to the fuelling point, to have five tons of coal dropped into her tender, before moving on to the water tower. There, she was filled with 3,500 imperial gallons of water, sufficient to cover the eighty-five miles downward to Southampton.

Albert and Edwin discussed the merits of the new engine, as they shunted her from the depot to the platform at Waterloo. He reversed carefully, until she gently touched the buffers of the leading carriage, one of the three second-class carriages, normally attached nearer to the engine. Edwin jumped down from the footplate and coupled the locomotive to the carriage.

By then, the time had crept round to a quarter to eleven. The guard came forward from the kitchen and brake van at the rear of the train. He stood on the platform, below Albert's left-hand side and they exchanged pleasantries, while one or two early passengers arrived to take their seats.

3.10

Rose paid the cab driver and carrying her small carpetbag and handbag, walked into the station entrance at Leyton, making her way towards the booking office. It was Friday, 17 October 1902, and she was starting her return journey to Ventnor. She bought a second-class ticket to Liverpool Street station. As she moved away from the booth, she placed the ticket safely in her handbag and looking up she stopped dead for a moment. She was startled and unsure what to do.

Ten feet in front of her stood Sidney, the draper's porter from Crockford's, his arms folded, looking at her with an expression of utter contempt.

'Well, well, well,' he said, 'if it ain't Scarlet Rose!'

'What do you mean?' snapped Rose as she approached him, trying to move further away from the queue.

'Don't come all high 'n mighty with me Miss Rose. We know all about you, "woman of ill repute", that's how we refers to you in the shop. "Scarlet Rose, the woman of ill repute" … and to think I used to believe you was so lovely and innocent.'

Rose started to flush and look embarrassed. Several people in the queue had overheard and were now waiting to see her reaction. 'You don't understand Sidney; you've no idea of these things.'

'Is that so?' he sneered. 'Tell you what I understand. You got yourself in the family way, didn't you, *Miss* Ince? That's what you did. Reckon you weren't so innocent after all. A soldier boy too, I 'eard: brother of John Williams. You should 'ave known better, you know. Thought yourself too grand for me, I s'pose. Told everyone you 'ad some posh job up West, but you had to leave in a bit of an 'urry now, didn't you?'

It occurred to Rose that Sidney felt scorned and rejected. He really had been carrying a torch for her. He must have been hurt when Mrs Robins spread the gossip about her.

'I didn't mean to upset *you*, Sidney. I'm sorry if you have that opinion of me.'

'Well, I certainly don't feel sorry for you, that's for sure,' he replied. 'Reckon you got what you deserved. No man, and now stuck with two nippers as well I 'ear, tuppence worth for the price of a penny!'

Sidney's last remark was too much for Rose. Out of rage, guilt, shame, and frustration, she slapped Sidney smartly on the cheek. With that, she turned and ran, as quickly as she could, along the London-bound platform, away from her confrontation with someone whom she had once regarded as a friend.

It was all too much. The tears streamed down her cheeks. She felt trapped. Her life was a mess; she needed to make a new start, but how? That was the problem.

She continued down the platform, away from Sidney, and waited for her train. She looked back up the line and saw her train in the distance. She stared down at the rails and then looked again at the approaching train. *I could end it now*, she thought. *It would all be over. It would be so easy, the torment would finish; no need to think about the future. The twins would be better off without me.*

She took a few deep breaths and pulled herself together. *Come now, Rose. Are you going to let some lovesick lad get at you like this? No, of course not. Now calm down.*

The train halted in front of her. Rose looked back in the direction of the ticket office and saw that Sidney was still there, watching her disdainfully. She opened the carriage door and stepped on to the train, out of his vision, and tried to put his words out of her mind.

Disembarking at Liverpool Street, Rose made her way on foot to the City underground station, where she purchased a ticket. She realised she must have looked distressed, because the concerned ticket clerk enquired after her well-being. She didn't answer and snatching the ticket, hurried away. The underground train took her directly to Waterloo. During the short journey under the River Thames, an older woman seated opposite stared at her before asking if she was going far. Rose muttered, 'Ventnor' and then moved to another seat, in order to avoid further conversation.

When she arrived at Waterloo train station, she had around twenty minutes to wait for her connection to Southampton. She recovered her composure and found the Waiting Room to be empty. She took a seat. Two ladies entered shortly after, taking in the fact that there were no men present.

'Damnation!' one of them exclaimed. 'Those infernal Hackney carriages or whatever they're called … why did my dress have to be caught in the door? That darn gust of wind, I guess. Oh, these so-called showers, it's been raining all morning! Martha, just look at my hem. It'll drag on everything now. Do you think we can get someone to repair it?'

Rose noticed that the lady had an American accent, but she looked as if she could have been Italian.

'Well I can't, Graziella dear,' the other replied. 'I don't have any thread, and anyway I just can't sew, simple as that.'

Rose noticed that her companion was American too. She took in the situation. She really wanted to be ignored and she didn't know why she asked, but she did. 'Can I help? I can stitch it for you, if you like. Let me see what I can do.'

Graziella sat down beside Rose, who quickly appraised the damage to the dress. She knew she could easily make a temporary repair. She opened her handbag and took out a fine needle and a small wooden bobbin of black thread, kept for emergencies. She expertly threaded the needle, knelt down, and started to stitch the ripped hem back into place.

'My dear, this is so kind of you. I can see by the way that you handle a needle, that you are fully accustomed to using one and very skilful with it too,' Graziella commented.

Rose thought she was probably in her fifties. She looked very smart and was expensively dressed. Her companion, Martha, was similarly attired.

'Yes,' said Rose. 'I'm a draper by trade. I served my apprenticeship as a seamstress. I used to make bespoke dresses for a living.' She barely looked up as she concentrated on her work.

'Is that a fact,' said Graziella, as more of a statement than a question.

'You sound as though you're American,' said Rose. 'Are you here on holiday?'

'Yes we are, but not for much longer. I'm with my husband. We're part of a group that came over together. We're all leaving London to go back to New York today. That's partly why I was annoyed. Our train leaves in fifteen minutes,' she said, looking at her watch. 'It's the express train to Southampton. We missed the earlier one – the one we should have caught – and we might even miss our boat if this train is delayed in the slightest.'

'Oh dear,' said Rose. 'I'll be as quick as I can. I'm catching the same train actually. I've a boat to catch too, but mine only goes as far as the Isle of Wight.'

'The Isle of where?'

'Wight. It's just across the Solent from Southampton. You'll pass it as your ship makes its way towards the English Channel. How are we doing for time?' asked Rose as she continued to concentrate on the repair.

'Fine, my dear. I can see you'll be finished pretty soon. Jim – he's my husband – and the other guys are hopefully talking to the driver as we speak. They headed off towards the engine, while we came in here. Jim can be very persuasive you know, especially if he waves a few bucks around while he's asking. He reckoned he could persuade the driver to make as much speed as possible, so that we catch the boat on time. Say, why don't you join us for the journey?'

'Aren't you in First Class?'

'Well, sure, but we could always squeeze in another.'

'No, I don't think that would be appropriate, but thank you anyway,' said Rose.

It took Rose no more than a couple of minutes to finish the hem. She cut the thread between her teeth and put the needle and remaining thread back into her bag. 'There we are, that should do,' she said. 'I don't think you'll have any further problems. I've even managed to conceal the small tear.'

'My, that's wonderful,' said Graziella, patting her dress admiringly and getting to her feet. 'Just wonderful. Thank you so much.' As she spoke, she opened her purse and brought out a gold half-sovereign. She offered it to Rose.

Rose refused her offer firmly. 'No, really, it was nothing. I'm glad to have been of assistance.'

Graziella looked slightly taken aback. 'But I feel I must offer you something for your trouble. You could buy yourself a first-class ticket.'

'No, absolutely not. I really don't want to take anything … really.'

'Have you ever been Stateside?' asked Graziella.

'No, I haven't,' said Rose.

'Well, look, here's my card. My husband runs our family clothing business in New York. If you ever find yourself over there and need some work, you be sure to look us up.'

Rose took the card, noting that the lady's name was Graziella Stefano-Silverman, and slipped it into her handbag.

The two American ladies left and Rose turned to the mirror above the waiting room fireplace to straighten her hair and hat. The small favour she had just performed had distracted her and lifted her mood a little. It was nice to do something for a stranger, but as she looked at her reflection in the mirror, her conscience brought her back to the present. *How could you not be looking forward to seeing your children? There's poor Louisa, absolutely heartbroken at losing Henry, and you, with two healthy children, regarding them as a hindrance, preventing you from pursuing your career. You should be ashamed of yourself!*

Rose started to feel sick again. A flood of guilt and confusion washed over her. She knew the train was almost ready to depart. She picked up her carpetbag and handbag and walked out on to the platform. A second-class carriage was directly in front of her. She glanced to her right, to the American party further down the platform, towards the rear of the train.

Why was her life in such a mess? Why did Frank have to get killed? Why had she ended up with two young children, with neither work nor income to support them? What was she to do?

She watched the wealthy Americans as they boarded their first-class carriage. Why couldn't she afford to travel first-class? One day she would, she promised herself. She gritted her teeth and took a deep breath. Yes, one day she would.

3.11

Albert Wallis glanced back down the length of the train as the guard walked away, and observed a group of four wealthy-looking men advancing along the platform towards him. One in particular appeared to be in command, and when the group came alongside the footplate, it was he who spoke, asking if he could climb up into the cab. Albert recognised his American accent. He thought it was an unusual request but nodded his assent. Once up on the footplate, the American introduced himself.

'Hello, driver, my name is James Silverman. This sure is an impressive engine you have here. Tell me, what speed can she do?'

'We'll probably touch sixty-five on the run today, sir. She could go faster, but we have to stick to the timetable you know.'

'Yes, I know there's a timetable, but we've got one too,' he said pointing back to his friends gathered on the platform below. 'We've missed the earlier nine-thirty express due to a mix-up by our cabbie over which station we were going to. It's confusing, you know, having more than one station here in London named Waterloo.'

'Yes, sir, I agree it is … bit of a music hall joke that one.'

'Sure, well, the thing is, we might miss our boat today if we don't get a move on and get down to Southampton as soon as possible … if you get my drift.'

'I have to stick to the timetable, sir. It's against company regulations to arrive before time.'

'Sure, but what if I made it worth your while? We think you only need to get us there a couple of minutes before schedule. We should just make it if you can. If we miss our boat, then we could be stuck in England for several more days …'

Albert turned to the fireman. 'Edwin, jump down and check the couplings will you? All the way back to the brake van, and don't forget to look for any broken axles on the coaching stock.'

Edwin left the cab as instructed. Meanwhile, the American gentleman put his hand in his pocket and brought out a cylindrical silver case, from which he extracted two gleaming gold sovereigns. 'Is this worth a couple of minutes?' he asked.

'I'm sure it might make a difference,' replied Albert as he pocketed the money. 'Rest assured, I'll get you down to Southampton ahead of schedule.'

'Excellent driver, excellent … let's see what she can do, eh?'

'I'll do my best, sir.'

With that, the smiling gentleman carefully climbed down to the platform to receive congratulations and a series of hearty slaps on the back at the success of his mission. They turned, laughing and talking with excitement as they walked away towards the first-class carriage at the far end of the train. Albert watched them join a group of well-dressed ladies, who were waiting expectantly for news of whether the attempt to persuade the driver to make haste had been a success.

At eleven o'clock precisely, with the last of the carriage doors shut, the guard blew his whistle and waved aloft his green flag. This was his signal to Albert Wallis, driver of the Waterloo to Southampton express, that all was in order and that the train was secured for the journey.

On the footplate, Albert opened the regulator, allowing the steam to enter the cylinders, forcing back the pistons and providing power to the four driving wheels. The huge engine weighing over eighty tons began to move, slowly at first, but with gathering momentum.

The train rattled and swayed slightly as it passed over a complicated series of points located just outside of the station, crossing connections to sidings and other platforms, before being channelled through to the Southampton track, which consisted of two lines. Before long, they passed a train coming towards them on the up line, the London-bound line. Although the express was not yet up to full speed, the combined closing speed of the two trains was still in the order of nearly ninety miles per hour. The drivers blew their whistles as they passed each other, a polite acknowledgement of their camaraderie and acquaintance.

151

The earlier rain that morning had disappeared and as the train gathered more speed, heading south-west, a little blue sky was showing in the distance. There was only one scheduled stop on the journey, at Basingstoke, approximately fifty miles away. Edwin shovelled coal continually into the firebox, maintaining the heat and the steam pressure, as the locomotive settled into its rhythm.

Timings were very important. The guard in the brake van noted the timings throughout the journey. In addition, each signal box they reached logged their passing. At the stations they went through, Albert knew that the station inspector, the parcel porters and the yard foreman would all be glancing at their watches, checking the time. Time was all-important on the railway. It governed everything and woe betides anyone who ignored its all-encompassing influence.

Albert patted his inside pocket and felt the outline of the gold coins secreted safely out of harm's way. He had caught on quickly to what the American wanted and that some kind of gratuity was likely to be offered. He had been right to send Edwin back to check the couplings. No witnesses to his little deal, that's how he liked it. Obviously, accepting a bribe, or gratuity, as he preferred to think of it, was completely against regulations, but who would know? What pleased him even more was that he was confident that he could arrive two minutes ahead of schedule and get away with it. He hadn't been called before the traffic superintendent for more than two years. His record on time keeping was good. He had the perfect excuse. If he found himself facing questions, he would blame his early arrival on his inexperience with the new engine. After all, the engine had no indicator of speed. Judging speed was subjective. They were guided by the need to match the timings at particular points on the journey, but it was not easy to be precise to the half-minute. On any given trip, they could lose time, which meant later on, they needed to make up time. There were ways and means, and the company largely left the means to the competence of their drivers, stipulating of course, that safety remained of paramount importance.

Passing the signal box one mile east of Basingstoke, Albert closed the regulator and the train started to slow down. Shortly after, they drew alongside the platform at Basingstoke station, where a handful of passengers was waiting to embark.

'Not many passengers today, Edwin,' commented Albert. 'Most of them must have caught the earlier express. Still, I'm sure we'll be full on the return this afternoon.'

They were one minute ahead of schedule; just right, Albert figured, to show that his inexperience in judging the speed of the new engine was apparent throughout the whole journey. As they waited at the platform, the stationmaster walked briskly towards Albert. He climbed up onto the footplate.

'Just had a message from Micheldever. Some sheep have strayed onto the embankment. They've found the farmer to round them up, but be prepared to slow down if required.'

'Right-oh,' replied Albert. *Damn!* he thought. *Let's just hope we don't get delayed.*

The guard on the platform blew his whistle and waved the green flag. Albert released the brake and let out the regulator once more. The locomotive crept forward and started to pick up speed. The weather was definitely clearing from the west, with the promise of a sunny afternoon.

They had covered eight miles, gained more time, and almost reached Micheldever when they spotted the distant-signal in the 'Stop' position. As they passed it, Albert shut down the steam and applied the brakes – not too forcibly, for this was not an emergency – just enough to slow the train, if they needed to halt at the next signal. Albert looked ahead and was disappointed to see that it too was in the 'Stop' position. He brought the locomotive to a halt just before it. They waited no more than one minute, but it seemed an eternity. Albert looked back along the train and could see several heads from the first-class carriage sticking out, looking anxiously forward in his direction, trying to determine the reason for the delay.

Suddenly, the signal's semaphore indicator clanked downward into the 'Go' position. Within seconds, they were moving forward and gathering pace once more. Albert considered his options, and where he might make up some time. He decided his best chance would be at

Dunley Bottom. This was situated at the foot of a long, shallow decline of a mile in length. Dunley Bottom itself consisted of a sharper than usual left-hand curve, before the line straightened into a steep half-mile incline out of the 'bottom'. There was a speed restriction of thirty miles per hour through the curve. All the drivers were aware of this, as they were periodically reminded in notices, which they had to read and sign.

Past experience told Albert that he could negotiate the curve at almost forty miles per hour, without a problem. The speed limit was far too low. If he could go through Dunley Bottom at forty-five miles per hour, it would give him greater speed to tackle the incline on the other side. If he judged the deceleration and the acceleration correctly, he was sure he could make up at least a minute. One mile out, they crested the ridge. He cut back the power and they started down the shallow gradient towards the curve at the bottom. Half a mile further on, he applied some gentle braking, aiming to take off about fifteen to twenty miles per hour from their speed.

Looking ahead, Albert could clearly see the left-hand curve at Dunley Bottom. He also noticed steam rising from the cutting leading down towards it, on the other side. This indicated the approach of a train on the up line. At the bottom of the gradient, just before the curve, Albert released the brakes and opened the regulator to full power. The couplings took up the slack, as the locomotive's influence changed from braking to pulling the train once more. Halfway through the curve, the smoothness of the track was interrupted by two sets of points, where sidings led to a chalk quarry. The two trains converged and the engines passed each other. They whistled a greeting. The other train was a goods train, consisting of flat-bed wagons loaded with wooden barrels. Albert could see it stretching back two hundred yards through the bend ahead of him.

As Albert's speeding engine crossed the first set of points, the jolt unbalanced it and it started to lean to the right, tilting awkwardly towards the goods train. For a second, Albert's engine hung in equilibrium, then its continued acceleration pushed it beyond salvation and it heeled over against the wagons travelling in the opposite direction. There was a sickening tearing sound, as metal tore through metal. The Southampton-bound locomotive, with Albert and Edwin at the controls, left the rails completely and instead of turning with the curve, continued straight ahead, cutting the goods train in two and partly compressing both itself and several wagons in a head-on collision.

Albert and Edwin were killed instantly. The leading second-class carriage, coach number one, concertinaed itself against the engine's coal tender. The next coach broke its couplings and slewed sideways onto the up line. The passenger body, unlike the steel chassis, was made of wood. The sides splintered and the glass in the windows shattered. As it came to rest, several barrels from the goods train that had been catapulted into the air by the force of the impact, rained down upon coach number two. The barrels contained paraffin oil, destined for the lights and fires of London. They split on landing and paraffin liquid was splashed extensively over the interior of the carriage. The unfortunate passengers inside had no chance. Those not killed by the force of the collision were enveloped in a fireball of burning vapour as a spark, possibly from the gas lighting, ignited the paraffin.

Passengers in coach number three suffered the least injury, because it slid sideways past the stricken coach number two. However, those in the fourth and final coach, the first-class carriage, were less fortunate. Coach number four came off the track and slid down the embankment, before being struck from above by the kitchen and brake van, which weighed twenty-three tons. Unfortunately, it ripped into the roof of the first-class coach causing many fatalities.

The driver of the goods train had noticed the excessive speed of the express. He looked anxiously back down the curve, after Albert had passed him. He saw the funnel of the express rise in the air as it made impact with the last few wagons of his own train. He felt the jolt and his coupling to the leading wagon break, releasing his engine from its load. He then had the dilemma of whether to stop and offer assistance, or whether to take advantage of the loss of his wagons and the opportunity to go at full speed to the next signal box, in order to raise the alarm. He chose the latter option. It was the right decision, but as he looked back, he and his fireman were horrified to see flames and a pall of black smoke rising from the collision.

'God knows whether Walter has survived back in the guard's van!' he exclaimed. 'I just hope that he has!'

Two weeks later, Colonel Fothergill, of the Board of Trade, Railway Department, published his findings into the circumstances surrounding the disastrous accident to a passenger train, which occurred about 12.13 pm on 17 October 1902, at Dunley Bottom, on the London and South West Railway. Extracts from his report read as follows:

In this case, the second daily express from London Waterloo to Southampton was travelling through Dunley Bottom on the down line, when the engine and coaches left the rails and came into violent contact with a goods train, which was moving in the opposite direction on the up line, causing the death of 14 persons.

The express carried 38 passengers. Additionally, there were on the train, a driver, a fireman, a guard, a ticket collector and a waiter. Of the passengers, 10 were killed or died as a consequence of their injuries and 5 were seriously maimed or hurt. The engine driver, fireman and guard were killed. The ticket collector and waiter were injured. To this long list of fatalities has to be added the guard of the goods train.

The locomotive was badly impacted and destroyed. The leading coach, number one, was severely compressed. Coach number two was damaged by collision and subsequent fire.

Coach number three came to rest on its side with the least damage. Coach number four, the carriage reserved for first class passengers was derailed and struck by the kitchen and brake van.

156

The majority of the victims were in the first-class coach, number four.

The cause of the accident was excessive speed on the part of the express driver. Contrary to instructions, he attempted to pass through Dunley Bottom at a speed in excess of the restriction, set at 30 miles per hour. It is not clear why the driver committed such a fatal error. However, the Company has admitted that the driver was unfamiliar with the locomotive that he was operating that day, it being the first time he had driven it.

From calculations made by the Company's Chief Mechanical Engineer, it has been noted that the extra height of the locomotive, over the examples to which the driver was accustomed, may have contributed to the accident. The centre of gravity, being higher, caused the locomotive in question to assume an unstable equilibrium at a lower speed than the driver may have expected. However, no such problem would have occurred if the driver had not exceeded the 30 miles per hour restriction. The Company's Chief Mechanical Engineer has further calculated that the engine would have had to exceed 47 miles per hour to cause an unstable equilibrium, and it seems from all of the evidence that this was the case.

I cannot conclude my report without an expression of deep regret for the loss of so many valuable lives in this disaster, and of sincere sympathy with the relatives and friends of those who were killed and with the injured.

Col. W. P. Fothergill.

The Assistant Secretary.

Railway Department, Board of Trade.

Dunley Bottom, being situated seven miles north of Winchester, fell within the jurisdiction of the Winchester Coroner, James Driffield, whose job it was, under English law, to investigate deaths,

157

particularly those occurring in unusual circumstances, and to decide whether a post-mortem should take place and whether to hold an inquest.

In relation to the train crash, he ordered both post-mortems and inquests. He worked in conjunction with the police and railway officials. His immediate task was to instruct the police to confirm the identity of each of the victims. Here, he came across a problem: two of the victims, located in coach number two, were terribly burned and facial recognition was impossible.

A temporary mortuary was established in one of the nearby outbuildings belonging to the chalk quarry. The bodies were removed, one by one, from the scene of the accident; each one labelled, to show from which coach it had been recovered.

By luck, the express train was lightly loaded with passengers on the day of the accident. There were only three passengers in coach number one, two of whom survived. The unfortunate victim was crushed to death on impact. He was identified by his daughter, who survived and received only minor injuries. There were two passengers in coach number two. Both died from burns and the inhalation of noxious gases. All of the twenty-five passengers in coach number three survived, although five were seriously hurt. In coach number four, the first-class carriage, the waiter and one American passenger escaped with minor injuries. The other seven passengers, all American citizens, lost their lives. The surviving passenger in the first-class carriage was able to identify his compatriots.

Where there was any doubt as to the cause of death, post-mortems were carried out. One of the Americans, James Silverman, survived the initial impact, but died two hours later. His post-mortem revealed that he had suffered a fatal heart attack, brought on, it was believed, when he was informed that his wife had perished.

The railway employees were formally identified by work colleagues. The two burned and disfigured bodies in coach number two defied initial identification. One was female and one was male. The fire had consumed any luggage that they may have had with them. The female's face and upper torso were particularly affected by the heat of the fire. From her remains and charred clothing, the police were able to determine that she was aged twenty to thirty-five, had black hair, was unmarried (no rings) and was travelling alone (her body was found at the other end of the carriage to the that of the gentleman).

The male victim, was older and a particularly tall individual. Close to his body, the rescuers found an inscribed silver watch presented to a Henry Dodd. His corpse was missing the small toe from his left foot. It was an old injury and the police were soon able to trace a relative, who formally identified the body as being that of Henry Dodd.

3.12

The day after the train crash, the story dominated the newspapers. John and Louisa knew nothing of it, until John opened his newspaper that Saturday morning. He realised instantly that it was Rose's train. He passed the paper to Louisa, who read the headline and paled. It was dreadful news, on top of the misery they were suffering from the loss of their son. Surely, Rose had not perished in such an awful accident. John comforted Louisa. They held each other, and hoped with all their hearts that she would be among the survivors.

The following twenty-four hours were a further ordeal for John and Louisa. The next edition of the newspaper gave the names of the dead and those of the injured, as well as those who had escaped the crash without injury. Rose's name was not listed. However, there was mention of one female victim, who had yet to be identified and this piece of news caused a shudder to pass between them.

John decided that he would contact the police without delay, to inform them of his suspicion that the unidentified female may be Rose. He went to the local police station, where a sergeant patiently took down the details.

The sergeant tried to calm John's fears, but was willing to admit that her death in the accident was a possibility. He noted the address of George and Charlotte in Ventnor and sent a telegram to the Ventnor police, requesting that they enquire as to Rose's whereabouts. He advised John to return home and await developments.

Later that afternoon, a police constable called at Apsley Street. John led him to the rear parlour where Louisa was ironing. He informed them that Rose had not arrived in Ventnor as expected. Louisa almost collapsed with grief. John supported her and helped her to a chair.

'Now sir, madam,' said the constable nodding to Louisa. 'We have no proof at this stage that Miss Ince was a passenger on the ill-fated express. Could you give me some more information and we'll make further enquiries.'

John then explained the timings of Rose's journey, of how she had left at about eight-thirty in the morning two days before, with the intention of catching the eleven o'clock express from Waterloo to Southampton.

'Do you have a recent photograph of Miss Ince, and can you remember what she was wearing when she left here? Was she carrying a bag or something?'

Louisa soon found a photograph. It was one given to her by Rose and was from the same set of portrait photographs, which Rose had commissioned for Frank.

'Ah yes, this should do well,' confirmed the constable. He turned it over and on the reverse noticed the name of *Douglas' Portrait Studio, High Street, Leyton*.

'When was this taken?'

'About two years ago,' replied John.

'Excellent,' said the constable. 'With luck, Mr Douglas still has the means to make a copy. If so, we can obtain some more photographs and perhaps enlarge them as well.'

Louisa recalled Rose's clothing as best she could. She remembered that she was carrying a carpetbag and a small handbag, both of which she described.

The constable noted everything down before leaving, advising them not to give up hope until the police had finished their enquiries.

The police soon established that Rose had purchased a ticket to Liverpool Street at Leyton station two days before. The booking-office clerk confirmed her likeness to the photograph and added that she had appeared to have a 'contretemps' with the draper's porter, who worked for Crockford's in the town.

They followed up his observation by calling at the shop to interview Sidney. He was asked if he had seen Miss Rosetta Ince at Leyton station, two days before.

'Yes, I saw 'er at the station. I 'ad a bit of a go at her actually,' he added sheepishly.

'Oh, why was that?'

'Well, she wasn't who we thought she was, that's all. Got 'erself in the family way, you see ... not married like.'

'Did she work here then? Is that how you know her?'

'Yes, that's right. Worked 'ere for about two years. She was very good at 'er job, a very skilled seamstress and draper.'

'And what exactly happened at the station?' asked the policeman.

'Well I spotted 'er buying a ticket and when she turned away from the booth I 'ad a go at 'er, told 'er what I thought of 'er.'

'And what was her reaction when you ... 'ad a go at 'er?'

'She didn't like it ... slapped my cheek and ran off to get 'er train.'

'Did you see her get on a train?'

'Yes.'

'And which train was it? Where was it going?'

'It was the train to Liverpool Street.'

'And what was the time?'

Sidney thought for a moment. 'It was nine o'clock. Yes, she caught the nine o'clock to Liverpool Street.'

'Very well, that's all for now,' said the policeman, closing his notebook.

The police continued with their enquiries. They further established that Rose had purchased a ticket for the underground at City station.

The ticket clerk recalled seeing her, because he noticed that she looked as though she had been crying and he had enquired if she was in distress. He explained that she had shaken her head and had hurried away in the direction of the electric underground train. There was no other destination from this station, as the line operated solely between City and Waterloo.

At Waterloo, the clerk could not recall seeing her, but one of the porters confirmed that he had seen her coming out of the waiting room, just prior to the departure of the express.

A lady contacted the police to say that on the morning of the crash, she had sat opposite a young woman in her twenties, matching the description given in the newspapers of the unidentified female victim. The lady had taken the electric train from City underground to Waterloo and thought her encounter may have been significant. She described how she had noticed a distressed young woman sitting directly opposite her in the carriage and had tried to engage her in conversation, but had only established that she was going to Ventnor, before the young woman had moved to another seat.

The police, at the accident scene, had deduced that the unidentified female victim was black haired, unmarried, aged twenty to thirty-five and travelling alone. Rosetta Ince's description matched the victim in age, height and build. They could find no evidence of any labels on her badly charred clothes, which indicated that they were probably home-made, rather than purchased from a retailer. That observation fitted with Rosetta Ince's occupation as a seamstress-cum-draper. The remains of her footwear matched the colour and style described by Louisa Williams. Furthermore, Rose had left Leyton on the morning of the crash and had not arrived at her destination in Ventnor.

All this evidence was put before the coroner, James Driffield, and he was satisfied that the body of the female found in coach number two was that of Rosetta Ince and he issued a death certificate accordingly. The body was released to the undertakers on the nineteenth day after the crash.

3.13

Louisa and John found themselves at a second funeral in four weeks. This time however, it took place in Ventnor. It was a very sad and solemn occasion. The local parish church was virtually empty. Florence and Arthur were present and so too were George and Charlotte, but that was all.

Florence complained bitterly that the family had seen enough misery and sadness. 'That's three deaths now,' she said. 'Let that be an end to it. We deserve some happiness; we've had our share of sorrow for the time being. I've had just about enough of being in mourning. I want to be able to pack these clothes away for a good long spell.'

Mrs Edwards had remained at Brindle Lodge to look after the twins. After the short but moving service, followed by burial in the little churchyard, the family returned to Brindle Lodge for a cup of tea, and to recover from the ordeal of the funeral. Charlotte and Louisa were desperate to see the children. They were a tonic to counteract the sadness that they were both feeling.

When Mrs Edwards had served tea and left the room, the family settled down to consider the future of Edith and Harold. The subject had already been aired by John and George the previous evening. A possible solution had been proposed and discussed exhaustively. Their wives were in favour, but they wanted to put it before Arthur and Florence, in order to gauge their feelings too.

George explained the proposal to Arthur and Florence, and all waited for their reaction.

It was Arthur who spoke: 'What you're saying is, that you want to separate the twins … have Edith remain here in Ventnor with you and Charlotte, and let Harold go with John and Louisa to live in Leyton?'

'Yes, that's about the long and the short of it,' confirmed John. 'What do you think?'

There was silence before Arthur spoke again: 'Florence and I have been wondering what might happen. Actually we came up with the same idea, but weren't sure how Charlotte would react to splitting the twins. We know how fond you have become of them, dear.'

Yes, I have,' said Charlotte, her eyes starting to well with tears once more, 'but the children are still young, too young to suffer lasting damage and we know Harold will be well looked after. I will miss him terribly and it will be hard, but I can't have children and poor Louisa has been told that she may not be able to have another. Why should George and I keep both children? It seems the best solution all round, and I am sure the children will not suffer as a consequence.'

'We are too old to take on these youngsters,' Florence began, 'and it will be a wrench not seeing Harold very often, but when everything is taken into account, we think this is a good idea, don't we Arthur?'

'Yes dear, we do. Frank's not here,' he continued, 'and we have to think what he would have wanted. We know he loved his brother and cousin dearly. In Frank's absence, we feel responsible for deciding the children's future. Edith and Harold are our flesh and blood and it seems only right that if we can't bring them up, then either our son or our nephew should do so. You know we have great affection for both of you and you are already their godparents. So, yes, if all of you are happy that the children can be separated with no lasting ill-effects, then you have our blessing to the arrangement.'

Two days later, John and Louisa returned to Leyton with young Harold in their charge. Louisa and Charlotte had spent the day after Rose's funeral packing his things, mainly clothes and a few easy-to-carry toys. Charlotte was quite tearful at times and it was obvious that letting go of Harold was painful for her, but she also recognised the needs of Louisa and John, who were devastated over the loss of Henry.

As the Williams family left Brindle Lodge, the emotion was almost too much for Charlotte and Louisa. George had taken the day off work to be there. The ladies were both in tears, but after the parting, each of them felt some relief. The dread of the moment of leaving had, for each of them, been building and after it was over, it was as if a new chapter was opening and it was time to move on and to plan for the future.

On the whole, they had all agreed, although difficult to cope with, it was an admirable arrangement. Charlotte and George had Edith, the child in the household that they had always wanted. Louisa and John had Harold, a replacement of sorts to fill the void left by Henry.

As the Williams family made their way back to Leyton that day, increasing the physical distance between the twins, they wondered whether Edith and Harold would ever again feel that bond of closeness with each other – the bond that had been there in the womb and from the moment of birth.

3.14

When Carol returned from Vestry House later in the afternoon, she had some good news for Nick Bastion.

'You were right! During the 1940s and 1950s, there was another voter registered at Harry Williams' address. Her name was Louisa Matilda Williams. I've checked the 1911 Census for Leyton and found Harry and Louisa Matilda living in Moses Street, West Ham. On the census, Louisa was Harry's mother and her husband, John Williams, was head of the household. They'd been married eleven years. There were no other family members living with them.

'Excellent,' said Nick. 'Have you tried looking for Louisa Matilda's death, as she has an unusual middle name?'

'Yes. I've just run a search for it and found one in the right area for 1962. The age given is ninety-two. I've also checked the probate records, but she didn't leave a will, so no clues from there.'

'What about the marriage? Have you found that too?'

'Already have … 1900 in Leyton … Louisa Matilda Crockford married John Williams.'

'Well done, Carol … well done.'

Carol was beaming. 'I'll order the death and marriage certificates first thing tomorrow if that's OK, or do you want to send Tom Furniss to the local register office to pick them up?'

'No, this case is old. Order them by post, but pay extra for the twenty-four hour service.

Peter Sefton moved forward ten years in his research on the marriage certificate, to the census of 1911, the most recent one available. He looked again for Frank Williams, born on the Isle of Wight, but once more drew a blank as far as definite identification. There were some possibilities but nothing more. He had calculated that by 1911, Frank would have been thirty-four and could have established himself anywhere in the world, so Peter's chances of finding him were quite low.

Rosetta Price had disappeared too. She'd probably married during the intervening years and unless he really wanted to go off on what could be a costly certificate-buying tangent, Peter decided it was probably as well to call off any more investigation of her for the moment.

He ran a search for *46 Apsley Street* and discovered that John and Louisa were no longer the occupants. He then searched, using their names, and found that they had moved to Moses Street in West Ham.

1911 Census Return

ADDRESS	NAME	RELATION	AGE	OCCUPATION	WHERE BORN
22 Moses Street West Ham	John Williams	Head	41	Engineer on dredger	Cowes, IOW
	Louisa Williams	Wife	40	Dressmaker	Leyton
	Harry Williams	Son	10	Scholar	Leyton

Completed years the present marriage has lasted: 11 years

Particulars of marriage for persons aged 15 years and upwards

John Williams   Married

Louisa Williams   Married

State for each married woman entered on this schedule the number of:

Children born alive:	1
Children still living:	1
Children who have died:	--

Peter chewed over the census information for a while. John was there, and for whatever reason, by 1911 he was no longer working for the prestigious Castle Line. He was employed as an engineer on a dredger. That seemed a bit of a comedown and they'd moved as well, closer to the docks. Perhaps, he'd changed jobs to avoid spending long periods at sea and away from home? As a dredger man, Peter reasoned, he would have been able to return home to his family each evening.

Peter also noticed that Henry, as he was named in the 1901 Census, was now referred to as Harry. He was aware that Harry was often used as a more familiar name for someone called Henry. He saw too that Louisa gave her occupation as 'dressmaker' and he wondered whether she did any work connected with her father's drapery business.

A novel feature of the 1911 Census was that householders were asked to fill in the census form themselves and to provide marriage particulars, as well as details of children, alive and dead. Peter looked to see if Harry had any siblings.

Obviously, no brothers or sisters, Peter thought, although it was strange not to find more children in the household. The couple had been married for eleven years and generally, families of that era were large. Perhaps, Peter considered, Louisa had miscarried, which would not have been recorded, but there was no way of finding out.

There was a possibility that although aged forty, Louisa may have had another child after the 1911 Census. Fortunately, this was easy to check, because from September 1911, the birth indexes showed the married and maiden name of mothers.

Peter ran a search on all Williams' births between 1911 and 1925 with the maiden name of Crockford. His search returned no results. Technically, there was a gap in his search period of five months, between the census in early April and the extra information given from September 1911, but he felt able to conclude with reasonable certainty that Harry was an only child.

168

3.16

Everything was just as Carol had hoped when she received the death and marriage certificates of Louisa Matilda Williams. The death certificate showed that Louisa was Harry's mother and that her husband John had died before her.

Certificate of Death

REGISTRATION DISTRICT	ESSEX SOUTH WESTERN
1962 DEATH	in the County of Essex

When and where died	Name and surname	Sex	Age	Occupation
Tenth December 1962, 59 Stephenson Steet Leyton	Louisa Matilda Williams	Female	92	Widow of John Williams, Chief Engineer (marine)

Cause of death	Signature,description and residence of informant	When registered
Coronary thrombosis, Certified by R L Chambers M.B.	Harry Williams, Son Present at death 59 Stephenson Street Leyton	Fourteenth December 1962

From the details on the marriage certificate, Carol knew she had the correct marriage and saw that it had taken place in Leyton. Unfortunately, she'd already ordered ten possible birth certificates for Harry – or Harold – Williams. She'd had a feeling that searching all of Essex had been too wide. She went back to examine the birth indexes and realised that of the ten certificates she'd ordered, only six applied to the West Ham district covering Leyton. In 1900, the birth indexes did not show the mother's maiden name, so she hoped that one of the six certificates would be the right one.

When the certificates arrived a few days later, they were all wrong. None of the births was to a Louisa Crockford. Carol sat back after studying the certificates and groaned with disappointment and frustration.

Carol looked again at her notes. Although she'd checked the 1911 census, she realised that she hadn't looked on the 1901 census too. She searched the index for 'Louisa Williams', and found an entry in the registration district of Leyton. Looking at the image of the census return, she noticed that this Louisa lived with her son 'Henry', not 'Harry'. She then checked the address: Apsley Street. It matched the groom's address on the marriage certificate. This had to be the correct Louisa, but who was Henry and where was Harry? Carol was confused.

She took the problem back to her boss. They discussed the progress so far and the problem that she appeared to have encountered. Nick came up with the answer and Carol inwardly kicked herself for her ignorance.

'Carol, I'm pretty sure that Harry and Henry are one and the same. Harry is a name often used as a more familiar form of Henry. Try a birth search for a Henry Williams.'

Carol left Nick's office. On her way downstairs she felt disappointed with her performance. She played back the conversation she'd had with Nick, trying to put her finger on something that had been nagging at the back of her mind during the meeting. She sat down at her workstation and was just about to search the last quarter of 1900 again when she realised what it was that didn't add up. Maybe she could redeem herself?

From the 1901 Census, taken on 31 March 1901, Harry's age, or Henry as he was called at the time, was shown as six months. If he had been born on the date shown on his death certificate of 8 October 1900, his age would only have been five months. Was it possible that the Coroner's Department had entered the date of birth incorrectly on the death certificate? What if he had been born before October? October is in the fourth quarter, whereas September falls within the third quarter. Following this train of thought, Carol bravely decided, on her own initiative, to search only the third quarter and identified five possibilities; three 'Henrys', a 'Harry' and a 'Harold'. She ordered five certificates and this time took it upon herself to use the express service. She almost counted the hours until they arrived the following day, praying and fretting that her theory would prove correct.

She opened each envelope with trepidation. When she read the entries on the third Henry, she let a loud whoop of joy and everyone in the office knew that she had found her missing birth.

Certificate of Birth

REGISTRATION DISTRICT	WEST HAM
1900 BIRTH	in the County of Essex

When and where born	Name, if any	Sex	Name and surname of father
Eighth September 1900 46 Apsley Street Leyton, Essex	Henry	Boy	John Williams

Name, surname and maiden surname of mother	Occupation of father	Signature, description and residence of informant	When registered
Louisa Matilda Williams formerly Crockford	Ship's Engineer	John Williams, Father 46 Apsley Street, Leyton	Eleventh September 1900

Nick was in the main office at the time and came over to congratulate Carol.

'Well done, that's a real step forward,' he said. 'You're making progress. I think we'll move this case up one level and put it onto a higher priority. We'll get Fred Howard over to the deceased's neighbourhood in Leyton to see if he can discover anything by knocking on a few doors.'

Carol was already thinking ahead. She had found Henry's birth and had identified his parents. The next move would be to look for full blood or half-blood siblings and failing that, move back a generation to uncles and aunts, or their offspring, who would be cousins. Carol was anxious to prove herself and to make up for her earlier lack of inspiration and ideas.

3.17

By coincidence, the copy of Henry Williams' birth certificate, which Peter had ordered, also arrived at the cottage during that same week in January 2011. He sat in the kitchen sipping coffee as he studied the entries. It was mid-morning and he'd needed a break from tracking his shares on the London market.

Henry, or Harry, as he seemed to have become known was born on 8 September 1900 at home, in the West Ham registration district. The gap between the wedding and the birth was around thirty-four weeks. It confirmed Peter's suspicions. Harry's birth may have been premature, but somehow Peter didn't think so. The likelihood was that Louisa was pregnant when she walked up the aisle.

Peter had been pondering the extremely unlikely possibility that Harry's mother could have produced a brother or sister between April and September 1911. If Harry had married, his marriage certificate might name a sibling as a witness. The death certificates of his parents, John and Louisa Williams, could also contain a lot of useful information and might show a daughter or another son as informant and thus reveal the existence of a sibling for Harry.

Peter decided to follow that route and to look for the death of one of Harry's parents. He first chose his mother, Louisa Matilda Williams, because her middle name was uncommon. He went back upstairs to his computer and started the search.

Almost straight away, he found Louisa's death, during the last quarter of 1962, in the registration district of Essex South Western. Did that mean that the district covering Leyton had changed from West Ham to Essex South Western or had she died in a different area to the one in which she'd previously lived? A minute later, he had the answer: the registration district *had* changed in 1935. He ordered her death certificate immediately.

He then turned his attention to finding the death of Louisa's husband, John. As expected, the number of possible deaths that his search query returned was too high and he had to abandon it. John Williams may have died in the Leyton area, but Peter couldn't be sure. All he knew for sure was that John Williams was alive in 1911. He hoped that Louisa's death certificate would show whether John was still alive in 1962. He'd have to wait and see.

When Louisa's death certificate arrived in the post, it was, like Harry's birth certificate, a piece of physical evidence with a direct connection to the individuals on the marriage certificate from the antiques centre.

It was proof that in 1962 Louisa was a widow and her son, Harry, was the informant, and not any other son or daughter. Peter decided to accept that Harry was an only child. His address was the same as the one at which she'd died and he saw that it was in Leyton. It looked as if the family had continued to live in the Leyton area.

However, for Peter, there were still many unanswered questions. What had happened to her husband, John? How long before Louisa did he die? What happened to Harry after his mother died? Was Harry married? Did Harry have any children? These thoughts swirled around inside Peter's head as he wondered where to go next. Finally, he decided to concentrate on Harry, because if he could find his death, then his death certificate might answer the last two of his questions.

He subscribed to a website, which made it possible to trace living relatives, as well as those who were deceased. The website's resources included scanned copies of telephone directories. The directory covering Leyton was searchable for the period 1960 to 1984. He had a name and he had an address, so he tried it.

'Bingo!' he exclaimed. He had found a phone number listed alongside the name of *H Williams, Stephenson Street, Leyton*. Harry Williams was alive in 1984 and by Peter's reckoning would have been at least eighty-three.

Peter then searched the death indexes and looked for a Harry Williams, aged eighty-three or older, who had died in the Registration District of West Ham, after 1983. Peter was feeling exhilarated and definitely on a roll. He waited patiently for the page to load, expecting when it did so, to scroll down a column of names … disaster, no match. He looked again – no match. What a disappointment!

He paused and checked the information he had entered. It seemed correct. Then he realised his error. The registration district for Leyton had changed from West Ham to Essex South Western. He tried again, this time searching the correct district and to his delight, found the entry for the death of Harry Williams, aged ninety-five, in the third quarter of 1996. Peter ordered the death certificate. Now all he had to do was wait as patiently as he could for a few days. He really felt that he was starting to get somewhere.

3.18

It was a beautiful August morning and the *HMS Kidwelly Castle* was off the south coast of the Isle of Wight, heading westwards to the Bay of Biscay and the South Atlantic Ocean beyond.

Former Chief Engineer, John Williams, now Lieutenant Williams, stood once more in his familiar position, from where he could look down upon the boilers and the reciprocating machinery propelling the ship. The scene below had changed little, apart from the hastily installed steel mesh to protect the cylinders and moving parts from falling debris. The sides of the engine room were heavily padded with layers of mattress, held in place by thick canvas sheeting; wedged and fixed to the ship's internal frame.

Twelve years had passed since John had last stood at his post in this vessel's engine room: twelve years, in which there had been important changes in his life; twelve years of relative calm and happiness, but all that was about to change, as he found himself on his way to Africa once again.

This time, he was at sea in profoundly different circumstances. There was no schedule to observe, so that the mail was delivered on time in Cape Town; no annoying questions from the first-class passengers on how fast the ship could go and was she at cruising speed? Things were wholly different, for the *Kidwelly Castle* was now an armed merchant cruiser, requisitioned from civilian duty and pressed into service by the Royal Navy. She was needed to provide additional strength to protect the country's maritime interests. It was 1914 and Great Britain was at war with Germany.

The familiar warmth, hiss, and pulse of the engines caused John's mind to drift a little. He reflected on the events that had occurred during the intervening twelve years. It seemed like only yesterday that he'd returned to London to learn of Henry's death. He remembered the expression on his beloved Louisa's face when he got home. She was distraught; blaming herself for not appreciating sooner the seriousness of Henry's condition, but no blame could be put upon her. It was a tragedy for them, but not something that could have been averted.

Then they'd lost their dear friend Rose. What a horrible end she had met: burned beyond recognition in that dreadful railway accident, but a silver lining in the form of Harry had come into their lives. What a joy and relief he had been.

John had made the decision after Henry's funeral, that he would resign his post with the Union Castle Line. He no longer wanted to leave Louisa for long periods and so he set about finding another job, a job that would enable him to return home each day, so that they could pass more time together as a family. He'd found a job locally, which although didn't have the prestige of being a chief engineer on a Royal Mail ship, sailing thousands of miles across the oceans of the world, meant that at least he returned home every day. His trips tended to be somewhat shorter, perhaps forty miles at the most. He'd swapped the *Kidwelly Castle* for a ship of an altogether different kind: a dredger no less, a Thames dredger called the *Woolwich Queen*.

She was a third of the size of the *Kidwelly Castle*. Instead of carrying passengers, her holds were filled each day with mud and sand scooped from the bottom of the Thames estuary. John had been forced to take a lower wage, but with Louisa's contribution from her dressmaking, and a move to a smaller house in West Ham, they'd managed. Harry had done well at school and just after his fourteenth birthday, had started as an apprentice patternmaker at the Falcon Foundry. With luck, if he progressed well, his choice of job, which happened to be a reserved occupation, would keep him from military service. The foundry had switched production from trains to the vital munitions and military equipment the country needed, to fight the war against Germany.

John had received his naval call-up papers just three weeks before. It wasn't entirely unexpected. He was in the Mercantile Marine Reserve after all. What had surprised him was that he had found himself back on his old ship, but when he thought about it, it made perfect sense.

The Royal Navy needed more ships to support and relieve its conventional warships. Each of the large civilian shipping companies was ordered to give up some of its fleet. Among those selected from the Union Castle Line was the *Kidwelly Castle*. Now, she sailed under the White Ensign and was commanded by naval officers, with her previous or existing senior crew given temporary commissions.

John's immediate predecessor had joined the Royal Navy proper and so his vacant post had to be filled. John at forty-four years old, although more mature than normally acceptable, was the natural and obvious choice, being given the naval rank of Lieutenant.

He had been delighted to renew the acquaintance of old shipmates and colleagues, many of whom had remained with the company during his absence or, like him, as reservists, had received their call-up papers in the post. He was pleased to see two of his old stokers, Albert May and Frank Butler. They were good men and could be trusted to keep the newcomers up to scratch. The purser remained, as before, his good friend George Corbett, whose Royal Naval rank was that of Paymaster.

John's reverie was broken by a command from the bridge requesting more speed. He knew he would need to get used to the new regime on board. The ship was vulnerable to attack from German submarines. They'd been forewarned by the Captain to expect constant changes in speed and direction, part of the strategy to avoid U-boat attack.

The *Kidwelly Castle* had undergone the transformation from mail and passenger ship to quasi-military vessel in just a few weeks. Gangs of carpenters and general workers had removed her fine furnishings and staterooms. The first-class accommodation, the dining rooms and smoking rooms had been gutted; the small swimming pool covered over. Throughout the ship, unnecessary fittings had been removed and flammable materials stripped out. Steel plating had been added to the wheelhouse, to protect it from shelling. The deck had been strengthened, in order to bear the weight and the recoil of the four-inch guns, two forward and two aft. *Maxim* machine guns had also been fitted at various locations on the superstructure. The passenger rails and stanchions had been dismantled to provide a clear line of sight for the gunners. Below decks, the holds had been converted into magazines and extra storage capacity for coal, the vital fuel she needed to keep her at sea. Hoists and lifting tackle had been installed to facilitate the loading and reloading of the guns.

Unfortunately, her top speed had not improved. She could still make seventeen knots, but this was slow when compared to the speed of the more modern German warships she might have to encounter and engage. Nevertheless, she was more than capable of transporting equipment and personnel, of looking out for enemy raiders, and of patrolling and intercepting neutral blockade-runners.

The first few days were intensely busy for the crew. The Captain was anxious that they practise and carry out numerous drills and training exercises. A call to action was possible at any time and he wanted to be sure that should the need arise, his crew would perform to the required level.

Night running was a new experience for John. In contrast to the peacetime state of brightly lit staterooms, filled with music and laughter, under wartime conditions the exterior of the ship had to remain dark. Dimly shaded lights lit the stairwells and the wheelhouse. Cabin windows and portholes were blacked out. Everything was done in order to conceal the ship from the enemy. The German U-boat threat was greatest in the western approaches, so in theory the risk of being torpedoed reduced as the ship passed Gibraltar and headed south towards the Canary Islands. However, the Captain was a cautious man. Wherever they were after dark, he preferred to keep his ship in such condition as least likely to attract the attention of a U-boat's periscope.

One evening, John remained in his cabin. He had started to write a letter to Louisa and Harry, although it was difficult in the poor light. The ship was due to call at St Helena; with luck, he could post the letter there. He cast his mind back once more to the times he had passed in this same cabin. He remembered vividly the conversation he'd had with Frank and the promise he'd made to his brother to look out for Rose and their child, if she had found herself pregnant. He considered the extent to which he had fulfilled his obligation and was content in the knowledge that he and Louisa could have done no more. Harry was well fed, well clothed, and most importantly well loved, and was being brought up in a secure and happy home.

It was a shame, John thought, that Harry hadn't seen his twin sister since the day they were separated. He and Louisa had never mentioned Edith to Harry, who had seemed to have forgotten her. They hadn't been over to the island for a long time. John recalled that the last time he went, it was on his own, in 1905, to attend his father's funeral. As they didn't have the money for holidays and long seaside trips, they took day trips during the summer. Southend was nearby; it was their favourite destination and Harry loved it there.

He had sometimes wondered if he should take Louisa and Harry to visit Florence, and had put the idea to Louisa on more than one occasion. They had discussed the implications and consequences at length. The problem was, that taking Harry to Ventnor opened up the risk of him meeting Edith. Such a meeting would be fraught with likely complications. Would they tell Harry who she was? Should

178

they have to tell him at all? If he knew of her, would that jeopardise the harmony and stability of their little family? After losing Henry, anything that might disrupt family life was to be avoided at all costs.

They both regarded Harry as their son and were intensely happy with the situation. Since moving house, the new neighbours naturally assumed that Harry was theirs. Harry referred to them as mother and father. Louisa had not been able to conceive a second time and so they blessed their good fortune in having him.

There had been no discussion with George and Charlotte at the time of separation, on whether to tell the twins of their true parentage. It was as though once the arrangement was made to separate them, each couple wished to retreat with their prize, into a form of denial and obscurity, assuming the role of parents and creating the perfect family environment. An unspoken assumption had been made, that telling each child too soon that they had a twin sibling, would cause problems of insecurity and unhappiness. As the years passed, there came a point when, for the very same reasons, John thought it was really too late to tell them. It seemed easier to keep the twins apart, in order to avoid any potentially unsettling questions or complications.

Florence of course, knew the truth but she chose not to divulge the secret. She concentrated her affection and attention on Edith, who had a striking resemblance to Frank. Harry's colouring was darker. He took after Rose. Florence was more than happy to dote on her granddaughter and as she got older, she felt no compulsion to make the long journey to London to visit John and Louisa. The years passed and the London and the Isle of Wight branches of the family grew far apart.

Coming back to the present, John finished his letter to Louisa and Harry. Censorship permitting, he'd brought them up to date with what news he could. He told Harry to look after his mother. By all accounts, the war would be over by Christmas, so his separation from them shouldn't be for too long. He signed the letter '*love Father*'.

3.19

The death certificate of Harry Williams, aged ninety-five, arrived in Peter Sefton's post. There was good and bad news.

The useful information included his occupation, his address at death, and the place of death, which were the same. So he'd died at home, Peter noted. He also noticed that the date of birth was exactly one month after the date given on his birth certificate. He put the discrepancy down to a clerical error by the informant or registrar. The bad news was that the informant was a council employee, not a relative, as Peter had hoped. This puzzled him. He looked on the Internet and discovered that where no person can be traced to pay for a funeral, local councils have the final responsibility to bury or cremate someone who dies in their area. *Oh well*, Peter thought. *That explains that.*

He pondered the intervention of the coroner, because usually a coroner only becomes involved if there is some uncertainty over the cause of death. There might have been a mention in the local press, he wondered, so that line of enquiry would be worth pursuing.

He also wondered what a patternmaker did. He searched online again and found that it was an industrial trade. Patternmakers made exact wooden mouldings according to engineering drawings. The moulds were then used to cast metal components. It was a job requiring the ability to interpret drawings, along with exacting and precise carpentry skills. It required an apprenticeship of around seven years.

Peter wondered where Harry had worked. There must have been some form of metal casting in the area. Again, he searched online and discovered that Leyton used to have a foundry, which produced steam locomotives. It was called The Falcon Foundry. He investigated further and learned that until the works closed in 1982, the foundry supported a thriving community, known locally as Falcon Village, which consisted of a number of streets of terraced houses, built by the foundry to house its workers close to the factory.

Harry Williams lived in *Stephenson Street*. It occurred to Peter that the name Stephenson was synonymous with railways. George Stephenson built The Rocket and established the first passenger railway between Stockton and Darlington in 1825. It made sense then that Stephenson Street was part of Falcon Village. Another quick search online confirmed this.

Peter spent some time following links on the subject of the Falcon Foundry. He spotted one, which took him to a website established by former employees to record the foundry's history. Reading through the introduction, he learned that the foundry used to have a quarterly news magazine called *The Falcon*. It featured company news, pictures of the trains they built and one section covered news of staff, including outings and family events.

He clicked on a link, which took him to a collection of *The Falcon* magazines. They had been scanned and posted online. Choosing one from September 1958, Peter noticed that in the staff section, there was news of a wedding and also a mention of a retirement. *What if there is a mention of Harry Williams when he retired?* thought Peter. *If he lived in Stephenson Street, then it follows that he probably worked at the foundry.*

Peter calculated Harry's retirement year and looked at the four copies covering 1965, but he drew a blank. He tried 1964 and again drew a blank. Deciding on one final look, he selected the issue for April 1963 and there it was: an article, headed 'Foreman Patternmaker Retires After 49 Years'.

Peter could hardly believe it, for not only did the piece outline Harry Williams' career, from starting out as an apprentice at fourteen to his retirement at sixty-three, it also showed a photograph of him.

Peter copied the photograph and printed it for his records. He read the story carefully. There was a sad note at the end. It mentioned that Harry had not been able to continue, until normal retirement at sixty-five, and complete more than fifty years' service, because he'd lost three fingers in an accident. The article praised Harry for his loyalty during two world wars and his contribution to the foundry was recognised and appreciated.

Peter imagined a man who had learned his trade as an apprentice and worked loyally for the same employer for forty-nine years, rising to foreman patternmaker. He'd only retired early due to an accident, possibly at work, which had robbed him of his practical dexterity and necessitated a premature end to his career. He wondered how the man felt at the time: sadness, frustration, disappointment, elation, relief, optimism or perhaps fear of the future? It was hard to appreciate.

It dawned on Peter, that when Harry was forced to retire, it was only about three months after his mother had passed away. Peter didn't know how close mother and son were, but that period of Harry's life must have been marked by personal loss and possibly a great deal of turmoil.

Peter wondered whether Harry Williams had owned *59, Stephenson Street*. Had he managed to buy it, or did he rent it from the foundry? Peter decided that there was a good chance that he'd owned it; after all, he'd lived there for thirty-three years following retirement. One would naturally think that an elderly single man, if he'd been a tenant, would have been more likely to end up in a council retirement facility, rather than remaining at home until the end of his life.

Peter considered how he might find out whether Harry had owned the house. First, he looked up the postcode for Stephenson Street. Then, he entered the postcode into the search box on a website showing the prices at which houses had been sold. He wanted to know if the property had been sold in the last ten years. He found *Cambria*, 59, Stephenson Street, described as a 'freehold semi-detached house'. It had changed hands twice, the first time in 2001 for £65,000 and then again, one year later for £165,000 but the information didn't help to confirm whether Harry had owned the house.

Peter thought that Harry could have been a tenant and that when he died, the owner had sold the house, but somehow he thought it more likely that Harry Williams owned the property. He would need to look elsewhere for any supporting evidence.

Assuming that Harry was the owner, Peter wondered if he had left his house to anyone in his will. He tried a search of probate records, but found no match. It then occurred to him that he could have died without making a will. *People die intestate all the time*, he thought. On a whim, he decided to look at the Treasury Solicitor's Bona Vacantia Division website, because it advertised unclaimed estates in the hope of finding heirs. If unclaimed after thirty years, the Government kept the proceeds of such estates. *Harry's name might be there*, he thought, but when he entered the surname 'Williams' into the main search box, there was no match.

Peter browsed through the website for a while. He read a note explaining that the Treasury Solicitor no longer published the values of estates, as there had been some problems with fraud. Then on one side of the page, he noticed a link to the complete list of unclaimed estates. He realised that so far, he'd only searched the current weekly additions. He clicked on the link, which took him to a large, multi-page document. Each page listed about eighty names, so he quickly estimated that the total number of unclaimed estates ran into hundreds, possibly thousands.

He could see that the names were organised in alphabetical order. He scrolled down to the pages covering the names beginning with W. There were three entries for the surname 'Williams' and sure enough, although hardly able to believe it, he found an entry for *Williams, Harry, 01/07/1996, Leyton.*

Peter recognised straight away the date of Harry's death. He'd no idea how long the estate had been listed on Bona Vacantia, neither did he know the value, but more importantly, the quest to find out what had happened to the couple on the marriage certificate had just taken a new and most intriguing turn.

He carefully read all of the information available on the site. It seemed that the Treasury Solicitor admitted claims up to twelve years after an estate was substantially administered. Peter wasn't quite sure what that signified. Did that mean twelve years after the death? If so, was it too late for anyone to claim? For a few moments, Peter felt completely deflated. He chewed the end of his pencil. If the logic of that advice was taken, then why would any estate be advertised more than twelve years after the deceased had passed away? Reading further, he was relieved to learn that the Treasury Solicitor can use his discretion to consider claims up to thirty years after the date of death, although in such circumstances, only the residue of an estate, without interest, is paid if a claim is successful.

Phew! thought Peter. He'd no intention of claiming it for himself. After all, he had no blood relationship to the deceased, or assumed he hadn't, but a germ of an idea was forming in Peter's mind, that he might actually attempt to trace a beneficiary.

Peter mulled over what he'd discovered about Harry Williams. He had no siblings, so who might be close kin? Obviously, none had been identified. Presumably, the longer an estate remained on the list, the less chance that any heirs would be found. Two questions kept coming to mind: how long had Harry's estate been advertised? How much was it worth?

He looked again at the Bona Vacantia website to find out when they stopped publishing the value of estates – December 2007 – what he needed was a record of the website before that date.

Peter remembered that whilst carrying out some investment research, he had once read of a trademark infringement case involving the unauthorised online use of a trademarked image. When the trademark owner complained, the offending website immediately removed any evidence of the mark and pleaded innocence. However, the owner was able to prove the act of 'passing off', by locating previous versions of the offending website. They were stored and recorded on the database of a web-based archive. The earlier archived versions of the website clearly showed the inappropriate use of the disputed trademark.

Peter searched online for such an archive and scanned the results. He selected one of them and arrived at a site, where he entered the domain address of Bona Vacantia into the search box. Within a few seconds, he was looking at list of stored versions of the Bona Vacantia website.

Peter knew that Harry had died in 1996, but had no idea how soon after his death the name had appeared on the list of unclaimed estates. Unfortunately, choices were limited, because the earliest version of Bona Vacantia shown in the archive was that of October 2001. He started there but soon realised that he was not able to see the complete list of unclaimed estates, but rather the weekly additions to it. The archived copies were no more than snapshots. He spent the next twenty minutes, carefully looking at each subsequent version. Sometimes, there were no names beginning with W so he moved on to the following page. At March 2002, Peter felt the hairs on the back of his neck stand up. He'd got lucky. It was the first time that the name of Harry Williams was added to the list and the value of the estate was £67,000!

Peter shut down his computer and went downstairs to talk to Felicity who was preparing dinner.

'You'll never guess what I've discovered.'

'What?'

'Only that Harry Williams – or Henry if you like – the son of the married couple on the marriage certificate—'

'Yes, I know,' she interrupted.

'Well, he died in 1996 and left no will. His estate is listed on Bona Vacantia, you know, that government website, part of the Treasury Solicitor's Department, which lists unclaimed assets.'

'What does Bona Vacantia mean?'

'Oh, it means ownerless goods or something like that.'

'Really? How interesting.'

'Well, there's more. They don't show the value of an estate anymore. I didn't know how much the estate was worth … you following me here?'

'Yes, yes,' she said, at the same time as draining a saucepan of potatoes over the sink.

'Well, I've just played an absolute blinder. I remembered that I once came across a website that archives web pages. They must send out little web bots, or whatever they're called, all over the Net and millions of sites are recorded and stored on their database. Well, I did

185

a quick search and found the site. It actually had some archived copies of the Bona Vacantia website from October 2001 onwards. I started going through them and would you believe it, in March 2002, Harry Williams' name first appears on the list of unclaimed estates. The estate was valued at £67,000. How about that for a piece of detective work?'

'Very impressive, but, so what? It doesn't mean you can claim it.'

'No, no of course not, but the point is, it's been there since 2002 – nine years – which means that plenty of heir-hunting firms have probably looked at it and given up. What if the marriage certificate is somehow the key to finding the beneficiaries? What if I could actually find an heir? That would be amazing, wouldn't it?'

'But what would you do if you did find an heir? Ask for a percentage or something? You don't know how to make a claim.'

'I know, but I'm sure I could find out. It can't be that difficult. The thing is, what's weird, is that I don't really know why I bought the certificate in the first place. I mean, what drew me to it? It just seems so amazing, as if fate has given me the opportunity to solve this mystery. I think I've got to at least have a go.'

'So, what are you going to do next?'

'Well, I reckon I ought to try and find out a bit more about Harry Williams. There might have been some mention in the local press at the time of his death. I've had a quick search online, but 1996 is a bit before the modern Internet and I couldn't find any information. It's strange you know, his house was sold in 2001 for £65,000. He must have owned it and the proceeds formed the bulk of his estate. Then it was sold again in 2002 for £165,000. In one year, that's a massive increase.'

'How old was he when he died?' asked Felicity.

'About ninety-five, I think … died at home.'

'Well, maybe he lived there as an old man and the house was run down, needing modernisation or something like that? Had he lived there long?'

'He was living there in 1962 when his mother died there …' Peter considered Felicity's idea. 'You could be right, you know …' His mind was racing and with excitement in his voice, he added, 'that would explain it ... if someone bought the house in need of renovation, did it up and then sold it on quickly for a profit. I bet that's the reason. Either that, or a dodgy estate agent sold it cheaply to a mate, for a share of the profit.'

'You're always so suspicious,' Felicity scolded.

'I think my next move might be to go over to Leyton and see if the nearest reference library keeps any back copies of the local paper. If not, there's bound to be a county archive. Perhaps they might have something. I might be able to find a death notice for his mother from 1962. That might mention siblings or close relatives, although I'm pretty certain that he didn't have any brothers or sisters.'

'How far is Leyton? Where is it exactly?' asked Felicity. Geography wasn't her best subject. Fortunately, she didn't have to teach it at school.

'Well, it's about two hours away, East London, north of the river. We could make a day of it. I can look to see if there's anything there you could do. Maybe there's a retail park. We could have a nice lunch out somewhere. What about one day next week, during half term?'

'Yes OK, but I'd ring up the library first if I were you ... might save a lot of time or a wasted journey.'

'Yes of course I will, but you see where I'm going with this. I'll get onto it first thing tomorrow.'

3.20

The hunt was closing in at Highborn Research and Carol felt that she was now making some real progress. She had identified the birth of the deceased, Harry Williams. He'd been born Henry Williams, on 8 September 1900, not 8 October 1900 as the coroner had said. Now she needed to identify any brothers or sisters, for they or their descendants would be his heirs and entitled to inherit his estate. She knew from the 1911 Census that he was an only child, but what about after that date? She checked the birth indexes for the next fifteen years to 1926, when Harry's mother would have been fifty-five. Her search proved negative and Carol was satisfied that Harry was Louisa's only child.

Meanwhile, Fred Howard, one of Highborn's travelling researchers reported on his enquiries in Stephenson Street. He'd managed to speak with a neighbour but there wasn't much to tell Carol. It seemed that Harry had lived at number fifty-nine from the 1940s up until his death in 1996. He hadn't married and had lived with his mother until she died there in 1962. After his retirement, he became extremely reclusive and the house was in an appalling condition at the time of his death. It was sold at auction, bought by a builder who completely stripped and renovated it, before selling it on eighteen months later.

The neighbour, an elderly lady, said that she thought the Williams family had Welsh roots. She vaguely recalled a connection with Kidwelly Castle or Pembroke Castle in South Wales, but wasn't sure.

Carol thought that snippet tallied with the background information from Leyton Council. She added Fred's report to her growing file on the Williams' case. She decided to go back one generation to Harry's parents, to see if they had any brothers or sisters. If she could find any uncles or aunts, their descendants would be rightful heirs and could legally inherit.

She found John Williams and his brother, Frank, living with their parents on the Isle of Wight on the 1891 Census. Frank was fourteen at the time, so she tried to find a marriage for him during a period of fifteen years from 1895 to 1910, the years when he would have been most likely to marry. There were nearly two hundred possible matches, far too many for her purpose, so she considered another tack. It was a long shot, but breaks in research often came from just such an idea.

Looking again at the marriage certificate of Harold Williams' parents, Carol noted the names of the witnesses. Frank was one of them and likely to have been best man too. The other witness's surname looked like Price, Rosetta Price. Carol quickly identified her on the 1901 Census. She was aged twenty-nine, living above a draper's shop in Islington. She was single and a draper's assistant.

Carol decided to look for a marriage for Rosetta Price during the following ten years. It was a gamble, but what if Rosetta had met and married the best man at the wedding? It had happened to one of Carol's friends the year before, so why not in 1900? People travelled little and tended to have a smaller circle of acquaintances and less opportunity to meet a potential spouse.

Carol noticed from the census that Rosetta Price had been born in Llanelly. She knew Llanelly was in South Wales. *Could that be the Welsh connection?* she thought. Searching through the marriage index, she found a Rosetta Price marrying in Llanelly in the last quarter of 1903. She studied the results of her query and clicked on the link to see all of the names on the relevant page of the Llanelly marriage register. There were eight names: four female and four male, making four married couples. Carol scanned the four male names. She knew that one of them would be Rosetta Price's spouse, but which one? One in particular – Francis Williams – jumped out at her. *Got you!* she thought. Carol was satisfied. Rosetta Price married the best man Frank Williams in her hometown of Llanelly in 1903. She ordered the certificate immediately.

3.21

Peter and Felicity arranged to go to Leyton on Wednesday of the following week, during Felicity's half-term holiday. They left at about nine. The early morning fog had cleared and the day promised to be cold and bright. They found the motorway traffic was relatively light after the morning rush hour and made good time. Even the notorious M25 was running smoothly and two and a half hours later, they were pulling into a large retail park on the outskirts of Leyton.

Peter dropped off Felicity, leaving her to enjoy some shopping for an hour or so, while he went to have a look at Apsley Street and Stephenson Street. He wanted to get a first-hand feel for the area. He arranged to pick up Felicity later for lunch.

He had previously looked up the postcodes for both addresses and entered them into the car's navigation system. The car was a BMW coupe, powerful and comfortable, not the sort of car he liked to just leave anywhere, but he had checked out the areas online beforehand. He felt reasonably sure that the car would be safe, if he needed to leave it unattended for a while. Otherwise, he would have driven their other car: a scruffy little hatchback.

Peter found Apsley Street within ten minutes and started to search for number fifteen. Apsley Street had a gentle slope to it, the upper part being furthest from Leyton town centre. He noticed straight away that the houses were grand Victorian constructions. It looked as if many had undergone conversion into flats, but there were a few which had escaped the developers' attentions and remained as large, substantial family homes. He drew up outside number fifteen – the home of Thomas Crockford in 1901 – and pulled in to the kerb. There were parking restrictions and he did not have a residents' permit, so he left the engine running while he surveyed the scene, keeping one eye out for parking wardens.

He could see a call panel just to the right of the front door of number 15. It had four buttons, which indicated that the imposing house had probably been subdivided into four flats. It did seem rather on the large side for a widower with a married daughter. Then Peter remembered that there was a son too, David. He'd brought along the printout of the relevant page of the 1901 Census and he looked down to check. No son was listed, so he realised that he must have been thinking of the 1891 Census, when they all lived above the shop. In 1901, Mr Crockford did live alone at number 15, because his daughter had married and moved further down the street to number 46. The single occupant of number 15 was in marked contrast to the adjacent properties. The census record showed a couple with six children and a servant living on one side, and a doctor, his wife, five children and two servants living on the other side.

Peter scribbled a few notes regarding the house. He took his camera from the glove box and opened the car door. He got out and stood on the pavement, looking to see if anyone was around. There wasn't. If there had been, he would have explained his interest. He took a several photographs of the house and of the street as it sloped away towards the town centre. The top end certainly had a view and that must have determined the location of the more expensive and prestigious residences.

Thomas Crockford was doing rather well to live here in 1901, Peter reasoned. He must have been the owner of the house, because he couldn't see why a man on his own would rent a house of this size. He had the shop for accommodation and may have bought the house as an investment or perhaps he intended to remarry. Peter could only speculate.

Next, he decided to locate number 46, the home of John and Louisa Williams after they married in 1900. It was obviously towards the lower end. He got back in and pulled away, cruising gently towards the bottom of the street. He was right and again he was lucky to find a parking space to pull in to. Most people, along with their cars, were at work at this time of day so there were plenty of spaces. He stopped directly outside number 46.

It was part of a terrace of five similar houses and the Williams' house was in the middle. It was much smaller and much closer to the road than those at the top of the street. It had a waist-high brick wall fronting the pavement, with a small wooden gate leading just a few yards to the front door. The downstairs front room had a bay window, just as in the agent's photograph he'd seen on the property website. Some of the neighbours had extended into the roof to create more space, but the former Williams' house appeared unaltered.

On the whole, the house looked to be in quite good order. It had retained its original cast iron gutters, sash windows, and part-glazed wooden front door. In the brickwork between two first floor windows, Peter noticed a stone. It read 'BHD 1898'. Most likely the initials of the builder and date of construction, he thought, and that explained why he hadn't been able to find Apsley Street on the 1891 Census.

Once again, he got out of his car and took some photographs. No one challenged him, but he couldn't help feeling a little furtive, even though his motives were completely innocent. It was that camera-induced guilt thing again, but this time he was holding the camera rather than being watched by one. *Well, bizarre or what?* he thought, using a phrase his teenage nephews and nieces would recognise.

He tried to picture the scene back in 1901. The street would have looked quite different, notably the absence of cars, parking restriction lines on the road and traffic signs. Instead, he could imagine a black and white photograph, showing a daytime scene of a horse drawing a carriage, gas lamps, and a few pedestrians on the pavement, with perhaps children playing in the middle of the road.

Once back in the car, he selected the Stephenson Street address on the satnav and set off again. Five minutes later, he was directed into a cul-de-sac and told that he was arriving at his destination.

Stephenson Street was different to how he'd imagined it. He thought it would look very similar to the railway village in Swindon. That was built by the Great Western Railway to house its workers, but he could see that Stephenson Street was probably built much later in the 1920s. The houses were terraced, but they had private front gardens and possibly rear gardens as well. He drove slowly down towards the end counting the odd numbers. They were on the left. He stopped outside what should have been number 59, but there was no number on the door, just the name *Milton*. It was at the end of a terrace and had a garden at the side too. *Of course*, he realised – *that's why it was described on the property website as semi-detached.*

Peter parked and again noted the parking restrictions. This time however, the sign allowed him thirty minutes. He switched off the engine and got out, taking the camera and his leather jacket. It had turned even colder and he zipped up his jacket, tucking a scarf around his neck. Number 59, or *Milton*, was almost at the end of the cul-de-sac. Immediately in front of the car, the road opened out into a 'bulb' shape, to allow a U-turn. Here the houses fanned out in a radial pattern with front gardens, which grew in width as they went back towards the front of the houses. Most of them looked tidy; just one house let the side down. Children's bicycles were strewn on the mud in front of the porch and an old van took up much of the front garden. The van's tyres were flat and it obviously hadn't been driven for some time.

Peter took some photographs of *Milton* and the street. He was reviewing them to check their quality, when an old man walked up to him.

'Got your number I 'ave; written it down and everything.'

Peter noticed the strong cockney accent. 'What do you mean?' he asked politely.

'Your car's registration number, and the make, and the colour. I'm in Neighbour'ood Watch, you see. They asks us to take note of strangers and anything unusual going on, you see.'

'Oh right, Neighbourhood Watch. I'm in that as well, in our village.'

The old man seemed a little deflated. He'd obviously hoped for a more confrontational reaction. Still, not to be deterred, he was straight back with, 'Not one of those DHS snoopers are you, checking up on those claiming benefit, like?'

'No, no, nothing like that. I'm doing some family history research. I'm interested in number 59, where someone called Harry Williams used to live, until about 1996. This one here, called *Milton*, was it number 59?'

'What, you mean like that television programme – where do you think you came from?'

'Well, sort of, but not quite the same,' answered Peter.

'You're not the first you know, what's come snooping round 'ere asking about Mr Williams what died in number 59. Mind, it 'as been a while. Early on, we 'ad several asking and such like.'

'Did you now? So how long ago would the last one have been?'

'Well, it must 'ave been seven or eight years, but funnily enough I tell a lie, there was a bloke 'ere last week.'

193

'Last week! Really?'

'Yeah, I didn't see 'im, because I was in town at the time. I always goes into town on Thursday mornings, but Mrs 'iggins at number 56, she challenged 'im and then she let me 'ave the details for my report. All this street is my watch you see,' he said proudly. 'I send anything of interest up to my local coordinator, you see.'

'And what did Mrs Higgins say?'

'Only that 'e was asking about old Mr Williams and said 'e worked for some London firm who was trying to trace any relatives. She told 'im they all gave up years ago because there weren't none.'

'I don't suppose he told her which firm he worked for?'

The old man paused and thought for a moment. 'Something like High Holborn Research I think.' He pronounced the name of the firm slowly with great emphasis the letter 'h'. 'Like I say, some London firm.'

'Have you lived around here for long? Did you know Mr Williams?'

'Yeah, I remember 'im, but I was a lot younger then and I knew 'im a long time before 'e died too. He kept 'imself to 'imself later on, you see, never went out, 'ardly.'

'Was Mr Williams married, or a widower perhaps?'

'Nah, 'e was never married ... 'e lived with his mother most of 'is life ... sort of looked after each other, really. She was a widow.'

'What happened to his father?'

'No idea, must 'ave died a long time ago.'

'Did Harry have any brothers or sisters?'

'Nah, can't 'ave done. No one never found any. I'm pretty sure 'e was an only child.'

'Your information could be really helpful to me. I don't work for anyone or do this professionally ... it's just a hobby really, but if you could spare me a few minutes, to tell me a bit more, I'd be more than happy to give you a drink, if you follow.'

'Yeah, OK. Can we sit in your car? Ain't never been in one of these.'

'Of course, no problem,' Peter said, as he opened the door and

194

invited the old man to take the front passenger seat. Peter came back around to the driver's side and sat beside him. The interior of the car was still warm and cosy despite the cold.

'So what was he like then, Harry Williams?'

'Normally 'e was OK ... was a senior patternmaker at the works ... a foreman when 'e retired.'

'Would that be the Falcon Foundry works?'

'Yeah, that's right. Harry was OK and then 'e 'ad this accident at work and lost some fingers off 'is hand. 'e couldn't carry on after that and Harry 'ad to retire early.'

Peter kept his amusement to himself at the effort made to pronounce the 'h' of Harry.

'Course, 'is mother 'ad died a few months before. They said 'e took his mother's death bad and 'ad a problem concentrating, you see. Maybe that caused 'is accident, but I don't know for sure. I mean, I worked at the foundry, but I was in the copper shop, so I never knew what 'appened directly.' The old man wriggled and settled down in the comfortable leather seat. 'Thing is, after 'e retired and what with his mother dying and such, 'e went right peculiar ... stopped going out ... never spoke to no one. Harry kept 'imself to 'imself ... very private 'e was. You should 'ave seen the state of this place when 'e died,' he said pointing towards *Milton*. 'Just let it go 'e 'ad, even though 'e'd bought it like, when 'e first became foreman. But 'e 'ad more money then I suppose, but when 'e retired, 'e just didn't want to spend on anything.'

Peter digested the information he'd just been given. So, Harry's accident in which he lost three fingers definitely had occurred at work.

'Were you around here when he died?'

'Yeah, we'd been moved in 'ere about eighteen months I think. I'd just retired myself, that was in 1995. I'm nearly eighty-one now you know ... 'adn't seen him mind. I'd been over a couple of times to see if 'e was OK, because Mrs 'iggins had told me who lived there, and I remembered 'im like, but 'e wouldn't answer the door. Mind you, even if 'e 'ad seen me, I doubt 'e would have recognised me, because it would 'ave been about thirty years since 'e'd last seen me, 1963 I should think ...'e left not too long after we finished building the *Cambria*, the very last steam locomotive we did at the Falcon. After that, it was all diesels and they weren't 'alf so interesting.'

Peter interrupted at this point, because he could see the conversation heading towards the merits of steam versus diesel. He hadn't much time left, either for parking or before he had to meet Felicity, but the information he'd gleaned so far was really useful. 'When you say he never went out or talked to anyone, would you say he was a sort of recluse?'

'Recluse, that's the word. Never wanted nothing to do with no one, apart from 'is milkman and the man at the corner shop. Used to go up there late for 'is shopping, just before closing. Never talked to no one. Proper recluse 'e was ... the 'ouse was in a shocking state too. The local paper 'ad a field day ... tried to blame the social services and us neighbours. They reckon 'e'd been dead three weeks before they found 'im like, but 'e just wouldn't let nobody 'elp 'im ... preferred to be left alone. It's strange you know, because before 'e retired 'e was quite sociable like ... used to run the bingo at the works social club. Collected ever such a lot for the lifeboats, but after 'e retired, like I say, 'e just went all recluse like.'

'I see the house is now called *Milton*, but back in 1996 it was called *Cambria* wasn't it?'

'That's right, it was. 'e named it after the steam engine we built. Suppose being the last one, 'e wanted to remember it by something. When they sold the 'ouse and the new owners moved in, they changed the name and everything. Don't blame them mind, after what 'ad gone on there ... 'e'd been dead three weeks. They reckon the smell was awful.'

'When you say "they sold it", who sold it?'

'The council, I think. It was in a right old state. They boarded it up straight after, like, but the vandals and druggies got in there. So the council did that compulsive purchase, you know, where they take it over and sell it, at an auction, I think. The council buried him too, because there was no one to pay for the funeral. Anyway, Bill Ward bought it ...'e's a builder and did it all up. Stripped it right back to bare brick and started again. When it was finished you wouldn't 'ave thought it was the same place and the new family what moved in after changed the name to *Milton*.'

'Look, that's really helpful. I could chat all day but I need to meet my wife,' Peter said, as he fumbled in his jacket for his wallet. He found it and took out a five-pound note, which he pressed into the old man's hand. 'Thank you very much,' Peter said. 'You've been very helpful.'

'That's all right, was no trouble.'

Peter jumped out and went round to the passenger side to open the door for him. The old man got out stiffly. 'Lovely car mister,' he said. 'Thanks for the drink.'

'That's OK, you treat yourself.'

'Yeah, reckon I will. Cheerio.'

'Cheerio,' said Peter climbing back into the car. He started the engine, turned around and headed off for his lunchtime rendezvous and only five minutes late! Still, Felicity would understand, especially when he gave her the details of the conversation he had just had.

3.22

Carol was desperate to open the envelope containing the certificate of the marriage of Francis Williams to Rosetta Price when it arrived on her desk, but her excitement was short-lived. The bride was correct, but the Francis Williams she married was aged forty and not the son of Arthur Williams, hotel keeper. He was the wrong Frank Williams. She was bitterly disappointed. 'Williams', she knew, was a very common name in South Wales. It was just an unfortunate coincidence.

She tried to imagine where Frank might have gone after the wedding in 1900. She couldn't find him on the 1901 Census, or on that of 1911. He could have been anywhere, home or abroad, she thought.

She didn't know his occupation. Perhaps, he never married? She really had so little to go on.

She decided to change tack. She knew from the marriage certificate of John and Louisa that Frank's father was Arthur Williams. What if she looked for his death and then tried to find a will? Again, it was something of a long shot, but wills often listed family members as beneficiaries. If Frank was listed on his father's will, then that might give her some clues.

She searched for Arthur's death and located it in Ventnor during the fourth quarter of 1905. Then she checked the probate calendars and found what she was looking for. The entry said: *Williams – Arthur. Cascade View Hotel, Marine Parade, Ventnor IOW. Died 14th December 1905 at Memorial Hospital, Cowes, IOW. Probate, Winchester, to Florence Williams, widow. Effects £327.*

Carol asked Tom Furniss to pick up a copy of the will on his next visit to the Probate Office.

She turned her attention to the Crockford family. Did Louisa have any brothers or sisters? The 1891 Census showed that she had a brother David, aged fifteen. She looked for a marriage of David Crockford from 1896 to 1914, but drew a blank. Neither could she identify him on the 1901 nor the 1911 Census Returns. She checked to see if he had died between 1896 and 1911, but again drew a blank. What could have happened to him? She then tried looking for the death of his father, Thomas Crockford, thinking David might be named in his will, but found nothing.

She started to get the feeling that this case might be unsolvable, but she had no intention of giving up, not unless she was instructed by Nick to drop it. So far, she felt that for every two steps forward, she met an obstacle, which pushed her one step back. That was obviously the reason the case had remained unsolved and listed on Bona Vacantia for the last nine years. Still, she consoled herself with the thought that if and when she did crack this case, the satisfaction would be all the greater.

Carol took a break and went to get some coffee. She sat back in her chair, sipping slowly from her cup and wondered what to do next.

She had an idea. As she had been unable to find a marriage or death for David Crockford, then perhaps he'd gone abroad, either for work or to live permanently. She decided to have a look at passenger lists for ships leaving British ports from 1890 to 1910. This time she was in luck. She found an entry for a David Crockford, listed as a passenger on the *SS Manitoba*, which sailed from London, bound for New York on 15 August 1894.

If this was the same David Crockford, brother of Louisa, then he would have been eighteen at the time, Carol surmised. What was even more interesting was the name of the passenger listed directly above his on the manifest. The name was Frederick Crockford, occupation 'Doctor'. Surely, it couldn't be a coincidence. There had to be a family relationship, between Frederick and David Crockford. Her imagination went into overdrive as she considered the implications.

3.23

Felicity was waiting at the kerb where Peter had dropped her off earlier. She was overloaded with bags; she'd obviously had a successful time. He pulled up and released the luggage compartment so that she could put the shopping out of the way. He got out to help her.

'You're late,' she said. 'I was just about to ring and see where you were.'

'I know, I know … sorry, but wait until you hear what happened.'

'OK, but are we going to have something to eat?'

'Yes, of course. I noticed a trendy restaurant on the way into here. It looked as if it might be OK.'

'That sounds fine and you need to eat. You've had nothing since breakfast.'

Peter drove the short distance to the restaurant and he chose a spot to park, where he could keep an eye on the car while they ate. They were shown to a table and quickly ordered. Felicity started to tell him about the bargains she'd found and how much she'd saved. He listened patiently and waited until she'd finished.

'Right, you'll never guess what I've managed to confirm and find out.'

'Go on.'

'Well, Harry Williams did have an accident at work. Remember he had to retire early because he lost three fingers?'

'Yes, but who told you this?'

'An old boy – one of the neighbours. He came out to challenge me when I was taking some photos of the house in Stephenson Street. He said he was in Neighbourhood Watch and that he'd written down the number plate. Anyway, we got talking. I told him that I was researching family history and asked him about Harry Williams. He knew him when he worked with him at the foundry, about fifty years ago.'

'Fifty years ago! However old was he?'

'Well, he said he was nearly eighty-one. He remembered when Harry retired. He confirmed that Harry was foreman patternmaker. He was definite that Harry never married, nor had any brothers or sisters. He said that he lived with his mother, that she was a widow, and that they looked after each other. He reckoned that Harry bought the house when he became foreman patternmaker, but I never thought to ask when that was. I also forgot to ask how long he thought Harry had lived there – damn! He told me ... and this is most interesting ... after Harry retired, and having lost his mother a few months before, he just shut himself off from everybody and became a recluse. Apparently, the house was in a shocking state when he passed away. Before that, he used to be quite sociable; ran bingo evenings at the works' social club, apparently, and raised lots of money for the Lifeboat Charity.'

Felicity started to say something, but Peter stopped her gently. 'There's more too. It seems that when he died, his body wasn't discovered for three weeks. The house was boarded up afterwards, but vandals got in there. So the council took it over and sold it under a

200

compulsory purchase order, or a "compulsive" order, as he described it!'

'What? ... and you found out all of this from talking to just one old man?'

'Yes, and there's even more!' Peter replied excitedly. 'He said that some chap, an heir hunter I suppose, was in the area the other week asking questions about Harry Williams. He spoke to Mrs Higgins, one of the other neighbours and told her that he worked for a company based in London, called High Holborn Research or something like that. The old man wasn't absolutely sure of the name.'

'How come this busybody didn't see the man?'

'Ah, well, it was a Thursday morning and he always goes into town on Thursday mornings.' They both laughed.

'Holborn Research? Have you heard of it?' asked Felicity.

'No, but I could try looking them up when we get back.'

The waitress arrived with their meals. As they tucked in, Peter went on to tell Felicity that apparently the local paper had made a lot of the story at the time, because Harry's body had lain in the house for three weeks. 'The paper blamed the social services and the neighbours for not caring about him. That means it should be worth trying to get hold of a copy, to see if I can dig up any other information about him. I'll try the local reference library this afternoon. You're quite happy to do some more shopping, aren't you?'

'Yes, of course I am, but get on with your food before it gets cold and don't talk any more about festering bodies, at least not until we've finished eating!'

3.24

Whenever her other work priorities allowed, Carol continued to work on the Williams' case. She had given up temporarily on Harry's uncle, Frank Williams, while she was waiting for the will of Arthur

Williams. For the moment, she had switched her efforts to Harry's mother's side of the family, specifically his uncle, David Crockford.

She knew that David Crockford had left London, bound for New York, in 1894. She was certain that he was accompanied by a relative, Doctor Frederick Crockford, but how was he related?

Carol searched the 1861 Census to see if she could find Frederick Crockford. She found him, living in Leyton in the same household as Thomas Crockford. Frederick was eight at the time and his brother Thomas was thirteen. Their father was a draper and everything fitted in nicely. Frederick therefore had to be David Crockford's uncle.

Unfortunately, for Carol, the fact that David Crockford had gone to the United States in 1894 opened up a whole new catalogue of questions. In order to answer them, she was going to need some assistance from one of Highborn Research's associates, based in the USA. First and foremost, she needed to find out if David had fathered any children. He would of course be dead by now, but any child of his would be Harry's first cousin, and any grandchild of David would be a first cousin, once removed. In English inheritance law, if there were no living first cousins, then first cousins once removed could inherit.

The following day, Tom Furniss placed an envelope on her desk. He knew she'd been waiting very patiently for it.

'There you are. Don't say I never do you any favours. Just got back from the Probate Office. I think that's the will you wanted, for Arthur Williams.'

'Oh, thanks Tom. I didn't think you'd be there until tomorrow.'

'Nor did I. Friday's my normal day down there, but there's a flap on – one of the cases on the Treasury List this morning. So, there you are, what service, a day early!'

Carol pulled out the three pages from the envelope. The first page was a copy of the grant of probate to Arthur's widow, Florence. The other two pages were of the will itself. It was brief and straightforward. Florence was appointed as executor. Arthur left everything to Florence apart from three specific bequests. To his son John, he left his gold pocket watch. To his nephew, George Morris, he left his silver cigarette case. In memory of his deceased son, Frank, he wished that a memorial plaque be erected to show Frank's name and those of his comrades from the Isle of Wight who fell in the South African War 1900–1902. The will set aside a sum of fifty pounds to cover the cost of providing it.

No wonder I couldn't find Frank on the 1901 or 1911 Census returns, Carol thought. *He was killed in the Boer War.* The will made no mention of Frank having a wife or children, but Carol needed to find out a little more about Frank and any children he may have had before she could eliminate him completely. She was able to check a database of British casualties of the Boer War. She entered his name into the search box and soon found the information she needed. Frank Williams died 5 October 1900, at Bloemfontein. He was a soldier in the City of London Imperial Volunteers.

Carol had never heard of the City of London Imperial Volunteers, but it was not something she needed to know. What she did need to confirm was whether Frank Williams had made a will and named a wife or child. She wrote down the details of the date of death and made her way over to Tom Furniss' desk.

'T-o-o-o-o-m,' she said in a husky, laboured voice. Playing on her sexuality a little always turned Tom into a sucker for the helpless female. 'Will you be going to the Probate Office again tomorrow?'

'Should be, that's the plan.'

'Well, could you see if you can find another will for me?' she asked in a sort of pleading, *I'll-make-it-worth-your-while* voice.

Tom didn't take much persuading and it was always flattering to have a pretty girl like Carol asking for a favour. 'Oh, go on then,' he said, 'give me the details.'

Carol passed a piece of paper to him with everything he needed to know. As she returned to her desk, she pondered the possible outcomes any will might reveal. She'd established that Frank Williams, Harry's uncle, was killed in 1900. She calculated that Frank's death must have occurred about nine months after Louisa and John's wedding, where he was probably best man. Carol thought it sad. If Frank did leave a will and mentioned neither wife nor children, then Carol could assume that he was a bachelor. Should that be the

203

case, Carol would be able to cross off Frank as providing a blood relative to Harry Williams. His line would be a 'dead stem'. That would clear the way for her to concentrate on David Crockford's line, as potential heirs to the Harry Williams' estate.

Tom Furniss approached her desk after lunch the following day. From his expression, she could see that he hadn't found what she wanted.

'No luck then?' she queried, despondently.

'No, sorry.' He watched her face fall and then with a flourish, pulled an envelope from his inside pocket.

'What? ... That's it? You found it after all!'

He grinned and winked as he passed it to her.

'You bugger!' Carol exclaimed. She stood up and gave Tom a peck on the cheek, grabbing the envelope at the same time. 'Thanks, Tom.'

After he'd gone, she opened it and read the details of the will it contained. It was another very short and simple last will and testament. A London solicitor had drawn it up in November 1899. Carol decided that Frank must have lived in London, and that explained why he was in the City of London Imperial Volunteers.

Reading the will, Frank left everything to his brother, John Williams of 46 Apsley Street. It mentioned some shares and some money deposited at a bank, but nothing more. The will had been proved and probate granted to John in January 1901. No wife or child was mentioned, so it was reasonable to assume that Frank was a bachelor. She'd now obtained what she needed to confirm that fact.

Her attention again turned to David Crockford. She checked incoming and outgoing passenger lists to see if he had returned from America after 1911, but found no match. She then double-checked the English and Welsh marriages and again drew a blank. She was pretty sure that David had settled in the United States.

One name she did notice when she searched the passenger lists was that of a Thomas Crockford going out to New York in 1917. She was certain it was David's father, as his age matched. She felt even more certain that David had stayed in the United States and had been joined there later by his father.

She brought up the 1930 United States Census on her computer and searched for David Crockford. She found him living in New York, married to Doris. They had a son, Michael, aged ten. She'd expected to find that David had got married in the States and the U.S. Census confirmed it.

She needed to bring Nick up to date, so she buzzed him in his office.

'Come straight up,' he said.

Carol quickly explained where she'd got to.

'Well done. I'm impressed. Now, we'll need to get on to our stateside associates Purdie-Gressl. Get a copy of the file prepared. I'll give John Gressl a ring, before we email the stuff over.'

'Is there no way I can continue from here?'

'Sorry, Carol, but they're best placed now for this one. That's heir hunting for you. Sometimes it takes us across international boundaries.'

When Carol had gone, Nick leaned back in his chair. It was a little disappointing that the trail had gone abroad. It meant sharing some of Highborn's commission with Purdie-Gressl, but the two companies regularly worked for each other. Purdie-Gressl would trace any heirs of David Crockford in the United States, or Canada, and sign them up on Highborn's contract, before returning the paperwork to Highborn for onward submission to the Treasury Solicitor.

3.25

After lunch with his wife, Peter made his way to Leyton's local library. He was directed to the local history section and was delighted to learn that the library had physical copies of the Leyton Chronicle for July 1996.

He recalled from Harry Williams' death certificate that Harry had died on or about 1 July, but his death had not been registered until three weeks later. Having spoken to the old man in Stephenson Street,

Peter assumed that Harry's death was a big local story and when he looked at the front page of the edition for the 19 July 1996, his assumption proved to be correct.

'Man's Decomposing Body Found in House' proclaimed the headline. The story was placed alongside a photograph of 59 Stephenson Street, looking extremely untidy and dilapidated. Peter scanned the details:

The partially decomposed body of 95-year-old bachelor, Harry Williams, was found yesterday at his home in Falcon Village. The alarm was raised by local milkman, Barry Purton, who asked a neighbour to phone the police. Two constables forced entry and discovered the body of Mr Williams in the rear sitting room. He appeared to have been dead for some time. The house in Stephenson Street has been sealed off, pending investigations, although the police stated that foul play was not suspected. It is understood that Mr Williams may have been dead for several weeks. Neighbours were said to be shocked.

Enquiries by the Chronicle have revealed that Mr Williams was a very private man, who kept himself to himself. He was a late-night customer at the local corner shop and was seldom seen out during the daytime. Some neighbours had never seen him and one said he was known as a recluse. Another neighbour even assumed the house was unoccupied.

Little is known about Mr Williams. He retired from the Falcon Foundry in the 1960s. It appears that he wasn't married and was not thought to have any relatives in the area. One neighbour told the Chronicle that she had always believed his family's roots were in Kidwelly in South Wales. Another confirmed that there was a connection with South Wales.

A post-mortem has been ordered by the coroner, although it is thought unlikely that an inquest will be required. Police are continuing their enquiries and attempts to trace relatives.

Peter went on to read the remainder of the report. Various neighbours were quoted on what they knew or recalled of Harry Williams, which was very little. The report finished by criticising the social services for abandoning Mr Williams and raised the question of how such a sad and lonely death could have occurred.

Peter brought Felicity up to date on the journey home. 'You were absolutely right about Harry's house being in a dreadful state. There was a photo of it from 1996. It looked awful, totally different to what I saw this morning. The old man told me that a builder had bought it and had renovated it. He did an amazing job, which would explain the big increase in value when it was resold in 2001. Apparently, the milkman alerted the police. The paper said that the police were trying to trace relatives. The neighbours thought that Harry's family came from Kidwelly in South Wales, but that's a complete red herring.'

'What do you mean by that?'

'Because in 1900, John Williams was on a crew list, as chief engineer of the RMS *Kidwelly Castle*. That's where the Kidwelly link comes from. The neighbours must have got their facts confused, which sent the police and any previous heir hunters on a wild goose chase to research the thousands of Williams' in South Wales! Obviously they got nowhere and the local council had to sort out his cremation.'

'So if the police couldn't find the right Williams family, how do *you* expect to get any further?'

'I'm not sure, but I'm not ready to quit yet. I know from the 1891 Census that John Williams came from the Isle of Wight. What is worrying me though is why a London firm should send someone round to Stephenson Street now, trying to trace relatives? I need to find out who they are.'

As soon as they got home, Peter went upstairs to his computer, while Felicity started to prepare a meal. He quickly identified which company the investigator in Stephenson Street worked for. It was Highborn Research, not High Holborn Research. Highborn were based in central London and were well established in the field of tracing heirs to unclaimed wills. He was a little daunted when he read about them on their website. They were big professional players. By taking them on, he as an amateur with limited experience and resources was pitting himself against one of the heavyweights of the industry.

Perhaps, he should just drop the whole thing, Peter thought. Obviously, he would have no chance in a race to find an heir against the likes of Highborn Research, but they didn't know that they had competition from him on the case; even if he was small fry. What puzzled him though was why they were investigating now? The estate had been listed as unclaimed since 2002 and no heir had been found. Had they obtained a new lead or was it just coincidence?

Peter toyed with the idea of abandoning it, but something nagged at him to continue. *Happenstance*, he mused. *Isn't that what they call it? That chance occurrence, when either through luck, fate or whatever, things come together.* What made him, an amateur genealogist, spot the marriage certificate in the first place? Furthermore, what subconscious force or motivation prompted him to buy it? He couldn't really explain it, other than the idea that it might be interesting to do some research on the certificate. *Look where it has taken me so far*, he thought excitedly, *to an unclaimed estate; to a mystery.*

Surely, he must continue, he reasoned. Something was pulling him along and he wasn't going to let go until it released him. He would carry on, but with the proviso of checking the Treasury Solicitor's list regularly. If Harry Williams' name disappeared from it, Peter would give up.

An alarm bell rang throughout *HMS Kidwelly Castle* calling the crew to action stations. The ship was on patrol off the West African coast, south of Cape Verde. Her orders were to intercept enemy shipping and keep an eye out for the German warship named *Karlsruhe*.

Light was fading and a sailing ship had been sighted. *HMS Kidwelly Castle* was gaining quickly, speed set to full ahead. There was just enough time before dark to close with the unknown vessel and board her if necessary.

The vessel turned out to be German: a three-masted barque with a crew of fifteen. She hove to without a fight, for she was no match for the *Kidwelly Castle*. She was boarded and the enemy vessel was taken as a prize. She was carrying three hundred tons of coal, along with stores and equipment. Although her master remained silent, there was little doubt that her cargo was intended for the *Karlsruhe*.

Escorted by the *Kidwelly Castle*, the captured vessel and crew were taken to Freetown in Sierra Leone to be handed over to the British representative.

During a short stopover there, they received new orders from the Admiralty and they departed for Cape Town with all haste. On the other side of Africa in the Indian Ocean, the Admiralty had learned of a German raider, the *SMS Salzenburg*, causing havoc to British shipping.

She was the guard ship for the German port of Dar es Salaam in German East Africa and had left port on 29 July, just prior to the outbreak of the war. Well-armed and fully fuelled, she had steamed north, sinking a British merchant ship called *City of Canterbury* on 6 August. It took a couple of weeks for the British authorities to learn of the loss. As soon as they did, they mobilised a number of ships to take part in the hunt for the *Salzenburg*. *HMS Kidwelly Castle* was assigned to that force.

She covered the distance to Cape Town in just over nine days. As she entered Table Bay, she exchanged signals with the shore authorities and refuelling and provisioning commenced as soon as she anchored. Again, the stopover was short and the crew had no opportunity to leave the ship. The mail they'd hoped to post at St Helena was taken ashore. John Williams sat on deck in the sunshine, chatting to George Corbett, as the loading derricks swung in nets full of stores and equipment. Meanwhile, a conveyor brought up coal from a barge moored alongside, delivering it directly into the ship's bunkers. Within a few hours, they were ready to return to sea, but on this occasion, the course would be a different one for John Williams. Rather than returning straight to England, this time the ship would first take him eastwards around the Cape of Good Hope, before turning northwards into the Indian Ocean, to join the hunt for the *Salzenburg*.

On 20 September, the German raider appeared off the coast of Zanzibar. Her captain had been tipped off that a Royal Naval vessel was immobile, undergoing boiler repairs. The British ship was soon located and sunk, having fallen easy prey.

News of the attack filtered through to Royal Naval Command. *HMS Kidwelly Castle* was sent to help patrol the Mozambique Channel, a sail of two days. She set course immediately. Meanwhile, the crew continued to carry out practice firing and battle drill. The plan was to rendezvous with two other Royal Navy warships. However, *HMS Kidwelly Castle* was alone when she first sighted the *Salzenburg* on the morning of 22 September. Both vessels spotted each other simultaneously and set themselves on a converging course. Their crews went to action stations.

The German warship was slightly smaller than the *Kidwelly Castle*, but much faster, being capable of twenty-three knots. She was more manoeuvrable too and could make a tighter turn. She had armour-plating and was equipped with a formidable array of heavy armament, as well as two submerged torpedo tubes. She out-gunned the *Kidwelly Castle* by a ratio of four to one.

The ships opened fire on each other as soon as they considered they were in range. Shells howled past the twin funnels of the *Kidwelly Castle*. In the heat of the engine room, the stokers were stripped to the waist. The bridge had called for full speed and they were trying to extract every last drop of power. John Williams monitored the pressure gauges and dials. He shouted orders and encouragement when needed. He was pleased. They had managed to squeeze a little extra power and judging by the revolutions counter, the ship was achieving nearly eighteen knots.

The *Salzenburg* drew first blood, striking the corner of the bridge on the *Kidwelly Castle*. The shell killed a machine gunner instantly. As the distance between the two vessels closed, the *Kidwelly Castle* landed several hits on the German ship, but they glanced harmlessly off her armour plating. The two vessels passed each other at full speed with a gap between them of less than fifty yards, close enough for the crews to see each other clearly. They fired furiously across the narrow stretch of water separating them. Then *HMS Kidwelly's* rear guns came into play. It was her rear gunners' chance to inflict some damage before she was hit again.

It may have been a lucky shot, but one of the *Kidwelly's* shells struck the *Salzenburg* in the stern, just above the rudder. The force of the explosion jammed the rudder hard to one side and immediately made the *Salzenburg* turn to starboard. For *HMS Kidwelly* this was just what the crew had hoped for. If the German ship was disabled, then there was a good chance of finishing her off.

The *Kidwelly's* Captain ordered a turn to port of 180 degrees, but here he made a fatal mistake. He was unaware that the German ship was armed with torpedoes. When the *Salzenburg* had almost completed her involuntary about turn, the German Captain ordered the launching of two torpedoes from her underwater tubes. It was a wild and desperate act. As the *Kidwelly Castle* made her turn, intent upon another attack, she presented herself broadside to the approaching torpedoes. The first one passed her bow, missing by a hair's breadth, but the second one hit *HMS Kidwelly Castle* below the waterline, in the area of the engine room. There was an enormous explosion and those in the engine room stood no chance. She shuddered, came to a standstill and started to list, all power gone and taking in water rapidly. Her Captain gave the order to abandon ship and the crew threw out lifebuoys and lowered two lifeboats.

The ships were stationary about one mile apart. The German crew cheered as they saw the *Kidwelly Castle* heel on to her side. They watched her survivors jump from her upturned hull, in the hope of reaching a lifeboat. Then her stern rose in the air, the White Ensign still plainly visible, and with a hissing of steam and a tremendous blast of air she slid below the surface forever. From the moment of impact by the torpedo, to the last sight of her White Ensign, no more than twelve minutes had elapsed. Of her full complement of twenty-four officers and ratings, ten were lost, presumed drowned. The Captain was amongst the missing, but John's friend, Paymaster George Corbett, survived.

Meanwhile, the German Captain ordered a damage assessment. The rudder was jammed and distorted, but the crew was already cutting part of it away, so that it could swing free. They were confident they could repair the steering mechanism to give some measure of control.

By then, it was midday and the sun was hot. The German sailors worked frantically, fearful that their position made them vulnerable to attack by other British warships. It took them two hours to make a temporary repair. During that time, both lifeboats were rowed across to the *Salzenburg* and the British survivors asked to be rescued. The German captain refused to allow them aboard. He was desperate to get away from the scene, as soon as possible. He ordered his crew to throw down some water canisters and canvass sheeting to the survivors. Leaving them to fend for themselves, he set a westerly course for the African coast, which was about fifty miles away.

As the German ship disappeared over the horizon, those in the lifeboats shared out the water and got beneath the canvas to protect themselves from the sun. Fortunately, early the following morning, the two Royal Navy warships with which *HMS Kidwelly Castle* had been scheduled to rendezvous, spotted the survivors and took them on board.

Part Four

4.1

In genealogical terms, Peter was up against a brick wall. He needed to find some more relatives of Harry Williams. As he hadn't married or had children, aunts or uncles were the key. He took some consolation in the fact that he was unlikely to be the first to research this case. If it had been easy to solve, then it would have been solved by now.

He checked the Bona Vacantia website again and was relieved to see that Harry Williams' name was still there. Highborn hadn't claimed it yet. *Phew,* he sighed. *Now let's review what I know and perhaps I'll get some inspiration.*

From the 1891 Census, he'd discovered that Harry had an Uncle Frank and an Uncle David. He'd already looked for Frank as far forward as 1911 and failed to find him, so he decided to try to find Louisa's brother, David. He got nowhere trying the Census returns. Maybe he went abroad? He hadn't searched passenger lists for Frank Williams, because the name was so common, but 'David Crockford', that was a different matter. Two minutes later he was elated to find someone called David Crockford as a passenger on the *Manitoba* bound for New York from London in 1894.

The entry on the *Manitoba's* passenger list was intriguing. Directly above David's name was the name of another passenger called Frederick Crockford, occupation 'Doctor'. It seemed reasonable to assume that they were related and a quick look at the 1861 Census confirmed that Frederick Crockford was the younger brother of Thomas Crockford. Peter was certain he had found the correct David Crockford. In 1894, Doctor Frederick Crockford would have been forty-one, and his nephew, David, eighteen. They were obviously travelling together.

Peter looked up Frederick Crockford in the British Medical Register of the time, but he was not listed. He may have had an academic doctorate, Peter reasoned, but he was certainly not a physician. Peter also tried the online record of passport applications, but drew blanks for both Frederick and David. Passports were not compulsory until 1914, so the absence of any record was no real surprise.

He then searched several international genealogy websites, in order to find them after they arrived in the United States. He found David Crockford on the 1930 United States Census. He was married with a son. For Peter this was not good news. He had very limited knowledge of how to trace relatives in the United States, but that would not be the case with a probate research firm like Highborn Research. They'd have associates out there. Maybe he didn't have much chance against them. Still, he had some other avenues to research. There was always Frank Williams, who'd disappeared and of course, Peter still hadn't discovered what had happened to John Williams, Harry's father.

Peter knew that in 1911, John was forty-one, yet he was dead by 1962, a gap of fifty-one years. The maximum age he could have reached would have been ninety-two. The neighbourhood watch busybody thought he'd died years ago. The problem was, how long ago was 'years ago'? Peter was reluctant to send off for the death certificates of every 'John Williams' aged between forty and ninety-two, who'd died during those fifty-one years. It was too expensive for one thing. He needed to reduce the odds a little, by looking in the most likely places first.

He could have started with all of the 'Leyton' deaths, but for some unknown reason Peter was drawn to the idea of looking at the records of the Commonwealth and War Graves Commission, otherwise known as the CWGC, to see if John Williams had died during the First World War.

Peter already knew that John was a chief engineer on a ship. In 1914, he would have been about forty-five, which was probably too old for the Royal Navy, but possibly suitable for the Merchant Navy. Peter typed John's full name into the search box on the CWGC website and selected the 'Merchant Navy' option. The search returned about thirty records matching his query. He scanned the list. He noted that by each name, the rank and age was given. One name stood out: 'John Williams, Lieutenant, Mercantile Marine, age 44'. He clicked on it for more details and when they appeared on his screen, Peter had found who he was looking for.

Name: WILLIAMS, John

Initials: J W

Nationality: United Kingdom

Rank: Lieutenant

Regiment/Service: Mercantile Marine Reserve

Unit Text: HMS Kidwelly Castle

Age: 44   **Date of Death:** 22/09/1914

Additional Information: Son of the late Arthur and Florence Williams; husband of Louisa Williams (nee Crockford), of 22 Moses Street, West Ham. Born in Cowes IOW. **Casualty Type:** Commonwealth War Dead

---

So, John Williams had sadly died in World War One, thought Peter, *and there's the name of the ship on which he served, HMS Kidwelly Castle.*

He was puzzled, because John Williams' previous ship was called the *RMS Kidwelly Castle.* Were they the same vessels? He soon found out that they were. In 1914, she was converted from a civilian passenger and mail ship to an armed merchant cruiser, under Royal Naval command. She was sunk off Zanzibar in September 1914, by the German raider, *SMS Salzenburg.*

He read with interest that before she sank, *HMS Kidwelly Castle* inflicted serious damage on the German ship and it wasn't until April the following year, that the *Salzenburg* was finally put out of action. After sinking *HMS Kidwelly Castle,* she limped into a river estuary on the East African coast, where she hid for a number of months, undergoing repair. The Royal Navy eventually found her. They set up a blockade to prevent her escape, while they brought up heavy weaponry to bombard and sink her, but the German Captain scuttled her, rather than have her fall into British hands.

Just then, Peter's phone rang. It was his contact in the antiques trade in Marlborough.

'Hello, Peter. I've got a couple of sovereigns if you're interested. They're nice ones too, in excellent condition.'

'Oh right, Nigel. Thanks for ringing. I'd like to have a look at them. Could you hold them for me, until tomorrow afternoon?'

'Yes, of course.'

'Great, I'll see you tomorrow then … about three o'clock.'

As he drove to Marlborough, Peter came up with an idea. Somehow, the marriage certificate of Harry Williams' parents had found its way to the antiques centre. The newspaper report from the time of Harry's death described his house as dirty and dilapidated, but implied that it was fully furnished and that the contents at the time of his death were intact. It was reasonable to assume that after Harry had died; everything in the house was disposed of, either by the council, or by the builder who bought the house for renovation. Peter couldn't be absolutely certain, but the clearance of Harry's house must have been the starting point, by which the marriage certificate had ended up in the antiques centre.

Maybe the vandals and drug takers who had broken in to the property had helped themselves to some of the contents. That was a possibility, but they probably only took items which they could turn into easy cash. They were unlikely to have been part of the chain along which the marriage certificate had passed.

Peter pictured the interior of the house. Items like marriage certificates were often kept in a box or suitcase and stored out of the way. There might have been other important family documents, photographs, and paperwork as well. What if some of those other items had also found their way to the antiques centre? What if the unit where he'd spotted the marriage certificate, had more family mementoes or records from the same source, from the home of Harry Williams?

Peter realised it was a long shot, but why not? Unit 14, where he'd found the certificate, actually specialised in postcards. Perhaps there was a postcard there, connected with the Williams family? Imagine if there was a postcard from David Crockford in the USA to his sister

Louisa. She might have kept it and stored it away with the marriage certificate. He decided that he would pay another visit to Unit 14 – it had to be worth a try.

His dealer contact was temporarily absent when he looked through the glass window into the interior of the shop on Marlborough high street. It was situated directly opposite the antiques centre and specialised in antique clocks and jewellery. A note was stuck at an angle on the door: *Back in five minutes.* Instead of waiting, Peter crossed the road to the antiques centre and went in.

When he entered, he took in the familiar atmosphere and surroundings. It was only a few weeks since his last visit and the weather was still cold. The place had an aroma of old musty objects and paraffin. The paraffin smell came from various portable heaters scattered throughout the rambling premises. There was no central heating. Peter recognised it as a sixteenth-century, timber-framed building with an uneven ground floor and creaking boards on the first floor. He realised that its conversion to its current use had been fairly basic and rudimentary.

When he approached the postcard unit, Peter found that three other people, avid collectors by the look of them, had taken up most of the space and he was forced to wander around elsewhere, looking at some of the other units to waste a few minutes.

He scanned numerous antiques and items of bric-a-brac on display, not looking at anything in particular, but hoping for an idea that might provide some inspiration or hint at some new path to investigate. He spotted a glass cabinet containing a pair of military medals from the First World War. He would be amazed to come across a medal with a family connection to the Crockford's or the Williams'. He peered at the information card beside the medals and saw the original owner's name. Unsurprisingly, they had nothing to do with his research.

He worked his way back to Unit 14. By then, there was only a middle-aged man still browsing and he could see that he was not looking through the box labelled 'USA'. Now was Peter's chance to have a quick look. It would only take a few minutes.

He carefully grasped half of the postcards from the 'USA' tray – a shoebox in a former life, Peter noted, smiling to himself – and holding about forty cards, he started to go through them methodically. He saw that most were relatively modern, from the fifties and sixties, nothing much before. He put them back and picked up the remaining cards. They came from all over the United States. He turned each one over to see the address and paused several times to read the messages. He thought it nosey, but some were quite interesting. It was surprising, the information that some of the cards included. One or two were very amusing, but none was addressed to Leyton or sent from David or Frederick Crockford. Peter put them all back, feeling a little deflated.

He left the antiques centre and crossed the road to see if the dealer had returned to his shop. He had, and Peter bought the sovereigns. They were both dated 1902. It was the first full year of the reign of Edward VII. Queen Victoria had passed away the year before. The British Empire was at its height. It was also the era, Peter recalled, in which John and Louisa Williams were getting used to married life.

Peter then walked down to the local branch of his bank and deposited the coins in safe custody. He looked at his watch and decided he still had enough time for quick sort through the postcards. Maybe if he browsed the categories, a germ of an idea would come to him.

The man who'd been looking earlier was still there. He seemed to be very focused and was searching intently. He'd already put five or six cards aside. Peter noticed that the boxes containing postcards from the English counties were some way to the right of the man. Peter decided that he could look at those, without interruption or the need to shuffle sideways, to allow anyone else to search beside him.

He spotted the box labelled 'Essex'. It was unlikely that someone living in Essex would receive a card from Essex, but he reasoned there might be a picture of St Martin's Church, Leyton. He grasped a handful and worked his way through them, but again he drew a blank.

He scanned the labels on the other boxes noting the names for each county and saw that the 'Hampshire' box had a sub-section tabbed 'Isle of Wight'. Suddenly, Peter's heart started to beat a little faster. The Williams family came from the Isle of Wight. What if a family member had sent a postcard to John and Louisa in Leyton?

He began to examine the Isle of Wight cards, studying the addresses on the back. He was halfway through them when he stopped and read one address again, this time carefully: *Mr & Mrs J Williams, 46 Apsley Street, Leyton, Essex.* It was postmarked Ventnor I.O.W. 28 July 1902.

The scene on the front was entitled 'Ventnor, Isle Of Wight'. It was a coloured picture of the beach and esplanade. Numerous bathing machines were drawn up in a line along the water's edge, extending towards the pier. Behind the beach, buildings dominated the face and top of the cliff.

The message on the reverse read:

Dearest John and Louisa,
Charlotte and I took Edith and Harold to the beach today. Lovely sunshine. They paddled and made sandcastles. Hope Henry is better now. George and Charlotte send their love.
Love from Rose
X

Peter studied the message. It was to John and Louisa from somebody called Rose. Who was she? Could it be a postcard from Rosetta, the witness named on the marriage certificate? Perhaps, she used the shorter form of her Christian name when writing to her friends? It was a possibility.

He felt a charge of excitement and searched through the remaining Isle of Wight cards. About twenty cards later, he came across another one sent to John and Louisa.

It was postmarked Ventnor I.O.W. 26 June 1902.

The scene showed the front façade of the Cascade View Hotel and the message on the reverse read:

Dearest John and Louisa,

How do you like our new postcards? Just had them printed and you are the first recipients. Saw Rose and children yesterday at Charlotte's. Edith is the image of Frank. C and G adore them. Shame they can't have their own. We've vacancies early next month, if young Henry's up to it. Hope you can get some leave. Send a p/c if you're coming.

Love from

Mother and Father

This is incredible, Peter thought. He could hardly believe his luck. He turned to the man who was still there. 'Excuse me, but do you know much about old postcards? Are you a collector?'

'Yes I am.'

'Do you know when postcards first started?'

'Well, postcards as we know them started in about 1902. By that, I mean cards with a divided back, in other words with two panels, one for the message, and one for the address. Before that, the back of the card was reserved exclusively for the address. If someone wanted to add a message, then they simply wrote it somewhere on the front, either on the picture or perhaps in some blank space at the side, if there was any room.'

'Really? So this one, for example, from the Isle of Wight in 1902 is an early one then?' Peter showed the man the postcard from Ventnor, with the bathing machines drawn up on the beach below the cliff.

'Yes it is, certainly for one with a divided back and you can see that the original picture was black and white. It was then hand tinted to give it some colour.'

'Do you specialise in any particular type of postcard or subject?' Peter asked, with genuine interest.

'I mainly collect postcards with a naval or merchant marine theme.' He showed Peter the ones he intended to buy. They were postcards of ships, several transatlantic liners, and a smaller passenger vessel.

'So, how come these ships were popular subjects for postcards?' asked Peter.

'Ah, well some were complimentary, but most were sold on board to passengers as a souvenir. They liked to send a card home from their ports of call. For some, it was to let family at home know where they were. For others, it was to show off by sending a picture of the ship they were sailing on and boasting of how far they'd travelled.'

As the collector was talking to him, Peter glanced over the man's shoulder and saw on the wall just behind him, a small glass cabinet with several postcards propped up on the shelves. They were obviously the rarer and valuable ones, as the door to the cabinet had a prominent lock. They were all postcards of ships.

'Oh, have you seen those in that cabinet? They're all cards of ships.' Peter pointed behind the man in the direction of cabinet, trying to be helpful.

'Yes I have,' he said, 'but thanks anyway.'

Peter, still looking over the man's shoulder at the postcards in the locked cabinet, noticed two things: first, the ship on one of the cards, the one directly in his line of sight was clearly named and was none other than the *RMS Kidwelly Castle*, John Williams' ship. Second, the same card had a brief message written on the front of it. It was in the white space provided by the impressive bow wave of the vessel. He could just make out the slanting signature at the lower right hand corner, one word: *Frank*.

At that moment, the postcard collector's phone rang. He fumbled in his pocket for it, before putting it to his ear. 'Yes dear, I know … meet you at the car in five minutes.' He turned to Peter, 'Sorry, have to go,' he said, 'my wife's waiting for me.'

'Mustn't let that happen!' Peter replied. 'Thank you for your help.'

As the man left, Peter stepped up to the cabinet. His nose was no more than six inches from the card. It showed the *RMS Kidwelly Castle* on the high seas, smoke and steam billowing from her twin funnels. He was able to read the message clearly:

10th February, 1900. Dear John and Louisa. Setting off for Orange River tomorrow. All in good cheer. Love to you both. Frank.

The postcard had a price label with £15 marked on it, but to Peter the price was irrelevant. His only concern at that moment was to get to the front desk as quickly as possible, so that he could buy the card before somebody else did.

When he got there, he had to wait of course, while the same elderly lady who'd served him a few weeks before, now served the man to whom he'd been chatting. The several minutes she took to carefully wrap and seal his postcards in a familiar brown paper bag, and accept the payment before handing him his change, seemed like an eternity.

Finally, she turned to Peter. He asked as quickly and politely as he could manage in his state of excitement. 'Could somebody bring the key to the locked glass cabinet in Unit 14?'

'Yes, of course. I'll get someone to unlock it for you. Hold on please, while I put out a call.'

Peter groaned inwardly. She went over to a microphone behind her. 'Ahem … could Tracy come to the front desk please? Tracy to the front desk, please.'

She turned to Peter. 'Tracy should be here in a few minutes.'

'Thank you … I'll be waiting for her at the unit.'

He made his way back to the display cabinet, glad to see that no one else was there. He took a deep breath.

Now think, Peter said to himself. *So far, you've found three postcards, which have connections to John and Louisa. Is there anything else here? You must make sure that you haven't missed anything. For all you know, several other cards or certificates with something to do with the Williams family might have already been sold. You've no idea how long they've been on display. It might have been two weeks or two years,* he thought. *Now look carefully for anything that you may have missed.*

Peter stared at the items fixed to the display walls of the unit. He recognised the ration book and the gold embossed luncheon invitation. They were both here last time, he recalled, but there were some new items as well. He tried to search methodically, starting high and working down in imaginary columns. Halfway down the centre column, he saw again the Post Office Telegram, with the message about someone passing away. He wasn't surprised to see it was still there. Who would want to buy something like that? His eyes couldn't help but read what it said, just as he had the previous time. The telegram was postmarked Leyton 9 Oct 02.

TO: Miss Rosetta Ince. 'Brindle Lodge', Beaufort Street, Ventnor, Isle of Wight.
Henry passed away yesterday. Please return Leyton urgently if possible. Louisa.

Peter's heart skipped a beat. What if Rose or Rosetta *was* the same person and her surname was not 'Price' but 'Ince'? What if he had misread her name on the marriage certificate? What if – and this was a huge 'what if' – what if *Henry* was a reference to John and Louisa's son, Henry?

Peter's mind started to run away with more ideas and implications, but he was interrupted.

'Are you the gentleman who wanted to look inside the glass cabinet?'

'Yes – yes, that's me,' Peter almost stuttered, returning to the present. 'That card there please, on the middle shelf. I'd like to look at that one, please.'

The assistant held up a string of about twenty keys, before making a choice. 'I think it's this key.' She tried it without success. 'It must be this one then.'

Fortunately for Peter, who was finding the delay somewhat agonising, it was. She opened the door and handed the postcard to him. He turned it over. The address took up whole of the reverse. It was addressed to: *Mr and Mrs J. Williams, 46 Apsley Street, Leyton, Essex.*

Suddenly things were slotting rather magnificently into place. *Eat your heart out Highborn*, Peter chuckled to himself.

The twenty-minute drive from Marlborough to home seemed like an eternity for Peter Sefton. His mind was whirling and he found he needed to make a real effort to concentrate on driving. Was Rose actually Rosetta? Was her surname Ince and not Price? What was Frank doing in South Africa? What was that about setting off for Orange River, 'all in good cheer'? Then of course, the big one … the telegram to Rosetta with news of Henry's death!

He roared into the driveway and parked near to the house – no time today to put the car away in the garage. Felicity had just arrived home from school. She started to say something to him as he came in the front door, but he shot upstairs to switch on his computer, racing back down again to kiss her and say hello.

'What's going on?' Felicity asked. 'What's the excitement? Have you got some shares you need to trade?'

'No, nothing like that. I've just come back from Marlborough. I've got some postcards and a telegram, would you believe, from that postcard unit. They're all connected with Harry Williams. It's amazing, incredible! I haven't got time to put the kettle on for you today. Can you do it? This is really urgent. I need to look up some things,' he shouted, already on his way back upstairs.

'Ooh, I suppose so. Service isn't very good around here!'

Peter sat in front of his computer and looked up the 1901 Census. He searched on the name of Rosetta Ince. He clicked on the result associated with an address on the Isle of Wight.

1901 Census Return

ADDRESS	NAME	RELATION	AGE	OCCUPATION	WHERE BORN
Brindle Lodge, Beaufort Street Ventnor IOW	George Morris	Head	37	Banker	Cowes, IOW
	Charlotte Morris	Wife	36		Cowes, IOW
	Rosetta Ince	Single	26	Lodger	Paddington
	Harold Ince	Lodger's son	5 mths		Ventnor
	Edith Ince	Lodger's daughter	5 mths		Ventnor
	Martha Edwards	Widow	56	Housekeeper	Lymington
	Emma Gilchrist	Single	18	Housemaid	Ventnor

Was this really the same Rosetta who was a witness at the wedding? Peter wondered. She had to be, especially if the 'Henry' mentioned in the telegram was Louisa's son. The census return showed Rosetta to be a 'Lodger', but additionally it revealed some startling information. Rosetta Ince was single and the mother of 5-month-old twins!

There were so many questions in Peter's head. Who were George and Charlotte Morris? Why were Rosetta and her children lodging in their house? Peter picked up the postcard sent to Leyton at the end of July 1902 and studied the message again.

'Rose' is a familiar form of 'Rosetta', he thought. The card is undoubtedly from Rosetta Ince, especially as it mentions Charlotte and refers to the children Edith and Harry. Peter looked again at the earlier postcard sent in June 1902 from the Cascade View Hotel.

Peter assumed that 'C and G' must be an abbreviation for Charlotte and George. The sender, presumably Florence Williams, John's mother, also referred to C and G's inability to have children. Florence must be related to them and obviously, Louisa was aware of their problem. It was hardly something one discussed with a casual acquaintance, outside of the family.

Suddenly, Peter was brought back from his thoughts by a physical sensation and he wondered why he had not noticed it before. It was a familiar odour, the smell of mothballs. He lifted the cards and the telegram to his nose. The smell was the same as the marriage certificate. There was no doubting that they had all come from the same place.

Peter considered what he knew. The 1901 Census confirmed that John Williams' parents, Arthur and Florence, ran the Cascade View Hotel. He guessed that the postcard had been written by Florence. He couldn't imagine a man writing a message of that sort. Florence referred to 'seeing Rose at Charlotte's'. Peter also knew that Rose and the children were staying at the Morris' house on the night of the 1901 Census. Florence referred to young Henry with 'if he's up to it'. That sounded like he had been unwell. She must be asking after Louisa's

226

son Henry. He must be the Henry who, according to the message in the telegram, had died.

When was the card sent by Florence? It was postmarked 26 June 1902, which was about three months before the telegram concerning Henry's death. Rose must have been staying at Brindle Lodge for quite some time. She was certainly there in March 1901, when the census was taken. She was there with the children in June 1902 when Florence visited and still there when the telegram was sent to her in October 1902. That covered a period of more than eighteen months. Were George and Charlotte Morris connected to Rose or to Louisa? And what of poor little Henry? What had happened to him? All of these questions needed answers. Peter turned back to his computer and settled down to find some.

For some reason, the questions surrounding the children, Edith, Harold and Henry seemed to top his imaginary list. If Henry was Louisa's son and he had died, then who was the child listed in the Williams' household on the 1911 Census – the son named Harry? What about the adults too? There were mysteries there.

Peter was in a quandary and deliberated for a few moments. He made a decision. He would concentrate initially on the young children, by finding births for Rosetta's twins and a death for Henry.

He searched the birth registers using the surname 'Ince' in the last quarter of 1900. He soon located their births, both in Ventnor IOW. He noted the reference details in readiness to order their birth certificates.

Next, he looked for the death of Henry, assuming that the 'Henry' in the telegram was Henry Williams, Louisa's son. He tried the West Ham registration district, where the John and Louisa lived. He looked at the third quarter of 1902 and was very disappointed to draw a blank. How frustrating he thought. Who was Henry? What was his relationship to Louisa?

He went over the information he had on Louisa. She was married to John. Her father's name was Thomas. She had a brother David and there was an Uncle Frederick. There wasn't anyone else. The Henry in question had to be her son. Unless Henry had been involved in a fatal accident, he had to have died from illness or disease. Peter recalled that Louisa had received two postcards with references to Henry's health in 1902. In June, Florence's card referred to, '... *if young Henry's up to it...*' and in July, Rose had written in her card *'Hope Henry is better now '*. Surely, it was more likely that young Henry had died through some form of illness.

Peter wondered what happened to sick children in 1902. He resorted to the web. He ran a search engine query and examined the results. He clicked on a link and came up with a possible answer. The London Hospital for Sick Children had been founded in 1852, in Great Ormond Street. Leyton was only a few miles away. Could Henry have been in the children's hospital? He searched the hospital's historic admissions register, available online, with the name Henry Williams. He found two matches.

He clicked on the first match. It gave details of the admission of a child called Henry Williams, aged two years, with severe diarrhoea on 12 June 1902. He was discharged after seven days with his condition 'relieved'. The second match also gave details of the admission of a child called Henry Williams, aged two years, with 'intussusception' on 8th October 1902. The result of his treatment said 'Died'.

Peter sat back from his computer for a few moments, to take in what he'd discovered. He looked up 'intussusception' and was disturbed to find out that it was a condition whereby the bowel folds in on itself. He needed to find a death certificate for this poor child to prove, for certain, that it was Henry, the son of John and Louisa Williams.

Great Ormond Street fell within the registration district of Holborn. It took him just a few minutes to find the death and note down the reference. He then ordered two birth certificates for Rosetta's twins and one death certificate for Henry, paying the supplement for the express service.

Next, Peter turned his attention to the adults. He wanted to establish any connections between George and Charlotte Morris, Rosetta or the Williams family. He knew from the census that Rosetta was born in Paddington, London, which made her an outsider when compared to the others. They had a common factor, in that they were all born on the Isle of Wight. They may have been friends or may have been related. Friendships were hard to prove in genealogy, but that was not the case with family relationships.

An easy relationship to establish was that of first cousins. Peter calculated that John Williams, Louisa's husband, was born in 1869. Taking a chance, he looked for a marriage of John's parents on the Isle of Wight, during the period 1864–1869. There was only one marriage, where the groom was called 'Arthur Williams'. He clicked to view the other names on the same page of the marriage register.

Well done, Peter said to himself. He had found the correct marriage, because the name of one of the brides was Florence Morris.

Then he looked up Florence on the 1861 Census and found her living as a young woman, with her parents and one older brother named George. Names were often passed down within families. Peter had a strong feeling that Florence's brother George would be the father of George Morris born about 1864, who married Charlotte. It took him just a few minutes, looking at the census returns from 1871–1891 to prove that he was right. John and Frank Williams were first cousins to George Morris. Florence was George Morris junior's, aunt.

The other result of the trip to Unit 14 was that Peter had the chance to learn more about Frank Williams. Previously, he had got nowhere, looking for Frank after the wedding. However, Peter now had a clue, namely South Africa, and that is where he decided to start his next search.

He studied the postcard from Frank, to John and Louisa and remembered that the *RMS Kidwelly Castle* with John Williams on board had sailed from London to Cape Town on 19 January 1900, only four days after the wedding. Peter's earlier research had shown that in 1900, the *Kidwelly Castle* was under commission to the War Office to transport troops to South Africa. Somehow, Frank had also got himself to South Africa. To be there on the 10 February, he also must have left Britain within a few days of the wedding, even perhaps on the *Kidwelly Castle*. It may have been a coincidence, but not impossible and furthermore, Peter thought, Frank had sent a postcard of John's ship. The most intriguing question though, was what was Frank

Williams doing in Cape Town? Was he a member of the British military forces? A few minutes later, Peter had the answer, but sadly, it was from a website that listed British casualties of the Boer War.

Name: Williams, F
Rank: Corporal
Unit: City of London Imperial Volunteers
Died, Enteric, 5th October 1900 at Bloemfontein

Peter quickly established that 'enteric' was now more commonly known as typhoid. It was rife throughout the entire campaign; poor sanitation, dirty water, flies and inadequate hygiene being the principal causes. A commentator of the day noted 'that enteric and dysentery killed by the thousand, whereas enemy action killed by the score'.

Peter left his computer at that point and went downstairs to join Felicity. He needed a break. The news of the deaths of young Henry and Frank Williams revealed a sad story. He explained it all to Felicity as he brought her up to date.

'Yes it is sad,' Felicity agreed. 'But you're making progress, even if some of it does make uncomfortable reading. Finding the postcards and telegram was a real coup.'

'You don't think I should give up then? Bearing in mind Highborn Research is also on the case.'

'No not at all ... luck seems to be on your side at the moment, and as you say, something made you buy that certificate in the first place.'

'Yes, spooky isn't it? I'm sure I'm being drawn along. I have to continue. The whole thing is becoming really fascinating. Who knows where it will end? I'm determined to find out.'

Peter lay in bed, unable to sleep. His mind was racing. He'd ordered Frank Williams' death certificate, but as the death occurred overseas, it could take three weeks to arrive from the General Register Office. He was now regretting his decision not to pay extra for a priority delivery. He was also waiting for a copy of Frank's will. Having identified the grant of probate to Frank's brother, John Williams, Peter was anxious to know the details. It would reveal whether or not Frank was married. Wills also took about three weeks to arrive, unless a visit was made in person to the Probate Registry in London. Unfortunately, Peter couldn't spare the time for that, so he would just have to be patient.

Never mind, he thought. *The death certificate of young Henry and the birth certificates of Rosetta's twins should arrive tomorrow in the post.*

Peter was looking forward to seeing what they revealed. Who was the twin's father? That was something he wanted to know.

The following morning, Peter was out in the garage when Desmond, the postman, crunched his way up the shingle drive. Peter went out to intercept him. Desmond personified the reliable, friendly village postman who loved to chat and normally, Peter would have been delighted to catch up on village news, but on this particular morning he recognised at least two of the envelopes in Desmond's hand.

At the first opportunity, Peter managed to end the conversation with Desmond, slightly prematurely perhaps, and relieving Desmond of the post, walked briskly into the house to open the two letters from the GRO.

The first contained the death certificate of Henry Williams. It confirmed that poor little Henry was the son of John and Louisa Williams and that he died of intussusception. The second envelope contained the birth certificates of Edith and Harold Ince.

Peter's eyes went straight to the entry for 'Name and surname of father'. The boxes were blank! That meant that the children were illegitimate and confirmed that Rosetta Ince was an unmarried mother, a situation, which at the time, would have attracted social disapproval. Peter checked the dates of birth. They were the same and next to the date, the time of birth was entered too, confirming that the children were twins. Edith was the older by about twenty-five minutes.

Certificate of Death

REGISTRATION DISTRICT	HOLBORN	
1902 DEATH	in the County of London	

When and where died	Name and surname	Sex	Age	Occupation
Eighth October 1902, Children's Hospital Great Ormond Street	Henry Williams	Male	2	Son of John Williams, Ship's Engineer, 46 Apsley Street, Leyton

Cause of death	Signature, description and residence of informant	When registered
Intussusception, exhaustion, Certified by T P Gilchrist MD	Thomas Crockford, Grandfather, 15 Apsley Street, Leyton	Tenth October 1902

Certificate of Birth

REGISTRATION DISTRICT	NEWCHURCH	
1900 BIRTH	in the County of Hampshire and Isle of Wight	

When and where born	Name, if any	Sex	Name and surname of father
Eighth October 1900 11h 15m PM Brindle Lodge Beaufort Street Ventnor IOW	Edith	Girl	

Name, surname and maiden surname of mother	Occupation of father	Signature, description and residence of informant	When registered
Rosetta Ince		Rosetta Ince, Mother Brindle Lodge Beaufort Street Ventnor	Twenty- third October 1900

232

Certificate of Birth

REGISTRATION DISTRICT	NEWCHURCH
1900 BIRTH	in the County of Hampshire and Isle of Wight

When and where born	Name, if any	Sex	Name and surname of father
Eighth October 1900 11h 40m PM Brindle Lodge Beaufort Street Ventnor IOW	Harold	Boy	

Name, surname and maiden surname of mother	Occupation of father	Signature, description and residence of informant	When registered
Rosetta Ince		Rosetta Ince, Mother Brindle Lodge Beaufort Street Ventnor	Twenty- third October 1900

Well, well, well, Peter thought wryly. He'd suspected from the start that Louisa had married in haste. Obviously, Rosetta too had fallen pregnant, but for some reason, she did not marry the father.

Something occurred to Peter: supposing Frank was the father of Rosetta's children? Rosetta was acquainted with Frank Williams, certainly from the wedding, if not before. Frank died in Bloemfontein, South Africa, nearly nine months after the wedding. Rosetta could have become pregnant around the time of the wedding in January 1900. The dates matched. She had twins, so they could have been born a week or two early. Frank died on 5 October 1900 and Rose's children were born on the 8 October. Could there have been a connection? It all fitted, but he knew it was supposition; he had no way of proving it, one way or the other.

Peter also noticed that 8 October must have been a significant day in the lives of the people he was researching, but for different reasons. It was the day that John and Louisa lost their son Henry, whereas for Rosetta Ince, it was the birthday of her twins Edith and Harry. Although the events occurred two years apart, it seemed a strange coincidence.

233

This story gets more and more interesting, Peter thought. He wondered how Rose had coped at the time, as an unmarried mother on the Isle of Wight. If Frank was the father, it might explain why she stayed at Brindle Lodge. Frank Williams and George Morris were first cousins. By staying with Frank's family, Rosetta may also have received some support from grandparents, Arthur and Florence. Rose's options, unless she had money, would have been severely limited. For most single mothers in 1902, the choice was stark; find someone to take on the baby, or go and live in the workhouse with your child.

Peter was desperate to know what had happened next, so he looked for Rose and her children on the 1911 Census. He couldn't find Rose. He searched for the twins, but was baffled when he found Edith Ince, but not Harold Ince. Edith was still at Brindle Lodge with George and Charlotte Morris. Next to Edith's name, was the abbreviation 'F.C.', which he discovered stood for 'foster child'. Of Rose and Harold, there was absolutely no sign. *That's bizarre,* thought Peter. *What could have happened? Where was Rose? Where was Harold?*

It was possible that Rose had married and consequently changed her name. Peter checked the marriage indexes from 1902 to 1911 without success. He decided he ought to make sure that she hadn't died; something he regarded as unlikely. He looked at the death indexes for the same period. He hadn't really expected to discover what he did. Rosetta Ince died during the third quarter of 1902, in the registration district of Winchester. The age matched. There was no doubt, he thought. It must be her.

Throwing caution to the wind, Peter ordered Rose's death certificate immediately, paying the supplement for the express service. He didn't look any further for Harold. Somehow, he thought he knew where Harold Ince was in 1911. He wasn't in the household at Brindle Lodge with his twin sister. He couldn't have been living with his mother, because she was dead. No, he was living in Leyton, with John and Louisa Williams!

Later, Peter explained his theory to Felicity, about how Frank Williams could have been the father of the twins and that his death in the Boer war was the reason for there being no father's name entered on their birth certificates.

'Couldn't a mother enter the father's name, even if they weren't married?' Felicity asked.

'I've looked into that. In 1900, a father who was not married to the mother had to be present at the time of registration in order to have his name entered on the birth certificate. It was a safeguard to prevent a woman falsely naming a man as the father. If later on, the mother and father married or the father wanted to establish his relationship to an illegitimate child, then the father's name could be added and a new birth certificate issued, but in this case, poor old Frank was not around later.'

'Yes, I see,' mused Felicity. Then she came out with something Peter had overlooked. 'Didn't one of the postcards say something about Edith being the image of Frank?'

'Yes, it did! You're right! I missed that!' Peter shouted excitedly, dashing upstairs to find the postcard. He looked in the folder where he was keeping a growing number of pieces of information relating to his quest. He pulled out Florence's card and found the phrase Felicity had quoted: *Edith is the image of Frank*. 'Brilliant! Brilliant!' he shouted. He rushed back downstairs to show the card to Felicity, his hand shaking. They reread it together.

'That proves it, doesn't it? asked Felicity.

'No doubt, as far as I'm concerned,' Peter replied. 'Frank Williams is the unnamed father of Rosetta's children, but to prove relationships in genealogy you really need certificates and as it stands at the moment, the birth certificates of the twins do not show the father's name.'

'But why do you want to know who the father of the twins is anyway?'

'Ah ... well ... that brings me to my other unproven theory.'

'Which is?'

'I think Harry Williams – the recluse who left the unclaimed estate, the estate Highborn Research is looking at – may really have been Harold Ince.'

'Really? Are you sure? What makes you think that?'

'Well think about it … John and Louisa's son, Henry, died when he was two years old. Henry and Harold were almost the same age, a month to the day between them. I know Henry was unwell for a few months before he died – that's in the postcards. I expect Louisa and Rosetta kept in touch all the time, especially if they were friends. Perhaps they exchanged postcards with little pieces of news? Then Louisa sent Rosetta the telegram telling her of Henry's death and asking her to come to Leyton urgently. OK, are you following me?'

'Yes,' Felicity said impatiently.

'Now here's the amazing part … Henry died during the last quarter of 1902 and during the same quarter, Rosetta Ince died in Winchester.'

'What? The same Rosetta?'

'Someone called Rosetta Ince died in the last quarter of 1902, aged twenty-seven – the right age. It has to be her. I've ordered the death certificate by the express service, so I should know for certain tomorrow … assuming no delay in the post of course. If I've found her death, it means that Edith and Harold were orphaned … you following me?' Peter asked.

'Yes.'

'Eight years later, on the 1911 Census, Edith is listed in the household of George and Charlotte Morris as a 'foster child'. Her brother Harold isn't there, in fact there's no sign of any Harold Ince, aged ten on the census. However, on the same census, John and Louisa have a son Harry, aged ten, but their son died. So who is Harry? He must be Harold Ince. They must have fostered him and completed the census return falsely, to show him as their natural son. It's possible, because that was the first census completed by the householder, rather than an enumerator. If Rosetta did die in 1902, then Edith remained with the Morris's and Harold went to live with John and Louisa. It all fits, don't you see? It all fits!'

236

'So how does this affect the unclaimed estate and Highborn Research?'

'What it means is, that if Harry Williams was really Harold Ince, then he had a twin sister. If I could prove that Edith was Harry Williams' twin sister then her descendants would have a strong claim to inherit Harry's estate.'

Peter continued with growing excitement, 'I can't imagine how Highborn would know anything about Edith and Harold. I've only found out through the marriage certificate, the postcards, and the telegram. They can't have the physical evidence I have. Maybe they're researching the Uncle David who went to New York. I'm fairly certain that Edith Ince, as a sister to Harry, would blow any claim from a descendant of David Crockford completely out of the water, but only if I could convince the Treasury Solicitor's Office that she is Harry Williams' sister.'

'But, if the Rosetta Ince who died in 1902 is not the mother of Edith and Harry, then all of this would fall apart, wouldn't it?'

'Well yes, it would … so let's keep our fingers crossed.'

Peter stayed indoors out of the way, when Desmond brought the post the following day. He couldn't bear the thought of getting into a long conversation with the postman whilst he held on to a vital letter from the GRO. The delay would have been torment. He waited until the post came through the letterbox and then dashed to see what had arrived. His heart was beating hard though excitement as he spotted the correct envelope and tore open the seal. He surprised himself. He hadn't realised just how involved he was becoming in the life of Harry Williams. It *was* the death certificate of Rosetta Ince.

Peter sat down and read the entries on the certificate once more. He turned on his computer and looked up the details of the accident. The train was bound for Southampton, when it collided with a goods train travelling in the opposite direction. There were fourteen fatalities in all. *Hence the inquest,* he thought. *Rosetta must have been on her way to Ventnor from Leyton.*

<table>
<tr><td colspan="2" align="center">*Certificate of Death*</td></tr>
</table>

REGISTRATION DISTRICT   WINCHESTER
1902   DEATH   in the County of Hampshire and Isle of Wight

When and where died	Name and surname	Sex	Age	Occupation
17th October 1902 Dunley Bottom on the London + South West Railway	Rosetta Ince	Female	27	Spinster of Beaufort Street Ventnor, IOW

Cause of death	Description and residence of informant	When registered
Met her death by derailing of London to Southampton Express on 17th October 1902, such derailing caused by excessive speed (open verdict death from injuries)	Certificate received from J.Driffield, Coroner for Winchester. Inquest held 20th October 1902 and by adjournment on 3rd November 1902	Fourth November 1902

The accident happened on 17 October and Rosetta was summoned to Leyton by the telegram on 9 October. *Could that mean,* Peter wondered, *that Rose stayed with Louisa for the intervening period of eight days? Including the funeral of Henry?*

He wondered if there was any way he could check. There might be, if the funeral was mentioned in the local paper. It meant another trip to Leyton library, but it would be worth it … *if* he found a mention in the *Leyton Chronicle*.

Peter turned back to the certificate. The age and address matched. It was definitely the correct Rosetta. She was a spinster. Her children were left with no mother and no legal father. He already knew that legal adoption did not exist before 1927. The children were separated. George and Charlotte fostered Edith. John and Louisa must have fostered Harry. Edith retained her mother's surname, the name under which she was born. John and Louisa, however, subjugated Harry into their household, giving him their surname, the name Williams and referred to him on the 1911 Census as 'son'.

A whole series of implications flashed through Peter's mind. Did Harry know that John and Louisa were not his biological parents? Probably not, certainly not as a child, but perhaps he was told later.

Did Harry know that he had a twin sister on the Isle of Wight? It didn't seem as if he had kept in touch with her, if he did. He hadn't made any provision for her in a will. In fact, he hadn't left a will and enquiries at the time of death obviously hadn't discovered the existence of a twin sister.

Peter contemplated whether John and Louisa deliberately deceived Harry, having him believe they were his parents. It was likely. They'd moved to Moses Street, West Ham by the time of the 1911 Census. The new neighbours would have assumed that Harry was their son. The move could have been a new start after the loss of Henry. What if John had left the Castle Mail Packet Company – or the Union Castle Line as it became known – to work locally on a dredger? He would have been there to support Louisa, rather than be away at sea. Perhaps, his change in work meant a pay cut and they needed to move to a smaller house, or to one more convenient for the docks.

Peter tried to imagine the situation. As the years went by, it may have become too late to tell Harry the truth about his true parentage. Sometimes things were best left as they were. Then John Williams was killed in 1914. Harry was all that Louisa had. She didn't remarry. Would she have risked jeopardising her relationship with him? No, of course she wouldn't. She needed him to look after her in her old age and that's what happened. She lived with him in the house he owned, until she died in 1962 at the age of ninety-two. He was present at her death and named on her death certificate, as informant and son.

Then, he supposed, after John died, Louisa's links with her late husband's family on the Isle of Wight might have been severed as time passed, especially if she managed to avoid family reunions and visits, or fell out with them. It was all quite plausible, Peter decided. He could completely understand how Harry may unwittingly have become estranged from the remainder of the Williams family and his twin sister.

What should he do now though? Peter contemplated his options. So far, he was piecing together a pretty convincing story that the reclusive Harry Williams, was in reality born Harold Ince. Legal adoption did not exist in 1902. A person could have been named anything they liked, but although Harry was known by the surname 'Williams', under inheritance law he would be regarded as 'Ince'. His assets should go to his bloodline and Peter had discovered that Harry had a twin sister, Edith. If she had any descendants, then they would be entitled relatives and could, in theory, inherit Harry's unclaimed estate.

There were a couple of things that Peter needed to do: find a death notice for young Henry Williams. It might show whether Rosetta was at his funeral, which could tie in with her ill-fated return journey to the Isle of Wight. Also, and perhaps more importantly, Peter needed to trace any living descendants of Edith Ince.

Before he got up from his computer, Peter remembered one other thing that he needed to check. He went to the Bona Vacantia website and once more looked down the list of unclaimed estates. Had Highborn beaten him to it? He was barely able to look and he felt his heartbeat quicken with angst as he looked at the names. He was greatly relieved to see that Harry Williams' estate was still on the list.

4.2

It was after midnight and the house lay in almost total darkness. Down in the small sitting room, next to the kitchen, the glow of a cigarette was the only sign in the blackness that someone was in the room. Harry sat in his favourite leather armchair. The clock ticked rhythmically on the mantelpiece above the fireplace. It was December and the ashes in the grate lay cold. The paraffin heater behind him emitted a feeble mixture of heat, moisture, and odour. However, the warm remains of a fire lay in the fireplace upstairs: the one in her bedroom, the one he had lit, before he went off to work as usual that morning.

Things were different now, Harry thought. In just a few hours, everything had changed. The world turned on its side; the very foundations of his life rocked by what she'd told him.

240

An hour before, the undertakers had brought her body downstairs. He heard them make their way down the hall, trying to be quiet and respectful as they carried her out to the shiny, black, unmarked van.

'Use Harringtons,' had been her last instruction to him and pretty much her last comprehensible words. The undertakers, Harringtons' Funeral Services, were a division of Harringtons' Department Store, which dominated High Street and included as part of its frontage, the former premises of his grandfather's drapery business. Only now, he wasn't *his* grandfather. Somebody else's perhaps, but not his. Not now, anyway, not after what she'd told him.

So, who was he? Not the son of John and Louisa Williams it seemed, and not the person he'd spent his whole life being ... well, for as far back as he could remember.

He'd found her lying on the floor in the bedroom when he'd got home; she was cold and confused. He'd managed to get her back into bed. She didn't weigh much these days. Ninety-two year old women are generally pretty frail and withered. Mother was no exception. Once back in bed, she seemed to come round and he'd relaxed a little.

'Are you all right, mother? What happened? Did you fall?'

'Yes,' she managed to croak, 'but I'll be fine now.'

'I'm going to the telephone box on the corner. I'm going to call the doctor.'

He found the doctor's number, grabbed his coat, and left the house. He took some coins to pay for the call. When he was connected, he explained the situation and the doctor agreed to come at once.

Harry returned quickly and went back upstairs to see how she was. He made her comfortable, plumping up the pillows and straightening the bedclothes. She started rambling and he began to worry that he should have called an ambulance rather than the doctor. He began to wonder if this might actually be it, the day he knew would eventually come; the day he had tried to prepare himself for in recent years. He knew that she didn't want to die in hospital.

241

Anyway, it was too late now for an ambulance, the doctor was on the way.

Harry went downstairs, made two cups of tea, and filled a hot-water bottle. He took them up to the bedroom and slid the bottle under the blankets near to her feet. She muttered something to him and so he sat on the bed beside her.

'Here you are, mother, I've made you some tea. Can you manage a drop?'

Her eyes opened and she looked steadily at him, but said nothing.

'Do you want anything, mother? I've called the doctor. Wouldn't you like some tea?'

'No,' she sighed. 'Not just now.' She closed her eyes again.

They were both silent for a minute. Then she turned her head towards him, opened her eyes a little, and spoke: 'Harry, there's something I need to tell you.' Her voice was weak. She paused to catch her breath.

Harry looked steadily at her, listening.

'I'm not your mother,' she said flatly.

'What do you mean? You're rambling. Of course you're my mother.'

'I didn't give birth to you, that's what I mean. It was Henry, poor Henry who I bore, not you.'

'What are you saying? Who's Henry?'

'Henry was our son. You're Rose's son.'

Harry was completely confused. Was she really saying this, or was she making it up. 'Who's Rose? Rose who?'

His mother paused again, trying to gather herself. 'My dear friend Rose, the one who perished in the train crash.'

Harry looked at her not knowing what to think, or what to say. 'But I'm your son. Are you saying that you and dad are not my parents?'

'That's right,' she said weakly. 'Frank is your father ... dad's brother ... and Rose is your mother, not me.'

'Rose who?' he shouted, 'Rose who?' Harry was getting annoyed now, but his mother seemed not to notice.

'Rosetta Ince, my best friend. She was my bridesmaid. She died in the train crash and we took you on, brought you up as our own. I should have told you … I'm sorry.' A tear rolled down her cheek and she closed her eyes. She turned her head away. 'We should have told you,' she muttered, her voice fading, before she drifted to sleep.

4.3

Peter's search to find living descendants of Edith Ince took him slightly longer than he had initially expected, but it was ultimately fruitful. He knew that she was born in 1900, so he began to look for her marriage in Hampshire and the Isle of Wight, during the period 1918 to 1930. When he drew a blank, it crossed his mind that she had either died or gone abroad. Undeterred, he tried the next ten-year period and found that she had married Charles Trigg in 1935.

The marriage was registered in Lymington, which he knew well as a pretty little fishing port and market town on the south coast of England. The town lay directly opposite the Isle of Wight and ferries carried passengers between Lymington and Yarmouth on the island. It was no surprise to Peter that Edith had married there.

Peter noted the GRO reference for Edith's marriage and then searched for any children of Charles and Edith. He found two where the surname was Trigg and the mother's maiden name was Ince. They were girls, both born in the second quarter of 1938, named Joan and Margaret. He noticed that the births were registered in Wiltshire, which wasn't quite as he'd expected, but it was only about seventy miles from Lymington. If the births were correct, it didn't take a genius to work out that they were twin sisters. Their grandmother Rosetta Ince had produced twins, so the trait was obviously in the genes. He knew that they were Edith's children, but the birth certificates would confirm it. Again, he noted the references.

He needed to find out whether Joan and Margaret were still alive, bearing in mind that each may have married and acquired her husband's surname. He examined the marriage registers between 1956 and 1979. There were quite a few 'Trigg' marriages, but none that matched. Their mother had married at age thirty-five. Surely, at least one of the daughters had married before she was forty, he thought. Failing that, the girls may have married abroad or died. He would need to hunt further.

Peter decided to try a different tack: checking the old telephone directories available online up to 1984. *What a fantastic resource,* he chuckled to himself, as he found an entry for 'M. Trigg' in the Lymington directory of 1984. No sign of a Joan Trigg, but he had made a start.

Next, he tried the electoral roll. He had to pay a fee, but it was worth it. He found an address in Lymington and to his joy, sister Joan, he presumed, as she was the only other person registered at the same address. With a fair degree of certainty, Peter had found an address for Margaret and Joan. If they were the two descendants he was looking for, then they were about seventy-two years old and living together, probably as elderly spinsters.

Just to complete that stage of his research, Peter looked for the deaths of their parents. He found the death of Charles Trigg in Wiltshire in 1967, aged sixty-eight when he died. The mother, Edith, died eight years later in 1975. Her death was notable in that it was registered in Lymington. It followed therefore, that after the death of her husband, she may have returned to Lymington, to live with her daughters. He'd only be able to confirm that, if ever he met Joan and Margaret.

Peter sat back from his computer. He couldn't believe how well he'd done and he knew that he had to meet Edith's twin daughters. He was as certain as he could be that they were granddaughters of Rosetta Ince. If he could prove that to be the case, then that would make them nieces of Harold Ince, also known as Harry Williams, whose estate rested in the hands of the Treasury Solicitor.

He ordered certificates for the births, marriages, and deaths he'd just found, once more paying a supplement for a rapid turnaround. *This is starting to get expensive,* he thought, *what with trips to Leyton as well*, but somehow Peter was feeling increasingly confident that he might be able to recoup his costs. In fact, the more he thought about it, he might even be able to make some money from it.

He knew that heir-hunting firms worked on a commission. He didn't know how much they charged, but it had to be somewhere between fifteen and thirty per cent. He mentally calculated that he might be able to earn between £10,000 and £20,000 if he could process a claim for the Trigg sisters and they were the only entitled relatives. *Mustn't count chickens*, he thought. *You are not a professional heir hunter. You don't have the legal agreements in place, nor the expertise to submit a claim and don't forget that a professional firm is also sniffing around.*

Peter decided it was better to play this carefully and see how it panned out. He needed to wait until the certificates arrived. If they confirmed what he believed to be true, then he would move one step closer to solving the extraordinary mystery that his quest had now turned into.

4.4

There was an impatient knocking on the front door. Harry got up from his mother's bedside and went downstairs to meet the doctor. He thanked him for coming and showed him up to the bedroom. The doctor asked some questions before examining his mother.

Harry left the room and went back downstairs to the sitting room. He wanted to keep out of the way for a minute, trying to understand what his mother had just told him. He gazed around the room and looked at the wooden framed photograph hanging on the wall. It was a black and white photograph of the *RMS Kidwelly Castle*. In the bottom right-hand corner, another photograph had been inserted behind the glass. It was a picture of his father, head and shoulders. He was wearing the uniform of the Castle Line and the caption read 'John Williams, Chief Engineer'.

Harry focussed on his father's face. *Does it mean that you're not my father*, he thought. *Who is Rosetta Ince?* He had never heard her name before. It was bizarre. *No, mother is confused*, he thought. *I am Harry Williams, everyone knows me as that. How could I be someone else?*

'Mr Williams,' the doctor called from the bedroom.

There, he reassured himself, *the doctor's just referred to me by my correct name*. 'Yes, I'm coming,' Harry answered, making his way back upstairs to his mother's bedroom.

The doctor met Harry on the landing and had closed the bedroom door. 'I'm afraid your mother is very ill,' he spoke quietly. 'Her pulse is very weak. How long has she been like this?'

'Since I found her – when I got back from work. She was lying on the floor, just inside the bedroom. She was fine this morning ... well, as fine as you would expect for a ninety-two-year-old. I always make the bedroom fire for her and put some bread and butter on the dressing table, before I go to work. She gets up later on and makes herself a sandwich. She takes all her meals in her bedroom now, you know. I make her some tea when I get home. I could see that she hasn't made a sandwich today, so maybe she fell when she got up this morning. She did seem very cold when I found her.'

The doctor glanced back to the bedroom door and continued, 'The shock of the fall and lying on the floor for some hours may have affected her. Do you want me to admit her to hospital? I will if you want, but I'm not sure what it will achieve. I'm sorry, Mr Williams, but she is very ill and I don't think she will get better. It may only be a question of hours.'

It was the 'Mr Williams' thing again. This time, much to Harry's surprise, it jarred his nerves.

The doctor misinterpreted his expression for one of dread at the thought of losing his mother. 'Would you prefer it if your mother went into hospital?'

'No, no, not if you really think she is unlikely to recover. Let her remain here until she ...' he paused, not wishing to use the obvious word. 'I know that's what she wants,' Harry continued. 'She's often told me she wants to stay here and not go to hospital.'

'I think that's wise,' the doctor reassured him. 'I can arrange for you to have some assistance to care for her. Would you like me to organise a nurse to sit with her?'

'Yes, that would be helpful, thank you.'

The doctor made his way downstairs with Harry following him. 'Ring me if anything happens. I'll arrange for a nurse to call later this evening, probably about ten o'clock.'

'Thank you doctor,' Harry said as he showed him to the front door.

It was just after seven in the evening. Normally, they would have had their tea by now, but Harry had lost his appetite. He went back upstairs to his mother's bedroom. He looked at her long and hard to check that she was breathing – she was; the bedclothes were rising and falling very slowly, almost imperceptibly.

He stared at her and recalled what she had told him. Was it really true that the two people in his life, the two people whom he had always known as his parents, were not in fact his biological parents? *I've been deceived*, he thought. *I should have been told. Why hadn't they told me?*

Harry didn't want to blame his father, though. He had died in the First World War, which had given his mother forty-eight years to tell him.

He tried to remember exactly what she'd said about who his real mother was. Someone called Rosetta Ince, her friend. She was her bridesmaid. He had no idea about any of it, or what it meant.

Harry went downstairs into the back sitting room. The alcove next to the fireplace was filled by a built-in wooden cupboard. He'd constructed it himself. The top formed a shelf and it supported a collection of miniature souvenir china jugs and vases, a fair number of which came from resorts on the Isle of Wight. He knelt on the floor and felt underneath the front of the cupboard. Finding the hidden screw head, Harry pinched it between his left thumb and forefinger, and pulled. A cleverly made section of the plinth below the cupboard came free. He put his hand into the void behind and grasped the old

247

biscuit tin, in which family papers were kept. He pulled it out and took it through to the kitchen table, where he opened it and began to examine the contents.

He wasn't sure what to look for, but guessed it was anything that would add some credence to what might be nothing more than the ramblings of a fading old lady. He found his parents' marriage certificate. He scanned the details. Then he noticed the names of the witnesses: Frank Williams and Rosetta Ince.

He sat down heavily at the table, took a few deep breaths, and looked at the marriage certificate again, this time, slowly and carefully. According to his mother, the two witnesses named on the certificate were actually his real parents, his biological parents. Uncle Frank's name hadn't been mentioned for years. He'd died long ago in the Boer War; at least that was what his father had told him. He'd never heard of Rosetta Ince.

Harry went back upstairs to the bedroom with the certificate. 'Mother, I've got your wedding certificate here,' he whispered urgently.

His mother turned her head towards him and opened her eyes.

'Are these two witnesses at your wedding – Frank and Rosetta – are they my real parents?'

'Yes they are,' she said weakly. 'I'm sorry Harold, I'm sorry.'

Harold? he thought. *That's strange; she's never called me Harold before.* 'Why did you call me Harold? You just called me Harold. You and Dad have always called me Harry. Was I named Harold?'

'Yes, you were ... Harold Ince.'

'Why not Harold Williams, if my father was Dad's brother?'

'Because your real parents weren't married. Your father, Frank, was killed before he came home to marry Rose.'

'Why have you never told me this before?' Harry's voice rose in frustration and shock.

His mother remained silent.

He left the bedroom. He was annoyed now. He needed to go down to the kitchen to get a cigarette. As he lit up and inhaled the smoke, he sat down at the table and continued to look through the contents of the biscuit tin. He spotted a telegram. He unfolded it and read the message.

> TO: Miss Rosetta Ince. 'Brindle Lodge', Beaufort Street, Ventnor, Isle of Wight
> Henry passed away yesterday. Please return Leyton urgently if possible. Louisa.

Harry went back upstairs. His mother hadn't moved. 'Mother, was Henry your son? The son who died?'

She turned her head slowly towards him and then stared at him with a vacant expression. Her thoughts were elsewhere. It was as if the name 'Henry' had sent her mind back into the past. She said nothing for about a minute, then she seemed to come back to the present and with great effort she simply said, 'Harringtons, use Harringtons, they're good.'

'But mother, was Henry your son?'

She didn't answer.

Harry watched as his mother closed her eyes. A few moments later, her breathing faltered and after a final exhalation, she passed away.

4.5

Peter left home early, aiming to be in Leyton by half past nine. He'd rung the reference library, to see if they offered a facility whereby he could pay a researcher to look up the information he needed. Unfortunately, that was not the case.

He'd asked how far back their collection of the local newspaper went, and was told that there was a complete set of the *Leyton Chronicle* available to the public, for the period 1901–1991, but only on microfilm. After that date, they had physical copies for reference.

Prior to 1901, the library had no records of the newspaper. That meant no chance of looking for any announcement of John and Louisa's wedding in 1900, but it did give him the chance to look for death notices for young Henry Williams in 1902 and Louisa Williams in 1962.

Peter made good time and had parked by just after nine-thirty. He locked the car and taking his notepad, he headed off in the direction of the library. Annoyingly, he had to wait until it opened at ten o'clock, so he popped into a coffee shop for a doughnut and cup of tea.

As soon as the library opened, Peter went straight to the reference section. He explained to the librarian that he needed to research the *Leyton Chronicle*, starting with 1962. She showed him the drawers containing the microfilm and demonstrated how to load the reel of film and use the viewer. Once he'd located the issues of the newspaper for mid to late December 1962, he scrolled through the newspaper, column by column. He was disappointed not to find any death notice concerning Louisa. He returned the film to its drawer and then took out the microfilm for 1902 and wound it on to the viewer.

The 1902 *Leyton Chronicle* had a completely different format to the modern version. Patent remedies dominated the advertisements and the front page consisted mainly of what one might refer to today as 'small ads'. The news itself began on page two. Peter found it fascinating, and it was easy to get distracted from his task. There were some interesting reports and it brought home to him how much times had changed. Personal notices, death notices, and obituaries were printed on page five.

Henry Williams had died on 8 October 1902 – a Wednesday. The newspaper came out each Friday, so Peter reckoned that any death notice or funeral report ought to be found in one of the three issues immediately following Henry's death. He found nothing in the edition published the day after Henry died, but in the next issue, the one for 17 October 1902, he struck gold. Midway down the third column on page five, he found just what he had been hoping for.

Funeral of Henry Williams.

The funeral took place on the fifteenth October at St Martin's Parish Church, Leyton, of Henry Williams, only son of Mr and Mrs J Williams of 46 Apsley St, Leyton. The service was conducted by Reverend T. Walter. The mourners were Mr and Mrs J Williams (parents), Thomas Crockford (grandfather), Mr and Mrs G Corbett (godparents), Miss R Ince (friend) and Mrs G Robins representing the staff of Crockford's Drapery Emporium. Floral tributes were sent by the Parents, the Godparents, Miss Ince, and the Staff of Crockford's Drapery Emporium.

Peter was delighted. He now had proof that Rosetta had attended the funeral of Henry. However, any elation was dampened by the knowledge of what awaited poor Rosetta on her return journey to Ventnor. Two days after the funeral, on the very date of the newspaper he was reading, he knew that she would be killed at Dunley Bottom, leaving her children, Edith and Harold, orphaned.

Peter asked whether it was possible to have a copy of the funeral notice.

'Yes we can copy individual pages. We have the original newspapers here, but they're not for public access. If you give me the details, I'll go down to the basement and make a copy of that part of page five for you. It will only take a few minutes. I'm afraid we have to make a charge of three pounds.'

'That's fine,' replied Peter.

When the librarian returned with a copy of the death notice, Peter checked to make sure it was what he wanted, and then paid the fee. Ten minutes later, he was back in the car and easing his way out into the busy traffic. Rather than returning home directly, he felt he had time to find the address in Moses Street where John, Louisa, and Harry were living in 1911. When he got there, he could see that it had been redeveloped. The Victorian houses had all but disappeared, replaced by three shabby concrete high-rise buildings, with interconnecting walkways. *No point lingering here,* Peter thought and just before two o'clock in the afternoon he was back home.

251

Opening the front door, he stepped over the day's post. There was more than usual scattered on the carpet. He spotted at least four white envelopes, which by their familiar shape and marking, he recognised as coming from the GRO. He shot upstairs to check the stock market on his computer, and then returned to the kitchen put the kettle on. He sat down at the table to open the post.

The first envelope contained the birth certificates of Joan and Margaret Trigg, confirming their father as Charles Trigg and their mother as Edith Trigg, formerly Ince. *Excellent*, he thought. The second envelope held the death certificates of Charles and Edith. He noticed that Edith's address, when she died, was the current address in Lymington of Joan and Margaret.

When he opened the next envelope, he found it contained the marriage certificate of Charles Trigg and Edith Ince. He didn't expect to find anything out of the ordinary, but it was the entry in the column for Edith's 'Father's Name and Surname' that made him sit up and grin. Edith's father was not named on her birth certificate, but here on her marriage certificate it said:

Father's Name and Surname: Frank Williams (deceased)
Rank or Profession of Father: Cpl. City Imperial Volunteers

Peter had heard of this before, where an illegitimate child puts the father's name on a marriage certificate. Somebody, perhaps George or Charlotte, or Edith's grandmother Florence, had told Edith whom her father was and she had taken the opportunity of her marriage to record his name on the certificate. Peter wasn't certain of her motives. It may have been connected with some form of pride and she wanted to see her father's name recognised. Alternatively, Edith may have felt embarrassed by leaving the entry blank and had entered Frank's name as a way of avoiding embarrassment. He would never know, but one way or another, this was a very significant discovery.

Peter now had a degree of proof that Frank Williams was the father of Edith Ince, which meant, of course, that he was the father of her twin Harold Ince. Providing Peter could convince the Treasury Solicitor that Harry Williams was born Harold Ince, then any descendants of Edith, his full blood sister, would be his entitled relatives.

Peter's run of success, however, wasn't finished. The last envelope from the GRO gave him the death certificate of a Corporal F Williams, the one he'd ordered nearly three weeks before. The details were taken from the 'Casualty Lists of the Natal and South African Field Forces 1899-1902'. It confirmed that he died of disease at Bloemfontein on 5 October 1902. Peter just needed Frank's will, to show that he had no other children. He'd ordered it the same day as his death certificate, so it had to be due any day.

Peter made himself a coffee and took it upstairs to his desk. He stared absent-mindedly out of the window while he considered his options to getting in touch with the Trigg sisters. He couldn't put off making some form of contact with them, not if he wished to see this project through. He didn't want to just drive down to Lymington and knock on their door with a cold-call. They might not be at home and if they were, it's unlikely they would be receptive to what he wanted to talk them about. Much better, he decided, to write to them first. If he couched his letter in a sincere and non-threatening manner, there was a reasonable chance that they would treat it seriously and agree to a meeting.

He gave some serious thought as to how he might phrase his letter of introduction. He didn't want to frighten them or give them any grounds for thinking that he might be some type of confidence trickster. He didn't want them to think that he was going to ask them for confidential information. He needed to assure them that initially he merely wanted to confirm some names and facts, in order to satisfy himself that the Trigg sisters were, as he believed, entitled relatives to an unclaimed estate. With these points in mind, Peter wrote his letter.

As he was about to pop it into the post box later that afternoon, he wondered to himself whether or not it would have the desired effect and if so, how long he would have to wait for a reply? *Fingers crossed,* he thought, *here goes.*

4.6

Harry leant over his mother and put his ear close to her mouth. He could hear nothing. He pulled her arm from under the covers and tried to find a pulse. 'She's gone. Oh, God she's gone,' he said to himself. He stood up and made his way to the bathroom. He suddenly felt sick and knew he was going to vomit. Afterwards, he wiped his face and saw in the mirror that his eyes were wet with tears.

Pulling himself together, he went downstairs for his coat and then walked quickly to the phone box again. He rang the doctor with the news.

The doctor returned to the house within fifteen minutes. He confirmed that his mother was dead. He explained the procedure to Harry, gave him a form, and advised him to call an undertaker. 'Are you all right?' he asked.

'Yes, I'm fine,' Harry lied.

'I'll send word to the nurse to stop her coming out.'

Harry made his third trip to the phone box that evening and called Harringtons'. After they'd left, he sat in the darkness in the back sitting room, smoking a cigarette.

He cast his mind back over the years. He'd always looked after his mother, but who was she? Technically, she was his aunt and that made his father his uncle. So, he'd actually been brought up by his aunt and uncle. *That wasn't so bad, was it?* Well, on the face of it, no; but why hadn't she told him before? It was as if she didn't want him to find out, in case it changed their relationship. She'd always been very possessive. 'No girl is good enough for my Harry', she used to say.

He'd had the occasional girlfriend back in his twenties and thirties, but things always went wrong once he brought them home to meet his mother. She pointed out their faults. She never encouraged him to get married and to have a life of his own. No, her life revolved around him. She cooked, cleaned, and did his washing, but when he thought about it, he realised everything was all very much on her terms.

Harry remembered that when he became a fully qualified patternmaker in his early twenties, she had encouraged him to get his name down for a Falcon Village house, just in case one should come up. *That suited her very well*, he thought. *Once I got a works' house, I was well and truly tied to the firm, and my job. Less chance for me to stray, and with her living here with me, she was in a perfect position to influence my social life and nip in the bud any threat from a developing romantic relationship. She needed someone to keep her.*

Later, the opportunity had arisen to buy the house and his mother had encouraged him to take on a mortgage, which meant even more responsibility. It all fitted.

He realised, bitterly, that throughout his life she had deceived him. He knew little or nothing of any relatives. She never spoke about the family. She'd now revealed that Uncle Frank was his father, but all that he knew about him was that he died in the Boer War. He knew nothing else. Mother had never socialised with any family members or anyone else in particular. Perhaps she'd been frightened that someone who knew her in her earlier life would let out the secret of his true parentage.

In the 1950s, one of the older ladies in the canteen at work had asked if his family was connected to Crockford's the drapers. She'd only said it in passing, but when he asked his mother for more information, she'd acted a little strangely. She'd seemed more interested in who the woman was who'd mentioned it, and what had made her ask. She certainly wasn't very forthcoming about any further details. All he'd gleaned was that his grandfather, Thomas Crockford, had a drapery business called Crockford's, on Leyton High Street, and that the economic pain he suffered during the First World War, culminated in him selling up in 1917 and emigrating to the United States, where he died in 1924.

She could have told me then, Harry thought, but now it seemed that Thomas Crockford was neither his grandfather nor any blood relation at all. He couldn't shake the feeling that he'd been duped and taken advantage of, tricked almost. The life he'd led had been a lie. He was Harold Ince really, not Harry Williams. Everything was so unsettling.

What was he going to do about it? First of all, he decided that he was going to go into work the following day and act as if nothing had happened. He wouldn't tell anybody. The doctor had given him a form to take to the local register office to record the death, but he wouldn't do that tomorrow either. *Leave it a day or so. No hurry there,* he decided. He would leave it until Friday afternoon. He would mention it to his boss on Friday morning and see if he could get a couple of hours off. He would call in at Harringtons' afterwards on the way back, to make the final arrangements. The funeral would be a very quiet and simple affair. He had no family, no family he knew of, and mother had certainly never kept up with any friends or acquaintances whom he ought to inform.

4.7

Joan heard the post fall on to the front door mat. She went to pick it up, leaving her sister, Margaret, in the kitchen. They'd just finished breakfast and Margaret was sitting in her wheelchair, with it drawn up to the table. She had switched on her laptop and was looking to see if they had any email.

Joan returned with the post. It was the usual junk mail, plus a water bill and a letter in a white envelope. The letter was addressed to both of them. The postmark was smudged, but it was possible to make out 'Wilts'.

'Not sure what this is or who it's from. It's from Wiltshire,' said Joan. 'We haven't heard from Doug and Moira for a while.'

'I wouldn't have thought it's from them,' replied Margaret. 'Don't forget, they're on email these days. It looks interesting though. Come on, open it!'

Joan went to a drawer, took out a knife, and neatly slit open the envelope. She returned to the table and sat down next to Margaret.

She laid the single page between them so that they could both read it at the same time.

Dear Miss Trigg and Miss Trigg

I hope that you don't mind me writing to you, but I have some information, which I would like to share with you and hope that it will be to your advantage. Please be assured that this letter is neither a hoax nor any form of request for money.

I am a private individual and one of my hobbies is family history research. Recently, I found a marriage certificate from 1900 in an antiques centre. Purely out of academic interest, I decided to see if I could ascertain what had happened to the married couple named on it. I might add at the outset, that I have no connection whatsoever with them, or with their families.

My research proved to be most interesting. I have discovered that an individual connected with the marriage died in 1996, without leaving a will. The deceased's assets are held by the Treasury Solicitor, a Government Department, responsible for looking after unclaimed estates whilst attempting to find missing heirs. I believe that you may be entitled relatives of the deceased.

I don't want to give too much information at this stage. There is the possibility that my research is flawed and I would not wish to raise your expectations or interest unnecessarily. To confirm my findings, I will need to ask you some questions about your family. I need to verify the names of relatives such as grandparents, uncles, and aunts, nothing confidential or not already in the public domain.

I would very much like to meet you and wonder whether it would be possible to arrange a meeting at your convenience. My telephone number and email address are shown at the foot of this letter. I would be able to make the journey to see you on any weekday.

My intentions in contacting you are genuine and born out of good faith. I would so much like to close my research on the marriage certificate, by bringing together an unclaimed estate and two possible heirs. It would be a most exciting finale.

Please let me know if you are agreeable to a meeting.

Yours sincerely

Peter Sefton

'Well, I never,' said Joan. 'What do you make of that?'

'It can't be right,' replied Margaret. 'There's no money in our family. He's made a mistake; either that or it's a wind-up.'

'Don't you think he's genuine then?' asked Joan.

'Well, normally I'd say no, but I suppose there is something about the tone … it's not like those emails asking for help in depositing money for a foreign general or something.'

'It's very polite and proper. I'd say it's written by an educated man,' stated Joan.

'That's the problem,' said Margaret. 'We don't want to be fooled. These fraudsters can be very convincing. Here, let me read it again.' She scanned the letter quickly. 'Which side of the family do you think he might be referring to? It's all very mysterious. We know about Dad's side fairly well. They were all from around here in Lymington, but we don't know much about Mum's side.'

'That's true,' confirmed Joan. 'She told us she was fostered and brought up by Uncle George and Auntie Charlotte.'

'But where did she come from before that? It's got to be something to do with Mum, it must be,' stated Margaret, putting the letter down. 'Mum was born in 1900, wasn't she?'

'Yes, do you think she's the connection or is that just a coincidence?' asked Joan, her mind working through other members of the family who might have been about the right age. 'Dad was eighteen months older than Mum, so he would have been born before this marriage. It's got to be something to do with Mum. Did she ever tell you much about her family? She never told me.'

'No,' answered Margaret, 'although one day we were watching something on television together; Dad was there as well. Something came on about the Boer War and Mum suddenly said that her father was killed in the Boer War. I started to ask some questions about him, but she just clammed up. Dad didn't add anything either. They glanced at one another, but neither offered any more information. Dad mumbled something about no point in raking up the past. It was strange, but by the next day, I'd forgotten all about it and nothing more was ever said.'

'Why didn't you tell me at the time?' said Joan with a hint of annoyance.

'Because they obviously didn't want to say anymore, that's why!'

'Anyway, what are we going to do about this letter?' asked Joan.

'I'll tell you what we'll do,' said Margaret. 'I'll do some research myself. I'll look online for information about the Treasury Solicitor and I'll also see if I can find anything about this Peter Sefton. He's given us an address, but can we be sure if it's his address?'

'OK, that's a good idea. I don't think we should rush to reply, but it might be worth digging around a bit first. We need to be as sure as we can that this is genuine.'

'Yes, we don't want to end up in the papers as two silly old spinsters who fell victims to a confidence trickster,' chuckled Margaret. 'On the other hand, if it is all above board, then how much do you think it might be? We could certainly do with some money, however much it is. Gosh, I think it's exciting really. Ooh, I hope it's true and he hasn't made a mistake.'

By lunchtime, Margaret had finished her online enquiries. She felt quite pleased with herself, quite the sleuth, in fact. As Joan set the table, Margaret told her what she had managed to find out.

'His address is correct. I managed to confirm that from the electoral roll. I had to pay, but it wasn't much and you can't expect that sort of information for free. I've also checked the telephone number and that's correct too. He's not ex-directory. I searched his name on the Net and he came up as a member and contributor to his family history society, which adds up.'

'So all in all, it looks like he's genuine then?'

'Yes, I think so. He says that the letter is not a request for money.'

'Did you find out anything about the Treasury Solicitor?'

'Yes, that adds up too. There's a website called Bona Vacantia, which apparently means "ownerless goods". It's run by the Treasury Solicitor's Department. They keep unclaimed assets for thirty years, after which they hand them over to the Exchequer. There is a sort of family tree diagram on the site. It should be on the printer.'

Joan got up and crossed the kitchen to the far corner, which Margaret kept as her 'office'. She brought the printed diagram back to the table.

'I see what you mean,' said Joan studying the layout. 'There's a hierarchy of entitled relatives. The closer you are to the top, the better, I suppose, your chance of inheriting. It's all very interesting, but can the names of the people who've died leaving unclaimed estates be found on the website?'

'Yes, they can,' confirmed Margaret. 'There are hundreds of them. For each name it says where they died and when, but no value unfortunately.'

'I'd no idea that anything like this existed. What do you think we should do?' asked Joan.

'I think we should make contact and hear what Mr Sefton has to say,' said Margaret. 'I could send him an email. He's given us his email address.'

'OK, let's just email him and tell him to come at a certain time ... one day next week. We can ask him to confirm the meeting.'

'Fine by me ... that will give me a few days to learn a little more about unclaimed estates. I'll email him straightaway. Ooh, this is so exciting. Wouldn't it be amazing if we could inherit some money?'

'It would be, but let's try and keep sensible about this for now. He may have made a mistake. We mustn't build up our hopes too much, not yet anyway.'

4.8

So it was that on Friday, 14 December 1962, Harry found himself sitting before the local registrar, providing the information necessary for the issue of a death certificate. As he feared, the question, he hoped he wouldn't have to answer, came.

'What is your relationship to the deceased?' the registrar asked.

He'd been in turmoil over this for the last few days. He wanted to say 'nephew' instead of 'son', almost to spite her in a way, to get his own back. The trouble was everyone knew him as Harry Williams. He couldn't suddenly change to being Harold Ince, nephew. Besides, he had no proof that he was a nephew. His mother had said that Frank and Rose weren't married, which made him a bastard. He didn't want that to get around!

In the end, Harry's courage and defiance slipped and he gave up a chance to get some revenge. He told the registrar he was her son. The death certificate was duly completed, signed, and issued accordingly. He took it down to Harringtons' and the following Wednesday morning the funeral of his 'mother' took place at St Martin's Church, Leyton. He was the only mourner, apart from a nosey neighbour whom he completely ignored.

By lunchtime, Harry was back at work just before the canteen closed. One or two workmates passed on their condolences, but he shrugged and made it plain that he didn't want any sympathy. He tried to throw himself into his work. They were making castings for what would be the Falcon's last steam locomotive, *The Cambria*.

A few weeks later, he had an unfortunate accident at the works. It was his fault. He'd been distracted and wasn't concentrating at the time. He'd been troubled by his mother's confession. At home, he'd removed all the pictures of his parents from view, even the one of his father's ship. He'd discarded the picture frames and put the photographs with the other family papers in the old biscuit tin behind the plinth. Looking at the photographs had been an unwelcome reminder of what his mother had said. He recalled her words constantly and he'd found it difficult to keep his mind on his work. The accident resulted in the loss of three fingers from his right hand.

After two months' sick leave, the stumps of his fingers healed and he returned to the foundry, but he could no longer grip and use his tools as before. His days as a foreman patternmaker were over. Harry was forced to take early retirement. He came home on the last day, deeply depressed, closed the door behind him, and slumped down in his leather armchair.

In the space of three months, his world had been turned upside down. He no longer knew who he was. He felt used and let down by the woman who had raised him. He'd suffered a painful and debilitating injury, forcing him to give up his hard-won trade. The works had given him some termination pay and a small pension, but in reality, they were glad for him to go and he knew he wouldn't be replaced. Times were changing. The old trades were disappearing – no job, no future, no one to share his life. The world could get lost, he decided. He'd have nothing more to do with it if he could avoid it.

Tears rolled down Harry's cheeks as he stared at the four walls surrounding him. At least they were his walls and no one could take those from him. He'd stay here. He'd shut the world out by shutting himself in. This he did until his death, thirty-three years later.

Part Five

5.1

Nick called Carol on the internal phone and asked her to come up to his office.

'Great news,' he said, as Carol came in. 'Sit down. I've just received an email from John Gressl in the States.'

'Have they traced any heirs?' she asked excitedly.

'They certainly have, well, one heir anyway, but one is good enough for us, makes the paperwork easier too!'

'OK, so who is it? What's the relationship to David Crockford?'

'They've found a grandson, Scott Crockford. He was born in 1941 and he lives near Boston. He's an only child. His father, Michael, another only child, was killed in Normandy in 1944. Scott's been signed up. So, we now have our heir. We'll be submitting the claim as soon as we have the documentation back from Purdie-Gressl.'

'Ah, I remember from the 1930 US Census that David and Doris had a son Michael aged nine. So he was Scott's father?'

'Yes, that's right. Scott was born just before Michael was called up, when the United States joined the war.'

'And Michael didn't come back … that's a shame. I wonder if his widow remarried.'

'She may have, but of course any subsequent children are not part of David's bloodline and can't inherit.'

'Yes, of course. Sorry, I was just thinking aloud. Have Purdie-Gressl found out what happened to David Crockford's father, Thomas, and his uncle, Frederick Crockford?' Carol asked.

Nick scanned the email he was reading. 'Just says that Thomas died in New York without remarrying, in 1924, and the uncle died without issue, also in New York in 1924. So David was the only live stem.'

'Oh, great. So that's it then,' replied Carol, who had secretly hoped that by some fluke the trail would have bounced back to England and given her a last stab at solving it.

'Yes, that should wrap it up Carol. Well done, you've worked well on this case. Pity you couldn't have solved the last part yourself, but that's heir hunting; no respect for international boundaries, I'm afraid. You did all that you could, so don't be disappointed. When the documents come through from the States, you can be responsible for putting everything together in order to submit the claim.'

'Thanks Nick. I'd really like to do that.'

'Great, and next time we get a case from Purdie-Gressl, I promise that you can handle it. OK?'

'Oh right, thank you. Yes, I'll look forward to that too.'

5.2

Peter checked his email and was delighted to see one from Margaret Trigg. The sisters had agreed to meet him and suggested one afternoon later that week at a convenient time. It was perfect. It gave him a day or two to collate his information and think about how he would approach the meeting.

Peter spent that evening scanning documents and certificates relevant to the sisters, and working out how they were related to Harry Williams. He wanted to persuade them to allow him to submit a claim on their behalf. He needed to make a good impression and to show that he knew what he was doing. Having come this far, he couldn't bear the thought of not finishing this off himself.

By now, Peter also felt he deserved something for his trouble, perhaps a small percentage, if possible. He knew that professional heir-hunting companies charged a commission. He prepared a letter of representation, which he hoped the Trigg sisters would sign. It would give him the necessary authority to act on their behalf. He also drew up a side letter, which granted him a percentage of anything received by the sisters, from the estate of Harry Williams. The amount of the percentage was left blank, to be filled in when, hopefully, he had agreed his commission with them. The issue of commission was a delicate one and not a subject he looked forward to broaching, so he decided that he would see how things went at the meeting.

Before he closed down his computer, he went to the Bona Vacantia website and was pleased to see that Harry Williams' estate was still on the list. Peter was feeling more confident now and each time he checked, he felt less anxious than the time before. He smiled to himself. *With luck,* he thought, *Highborn Research has hit a brick wall and hasn't found a way around it.*

Peter was driving through the New Forest in Hampshire, heading towards the south coast and Lymington. Snowdrops were just coming out and weak sunshine had burnt away the overnight mist.

Behind him, locked securely in the luggage compartment, his briefcase contained the documents he wanted to show to Joan and Margaret Trigg. They included the will of Frank Williams, which had finally arrived the previous day. Thankfully, it had contained no surprises. Frank had left everything to his brother John. There was no mention of a wife or child. Peter felt it safe to assume that there was no competing interest from Frank's side of the family to Joan and Margaret, as entitled relatives of the estate of Harry Williams.

Peter arrived on the outskirts of Lymington just before lunch. He wanted to eat before he saw the sisters, so when he spotted a quaint looking pub, he pulled in. He gave himself an hour, which still allowed plenty of time for his meeting. As he ate, he mentally ran through what he intended to say to the sisters.

At just before half past two, he drew up outside a small bungalow in a quiet avenue of similar properties, about a mile from Lymington town centre. Carrying his briefcase, he opened the wrought-iron gate and walked up the pathway to the front door. The small garden was neat and tidy, with early daffodils just showing through the soil below the south-facing bay windows on either side of the porch. He estimated that the bungalow had been built in the 1930s, although the door looked more recent and there was a ramp instead of a doorstep.

Peter rang the bell and as he waited for someone to answer, he took in the battered hatchback parked in front of the single garage. It

266

wasn't obvious whether the dents were wounds received or self-inflicted, but instinctively he knew it was the type of car he avoided when he was looking for a space in a car park.

The door opened and a tall, elderly lady stood before him.

'Hello, I'm Peter Sefton. Miss Trigg?'

'Hello, Mr Sefton, I'm Joan Trigg. Do come in and meet my sister.'

She closed the door behind him and led him down a short hallway to a large kitchen overlooking the garden at the back of the bungalow. Margaret Trigg was waiting for him, seated in a wheelchair. The kitchen was warm and cosy, heated by a large range, which looked as if it was also used for cooking.

'Margaret, this is Mr Sefton. Mr Sefton, this is my sister, Margaret.'

'How do you do, Miss Trigg?'

'Pleased to meet you, Mr Sefton.'

Peter could see instantly that they were twins. They weren't identical, but their faces were strikingly similar. Of course, there the similarity ended, because while Joan seemed fit and able, it was certainly not the case for Margaret. Peter wondered what had caused her to be in a wheelchair. Hopes of asking the sisters for a large share of any inheritance started to fade. He was offered a seat at a table, next to Margaret, on which to put his briefcase. Joan meanwhile, put the kettle on the range.

Peter started his well-rehearsed explanation. 'I expect you wonder what this is all about. Do you have any idea to whom I was referring, when I said in my letter that you might be entitled relatives to an unclaimed estate?'

'No, we haven't' said Margaret. 'We've racked our brains. All we can think is that it must be someone on our mother's side, because that side of the family is rather mysterious.'

Peter smiled. 'Well you might be getting warm there. I think I ought to explain my position at the start. I'm not a professional heir hunter, only an amateur genealogist. I enjoy researching family history. After Christmas, I found a marriage certificate in an antiques centre. It was from 1900 and I was curious. Don't ask me why, but I bought it, for the huge some of five pounds! For some reason, I felt drawn to it and I decided to try to find out what had happened to the couple who married. Now, could I ask you a few simple questions about your family, just to confirm my research?'

'Yes, of course,' Margaret said, looking towards Joan who nodded in agreement.

'What was your mother's name, married and maiden?'

It was Margaret who led the replies. 'Edith Trigg, but her maiden name was Ince.'

'Good,' said Peter. 'Now do you have any brothers or other sisters?'

'No, there's just the two of us.'

'What about your mother, did she have any brothers or sisters?'

'No, she was an only child.'

'Now, do you know the name of your maternal grandmother?'

'Yes we do,' replied Margaret. 'Her name was Rose. She was killed in a train crash when mum was very little.'

'Mum was brought up by Uncle George and Auntie Charlotte,' added Joan, anxious to play a part, and not be left out.

'Do you know the maiden name of your grandmother Rose?' Asked Peter, using a softer, more sympathetic tone of voice.

There was a pause of a few seconds. The sisters looked at each other unsure whether to continue. Peter was right to assume that parts of this meeting might be a little delicate.

It was Margaret who spoke. 'Her full name was Rosetta Ince. She wasn't married to mum's father. Mum never liked to talk about it, but one day she did say that her father was killed in the Boer war. When I pressed her to tell me more, she wouldn't.'

Peter opened his briefcase and removed the marriage certificate from its protective sleeve. 'This is the marriage certificate which I bought at the antiques centre.'

He passed it to Margaret. Joan slid a chair in beside her and sat down. They both looked at it closely, but gave no hint that they understood its significance.

Peter pointed to the section showing the names of the witnesses. 'There's your grandmother's name, Rosetta Ince.' He let it sink in for a few moments. 'That, I believe, is the name of your maternal grandfather, Frank Williams. He died in the Boer War at Bloemfontein in South Africa, three days before your mother was born in October 1900.'

He gave them a little while to take in everything.

'Is it true that grandmother Rose was killed in a train crash?' asked Joan.

Yes, it is,' he said quietly. 'It happened near Winchester in 1902, when she was on her way back to Ventnor having been staying in Leyton, Essex.'

'Mum came from Ventnor,' Margaret chipped in.

Joan, meanwhile, was studying the marriage certificate. 'It says here that this wedding took place in Leyton. Rose obviously knew the couple who married, so had she been to see them? Is that why she was coming back from Leyton when she was killed in the accident?'

'Yes it was,' replied Peter. 'She'd been to a funeral, the funeral of the couple's son, Henry. His funeral had taken place just two days before the train crash. He was born one month to the day, before your mother.'

'Gosh … he must have only been about two years old then. What a terrible loss for them,' stated Margaret.

'That's right,' Peter confirmed. 'He was just two years old.'

'I see the groom's name is John Williams. Was he Frank's brother by any chance?' asked Margaret.

'Yes, he was, making him your great uncle.'

'Fascinating,' said Joan as she got up and went over towards the kettle. 'Would you like some tea, Mr Sefton?'

'Yes please, thank you.'

'So who is the mystery relative who's died?' Joan asked, pouring milk into the cups.

'Look,' Peter said. 'I'm probably going to tell you some things about your mother's family which I don't believe you know. Some of it could be upsetting and I don't want to seem uncaring, as it's not my family. You just stop me, if I go too fast or you find it difficult.'

'Yes, of course,' said Margaret again looking over to Joan for reassurance.

'First of all,' he said, 'and I'm sorry if this might come as a shock, but did you know that your mother had a brother – a twin brother?'

There was a silence and the two sisters exchanged a surprised expression. Joan looked more taken aback than Margaret.

'No, not at all,' replied Joan. She came back to sit with her sister. 'Are you sure? We had no idea?'

'Yes, I am,' said Peter. He passed over the birth certificates of Edith and Harold. 'Here's your mother's birth certificate and also her brother Harold's. If you look, the time of birth is entered. Edith, your mother was about twenty-five minutes older than Harold, your uncle.'

'We've never heard of Harold. What happened to him? Is he the mystery relative?' asked Joan.

'Correct,' said Peter. 'It's quite a long story.'

Joan went back to the teapot. 'Let's have some tea, shall we, while we hear what Mr Sefton has to say.'

Peter began to feel more relaxed, having got over the initial awkwardness of meeting the sisters for the first time. He described how Edith and Harold had been born in Ventnor, to Rose, who was not married. He showed them their parents' marriage certificate, which they had never seen before. He pointed out that 'Frank Williams (deceased)' was entered on it as Edith's father, despite her birth certificate not showing a father's name. He then went on to explain his theory that following the death of Rose, the family must have come to some form of arrangement over what to do with the orphaned twins. Harold went to live with John and Louisa Williams, and George and Charlotte Morris fostered Edith.

When he got to the part of his story, which covered Henry's funeral, he showed them Henry's death certificate and pointed out the place of death – Great Ormond Street Children's Hospital. He also passed over the death notice, which listed the mourners proving that

Rose was there. He then got out the relevant pages of the 1901 and 1911 Census Returns, showing that the Williams family had changed address during the intervening period.

Peter continued. 'We know that Henry died in 1902, aged two, yet in 1911 the census shows a son in the household called Harry, aged ten. You can see here that John Williams put a dash through the box recording the number of children who had died during the marriage. I've checked to see if Louisa had another child, but she didn't. No, the only reasonable explanation is that they looked after Harold after the death of your grandmother, Rose. They regarded him as their son. I expect when they moved house after taking on Harold, the new neighbours had no reason to believe that he was anything other than their natural son. Don't forget too that the name "Henry" is often changed with familiarity to the less formal "Harry". John and Louisa, it seems, maintained the pretence that he was their son, whereas George and Charlotte respected your mother's true parentage. On the 1911 Census, your mother is described as a "foster child". She kept her birth name and someone, at some point before she married, told her that Frank Williams was her biological father.'

'But surely John and Louisa adopted Harold and they changed his name?' Margaret asked.

'Ah, there was no such thing as legal adoption before 1927. Harry Williams was born Harold Ince and under inheritance law, I believe that he was still Harold Ince when he died in 1996.' Peter was getting into his stride. 'I'm not sure whether he knew his real name or not, but sadly after his mother died, or should I say foster mother, Louisa … after she died in 1962, he became a recluse.'

Seeing that the sisters were enthralled, Peter continued. 'Mind, it wasn't the only sad event to happen to him around that time. Not long after she died, he had an accident at work. He was a skilled patternmaker and the injury forced him into premature retirement.'

'How awful,' murmured Margaret.

'Who told you that?' asked Joan.

'I went over to Leyton one day and spoke to one of the neighbours in Stephenson Street, that's the street where he used to live. He remembered Harry from the Falcon Foundry where they both worked. There was a piece about his retirement in the works' magazine too.' Peter looked among his documents and produced the photograph he had copied from the Falcon magazine. He showed it to the sisters. 'I think that was taken around the time that he retired. He looks about sixty.'

There was silence for a moment. They studied the photograph. Peter could see that Joan was struggling with her emotions.

Margaret spoke. 'He is very like our mother, darker colouring, but the eyes and the mouth are very similar. If you look over there on the dresser, there's a photograph of our mother.'

Peter walked over to the dresser and studied the face of the lady in the picture. It was obvious that she was related to Harry Williams.

He returned to his seat. 'There's no doubt in my mind that your mother and Harry were related.'

'Can you tell us anything else about Harry Williams?' asked Joan, who seemed to have regained her composure.

'Not much I'm afraid, and what I do know is rather sad. I paid a visit to the local reference library in Leyton and found a newspaper report from July 1996 ... that was when he died. It seems he became a recluse and let his home deteriorate. He lay dead in his house for about three weeks before his body was discovered. The paper put the blame on the social services for neglecting him.'

'Gosh, all this is almost unbelievable and so awfully sad,' Margaret said, her voice wavering.

'It is sad,' said Peter. 'The whole saga has been dreadfully sad. I've gone from one tragedy to another with my research. Life was tough then. People were less tolerant too and moral attitudes would have made life hard for Rosetta, or Rose, as an unmarried mother. She probably had a very difficult time.'

'Do you have any other evidence to back up your theory?' asked Joan.

'Lots,' he said. 'Apart from the timings of the various events, like the wedding and the subsequent births of the children, I also have some postcards and a telegram which link Rose, John's parents, and

272

George and Charlotte to John and Louisa. By the way, George was John's first cousin.'

Peter passed the postcards and telegram over to the sisters for them to examine. He continued. 'Yesterday, I received a copy of Frank Williams' will, in which he left everything to his brother John. Frank wasn't married and had no other children. He and Rose must have had a … relationship, at around the time of the wedding. I assume he was John's best man and Rose was Louisa's bridesmaid. Perhaps that's when they fell for each other. It still happens today, and remember, in 1900 there were fewer opportunities to meet a potential partner or have an affair.'

'Did you find a report of the wedding in the local paper?' asked Joan.

'No. I looked but the local reference library only holds copies of the *Leyton Chronicle* from the reign of Edward VII in 1901. I managed to find the notice for Henry's funeral in 1902, but not the wedding in 1900. I'll tell you what though,' he said. 'I think the wedding may have been arranged hastily.'

He pointed to the marriage certificate. 'You see here, it says, "Married by Licence", which may imply that they had insufficient time to read the Banns. I think Louisa was already pregnant and they had to get married before John went back to sea. Henry was born one month before your mother had Edith and Harold. The other thing is that Frank must have gone out to Cape Town almost straight after the wedding. Judging by the date of this postcard …'

Peter picked out the postcard of the *Kidwelly Castle*, postmarked 11 February 1900, Cape Town. 'This is John Williams' ship. Remember, he was the groom. He was a chief engineer on the ship. He left London for Cape Town just four days after the wedding. I suspect that Frank may have gone down to the Cape on his brother's ship, but I've no proof … if not his ship, then on another one within a day or two.'

'And you think that Frank went off to the Boer War leaving Rose pregnant?' asked Margaret.

273

'That's right, but I doubt he would have known, because he must have left soon after the wedding … assuming that's where he and Rosetta met.'

'And you've managed to find out all of this?' queried Margaret.

'Yes,' replied Peter. 'It hasn't been easy, but I've had some luck along the way.'

Joan said, 'What I don't understand is, you say that all of this connects us to Harry Williams, who died in 1996 and left an unclaimed estate?'

'Yes, that's right.'

'But why hasn't someone else found this out before?' she asked.

'Ah, well, there are several reasons, because I'm sure others have tried. I know for example that one of the big London heir-hunting firms has been looking into it recently. The neighbour told me when I went to Stephenson Street. Partly, it's the surname "Williams" that may have defeated, or deterred, previous attempts. As far as family research goes, it's an awful name. Apparently, it's the fourth most common surname in Britain; about 400,000 people share it. Also, the case was first advertised nine years ago. I reckon that the longer a case remains unsolved, the stronger the deterrent for someone to take a fresh look at it, although I am slightly perplexed as to what has attracted the current interest and competition. The local paper seemed convinced that the Williams family came from South Wales, which was a red herring. I started from 1900 and had an immediate advantage. I already had the marriage certificate of his adoptive parents, not that I knew that at the time. Those starting from 1996 had to get over that hurdle first of all.'

Peter took a sip of tea. All the explaining and excitement had given him a dry throat. 'Then, I had the luck to find the postcards and the telegram at the antiques centre, because they gave me the true surname of Rose. From the marriage certificate, I thought her name was "Price" not "Ince",' he said, pointing to Rosetta's name.

'Umm … I see what you mean,' agreed Joan.

'Yes it does look more like "Price" than "Ince". I would have assumed it said "Price",' Margaret added.

Peter took another sip of tea and carried on. 'Confusingly, on the 1901 Census, there is a Rosetta Price who was a draper's assistant. She was born in South Wales and she was about four years older than your grandmother was, but I only discovered she was the wrong Rosetta from the telegram, when it proved that our Rosetta's surname was "Ince". Then everything started to fall into place. Now, I think it unlikely that someone else could have made that connection.'

'But could anyone else have found out that Harry wasn't Henry, their real son? You said Henry died,' Joan stated. She was really getting into detective mode now, looking for any weaknesses in Peter's argument.

'Unlikely, I'd say,' replied Peter. 'First of all, they would have had to find Henry's birth; not an easy task in itself. Let me explain. From Harry's death certificate, his date of birth is 8 October 1900. That is interesting, because that is the correct birth date of Harold Ince. Presumably John and Louisa allowed him to celebrate his birthday on the correct day, rather than that of their son Henry, who was born a month before. Incidentally, the 8 October was also the anniversary of Henry's death, but there we are, we can only imagine how they coped with everything. Anyway, sorry, I'm digressing. The General Register Office divides the year into four quarters. October is in "Q4". Now, Henry was born on 8 September 1900, which is in "Q3". Anyone searching for the birth using the information on the death certificate would look in "Q4", and of course, wouldn't find it. They'd be looking for a Harry or Harold too. They'd have to widen the search and increase the cost to stand any chance of finding it, and as Harry didn't marry, they wouldn't have had his parents' names from a marriage certificate.'

The sisters listened intently as Peter carried on with his explanation.

'Even if the parents were identified by an heir hunter, Henry didn't die in Leyton, where his parents lived and married. That was unusual. His death was registered in Holborn, because he died at Great Ormond Street Hospital. His surname is very common and his death would be less easy to spot. Also, the 1911 Census shows a son of

275

the right age in the household and as we know, boys named Henry are often called Harry. He appears to be alive in 1911 so why look for his death? For these reasons, tracking down Henry would have been difficult enough, but to then realise that he had died and that Harry is not Henry is stretching it a bit. That's why it hasn't been claimed. At least that's what I believe. Maybe there are other reasons, but I've been checking regularly, last night in fact, and the estate is still listed as unclaimed.'

'Can we check now, just to make sure?' asked Margaret.

'Of course you can,' replied Peter.

Joan made room on the table for Margaret's laptop.

Peter was impressed with the speed with which she found the website. 'Click on the tab there, for the complete list,' he said. There was a pause while the page loaded. 'Now scroll down towards the end to the names beginning with "W".'

'There we are! There we are!' exclaimed Joan who was peering over her sister's shoulder. 'That's it, Williams Harry, died Leyton, 1996!'

'How much is the estate worth?' asked Margaret. It was the first time this aspect had been touched upon, which was surprising given the reason for the meeting.

'It was first advertised in March 2002, with a value £67,000,' replied Peter. 'Unfortunately, the Treasury Solicitor only reveals the value to a claimant, when the claim is accepted or admitted as it's termed. It's possible that much of the administration of the estate has been completed by now, which might have reduced it a little. I understand there's a fee of £180 plus costs and disbursements … and any accrued interest would have been deducted.'

'Is there a time limit for making a claim?' asked Joan with a hint of concern in her voice.

'Yes, twelve years after administration, but I think we should be within that.' Peter said reassuringly. 'Also there's a discretionary policy, whereby the Treasury Solicitor can admit claims up thirty years from the date of death.'

'A windfall like that would be marvellous for us,' Margaret said excitedly. 'I'm confined to a wheelchair through polio. I caught it as a teenager. Joan is so good to look after me, but we could use some extra cash, couldn't we?' she said, looking at Joan.

'Yes, it would be useful. We've always wanted to adapt the bathroom for Margaret. She could do with an electric wheelchair too and we would love to change the car for something more suitable, ideally one of those with a ramp or lift. That would be such luxury, but we mustn't complain, must we dear?'

'No, we mustn't ... but oh, if we could afford a carer for a spell, Joan could have a break, take a holiday or something, which would be marvellous,' added Margaret.

'Now don't you go worrying that I need a holiday,' Joan replied almost scolding her sister. 'We're fine; it's you who could do with a change of scene. I'm not cooped up in here most of the time like you.'

Peter decided to intervene. He was satisfied that they could do with a windfall and had no intention of asking them to pay him a commission. No, the sisters were lovely and it would be pleasure enough just to get anything for them.

'Listen, I would very much like to see this through to the end, after having done so much research. Would you be willing to give me permission to submit the claim on your behalf and deal with the Treasury Solicitor in the first instance as your representative? If your claim is accepted then you can take over dealing with it yourselves.'

This is the moment, Peter thought ... he didn't have long to wait. Joan and Margaret looked at one another for a second, before nodding in agreement. *Splendid*, he thought, *I really will be able to see this through to its conclusion.*

Peter read out the text of the Letter of Representation he had prepared. It gave him authority to submit the claim on their behalf and to deal with any queries, but not of course to receive any of the proceeds, should the claim be admitted. The sisters listened carefully and then each of them signed in the appropriate place.

It was Joan who spoke. 'Mr Sefton, you've done so much work on this and I know Margaret will agree too, that you should get some reward. How much do you want to charge?'

'Nothing,' Peter replied. 'If we're successful and you get a reasonable amount, then perhaps you would consider a donation to a charity of my choosing, but only if you receive enough for the things you've just told me about.'

'Do you have a specific charity in mind?' asked Margaret.

'It seems that Harry Williams, or should I say Harold Ince, used to run bingo evenings at his works' social club and raised a lot money for the Lifeboat Charity. That might be appropriate but we'll see, eh?'

'Oh, Mr Sefton, do you really think we may have a chance?' Joan asked, the hope evident in her voice.

'I can't say, but it has to be worth a try. The thing is, Harry Williams was not the son of John and Louisa. Their son, Henry, died. So where did he come from? I think there's enough circumstantial evidence to show beyond reasonable doubt that he was the son of Rosetta Ince. He and his twin sister were orphaned. Harry was taken on by John and Louisa, but not adopted. According to inheritance law … at least as I understand it, his estate should go to his blood relatives. If the Treasury Solicitor accepts that he was born "Harold Ince", then his sister is a full blood relative and her descendants are entitled kin.'

Peter paused before asking, 'I don't suppose you have a photograph of your mother when she was about sixty, the same age as Harry was when his photo was taken?'

Joan got up and left the room. She returned a few moments later with a portrait photograph of their mother. 'I think this will do.'

Peter could see that Joan was correct. The likeness of Edith to the photograph of Harry Williams was remarkable. Her hair was lighter, but the expression was very similar.

'Do you think I could take this with me and copy it for inclusion with the other evidence? I'm sure it will help our case.'

'Yes, of course,' said Joan, looking at Margaret, who nodded.

278

'Absolutely,' said Margaret. 'Let's go for it and give it everything we've got.'

'Yes, go for it, Mr Sefton,' agreed Joan. 'Do your best.'

Peter rang the Treasury Solicitor's Department late the following morning. It was Friday. He spoke to a Case Officer. Peter had just finished writing a detailed explanation of how he believed Harry Williams to be Harold Ince. He'd gathered together copies of documents, photographs and other evidence in support of his claim, all of which he intended to include. He wanted to know whether he needed to send the originals of the postcards and the telegram, or whether copies would suffice.

'Copies will do initially,' was the reply. 'For which unclaimed estate do you intend to submit a claim?'

'Harry Williams, died 1996, in Leyton,' replied Peter. There was a pause and he could hear the tapping of keys on a keyboard. 'Have you already submitted any documents on this case?'

'No, I haven't,' said Peter, starting to feel slightly concerned. A nagging doubt was forming at the back of his mind. Had Highborn Research, or somebody else, beaten him to it? 'I've just checked and the estate is still listed on your website.'

'That cannot be taken to mean that we have not already admitted a claim. It can take a while to update the list.'

Peter felt sick.

'Is the claim for yourself?' the officer asked.

'No, but I have a Letter of Representation to act on the claimants' behalf.'

'Is the claim fully documented?'

The question only aroused more anxiety for Peter. He started to worry. Was the officer looking at something on his screen?

'I believe so, but it takes some explaining and there is quite a long trail to follow,' Peter replied nervously.

'You have documents such as certificates and census returns to prove the claim?'

'Oh, yes. The claim is strong, certainly strong enough to beat any other competing claims.'

'What do you mean by competing claims?' queried the officer. 'We only accept one claim per estate.'

'Well, if you were examining two claims for the same estate at the same time … I know it's unlikely … but if you were, you'd accept the one from the claimant who was the closer kin to the deceased, wouldn't you?'

'We admit the first fully documented claim we receive.'

'So you wouldn't look at both claims and go for the stronger one?'

'We only admit the first fully documented claim we receive.'

Peter suddenly felt a cold sweat wash over him. 'Are you currently examining a claim on the estate of Harry Williams, died 1996?' he asked, holding his breath for the answer while he waited for what seemed an eternity for the reply.

'At this moment, we have no kin claim under examination for that particular estate.'

Peter sighed with relief. He thanked the officer for his assistance and put the phone down. He tried to calm himself. He realised that he had been lulled into a false sense of security. He'd wrongly assumed that if Harry's name remained on the list, it meant that his estate was unclaimed, but he'd now learned that that was not necessarily so. He'd also assumed that even if he submitted his claim while another was under examination, then his claim, which he was sure would be the stronger, would prevail. However, he'd just learned that the Treasury Solicitor admits the first fully documented claim, nothing more, and nothing less.

Therefore, the only way to be certain that the claim from the Trigg sisters could be admitted was to ensure that it was the first fully documented claim received by the Treasury Solicitor. He rushed upstairs to gather the documents and other proof he'd assembled. His original plan had been to post everything, but now time was of the essence. He left a message for Felicity on her voicemail. Ten minutes later, he was nosing out of the driveway, destination central London and the Treasury Solicitor's Department in Kemble Street.

5.3

Nick Bastion sat back from his computer with a satisfied expression. It was late Friday afternoon and he'd just received a reply to the email he'd sent to Purdie-Gressl in New York. John Gressl was delighted to hear that the claim on the Harry Williams case had been sent to the Treasury Solicitor's Department earlier that afternoon.

Highborn Research had a reputation for solid professional work in the field of heir hunting and were not prone to frivolous or unsupported applications. Their evidence spanned the years from Victorian England to the 1940s in the United States. Carol had carefully put together a fully documented claim to make the examiner's task as straightforward as possible.

Nick was confident that the contents of the package couriered to Kemble Street earlier that afternoon would convince the Treasury Solicitor that Scott Crockford, grandson of David Crockford, was entitled to claim the estate of Harry Williams.

John Gressl, in his email, noted Nick's caution in assuming that everything was 'in the bag', but was reassured to know that Nick was reasonably confident of a successful outcome. Nick had told him that the value of the estate, after costs and deduction of interest, was likely to be in the region of £60,000. John finished by saying he was looking forward to a successful outcome and wished Nick a good weekend.

5.4

Peter was stuck in traffic. It was just after two o'clock. He was about two miles away from his destination, and despite his frustration, he had no choice but to stick with the slow grind that he had become part of. He hated driving in London, especially on Friday afternoons. It took so long to get anywhere and it was expensive too, with the congestion charge and the cost of parking. He kept an eye out in his mirrors for cyclists and motorcyclists, who were in the habit of riding between the lanes of almost stationary traffic. He didn't want to have an accident injuring someone. Neither did he want to get his precious car scratched, or have a wing mirror broken by a motorbike trying to squeeze through.

Almost from nowhere, a motorcycle courier, panniers stuffed with packages weaved past him and then cut in front of him. Peter cursed silently, noting the bike's distinctive white fairing. The rider had a white helmet too and a full-face tinted visor. The matching white panniers were marked horizontally with a stripe of orange reflective tape. To a casual observer, it closely resembled the motorcycles used by the police. Unbeknownst to Peter, one of the packages carried by the rider was from Highborn Research.

Five minutes later, Peter had broken free of the main congestion. He was moving again, switching lanes and charging with the rest of the drivers through a sequence of green lights, hoping that his luck would hold. He didn't notice the distinctive white motorcycle, parked with others in front of a snack bar a mile short of Kemble Street, as he sped by.

He parked his car on a meter just off The Strand, paying the parking fee with his mobile phone. Then he retrieved the large envelope containing the evidence supporting the claim from the back of the car and walked smartly around the corner, to the office of the Treasury Solicitor.

When he returned to the car, he sat down behind the wheel and breathed a sigh of relief. He'd done it … logged and accepted. The claim was in. He was thankful that there hadn't been any complications. He rang the Trigg sisters and spoke to Joan.

'I'm in central London and have just submitted the claim to the Treasury Solicitor.'

'In London?' Joan repeated incredulously.

'Yes. I rang the Bona Vacantia Division from home this morning. It seems that just because a name is on the list of unclaimed estates, it cannot be assumed that they have not recently admitted a claim for it.

282

I decided not to take any chances, so drove up here myself to make sure it goes in.'

'Gosh, Mr Sefton. What can we say? Thank you very much … did they say how long their investigation would take?'

'Only that they try to admit or reject a claim within ten working days,' replied Peter. 'I'll let you know as soon as I hear anything and you let me know if you hear from them too.'

'Yes of course, Mr Sefton. We'll have to be patient and cross our fingers in the meantime.'

Peter switched off his phone and buckled his seatbelt. He started the car and pulled out into the traffic. He had to stop at the next set of traffic lights. He waited patiently, recognising the same motorcycle courier flash past him going in the opposite direction towards Kemble Street. Peter smiled to himself. *I bet he enjoys confusing some drivers into thinking he's a motorbike cop.*

The lights changed and Peter was on his way again, heading for home. *All that work,* he thought. He tried to rationalise what he'd included and to reassure himself that the claim was well supported. He could have done no more. Everything hung on the strength of his submission and the decision of the Treasury Solicitor.

A week later, Peter received a letter from the Bona Vacantia Division. It was quite formal and intriguing. In no way did it admit the claim nor did the letter reject it, but instead asked Peter to supply additional information.

Firstly, they wanted to see original documentary proof of Frank's postcard from the Cape, the two postcards sent from Ventnor during the summer of 1902 and the telegram sent to Rosetta with the news of Henry's death.

Secondly, and this was part that worried Peter, they wanted to know if he had any evidence relating to the baptisms of the twins, Harold and Edith, which might name Frank Williams as their father. Peter considered this request for a while. He had to admit that it was something he had not thought to look for and wasn't sure where it might be found, if at all.

283

He decided to ring the Trigg sisters to see if they had any ideas. It was Margaret who answered this time. Peter explained the contents of the letter he had just received. 'Do you have any idea whether your mother was christened?' he asked.

'Yes, I'm sure she was. She was confirmed too and was very keen to make sure we were as well. I don't think you can be confirmed without being christened.'

'Have you any idea where she was christened or confirmed?'

'It must have been at the parish church in Ventnor. Auntie Charlotte and Uncle George brought her up and they did go to church sometimes. I can't think where else it could have taken place.'

Peter was thinking aloud. 'Your mother was born at their house, Brindle Lodge. From postcards and census returns, I'm fairly sure both your mother and her brother lived at Brindle Lodge until Rose's death. So, I think you're right. If they were baptised, then it had to have been at the parish church in Ventnor. I'd better get over there and see what I can find out.' Peter paused for a moment. 'Just an idea here, but if you're up to it, would you and your sister be interested in meeting me in Ventnor? You never know what we might turn up.'

'That does sound rather exciting,' Margaret, replied. 'I'll need to ask Joan first, because it will mean a lot of work for her and she'll be doing the driving. I think she'll say yes though, because she is finding all of this as exciting as I am. We'll call you back.'

A few minutes later, Peter's phone rang and it was Joan ringing back to arrange the trip. Assuming Peter could confirm with the vicar that the church had the baptism records for 1900, they agreed to meet at Saint Matthew's in Ventnor at eleven o'clock the following day. Peter said he would find somewhere for them to have lunch afterwards.

Twenty-four hours later, having crossed the Solent from Southampton, Peter was waiting in his car outside Saint Matthew's Church, Ventnor. He kept an eye out for the sisters and after a while the battered hatchback appeared hesitantly around the corner and pulled up behind him. They had a few minutes to spare before their appointment with the vicar.

Peter got out of his car and walked back to their car. 'How did the ferry go? Smoothly I hope?'

'Fine,' Joan replied. 'Thirty-five minutes, Lymington to Yarmouth. We haven't been over for quite a few years. It's a bit of an adventure, isn't it Margaret?'

'Yes, it is. Amazing though, how much one remembers,' piped Margaret. 'Of course, we came here to this very church for the funerals, you know, both Uncle George's and Auntie Charlotte's. They both died when we were in our early teens. It was before I got polio.'

Joan got out and opened the tailgate. She lifted out Margaret's heavy wheelchair. Peter was unsure whether to help Joan, as she prepared the chair before pushing it around to the passenger door. He felt slightly awkward, but could see that she was used to it and he stood back, for fear of getting in the way or giving Joan the impression that he doubted her capabilities in dealing with the needs of her disabled sister. Margaret slid into the chair and all three of them made their way to the adjacent vicarage.

Reverend Cartwright welcomed them at the door and introductions were made. Fortunately, the access was suitable and Joan was able to push Margaret as they followed the vicar into a room reserved for parish matters. In the centre, a large circular table easily able to accommodate ten people, dominated the room. Laid out in readiness was a heavy leather-bound book, recording the parish baptisms.

'Now, what was the name you wanted to check?' the vicar asked.

Peter took the lead. 'It's two names actually, twins, a boy and a girl. We believe they may have been baptised here between September 1900 and December 1902. The mother's name was Ince, Rosetta Ince.'

'What about the father's name?' asked the vicar as he turned his attention to the book, looking for the relevant pages.

'Well, we think the father's name was Frank Williams, but they weren't married,' replied Joan.

'Frank Williams?' I've heard that name somewhere,' the vicar muttered, 'and what about the children, what were their Christian names?' He didn't seem at all concerned about the fact that the children were illegitimate.

'Edith and Harold. Edith was our mother,' answered Margaret.

By then, the vicar had found the correct pages and was sliding his finger down the column of entries. He checked the first page but found nothing. He turned over and continued to check the names. His finger stopped.

'Here we are,' he said with satisfaction. 'I've found it: 26 August 1901. Edith and Harold Ince. Mother's name, Rosetta Ince. Father's name, Frank Williams, deceased. Godparents of Harold were John Williams and Louisa Williams. Godparents of Edith were George Morris and Charlotte Morris.'

'Did you say that the father's name was Frank Williams, deceased?' asked Peter.

'Yes. It seems unusual for illegitimate births of that time, but the vicar entered the father's name.'

Peter and the two sisters looked at one another in excitement and satisfaction. This information was priceless. It proved the family relationships and hopefully, it would impress the Treasury Solicitor too.

'Would it be possible to photocopy this page?' Peter asked the vicar.

'I'm sorry, but we don't have any copying facilities and I can't let you take the book away.'

'Do you think it would be in order for me to take a photograph of the relevant page?' asked Peter.

'Of course,' replied the vicar. Go ahead. Why do you need it?'

'It's all to do with an inheritance and the need to prove close kinship,' explained Peter.

As Peter focused his digital camera over the page, the vicar suddenly exclaimed with a note of triumph. 'I've got it! I know where I've seen the name Frank Williams.'

'Really?' asked Joan. 'Where?'

The vicar tapped the side of his nose with a finger. 'All will be revealed presently,' he said.

286

Meanwhile, Peter took several close-up photographs and then checked to see that the images were clear, which they were.

'Thank you Reverend Cartwright ... that should do, but could I ask one other favour? If I print out a copy of this page at home and post it to you in a stamped addressed envelope, would you mind signing it as a true copy of the baptismal register and then returning it to me?'

The vicar closed the book. 'No, not at all ... now come on,' he said, 'follow me, I want to show you all something.'

The vicar led them out of the side entrance of the vicarage and down a path leading to the church. He opened a heavy wooden door decorated with iron studs and they entered. Peter helped Joan with Margaret's wheelchair. Reverend Cartwright then took them along a side aisle, passing several rows of pews before drawing them into a small alcove. He pointed to a wooden plaque fixed to the wall.

'Here we are!' he said triumphantly. 'Would you care to read that?'

This Memorial was raised in grateful memory of the men of this Parish, who gave their lives for the Empire during the South African War 1899 - 1902

Pte. Charles Robson Edwards: Imperial Yeomanry

Pte. Wilmot Potter: Imperial Yeomanry

Cpl. Frank Williams: Mounted Infantry of City of London
Imperial Volunteers

The words on the memorial were simple and poignant. The sisters were silent; this was, after all, a memorial to the sacrifice their grandfather had made. Peter could sense their emotion.

Joan broke the silence. 'Would he be buried here?'

'He died at Bloemfontein and would have been buried there,' Peter intervened. 'Unfortunately, the bodies of soldiers were not repatriated then, as happens nowadays.'

There was a further moment of silence before Margaret asked the vicar a question. 'Do you have any records of burials in the graveyard, for the end of 1902?'

'Yes, we have. Why do you ask?'

'It's just occurred to me that our grandmother, Rosetta Ince, could be buried here. Do you think you could look to see if that's the case? Her death occurred in October 1902. She was a victim of a railway accident.'

'Certainly, I'll go back and look it up for you. Give me five minutes. If you want to start searching the graveyard yourselves, I can tell you that most of the graves on the north-west side of the church date from around the turn of the twentieth century. That side over there,' he said, pointing to the direction where they should look first.

Joan pushed Margaret back down the aisle and out into the fresh air with Peter following respectfully behind. Something he hadn't considered when he'd invited them to join him that day, was that the sisters were investigating their own family and that there might be emotional complications. For him, it was different and he was more detached. However, he had to admit that from the moment he first saw the marriage certificate, he'd felt part of something that was pulling him along, and right then, he started to sense a renewed burst of that same feeling.

All three of them followed the flagstone path skirting the outside of the church, until they reached the north-west corner. The boundary wall ran quite close to the path at that point, so none of the headstones was more than fifteen yards away. Peter volunteered to walk amongst them to see if he could find what they were looking for. The grass underfoot was damp and spongy and in no way suitable for the wheelchair. Some of the headstones were difficult to read, either through erosion or from a covering of lichen. He'd looked at about a dozen when the vicar reappeared, walking briskly towards them, a piece of paper and a folder in his hand.

'Rosetta Ince *is* buried here,' he announced. 'I've got the plot number and the plan. We should be able to locate her grave.'

He stood and looked at the graves and then turned his plan to match the layout on the ground. With Peter behind him, he paced carefully between two rows and counted seven headstones, before swivelling left and bending to inspect the one at which he'd stopped. Peter knelt beside him and helped to rub off some of the moss. It was the correct headstone. Its inscription said: *Rosetta Ince – Aged 27 years – Laid to rest 7th November 1902.*

Joan made her way over to the grave. Poor Margaret had to remain in her chair as a spectator. The vicar stepped back to make more room. He offered his condolences and then explained that he needed to return to the vicarage. Peter accompanied him to the path and thanked him for his assistance, confirming once more that he would post a copy of the baptism record for authentication.

Meanwhile, Joan had returned to Margaret's side. They had linked hands and he could see that each was using a handkerchief to wipe away a tear. In the space of a few minutes, they'd received confirmation of their grandfather's name, seen his memorial and now were close to the spot where their grandmother lay, an innocent victim of a tragic railway disaster. Their reaction was completely understandable and Peter remained at a respectful distance, in order to allow them some privacy in their grief.

The sisters however, were not ones to dwell on sadness for long. Joan approached Peter. 'Stiff upper lip and all that, eh, Mr Sefton?' she said.

'No, please,' he replied, 'I remember when I found my great great-grandfather's grave. He died in a coal mining disaster in Lancashire in the 1870s. Something like this experience today takes you back in time, to the tragic circumstances in which they lost their lives. I understand your reactions perfectly and you have my sympathy.'

'Thank you, that's very kind. Do you think you could take a photograph of our grandmother's grave and headstone? It would mean a lot and be something to keep.'

'Yes, of course,' replied Peter. 'Would you like me to photograph the memorial plaque as well?'

'Yes, please do,' answered Margaret, who had recovered her composure and had managed to wheel herself over to join them.

Peter quietly took some photographs of the grave and then went back into the church to photograph the memorial. Afterwards, he met the sisters by their car. Margaret was already installed and her wheelchair had been stowed in the back.

'Look, I had booked lunch for us. I quite understand if you would prefer to head straight home if you don't feel like eating. I can cancel our table,' Peter explained.

'No, we think a nice lunch would be just the ticket,' said Margaret with enthusiasm. 'We could do with a distraction and a spot of lunch sounds perfect.'

'Right, let's go then,' he said. 'You follow me. It's a restaurant called "Brindles", would you believe, and it's about two miles away. There's plenty of room for parking and they have wheelchair access. I checked.'

'Perfect, Mr Sefton,' confirmed Joan, putting on her driving gloves.

Not something that most drivers wear nowadays – apart from racing drivers, Peter thought wryly. 'Lead on.'

A week passed with no word from the Treasury Solicitor. Peter couldn't decide whether that was a good sign or a bad one. On balance, he decided it was a good sign, because surely, if they were going to reject the claim, then they would have done so sooner.

As requested, he had forwarded the authenticated copy of the baptism register from Saint Matthew's Church, along with the originals of the postcards, and the telegram. Everything was sent by registered post, just to be safe. Peter was convinced that the naming of the godparents in the baptism register ought to clinch the decision in their favour. It proved the relationship between each of Rosetta's children and their foster parents. Just after breakfast the following morning, the phone rang. It was Margaret. She was breathless with excitement.

'Mr Sefton! Mr Sefton!' she exclaimed excitedly. 'We've got it! We've got it!' she squealed.

'They've admitted the claim!' shouted Joan in the background, sharing in the excitement.

'Yes, we've just opened the letter. Oh it's wonderful news, thank you so much,' added Margaret. Peter could tell that she was on the point of breaking into tears.

It was his turn to be excited now. 'What? You've had a letter this morning?'

Joan wrested the handset from her sister. 'Yes! Yes! Isn't it wonderful! How will we ever thank you?'

'That's amazing!' shouted Peter, punching the air with his free hand. 'I'm so pleased for you, I really am! How much are you going to get? Does it say?'

'Yes, the residual value of the estate is £64,376. The Treasury Solicitor has agreed to accept our claim. One of us has to apply for Grant of Letters of Administration. That'll be Margaret, she's best with things like that. Oh, we can't believe it, Mr Sefton. We just cannot believe it!'

'Well, you believe it. They wouldn't make it up. You and Margaret are entitled. I expect I've got a letter on the way too, but my post doesn't arrive till lunchtime.'

They chatted on for some time and later in the day Peter rang back to say that he too had received confirmation that the claim to the estate of Harry Williams had been admitted in favour of Joan and Margaret Trigg. It was fantastic news and Felicity was equally impressed when he telephoned her at school during lunch break. He felt ecstatic and remained on a high for days afterwards.

Peter chatted on the phone to the sisters on many occasions over the next few months. The legal hurdles took about seven months to complete and the sisters were thrilled when the estate was finally released to them. They immediately sought quotations to remodel the

291

bathroom and install full central heating in their bungalow. It was gratifying for Peter to know that the money would be put to good use.

During one telephone conversation, Margaret broached the subject of donating to a charity on Peter's behalf. Peter hadn't liked to mention it himself, but was pleased when given the opportunity to discuss it with her. He explained again that Harry Williams had been a keen fundraiser for the Lifeboat Charity. Peter wasn't sure why that was so, but said that he suspected it might be connected with the loss of his 'father', John Williams, at sea. Peter was amazed when Margaret announced that they wanted to donate £5,000.

'Are you sure that's not too much?' he queried. 'You need that money, I know you do. I was thinking more along the lines of about £500.'

'No, we've discussed it and we believe a charity should share in our good fortune. We have tried to think what Harry might have done with it and we agree that your suggestion is an excellent one. Although we never knew him, we would like to think that a donation of £5,000 would be a fitting tribute to his memory.'

'Well, that is extremely generous, I must say,' added Peter.

'We'd like you to come down for the presentation. Do you think that would be possible and you could bring your wife too if you wish?' asked Margaret.

'What presentation?'

'The presentation of the cheque; you know, one of those big cardboard ones, to the Lifeboat Charity. We've already set the wheels in motion. The local paper is going to host a small reception and they'll take a photograph of you with us. Please do come. They ran a little piece in the paper last month about our inheritance. We'd like you to be there with us. We've made it clear that the donation will be made by us, but on your behalf.'

'That's very kind,' Peter replied, almost at a loss for words. 'I'd be delighted to come down and I'm sure my wife Felicity would be delighted to accompany me.'

Hence, one day during the following month, Peter made a return trip to Lymington. Felicity was with him. Outside the building, which housed the offices and printing works of the local newspaper, they found a small crowd gathering. Peter couldn't help but notice a very smart new vehicle parked in a space reserved for the disabled. It matched the description Margaret had given him over the phone. It was especially adapted, with a rear door accessed by a ramp. Neat, compact, and functional, it was exactly what Joan and Margaret needed and Peter was delighted to see it.

Inside the reception area, he sensed the excitement and anticipation. Drinks and refreshments were on offer and several local dignitaries were in attendance. Peter spotted the sisters on the other side of the room. Margaret was seated in a brand new electric wheelchair. When they saw Peter, they waved excitedly and made their way over to welcome him. He introduced Felicity to the sisters who were delighted to meet her, and Margaret gave a quick demonstration of her skill and mastery of her new chair's controls.

The presentation ceremony went very smoothly. The newspaper and the local bank had organised the making of a giant two-metre long cardboard replica cheque, showing the amount of £5,000 payable to the Lifeboat Charity. One end of the cheque was held by Margaret, with Peter and Joan standing immediately behind her. The other end, the receiving end, was held by a representative from the charity. Photographs were taken and Joan gave a brief speech that concluded as follows:

'Above all, my sister and I are indebted to the kindness and amazing detective work of Peter Sefton, without whose efforts we would never have had the good fortune to be united with an inheritance from our late uncle, Harold Ince. We now know, through Peter's research, that Harold worked hard to raise funds for the Lifeboat Charity and for this reason, as a fitting tribute to the memory of our uncle, we are delighted to make this donation on behalf of Peter Sefton.'

5.5

New York Times, Obituary, Wednesday, April 21 1937

Rosetta Vincenti
Founder of The Silverman Skirt Company

Rosetta Vincenti passed away Monday at her apartment on Central Park West after a short illness. She was 62 years old.

She emigrated from Liverpool, England, in November 1902 and became a naturalized US citizen in 1913. On arrival in New York, she joined the business of Stephano-Silverman Costumes. In 1906, she became a partner in the firm. In 1912, she bought out the surviving partners to become the sole proprietor. Under her direction and ownership, The Silverman Skirt Company became a well-known manufacturer of skirts and dresses. The business expanded into retail and relocated to Fifth Avenue in 1922. She retired in 1932, selling the business for a sum reputedly in excess of $1,000,000.

It is understood that under the terms of her will, her entire fortune has been left to a number of children's charities.

Her funeral, which will be simple in accordance with her wishes, will be Tuesday morning at 10 o'clock from the Joseph C. Robinson Funeral Establishment at Broadway and Sixty-Sixth Street. She requested that no flowers be sent.

THE END

5037596R00166

Printed in Great Britain
by Amazon.co.uk, Ltd.,
Marston Gate.